WE ARE THE
Wildcats

ALSO BY SIOBHAN VIVIAN
Stay Sweet
The Last Boy and Girl in the World

SIOBHAN VIVIAN

SIMON & SCHUSTER BFYR
New York London Toronto Sydney New Delhi

SIMON & SCHUSTER BFYR
An imprint of Simon & Schuster Children's Publishing Division
1230 Avenue of the Americas, New York, New York 10020
This book is a work of fiction. Any references to historical events, real people, or real places are used fictitiously. Other names, characters, places, and events are products of the author's imagination, and any resemblance to actual events or places or persons, living or dead, is entirely coincidental.
Text copyright © 2020 by Siobhan Vivian
Cover illustration copyright © 2020 by Dana Lédlová
All rights reserved, including the right of reproduction in whole or in part in any form.
SIMON & SCHUSTER BFYR is a trademark of Simon & Schuster, Inc.
For information about special discounts for bulk purchases, please contact Simon & Schuster Special Sales at 1-866-506-1949 or business@simonandschuster.com.
The Simon & Schuster Speakers Bureau can bring authors to your live event. For more information or to book an event, contact the Simon & Schuster Speakers Bureau at 1-866-248-3049 or visit our website at www.simonspeakers.com.
Interior and cover design by Lizzy Bromley
The text for this book was set in Adobe Caslon.
Manufactured in the United States of America
First Edition
2 4 6 8 10 9 7 5 3 1
Library of Congress Cataloging-in-Publication Data
Names: Vivian, Siobhan, author.
Title: We are the Wildcats / Siobhan Vivian.
Description: First edition. | New York : Simon & Schuster Books for Young Readers, [2020] | Summary: "A toxic coach finds himself outplayed by the high school girls on his team in this deeply suspenseful novel, which unspools over twenty-four hours through six diverse perspectives"— Provided by publisher.
Identifiers: LCCN 2019024571 (print) | LCCN 2019024572 (eBook) | ISBN 9781534439900 (hardcover) | ISBN 9781534439924 (eBook)
Subjects: CYAC: Field hockey—Fiction. | Coaches (Athletics)—Fiction. | Friendship—Fiction. | High schools—Fiction. | Schools—Fiction.
Classification: LCC PZ7.V835 We 2020 (print) | LCC PZ7.V835 (eBook) | DDC [Fic]—dc23
LC record available at https://lccn.loc.gov/2019024571
LC eBook record available at https://lccn.loc.gov/2019024572
ISBN 9781534467040 (export paperback)

Ada Limón, "How to Triumph Like a Girl" from *Bright Dead Things*. Copyright © 2015 by Ada Limón. Reprinted with permission of The Permissions Company LLC on behalf of Milkweed Editions, milkweed.org.

FOR ZAREEN

WE ARE THE
Wildcats

HOW TO TRIUMPH LIKE A GIRL
By Ada Limón

I like the lady horses best,
how they make it all look easy,
like running 40 miles per hour
is as fun as taking a nap, or grass.
I like their lady horse swagger,
after winning. Ears up, girls, ears up!
But mainly, let's be honest, I like
that they're ladies. As if this big
dangerous animal is also a part of me,
that somewhere inside the delicate
skin of my body, there pumps
an 8-pound female horse heart,
giant with power, heavy with blood.
Don't you want to believe it?
Don't you want to lift my shirt and see
the huge genius machine
that thinks, no, it knows,
it's going to come in first.

It is tradition that the fifth and final day of tryouts for the Wildcats' varsity girls field hockey team be the most grueling of all. Though, real talk? It's not like the others were a walk in the park. Roughly half the girls arrive to the field with a vague sense of what's coming. The rest show up clueless. But there's no telling the two groups apart because—knowing or not—this is it. Today is everyone's last chance.

The girls mill around on the sidelines, taping up their sticks, their wrists, their ankles, cinching loose tank tops tight with little knots at their backs, rinsing out yesterday's nasty from their mouth guards with squeeze bottles of icy water. It's early enough that the air remains somewhat cool and the turf looks almost like real grass, with indifferent dewdrops clinging to blades of bright green plastic.

Summer break is just about over. Come Monday, a new school year begins. There is much the girls could discuss first-day outfits, class schedules, summer gossip—but not a lot of chitchat happens, because Coach doesn't want chitchat. He wants focus. And there's really no need for team bonding yet because there is no team. Every varsity spot is up for grabs. Even girls who lettered last year aren't safe. Even the ones who bled to bring home a second-place trophy at states could be cut.

Maybe *should* be cut.

At eight o'clock, a velvety knell rings out from the upper school's bell tower. With it, heads collectively swivel, ponytails swish. Every eye is on Coach as he pushes open the heavy metal doors of the athletic wing and stalks toward them, clipboard in the crook of his arm, a can of Red Bull in hand, a baseball hat pulled down low over his shaggy blond curls.

Both the JV and freshman coaches nip at Coach's heels. They are two much older and rounder versions of Coach, dads essentially, embarrassingly eager to assist him today. Dark wounds of sweat already bleed through their T-shirts.

The girls need no instruction. They quickly circle up and begin to stretch, clapping a slow-and-steady pulse for each position change. As they press and lean through lingering soreness, they watch-but-don't-watch Coach inspect his field. Trying to gauge his mood. Sense what he might be thinking. They get only reflections of their own longing in his mirrored sunglass lenses.

Some girls spent the past summer secretly worried—rightfully so—that Coach would not be returning to West Essex this year. There is always the fear he will leave them for some better opportunity. He's honestly too good to coach at the high school level, and especially a girls team. The very least they can do is win for him. Whether his decision to come back was because of them or in spite of them didn't much matter. He came back. Thank God.

Coach lifts a silver whistle to his lips.

Warm-ups begin. Always the same circuit. A brisk mile run around the field's perimeter. Then twenty-five push-ups. Then twenty-five crunches. Then twenty-five scissors. And lastly, a set of suicide sprints to lace the lines of the pitch.

It is now 8:30 a.m. Their hearts warm with blood, lungs flush with oxygen, the girls fetch their sticks and listen for Coach to call a skill drill. They gamely hope he goes with Tic-Tac-Toe or maybe Slalom, something chill to start things off. Instead, he cups his hands and bellows, "Figure Eights!"

This is the first sign they are in for it.

The other two coaches rush to set up cones, dotting the field with one for each player. Then, at Coach's next whistle, the girls hitch forward at their hips and begin pushing their orange balls with their stick blades in a tight, controlled infinity loop. Over and over they dance this twirl, eyes pinned on those orange balls to steady the spinning world, their abs and thighs and asses all fires stoked white-hot.

Fifteen grueling minutes later, Coach blows his whistle. It takes the girls' brains a few nauseating seconds to register they are no longer in motion.

If this were any other day of varsity tryouts, the girls would now pause for a quick water break while Coach handed out mesh pinnies in either white or navy for a scrimmage. Scrimmages are how Coach works through a Rubik's Cube of roster possibilities, swapping players in and out of potential lines and positions, whittling these forty or so hopefuls down to his final squad of twenty.

Except today there will be no scrimmage.

There never is on the final day of tryouts.

Instead, the seniors drop their sticks and immediately set off on another mile run around the field's perimeter, a thunder of tanned, toned legs. They are trailed by any juniors and sophomores who have endured this annual tradition before.

It always takes the new girls a few seconds to realize what's happening. Some are already chugging water, some have gone to their bags for a towel to wipe their sweat or—the brave ones—to sneak a discreet look at their phones. Once they do realize, they sprint off in a panic to catch up to the pack. This elicits a chuckle from the experienced girls, but then it's right back to business. There are twenty-five more push-ups, twenty-five more crunches, twenty-five more scissors, and another set of suicide sprints to complete.

It is 9:00 a.m.

Another whistle. Coach calls for "Shuttle!" next.

Groups of six girls quickly line up to sprint, receive, pass, sprint, receive, pass, sprint, receive, pass for fifteen minutes, until Coach's next whistle starts the warm-ups over again, their third mile run, twenty-five more push-ups, twenty-five more crunches, twenty-five more scissors, and another set of suicide sprints.

At nine thirty he calls out "Clover!" and the cycle begins anew.

At ten, "Forehand Fades!"

At ten thirty, "Snake!"

They are ants scurrying under his magnifying glass. Every move examined, dissected. Coach shouts for them to keep their form, to increase their speed, to stay sharp, to dig deep. This despite the girls' passes becoming sloppier, dragging as they grind on, the sun now searing high above them. The entire field gets unsettlingly quiet, save for the wooden slap of sticks against sticks, the pounding of cleats on turf, the groans of fatigue. And, of course, the trill of Coach's unrelenting whistle.

The girls give everything they've got, knowing Coach doesn't ask of them what he doesn't believe, deep down, they can deliver.

So they deliver.

That's Coach's magic.

That's why the Wildcats win, year after year after year. Waist-high trophies. Team pictures on the front page of the local newspaper. Invitations to play around the country. Full-ride scholarships to Ivy League universities.

At eleven, "Chop Shots!"

At eleven thirty, "Triangles!"

Through portholes wiped in the fogged-up windows of the weight room, the varsity football players watch the girls, jaws hanging slack and stupefied. To them, and the student body at large, there's something cultish and unsettling about the varsity girls field hockey team. Their devotion, their focus, their unquestioning commitment to Coach and to one another. For the duration of their season, their squad is impenetrable.

It should be said that West Essex's football team has not made it to states in over a decade. Their last championship banner hangs dusty and faded from the gymnasium rafters. Yet it never strikes the boys as odd that they still dominate the fall pep rally, always announced last by the principal. The boys don't question if they've actually earned the bleacher-stomping applause that beckons them, dressed in their jerseys and jeans, to burst through banners of butcher paper. Their arms simply lift in V shapes at varying intervals, summoning the student body to their feet. A reflex.

Boys default to kings. Their sovereign right to rule is never questioned.

The football players wait to be noticed, eager for their gaze to have some kind of effect on the field hockey girls, preferably embarrassment. That the girls never do annoys them, and eventually, they retreat from the windows. A silent acknowledgment that this is one kingdom beyond their reach.

This is why the field hockey girls would live on this field forever if they could. This blessed rectangle where their worth is wholly quantifiable, statistical, analytic black and white. How incredibly freeing it is to live a few hours each day where they don't worry about being beautiful or sweet or modest or smart or funny or feminine. The only thing required of them here is to play their absolute best.

And so, on this day, one girl always pukes.

One girl always cries.

One girl always falls.

But they all keep going. Because being a Wildcat means everything.

At noon Coach blows his whistle one final time. The girls—cheeks mottled, drenched in sweat, muscles twitching, stomachs sour, chests heaving—fall to their knees and look around at one another in awe. It seems almost cruel that not every girl who survived this will make the team.

But that's how it is. Winners and losers.

They rise on wobbly legs, silently collect their belongings from the sidelines, and file from the field out to the paved cul-de-sac ringing the stately front of West Essex Upper School, turf cleats clicking atop the pavement. There, underneath the flag, they stand shoulder to shoulder, hearts paused in their chests, as Coach reads the names of his chosen ones.

In exactly twenty-four hours, this brand-new Wildcats team will take to the field for their first official scrimmage of the season, against the Oak Knolls Bulldogs. Scrimmages typically don't mean shit, but it was Oak Knolls who beat them at states last year. It was the first time the Wildcats had lost a championship since Coach arrived at West Essex six years ago. And the girls would love nothing more than to start their new season by whooping some serious Bulldog ass. For Coach as much as for themselves.

Maybe more.

The newest members joining this team—plucked either from the JV squad, like Grace, or the freshman team, and one lucky eighth grader named Luci—are green, but their inexperience may well be an asset. The girls who played varsity last season each still nurse a secret wound, the thinnest of scabs capping a mountain of scar tissue. Mel, for not stepping up. Phoebe, for lying. Ali, for losing her head. Kearson, for treason.

The only way the Wildcats will manage a win tomorrow is if all the varsity players—new and returning—come together and bond as a team. They must believe with their whole hearts that they're in this together. Know without question that they'll have one another's backs until the final whistle. As Coach says, *Team first, always.*

That's why they lost last season. That's what broke them.

Luckily, there's a tradition for this, too. A secret celebration that will take place tonight on this very field. It is the single facet of being a Wildcat that belongs entirely to the girls.

At least, that's how it used to be.

FRIDAY, AUGUST 26
12:27 P.M.
LUCI

"*Bite down* as hard as you can."

Luci Capurro sinks her teeth into a perforated metal tray packed with pink clay. The overflow pushes through the tiny holes and streamers of orthodontic Play-Doh quickly fill the empty spaces inside her mouth. Luci gags, but thankfully the other girls—her new teammates—don't notice.

A celebration is brewing across the classroom.

Desks are bulldozed into corners. A platter of still-warm bagels and tubs of cream cheese carried away. A cooler with mini bottles of orange juice dragged across the linoleum. Someone turns up the volume on a cell phone and drops it into an empty plastic Solo cup. The vibrating plastic warbles the lyrics incomprehensibly, but it was *the* song of this summer. Everyone already knows the words.

As quickly as the dance floor appears it is filled by returning players. Luci identifies them as such by the varsity Wildcat gear they already possess. Dropped duffel bags from different regional tournaments. T-shirts boasting championships won before Luci moved to this town, boxy unisex styles snipped into more flattering silhouettes, like loose window dressings for their sport bras.

Though damp with sweat, they happily drape themselves onto each other and dance, paw, pinch, prune, grind, hip check. They seem so much older. Practically a different species of girl. The intimacy between them makes Luci feel like a creeper for staring.

But she is not the only one.

A smaller group of girls stands pressed against a table of computers, the dim monitors a contrast to their bright, adoring smiles. They must be the new players promoted from last season's freshman and JV teams, Luci decides. The veteran players shimmy over and take their hands. There is not a sneaker squeak of resistance. Even the shy ones close their eyes and dance.

No one notices Luci. It is not a slight. Luci is the only incoming freshman—technically still an eighth grader until Monday—to have made varsity. She is grateful that the dental tech's body mostly shields her from view, grateful she could point to the tray in her mouth if she were seen and beckoned to the dance floor. At this moment Luci doesn't have the courage to join in the fun. It took every last drop she had to bring her this far.

"And open." The dental tech pokes inside her mouth with his bitter rubber-gloved hand, scooping out the excess clay with his fingers and then checking the fit. "Okay, Luci, this looks good. Go ahead and close again. No talking for five minutes while the mold sets."

The song ends but the girls continue the beat, drumming on desks and walls, stomping their feet on the floor. The tech rolls his eyes and flings his used gloves into the trash. No one notices or cares that he's annoyed. The beat gets faster, building, blurring, until an impromptu cheer suddenly breaks out and nineteen teenage girls scream-sing the Wildcat fight song.

Luci hasn't memorized the words yet. It didn't feel particularly pressing. She wasn't making the team.

What a difference an hour makes.

Luci threads some stray wisps of hair behind her ears. Lowers her chin to her chest. Listens close.

We are the Wildcats, the navy blue and white,
We are the Wildcats, always ready for a fight!

Luci needs to learn names, too. She's picked up only a few. Not from any introductions or pleasantries but because the best players simply make themselves known.

One, a senior named Phoebe, breaks the horizon of bobbing heads by hopping up on a classroom chair. Phoebe's knee is double wrapped—an Ace bandage under a compression sleeve—and by her euphoric grin, you'd think she'd reached the summit of Everest. Phoebe reaches down into the crowd and starts pulling another girl up with her.

Mel. The Wildcats' varsity team captain.

Luci watches Mel try to gently wriggle free, but it is no use—Phoebe won't let her go—so she relents. The two girls then deftly negotiate their small, shared platform, finding their balance, turning butt to butt so they both can fit, their toes cantilevered off the seat's edge. Mel knots up her silky chestnut hair, lifts a fist, and punches the air with a cheerleader's precision, her face beaming joy and hope and pride.

Don't mess with the Wildcats, we won't accept defeat,
For we are the Wildcats, and we just can't be beat!

Arms are thrown over shoulders, zipping the cluster into a

tight, impenetrable spiral. They sing the last verse to one another.

Three cheers for the Wildcats, your honor we'll defend,
'Cause when you're a Wildcat, you're a Wildcat till the end!

The chant fades like a summer firework and everyone exhales a breath collectively held for an entire week. The girls slowly untangle themselves from one another, though not before one last bit of tenderness. Squeezing each other's hands, patting each other on the head, swatting a whip of ponytail.

Even from across the classroom, Luci feels the warmth.

Coach enters the room a moment later. He signals for Mel to follow him with a crooked finger. The other girls get busy straightening desks, resuming order.

The dental tech checks his clipboard. "Grace Mosure! You're up next!"

Luci recognizes the girl who walks over. During most of the scrimmages, Grace played defense to Luci's offense. Grace operated at one speed—full-throttle charge—and she was relentless in trying to strip Luci of the ball. Most intimidating were Grace's eyes, wide and desperately hungry behind the metal cage of her face mask, like a stray dog's. Now that the mask is off, Grace exudes a cooler, more relaxed vibe, though a faint pink ring remains etched in her skin from its suction.

Grace hops up on a desk and pulls her mousy hair into a sprout of ponytail at the top of her head. After scribbling a signature down for the dental tech, she gently peels the tape back from the rims of her ears, exposing on each a ladder of tiny silver hoops climbing the cartilage.

Grace's style is definitely edgy. Not what Luci has come to think of as the typical West Essex look. And yet Grace eagerly bites off the tag on a new Wildcat windbreaker and pulls it over her head. It is navy blue with a white zipper, a white paw print over the heart, and "Varsity Field Hockey" across the shoulder blades in blocky white letters. Grace cracks the entire length of her spine peering over her shoulder to admire it.

Grace becomes yet another piece of the puzzle Luci's trying to solve on the fly. Despite her incongruence, Grace clearly fits here somehow. It gives Luci hope that she might too.

Behind them, navy-blue-and-white Wildcat gear is bricked in neat stacks, along with folders of permission slips to be taken home for signature. Lastly, twenty white three-ring binders. *The Wildcats Varsity Field Hockey Playbook.* Luci takes one into her lap, opens it with reverence.

The first page is their schedule. For the next three months, there will be games once or twice a week and nearly every Saturday afternoon.

Luci turns the page and finds the Wildcats Varsity Field Hockey Code of Conduct. Any hairbands, wristbands, or headbands must be either white or navy. Makeup and jewelry and perfume are expressly forbidden from practices and games. Varsity players are expected to dress up for school on game days. Skirts or dresses, no jeans. There is a mandatory 10 p.m. curfew imposed on nights before games. Attendance at Psych-Up Dinners is mandatory. Attendance at practices and meetings is mandatory. There are many, many more.

Centered at the bottom of the last page, in capital letters, a catchall:

TEAM FIRST, ALWAYS.

Me, Luci thinks, dumbfounded. *This includes me.*

The remaining pages, comprising the bulk of the binder, each depict a different chaos, Xs and Os and arrows zooming across a rectangular representation of the field. Squinting, Luci wants this section to make more sense than it does. Maybe she's dehydrated? Her temples throb. She pinches the bridge of her nose.

If only.

She closes the binder and sees that Grace is watching her.

Luci tries to smile around the dental tray. A trickle of drool drips from the corner of her mouth.

Both girls laugh.

Grace benevolently says, "Supposedly, these custom mouth guards are amazing. You have to spit, like, significantly less. A dentist in town makes them for the varsity players every year, free of charge. His daughter got a full ride to play at Falk." Grace swings her legs, childlike. "I'm Grace, by the way. I'm new too. I started JV last year as a freshman."

The dental tech's watch beeps and Luci's mouth guard mold is popped out with more force than she was expecting. She runs her tongue across her teeth, makes sure her braces are still attached. "I'm Luci," she says, massaging her jaw.

"So . . . do you know who's taking you home yet?"

"My mom. Why?"

Grace holds up her hand to prevent the dental tech from inserting the tray into her mouth. "No, see. It's kind of a Wildcat thing that the younger girls who can't drive yet get adopted by the older girls with cars. You basically never have to worry about getting a ride home from practice or a game." Grace discreetly points across the room. "Ali Park picked me," she whispers, almost giddy, a strange show of emotion for someone projecting that much cool. "Ali was all-state goalie last year. Practically unstoppable for most of the season. Except . . . well. You know."

Luci doesn't. What happened? She's too insecure to ask. Luckily, Grace keeps talking.

"Anyway, I bet Mel already called dibs on you. She made varsity as an incoming freshman too. Plus you're both left forwards. Kinda makes sense she'd take you under her wing this season."

Luci scans the classroom and finds Mel seated at a desk near the front, dutifully copying what appears to be some of Coach's notes onto a strip of white stick tape. To Grace, she says quietly, "So I should tell my mom I'll meet her at home? Even though Mel hasn't said anything? I really don't mind not getting a ride. I might be out of the way, and—"

Full of confidence, Grace explains, "That's how it works on this team. The Wildcats look out for each other."

"Right." Luci digs in her bag and finds her phone is dead. She looks to the classroom clock—12:45. Her mother is likely already here. She'll have to run outside. "Hey, thanks for clueing me in on this stuff, Grace."

The dental tray has already been pushed into Grace's mouth but it doesn't stop her from answering, "That's what teammates are for."

Luci gingerly approaches the front of the classroom. Coach's desk has a throne-like quality thanks to the two trophy cases glittering behind it. His baseball hat is off, his sandy hair lightened blond by summer. He's on his laptop, typing, chewing a piece of gum fast and hard, almost compulsively. He could be a grad student cramming for an exam.

"Excuse me, Coach?"

He looks up, momentarily annoyed by the interruption. But then, in a flash, he's smiling warmly. "Lucianna."

"Oh. Ha. Only my grandmother calls me that." Luci lifts her

arms to fix her sagging ponytail but, realizing her armpits probably have sweat rings, lowers them. "Everyone calls me Luci."

He leans back in his creaky teacher's chair, old dark wood. "You're Argentinean, am I right?"

Luci cocks an eyebrow. "Yes. My mom's side." She was pretty sure everyone at West Essex assumed she was white.

Coach stretches, pleased with himself. "Did you know that you share a name *and* a heritage with arguably the best female field hockey player of all time? Luciana Aymar."

Luci laughs loudly. Practically a bark. "Um. No. And . . . in that case, for sure call me *Luci*. I don't want to get anyone's hopes up."

"Too late."

She has a hard time keeping eye contact with Coach. He sorta looks like a grown-up version of Mike Roy, a classmate who Luci secretly crushed on third quarter. "Sorry. I guess I'm just overwhelmed?" Her upspeak is like nails on a chalkboard. She hears now why her mother gets on her case about it. It makes her sound like a ditz. She forces a swallow. "I'd never even held a stick before the field hockey unit in Mr. Yancy's gym class last spring. So it's a little crazy to be standing here right now."

Mr. Yancy is the West Essex Lower School's gym teacher, and also, it turns out, the freshman field hockey coach. Over the summer, he mailed Luci info about a free skills camp for incoming freshmen. Luci decided to go, mainly because it would be a chance to see her classmates before high school started, have another crack at making friends with them. She'd been a midyear transfer during eighth grade, was still a little lost, and had spent most of her summer alone, guzzling Cheetos and Netflixing on her phone.

The skills camp had turned out to be good fun. They did drills, mostly, not the most exciting stuff, but Luci was a quick learner, and Mr. Yancy would often praise her good instincts. It was borderline embarrassing how good Luci felt to have something in her life clicking.

Coach leans forward on his elbows and laces his hands. "Luci, I know you're green but you've got a hell of a lot of raw potential. Believe me, I don't normally bother checking out the incoming freshman players. But Yancy called me and said, 'Coach, you have to see this girl play. She's a natural.' And he's right. You are."

Luci had heard whispers during the first day of skills camp that the high school's varsity coach was not like a typical teacher. He was hot. Also young and cool. In the abstract, Luci couldn't picture it. But on the second day, someone pointed Coach out to Luci, standing with his arms folded at the chain-link fence, watching them play. He didn't stay long—maybe ten minutes—but he spoke with Mr. Yancy before he left. His eyes were on Luci the entire time. And her cheeks flushed as brightly then as they probably are right now. The next day, before Luci even set down her gear, Mr. Yancy sent her to the upper field, where varsity tryouts were already in progress.

"I'll admit, I threw you into the deep end this week. But you more than held your own. Sure, I could have left you on the freshman team, given you a season to get your bearings. Or bumped you to JV and let you be their star. But playing at the varsity level and, frankly, having *me* be the one to coach you will raise your game much, much faster."

Luci feels herself stand taller. "I think it already has."

Not to say that she hadn't spent those three days of varsity tryouts expecting any minute to be pulled off the field by Coach. She was fast only because she was scared of getting a stick to the shins.

She never stood in the right place, even if she did score. And the language everyone spoke on the field was completely foreign to her.

Help side!

Get through!

Read it!

Pressure pressure pressure!

The girls would help Luci when they could, discreetly whispering tips, lifting their chins to show Luci where to stand. Little by little, the game began to feel more instinctual, the stiffness of drills smoothing during play. And when Luci completed one turn-and-shoot move, managing to sail the ball into the back of the net during a scrimmage, every girl, regardless of what color pinny they wore, swarmed her, slapping her back, mussing her hair. It was pure joy.

When she stood around the flagpole this afternoon, Luci desperately wanted to hear Coach say her name.

Coach nods, pleased with her validation. And perhaps, as a reward, his voice downshifts to something lower, more conspiratorial. "Tell you the *complete* truth, Luci, I'm being selfish. I haven't been this excited to coach someone in . . . well, it's been a while." His eyes drift over her shoulder, focusing briefly behind her.

Luci turns.

Mel, still sitting at that front-row desk, sets her pen down and begins to smooth the tape onto her stick handle, pressing the edges, careful, precise. Mel is definitely close enough to have heard their conversation, but if she's been listening, Luci can't tell.

"Anyway, Luci." Coach's voice is at a normal volume again, and Luci spins to attention. "I want you to start thinking about goals for this season. Lay out what you want to accomplish."

"You mean like . . . learn a lot?"

Coach's face crinkles with polite embarrassment. "I'm talking about setting some stat goals to get you on the college scouting radar. It wouldn't hurt to make a list of top schools. D1 and D2. More and more high school players aren't waiting to commit anymore. This summer, a sophomore at Ellis signed a letter of intent for DCU, full ride."

Luci bites down on her smile. This conversation feels impossible—she hasn't even played a single game yet—but if it *were* true, if there were even a remote chance at a scholarship, it would majorly help her mother, who was already drowning in med school debt.

"Now, you came over to ask me something, right?" He rolls his pencil through his fingers so fast, it's a yellow blur.

Right. Her mother. Still outside waiting. Luci thinks of a quick excuse, instead of telling Coach the truth, because she doesn't want to seem babyish. "May I please go to the bathroom?"

She winces. *Smooth, Luci. Real smooth.*

Coach laughs at her, but to his credit, attempts to disguise it by clearing his throat. "Just make it quick."

Luci's been in the upper school only once, for the holiday concert. She never walked the halls or peeked inside a classroom before this. It feels like high school here. Serious. Straightforward. Smart Boards. Meanwhile, at the lower school, her eighth grade locker had been directly above a kindergarten classroom, and once, as she searched for a tampon in her book bag, she'd heard children singing their ABCs. This memory only makes Luci happier to be here now, as if a paper-chain umbilical cord tethering her to childhood has at last been snipped.

She hurries past the bathroom and into the stairwell, quietly pushes on one of the metal doors leading outside, and then sprints toward her mother's car idling in the parking lot. Every muscle feels sore.

Her mother is in the front seat, dabbing at her white lab coat with a Clorox bleach pen. The plan was to grab lunch together before her shift. When she was still in med school, Luci's mother kept more of a normal schedule, but now that she's begun her residency, she's on two to eleven. Once school starts back up, they'll be running on entirely opposite schedules.

"Sorry to keep you waiting, Mom. I thought I'd be dismissed by now."

"No sweat. If we don't have the time to sit down someplace, we'll hit a drive-through."

Lots of people comment that Luci and her mother look like sisters. Yes, her mother is young, and that's part of it. Both have skin that will tan in the weakest sunshine, eyes the color of honey, brown hair streaked with copper and gold. Still, Luci knows it's a generous compliment, because her mother is full-bloom beautiful while she's a bud.

"Actually ... there's this thing about the older girls giving rides to the new girls on the team." Luci shyly adds, as a way to not feel like such a jerk, "I made varsity. The only one from my grade."

Her mother tosses her bleach pen aside and squeals. "I didn't want to ask, just in case! Wow, Luci! This is a big deal, isn't it?"

"Kinda. Coach is already talking to me about college scholarships and stuff."

"For real?" Luci dodges as her mother tries swatting her through the open window. They both laugh giddily, because even after these last few days of tryouts, it still feels surreal—practically divine—to discover that Luci might be gifted at something she only just tried. Her mother kisses two of her fingers and presses them to the cross that dangles from the rearview mirror. "Okay, well, if you're sleeping when I get home from the hospital, I'm waking you up. I want all the details."

Luci bites her lip. "Actually, there's a mandatory team sleepover tonight. They call it a Psych-Up. Our first scrimmage is tomorrow afternoon." There's a dip in her mother's gorgeous smile—the one Luci hopes to have when, at last, her braces come off—because she'll need to be back at the hospital. Luci leans half inside the car window and hugs her mother tightly, absolving her. "Don't worry. I doubt I'll even play. Anyway, the season doesn't officially start for another two weeks." Luci then jogs backward from the car, calling out, "Bye, Mom! Love you!" before she spins and runs full sprint back toward the high school. She's been out here too long already.

Luci pulls on the same door she exited from and is aghast to find it has locked behind her. *No no no no no.* She races to another set of doors a few feet away and finds them locked too.

Her heart beats a second pulse in her ears. Luci might not know much about being a Wildcat, but something instinctual kicks in, the heightening of senses when you suspect you may be in danger. She bangs her fists against the small glass window, kicks the base of the door with her foot, feeling pain from neither, only the desperate hope that someone will hear her and let her back inside.

Mercifully, the door opens.

Mel has changed out of her practice gear and into pale blue denim cutoffs and a pretty floral tank. She looks like a girl from a movie about girls.

"What are you doing out here, Luci? Coach is waiting on you."

"I, um, got lost looking for the girls' bathroom."

Mel tilts her head, as if contemplating this ridiculous possibility. "Well . . . you're lucky I'm here to save you."

It is said not unkindly. More like a gentle warning, which Luci gratefully heeds, lowering her head to slip under Mel's arm. Once inside, Luci takes off down the hall as fast as her leaden legs will carry her.

"And hey!" Mel calls out. "Just so you know, I'm your ride home!"

Luci thinks she hears a hesitation in Mel's voice. As if Mel extended this invitation despite some lingering reservations. Or perhaps Mel isn't sure if Luci can even hear her now that Luci's rounded the corner.

Whatever the reason, Luci doesn't slow down.

FRIDAY, AUGUST 26
1:12 P.M.
GRACE

Even with the roof off, the Jeep is a vanilla hotbox. No fewer than seven air fresheners dangle from the rearview mirror, a forest of yellow cardboard trees. And Grace Mosure, buckled snugly into shotgun, is delightfully high.

Ali Park is next to her, kneeling on the driver's seat, squeezing the trigger of a Febreze spray bottle rapid-fire, and misting the back seat, where Ali's enormous goalie bag takes up any remaining passenger space.

"I'm kind of obsessed with making sure my gear doesn't get stinky," Ali admits. "Some goalies? I swear you can smell their BO from across the field." She pauses, her finger on the trigger. "Which, come to think of it, might be some weird strategy. Anyway. You'll want to hold your breath for a second."

Instead, Grace closes her eyes and deeply inhales.

She is a world away from her brother Chuck's beater Honda, the grimy interior camo'ed in peeling stickers placed to suture splits in the vinyl seats, the back left passenger window forever sealed, its missing crank rolling around somewhere underfoot with empty cigarette packs and crushed soda cans. When their grandfather lost the ability to drive, Chuck was granted full automotive privileges with the caveat he would give his sister rides anywhere she needed to go. A promise Chuck has mostly kept. But when he picked up Grace from tryouts this week, usually on his way home from being out all night, Grace had to ride perched as delicately as she could on one of Chuck's sleeping bandmates' laps, hoping she wouldn't wake them up by sweating on their glitter-dusted skin.

"Okay, that should do it," Ali says, tossing the spray bottle aside, spinning around, and dropping into her seat. She turns the key and her stereo kicks on mid-song, hip-hop bass thundering. A cluster of her JV teammates turn toward the music.

Ahem.

Former teammates.

Grace hadn't expected them to still be lingering near the flagpole more than an hour after Coach had read his varsity picks, stunned to near paralysis by the disappointment of having not made the cut. This must be a rare situation for girls like Marissa Szabo and Quinn LaPlace. To be on the outside when they're so used to being in. Their already hushed conversation had quieted completely when Grace passed by with Ali on the way to Ali's Jeep.

The JV team is majorly cliquey, and for the past year Grace felt barely tolerated at team activities. The slights were small though numerous. A seat not saved. An invitation delivered at the last possible minute, if at all. An inside joke never explained.

Grace began varsity tryouts on Monday cautiously optimistic.

Knowing there were two spots open on varsity defense, she played the very best she could on the field. But Grace also took it upon herself to carry the huge Gatorade cooler in and out of the athletic office each day of tryouts, and picked up any discarded stick tape or trash from the sidelines before heading home, all in the hopes Coach would notice her extra hustle. She would have done anything, honestly, to make it off JV.

When she did, Grace expected no congratulations and received no congratulations from the other JV girls. But she wonders if they will at least try to fake some happiness when they see Kearson Wagner. It wouldn't even be hard to fool her, since fake is all she's ever known.

Poor Kearson probably still has no idea the shit her "friends" secretly talked about her last season. They pretended to be thrilled for her, of course, when Kearson first got called up to varsity to cover for Phoebe Holt after she sprained her ACL. But when Kearson completely choked, the JV team barely concealed their glee. Grace saw it firsthand, the way they clutched each other in the locker room, grins equal parts euphoric and morbid, as a classmate who'd been at the varsity game texted all the lowlights of Kearson's debut. It was beyond gross.

Grace wriggles in her seat. It's a relief to leave those girls behind. The varsity squad doesn't operate that way. Coach wouldn't stand for it.

"Ready, Grace?" Ali asks.

"Yup." Grace's smile widens, as if controlled by the stereo volume dial, which Ali turns up even louder. And feeling as much glee as relief, she discreetly watches in the side-view mirror as the JV girls crane their necks, tracking the Jeep until it's gone from the parking lot.

"You said you live on Dormont Road?" Ali shouts over her music.

"Dorchester."

"Right, sorry." Keeping one hand on the wheel, Ali reaches into the center console and unzips a small makeup bag. Inside are a package of Korean face wipes, the same ones Chuck swears by, and she uses a sheet to blot her forehead and the sides of her nose. "Grace? Remember the girl you elbowed yesterday? What was her name?"

"Marissa Szabo."

"Is she the one who went to prom with Ryan Durst?"

"I . . . I'm not sure."

"Yeah. I think she did. I remember her dress was cute." Ali wrinkles her nose. "Wait. Except the back was weird. It had these crisscrossing straps."

"Just so you know, I didn't elbow Marissa on purpose," Grace clarifies. Even though Marissa's been a total bitch to her since basically kindergarten, Grace still felt bad about the accidental contact, especially when Marissa made a big show of rubbing her jaw and wincing afterward.

Ali waves away Grace's concern. "Oh. Without a doubt. I mean, if Marissa still hasn't figured out that she needs to look at who's coming at her and not down at the ball after a year of playing JV . . ." She pauses and shrugs half-heartedly. "She's kind of a lost cause, you know?"

Grace presses her palms lightly to her warm cheeks. Everything Ali said is the truth, and yet this conversation feels surreal. Though Marissa and Grace are the same age, Marissa has already dated a senior *and* gone to prom *and* gotten a solo during the holiday concert. In any normally functioning high school social universe, Marissa would be the one in Ali's Jeep, forging a friendship, not her.

And yet, Grace had barely stepped inside Coach's classroom before Ali made a beeline for her, as if she'd already picked Grace out from the other new girls who'd made the team, the scrappy mutt puppy she was set on adopting. It had to be for how hard Grace had played this week. Any time that Coach had put Grace on the same team as Ali for a scrimmage, Grace busted her butt to clear every single ball she possibly could before it ever reached Ali in the goalie crease.

This is the magic of the Wildcats. The comradery of the West Essex varsity field hockey girls obliterates all other high school social hierarchies. In fact, while other sports teams at West Essex wear the same school colors and share the same mascot, it is only the varsity field hockey girls who are referred to as, simply, Wildcats. That's how tight they are.

Ali stretches past her open roofline, momentarily changing the sound of the air. "Anyway, Grace, when I saw you strip that pass from Marissa, I *knew* you'd make varsity." She reaches over and pinches Grace's arm playfully. "I bet Coach starts you tomorrow."

Though today's workout was maybe the hardest thing she's ever physically endured, Grace feels a sudden zip of new, excited energy pumping through her body, a transfusion brought on, perhaps, by so many of her dreams coming true in quick succession. She twists in her seat so she can look at Ali head-on. "Well. If I am that lucky, I want you to know that I'm going to be *all over* Darlene Maguire tomorrow."

Ali stiffens. "Do you know her?" She turns down the volume of the music.

Grace clears her throat. "Me? No. Not personally." But everyone knows *of* Darlene Maguire. She is the reason why the Oak Knolls Bulldogs beat the Wildcats in the championship game last season. Darlene scored on Ali twice, the only two goals of the match, a couple of seconds apart, near the end of the second half. Grace now wishes she hadn't mentioned Darlene Maguire, but for whatever reason, she keeps talking, explaining. "I made a point to watch her at Kissawa this summer. She has basically one move, which is to make defenders think she's slowing up to take a shot, but then breaking into a sprint and beating them into the key."

Ali manages a small nod, too small for Grace to pretend it affirms anything she's just said. Instead it appears to be punctuation in a conversation Ali is having with herself.

Grace turns back to the windshield. *Shit.*

Ali eventually says, "I went to a special goalie skills camp this summer. That's why I wasn't at Kissawa." She swallows. "I mean, I don't know if anyone said anything about me not being there...."

"No," Grace says. "No one said anything to me."

She feels bad for even bringing any of this up. Of course Ali would take the Wildcats' championship loss super personally. Though it's not just on her. The defenders didn't have her back. The offense didn't score. Mel hadn't managed a single goal after Phoebe's injury, which was why the Wildcats tied the last two regular-season games *before* the championship game zero to zero. Though if Kearson had stepped up and played better in Phoebe's stead, maybe Mel could have?

But there's no way Grace is going to dig into any of that right now. Not when the atmosphere in the classroom post-tryouts was so exuberant. Not when Phoebe has been cleared to play again. Not when Coach came back for another season. Not when the Wildcats seem more determined than ever to make a comeback.

Ali seems to be thinking the same thing. She takes a deep, cleansing breath. "It's going to feel so good when we beat Oak Knolls tomorrow."

"So fucking good," Grace says.

Ali cracks up laughing. And any lingering awkwardness floats up and out of the Jeep's open top.

Grace kicks the front door closed behind her. "Nana! I'm ho-ome!" she sings, and sashays into the living room, excited to spill her good news.

Nana's not in her favorite armchair, though the seat cushion remains concave despite her absent weight. Instead, Grace finds Chuck—or a lump of blankets she assumes is her brother—sleeping on the living room couch. He has the window shades pulled down, cartoons flashing bright colors on mute.

"Nana went to the store." Chuck rolls over under the blankets.

"Shit. Sorry." She sets her gear down quietly, leans her stick against the wall. "I didn't think you'd be home."

Before he ventured into the city with his friends last night, Grace told Chuck she wouldn't need him to pick her up at the high school the following day. Her thinking? If Grace made varsity, one of her new teammates would take her home. And if she didn't, she wouldn't have to cry about it in front of him.

A couch cushion muffles Chuck's yawn. "What's got you so cheery?"

"Oh. Nothing. Go back to sleep." Before tiptoeing out of the room, she picks up her field hockey stick and, with a quick flick of her wrist, fires one of Nana's crossword puzzle books stacked on the side table at Chuck's body. "Sweet dreams."

Grace knows plenty of siblings who spend their adolescence

totally ignoring each other. But Chuck, perhaps out of lonely necessity, was always more than willing to share the things he loved with his little sister. And Grace, a thirsty sponge, was more than happy to soak those things up. Some of her favorite memories are when Chuck invited her into his bedroom to play a new song, and the two of them would dance around with their eyes closed, bumping into each other every so often. Or the times the two of them would sit across from each other on the bathroom floor, their heads slick with colorful dyes, and passionately debate whether Remus's death was justified or if Thor's hammer could be lifted by an elevator. Grace harbors no regrets that her formative years were shaped by her brother. If anything, she feels lucky. And, as she's grown up and developed her own tastes, she's been able to open Chuck's eyes to some of the things she loves too.

Field hockey, however, isn't one of them. For someone like her brother, someone who lived on the fringes of West Essex—as a blur of bright hair on the edges of the hallway, a faint smell of clove left behind in a classroom, a backpack abandoned on one of the study tables in the library, covered in patches naming bands no one at their high school had heard of—it's nearly impossible for him to get that, when she's playing, Grace feels like the best version of herself.

Though, after her experience on JV last season, it became easier for Grace *not* to explain. Because if Chuck knew how shitty her JV teammates made her feel on a daily basis, he would have wanted her to quit. So Grace kept her head down, ignored the drama, played hard, got better. She felt about JV the way her brother felt about his four years at West Essex. Something Grace needed to survive in order to find her people.

Now that high school is over, Chuck has a scene, a band,

friends who get him. It's been great to see her brother in a place where he can turn his volume up as loud as he wants.

Grace believes she's found that with the Wildcats. Without a doubt. She's seen it from a distance, and now up close, today, the way the girls have already embraced her. It's a culture Coach has created, and where Grace intends to thrive.

Tonight's sleepover is a perfect example. Even if it wasn't mandatory, she'd be excited to go, but Grace appreciates that Coach *has* required that every girl on the team attend. It leaves no chance for someone to be excluded. What a relief to know that every weekend from now until Christmas break, she'll have plans.

In her bedroom, Grace begins packing. She's pleased to find Nana's washed her favorite thing to sleep in—a Ramones concert tee that Grace's uncle passed down to her on her thirteenth birthday. "That's the real deal," he told her, with love and caution. "July seventeenth, 1981, the Palladium in New York City. I was there with your dad." It's perfect for summer nights, thin and soft and raggedy in the best way. But also maybe a little short for a nightgown? She neatly folds a pair of spandex shorts and places them on top.

Grace shouts, "Hey, Chuck? Where's the sleeping bag you took to camp out for those concert tickets?"

From the living room he shouts back, "James's house, maybe? Why?"

She sits back on her heels. She could ask Chuck to pick it up for her, but it was on the city sidewalk for a night, and she might not have enough time to wash it. "Never mind!" Grace will bring some blankets to sleep on instead. Nana, for whatever reason, has hundreds and hundreds of blankets.

Chuck suddenly appears in her doorway, a blanket tight

around his head like a hooded cape. His eye makeup is smeary and raccoon-ish, though Grace isn't sure if that is from his nap or a look he created on purpose. "Hey. Was today the last day of tryouts?"

"Yep."

"So . . . are you going to tell me how it went?"

"It was fine." She smiles shyly up at him.

Chuck groans, marches into Grace's room, and sits on her bed. "So does that mean you made varsity or what? Because you're being super cryptic."

She's touched, and even a little weirded out, that he's this worked up over it. "Yes. I made varsity."

Chuck's mouth lifts into a smile but then it stalls out. He hesitates, chews the inside of his cheek. "What about those JV bitches?"

Grace laughs. "A couple of other JV girls got spots too. But not the meanest ones." Chuck lets out a long sigh. "Anyway, you don't have to worry about me. I can handle myself."

He stands up. "I was worried about me, actually."

Grace sets her bathing suit aside. "What?" Her eyes track Chuck as he heads out of her room. "Why?"

Pausing in her doorway, his back to her, Chuck glances over his shoulder and says, "Because if you hadn't made varsity, I would have felt embarrassed going out in public like this." In a flash, Chuck casts aside his blanket cape with the flourish of a matador.

Grace's hands fly to her mouth.

When her brother left the house last night, his hair had been colorless, bleached so blond it was practically translucent. But sometime between then and now, he's dyed it blue. Bright blue.

Wildcat blue.

Through her fingers she says, "You did that for me? But what if I didn't make varsity?"

Chuck shrugs his bony shoulders. "I may not know shit about sports, but there can't be another Wildcat wilder than you." And with a level of pep Grace didn't think was chemically possible for her brother, he lifts his arms and shouts, "Gooooo, Grace!"

She jumps up and smothers Chuck in a hug.

"I can't believe you made me drag it out of you. It was so hot under those blankets!"

"I didn't want to make a big deal about it."

"Umm, have you forgotten that I went to West Essex? This is a *huge* deal." Chuck shakes his head. Pridefully, he says, "I can't believe my sister is a Wildcat."

Finally, Grace lets herself release some of the giddy fizz inside her. "We have our first scrimmage tomorrow. And Ali Park told me she thinks Coach might start me." Her brother's eyes widen. "Ali actually drove me home. We're tight now," she says with a wink.

"Well, Nana and I will be there. Maybe I can convince her to dye her hair blue too."

Grace follows Chuck into the hallway, both of them laughing because there's a good chance Nana might do it. Then she ducks into the bathroom to get a swim towel from the linen closet. While grabbing her toothbrush, she meets her eyes in the vanity mirror. Her hair is still in a stubby little tuft at the top of her head from tryouts.

Grace takes out the elastic and rakes her fingers through it. She'd always had short hair—a chinlength bob with bangs, usually—but she'd dyed it so many times during eighth grade, the hair started to break off on her pillow. So the summer before high school, she buzzed it into a pixie and began growing it out.

At West Essex, basically every girl has long hair. Grace would be lying if she said that didn't factor into it too. That maybe if she looked a little more like the other girls on her team, they'd do a better job remembering she was on it.

Of course, they didn't.

Grace actually likes the length. Past her shoulders now, after a full year of growing it. She can braid it or twist it up if she chooses. It's the color that makes her feel like a poseur. Mouse-belly brown. The lamest camouflage.

Underneath the bathroom sink, she finds a squeeze bottle holding what's left of Chuck's blue dye. The color looks so good. The perfect shade. And, with about half a bottle left, likely just enough.

She no longer needs to hide who she is. Grace is a Wildcat now.

And like Chuck said, maybe even the wildest.

FRIDAY, AUGUST 26
1:39 P.M.
ALI

Ali Park pulls along the curb in front of her house, turns off her Jeep, and sits. Her parents haven't left yet. Their sedan is still parked in the driveway, the trunk stuffed so full of presents—rivaling the back of Santa's sleigh—that it can't properly close. Her father has used a bungee cord to secure it.

She should go in. See them off. Make sure her father has the right GPS app on his phone, the one that updates live for traffic.

Instead Ali sinks low in her seat and pulls out her phone.

There's no other way to put it. She's turned into a stalker.

She can't even remember what she used to look at before finding Darlene Maguire on social media. Since then Ali can pass hours like minutes scrolling through Darlene's posted pictures, reading and rereading the comments people have left. Ali's found Darlene in pictures posted to other people's accounts. Friends, relatives. Figured out that the boy who took Darlene to formal was likely just a friend. She's read Darlene's field hockey stats back to when she was in middle school, read a movie review

Darlene wrote freshman year for the Oak Knolls student newspaper. She's found the fax number for Mr. Maguire's accounting office, found a fundraising page Darlene's mother set up to purchase beanbag chairs and a throw rug to make a reading nook in her second-grade classroom.

Or maybe this isn't too different from how Grace scouted Darlene at Kissawa. Studying the way she played, noting Darlene's favorite moves, like that breakaway fake out, so that when the time came, Grace would be ready.

The thing is, Ali could already tell Oak Knolls was about to score on her. Like some weird sixth sense, the warning manifested in a physical way, a muscle that progressively tightened in her gut.

The championship game had been scoreless for the first half. It was a grind befitting the two best teams in the division. Hardly any breakaways, hardly any passes rolling out of the midfield. Ali faced maybe three shots on goal, and none of them were direct hits. More like desperate chips.

But the Oak Knolls strikers came hard and fast at Ali in the second half. They showed zero fatigue, no trace of exhaustion. As if it were the first week of September and not the end of December. All swagger, even though the Wildcats had bested them in their two previous regular season outings.

The Wildcats, in comparison, were nervous, unsure, tentative. Her defenders kept getting beat. Ali, who normally manned her goal in silence, had taken to screaming her throat raw for the last seven or so minutes.

Right side! On the left, the left, the left! Watch her!

Ali kept glancing over at the sidelines. It was so quiet, she wasn't sure if Coach was even still there. Maybe he'd gotten too disgusted and left.

But no, Coach was there, arms crossed in front of his chest, his mouth a firm horizontal line.

And then, off Darlene Maguire's stick, the orange ball came whizzing. If she'd been looking at the field, Ali probably could have stopped it. But with her reaction time delayed, she only managed to get a fingertip on it, enough to shift the angle at which it hit the back of the net by a few meaningless degrees.

The Bulldogs erupted in screams and fell all over themselves. The undulating hug pile was practically a simultaneous team-wide orgasm. And Ali, alone in her goal, was choked with a painful, shameful impotence.

That's the thing about being a goalie. Any point scored is ultimately your fault. The buck stops with you. Or it doesn't.

Sometimes Ali will do the same kind of deep dive on herself. She'll look at every picture she's posted, read the comments, find herself tagged on other people's pages. Photos of her parents, her two older brothers, John and James. Of her sister-in-law, Susan, and her wedding to John two years ago, first a ceremony at Susan's family's church in New Jersey in traditional hanboks, and then later a chic champagne celebration at the top of a New York skyscraper. Of Ali and baby John-John, heavy on her lap, on Ali's seventeenth birthday. John took the train down from New York City with Susan and John-John. Ali's brother James, who would normally get a pass because he lives in Seattle, flew in on a red-eye, tacking on a few days at home before beginning an overseas business trip.

But it's a pointless exercise. Ali's account has always been locked, friends only. Still, she wonders if Darlene did any recon on her? Figured out ahead of time that Ali was weaker on her right side than her left? Was she actively looking for a vulnerability to exploit? Or did she just stumble upon one?

Ali hears the front door of her house close, the lock click. She turns off her phone. Her father pulls two roller bags toward the car, her mother following with a hanging bag holding her new dress, a pink-and-black houndstooth tweed shift with black enamel buttons running up the back. Ali had been with her mother when she bought it. The dress was so expensive it gave Ali pause, but her mother didn't hesitate. When it came to anything related to John-John, she needed no justification to splurge.

Not to mention, this was John-John's first birthday, a big deal for any Korean. Her brother John and Susan had rented out a restaurant overlooking Central Park. Susan had three aunts and an uncle flying in from Seoul.

"They're staying for three months," John had whined when they last FaceTimed. Ali had sat at the breakfast bar while her parents drank smoothies before heading to the golf course. She could watch John-John for hours, the plump rolls of his cherubic body, the way he waved at her with his meaty hands and cooed when Ali sang to him.

Susan, who was on the couch behind John, threw a stuffed rabbit at her brother's head.

"What? I love when they visit! I just hate doing the touristy stuff. It's like, how many times in my life do I have to go to the Statue of Liberty?"

Ali let out an anguished cry. "You promised that the next time I came to New York, you'd take me to the Statue of Liberty!"

John and Susan both leaned toward the camera. "Does that mean you're coming to John-John's dol?"

Ali grimaced.

Of course she wanted to say yes. So much so that she waited

until the last possible minute—until she heard that Coach was for sure coming back—to tell her family no.

Playing field hockey at Ali's level is a year-round commitment, and there are always things you miss out on. Ali's declined countless party invites and weekend trips with friends, and she even missed the Spring Fling her sophomore year for traveling team. Sacrifices she never thought twice about. But John-John's first birthday was a special moment for her entire family, an important and revered Korean tradition. Having to miss out on it was like salt in a wound Ali was pretending not to have. Still pretending.

All this to say, it would have been a difficult decision for Ali, had it been hers to make.

Ali hurries up to meet her parents in the driveway, the strap of her heavy gear bag tipping her body visibly to the left. She kisses and hugs them, combining her hello and goodbye.

"Please take lots of pictures, okay? Like, double what you think is enough," Ali tells them. She moves her gift for John-John from the trunk into the back seat. She doesn't want it to be crushed. She wrapped the gift in an adorable paper—one with illustrated animals in silly party hats—bought from the specialty stationery store in town. And Ali tied the ribbon four times before she was satisfied with the loops on the bow. "And take a video of when John-John opens my present. Oh, and another one of the doljabi stuff too! I want to see what John-John picks up."

"He'll pick up the book, like me," her father says.

"First and last time you did," her mother teases.

Her parents speak to each other. Not to Ali. Still, she's quick to chime in, "I picked the ball, remember?"

Her mother deadpans, "As if we could forget."

Ali knows they are still angry she didn't press the issue with Coach. After all, this was a onetime, one-game miss for a family obligation.

"My team needs me," she tried explaining. That she hadn't actually asked Coach would only make it harder for her parents to understand, so she didn't mention it.

It did feel good to be back playing with the girls again, especially after skipping out on Kissawa this summer. Despite how things ended last season, the Wildcats are looking strong. Grace did great against the freshman Luci, shutting Luci down from getting off a shot most times, though Luci got better each day. Mel was unstoppable, especially now that Phoebe was back chipping her perfect passes from midfield, which allowed Mel to really use her speed, sprinting ahead with full confidence that the ball would land where it needed to. Mel's shots on goal flew like fiery orange comets. Ali caught them hot in her goalie gloves, slapped them back into the atmosphere with her stick. She held her own. *More* than held her own.

She was damn near perfect.

"Call me when you get there," Ali says.

Her father kisses her on the top of her head. "Good luck tomorrow."

Her mother squeezes her. "We'll miss you."

"I'll miss you too." Ali feels something catch in her throat.

It really does suck not to be going.

But on the upside, her parents will miss tomorrow's scrimmage, which is a huge relief. Ali didn't need that worry on top of everything else.

After the drive away, Ali takes the stone path into the backyard. She kneels on the warm patio stones, unzips her bag, and removes her goalie pads one at a time, laying each out to bake in the afternoon sun.

First out are the pads that strap to Ali's legs, thick U-shaped foam blocks that cup the tops of her feet up to her mid-thighs. Next are the pads circling each of her arms, wrist to elbow. Next is Ali's chest pad, which she slips over her head like a sandwich board before putting on her varsity jersey. Her helmet and the plastic piece that hooks under her chin, protecting her neck, come out next.

Last are her goalie gloves, far and away the nastiest pieces of gear, but they are Ali's prized possessions, passed down to her by the previous Wildcat goalie, Livvy Mills, after her last game. The foam inside is turning to dust, so cleaning them must be done with care.

She stands up, and from that angle, the assembled pads are like a black exoskeleton, the discarded shell of a teen-sized locust. Her cocoon.

With it all strapped on, the shape of her body completely changes, taking on the bulky squared-off look of a Lego person. No hint that her breasts are full C cups, that her thick black hair gleams and hangs to the middle of her back. The scar on her hand where her grandmother's dog bit her is hidden, as is the splotchy birthmark on her right thigh. You can't tell that Ali's posture is impeccable, that her limbs are long and lean, benefits of having studied ballet through grade school.

This is the reason why she hates watching game film. How awkward she looks lumbering out from the goal when Coach calls them in for a time-out. It's hard to even take a drink of water. She has to set down her stick, flick off her gloves, unhook the neck piece, lift her helmet up.

That said, it is necessary protection. Protection that makes her brave enough to stick out an arm, lift a leg, take a shot off her chest. The field hockey balls fly hard and fast, hit your skin like bombs. Ali's teammates are far more exposed in their pleated kilts, bloomers, knee socks, and polos. Sure, they look way cuter, but she's seen their skin swell, bruise, split on impact. She's seen girls lose teeth, crack bones.

Really, the only bit of Ali that's still visible is behind the cage of her helmet—her eyes, the bridge of her nose, her cheeks. But that's all you need in competition. Some small, vulnerable spot to exploit. Just ask Achilles.

FRIDAY, AUGUST 26
2:25 P.M.
MEL

Melanie Gingrich pulls up to the West Essex Starbucks and counts the cars idling in the drive-through lane. Six, which makes her white Mini Cooper number seven, annoyingly the norm for this location. For whatever reason, it's always busy.

But the parking lot itself is surprisingly empty. Mel scrunches up her nose. The decals plastered to the store windows make it hard to see inside, but she thinks she spies a few empty tables.

She reaches over and squeezes the shoulder of her very best friend, Phoebe Holt, slouched low in shotgun, refreshing her email on her phone.

"Phoebs, let's ditch drive-through and grab a table inside instead."

Phoebe's blue eyes light up but she pauses before unbuckling her seat belt. "You sure you don't need to get home?"

Since Coach dismissed them from his classroom, Mel's been dashing around town, slaying the last of her to-do list, with

Phoebe ready to assist just like on the field. There are still a few loose ends to tie up, but if she runs out of time she can always pin her hair up instead of blowing it out with a round brush, the way she'd been planning to wear it tonight. It feels ungrateful not to accept this serendipitous gift bestowed upon them by the Starbucks gods, a chance to properly toast the long-awaited return of Mel and Phoebe, the Wildcats' dynamic duo.

She zips out of the drive-through line and into a parking spot, though Mel doesn't turn off the car right away. Instead, she announces, "I wanna hear the rest of this song," and ticks the already loud volume a few notches louder. She hasn't listened to it in forever and somehow forgot how much she loves it. Mel reclines her seat and stretches out.

"Last track," Phoebe informs her, lowering the back of her seat to match the pitch of Mel's, and begins to sing along.

Mel closes her eyes and sings too, totally not caring that her voice never stays in key. With the sunshine streaming in her open sunroof, all Mel sees and feels is warmth.

This mix was a surprise gift from Phoebe. Their personal greatest-hits soundtrack, *Wildcats Season 1*. Phoebe stealthily connected her phone to the car's Bluetooth while Mel drove them out of the high school parking lot. When Phoebe pressed play on the first track, Mel legit gasped, and then the two best friends busted out the dance they used to do on the varsity team bus to burn off their nervous energy. Despite being restrained by seat belts, not a shoulder shimmy or hand gesture popped off-beat.

Mel could have fooled herself into thinking no time had passed between that first season and this one, if not for the glimpses she caught in her rearview mirror of their newest and youngest teammate. Luci, wide-eyed and rod straight, in Mel's back seat, her hands tucked under her thighs.

Phoebe twisted around, stunned that Luci didn't know the song, even though Luci would have been only like nine or ten when it came out. Despite Mel's protest, Phoebe abruptly skipped to the next track, another favorite. At first Luci played like she'd heard this one before—clearly wishful thinking, because by the chorus, it was obvious she hadn't. Before Phoebe jumped ahead to the third track, Mel shut her car stereo off and didn't let Phoebe turn it back on until after they'd dropped Luci at her house. These were their love songs after all, and with everything their friendship had endured in the last few months, Mel didn't want to squander a single note on a third wheel.

When this last song ends, Mel opens her eyes and turns her head to face Phoebe. The girls smile at each other. It reminds Mel of this very night three years ago. Mel and Phoebe, pre-boobs but post-periods, wearing their brand-new varsity jerseys like nightgowns, were tucked in their sleeping bags, smiling at each other through the dark while their teammates snoozed around them. They felt like the two luckiest girls in the whole world.

And really, all things considered, they still are.

Phoebe turns her head and says, "I can't believe this is our last season."

Mel nods. "It'll be a miracle if I get through tonight without crying." She's quick to add, "Happy tears," despite already knowing she'll cry tears of sadness, too. How could she not, when it marks the beginning of the end of her time as a Wildcat.

Mel cuts the engine and grabs her wallet from the center console. Phoebe heads straight for the entrance, but Mel circles around and clicks open her trunk to grab a hoodie. This Starbucks is always freezing. She's got so many packages and shopping bags stuffed inside—plus her and Phoebe's field hockey gear—that it takes a bit of digging before Mel eventually pulls out a slouchy cotton sweater instead of a hoodie. Which is fine.

She slips it over her head and checks her reflection. Maybe cuter, actually.

Mel quickly adjusts whatever stuff she disturbed, though she takes extra care when repositioning an enormous gold piñata, making sure it won't get crushed when she closes the hatch.

It was a last-minute impulse buy—not accounted for in Mel's carefully laid plans, a bullet-pointed rainbow of ink copied in her very best penmanship—but this piñata might very well come to define her entire Wildcat legacy. She runs her hand lightly over the shimmering paper, her reflection mirrored in the hundreds of metallic snips. The confidence she's known for comes back from whatever mysterious place it drained to.

Mel feels ready. And not a moment too soon.

Tonight is the first Psych-Up of their brand-new season.

Coach has always been brilliant at coming up with different ways to keep his field hockey girls close. At the very core of his coaching philosophy is the belief that cultivating bonds off the field translates to bonds on the field. But Coach's implementation of Psych-Ups is, undoubtedly, his most genius idea. It's become such an important and beloved tradition, she can't imagine it would ever be abandoned by the Wildcats, not even when Coach eventually moves on and coaches somewhere else.

Psych-Ups are when the entire varsity Wildcat squad is invited to a senior player's house for a team dinner and sleepover before their weekend game. So either a Friday or Saturday night, depending on the schedule.

Coach always shows up for the dinner part. And depending on the vibe or what else he has going on, he sometimes sticks around and hangs out for a little while afterward.

A good bet is to get him talking about field hockey. Movies are also one of Coach's favorite topics. The girls have fun winding him up about famous movies they haven't seen. He can't believe they'd rather watch garbage reality TV instead of whatever cinematic masterpiece is currently streaming on Netflix. But it's not like getting stuck talking with one of your parents' friends, because Coach isn't butchering some hugely famous person's name. He listens to the same music, he doesn't need someone to explain why certain texts show up in blue bubbles and some in green bubbles. It's just... super chill.

Either way, before Coach takes off, he'll make a speech about the next day's game, get them fired up not simply to play but to win.

After he leaves, all twenty girls cram themselves into a den or family room and spread out their sleeping bags. Then they watch a movie of the senior host's choosing as a way to unwind, multiple bags of microwave popcorn in orbit. Sometimes they make it to the end credits. But at most Psych-Ups, the movie gets shut off well before. Coach expects everyone in bed, with lights out, by ten o'clock.

Every senior holds a Psych-Up at some point during the season—sometimes two—but first-night hosting duties always fall to the team captain. Mel's parents are going all out tonight—caterers booked, a white tent erected in the backyard, dozens of white rose arrangements, helium balloon sculptures assembled in Wildcat colors. Even still, Mel's Psych-Up will follow the structure of any other.

Until the clock strikes midnight.

That's when, at Mel's direction, the Wildcats break Coach's curfew for the first and only time all season to hold their own secret season kick-off celebration on their home field, underneath the twinkling stars.

It's not to undermine his authority. This is in no way a rebellion. If anything, it's about the girls doubling down on the values Coach works so hard to instill in them. Loyalty. Pride. Grit.

Team first, always.

The captains have plenty of opportunities to put their own spin on the festivities. What music they'll listen to, what bonding games they'll play, what late-night diner to stuff their faces at afterward. But the night always, always culminates in a special ceremony where the captain presents each of her teammates with their varsity jersey. And, in accepting those jerseys, the girls pledge their hearts to the Wildcats.

It's a beautiful thing.

Mel is a golden girl, a top player of not just the Wildcats but all high schools in their state. Naturally, she aspires for her Psych-Up midnight celebration to be the greatest yet. That she's had less than a month to prepare for it—while previous captains got an entire off-season—has only made Mel more determined to exceed expectations.

But that wasn't the only challenge Mel faced with her Psych-Up plans. There's another horrible kink she needed to account for.

Until last season, the Wildcats have always been champions.

The best strategy Mel could come up with was to avoid, avoid, avoid, and instead keep her teammates focused on the future. In fact, she planned to expressly forbid any mention of last season's disastrous end during her Psych-Up. This was how Mel herself survived the off-season, embracing whatever methods of distraction necessary to put it out of her mind. And she suspected she wasn't the only one.

Mel and her teammates each swallowed the same bitter pill of disappointment, forced it down, and tried to move on. Was it really such a big deal if the loss was still there, a lump bobbing in the backs of their throats?

Mel's answer remained a firm *nope*, even after tryouts began this week and the girls who were on last year's varsity team were reunited after the different leagues and camps and club teams that scattered them in the off-season.

They seemed nervous to be around one another again. But in the aftermath of last season, the girls had never turned on one another, never pointed fingers or threw blame at another player's feet. So it didn't take long for things to warm back up. Muscle memory to kick in.

Mel felt this most acutely with Phoebe. Those nine long months of having not played together compressed into seconds as soon as Coach blew his whistle Monday morning. They knew each other again.

Technically speaking, this week the girls performed as well as maybe they ever have. Each of Mel's teammates was sharp, focused, committed, determined. They played like they had everything to prove.

Which apparently they did.

What else could explain Coach's punishing final workout today, which lasted almost twice as long as years past? Her teammates probably accepted it as an overdue penance. But Mel suspected there was more to Coach's methods. It was as if he were trying to physically wring any lingering effects of last season out of their bodies. As if he could see, somehow, that they still carried it with them, a shadow stapled to the turf on a week of sunny summer days.

Standing with her teammates around the flagpole this afternoon, Mel had a nagging feeling that she'd made the wrong call with her Psych-Up approach. That she, as team captain, could hinder Coach's efforts instead of help, was completely out of the question.

Even though the returning players had individually dealt with last season's losses, they hadn't ever processed it as a team. Maybe they needed to. The timing wasn't ideal, especially with so many new players, who had nothing to do with the championship loss, joining them. But it might be good for the new players to see—up close and unvarnished—how deeply it still mattered to the ones who did.

It was a delicate situation, sure, but when Mel finally let Phoebe pull her up onto the classroom chair, she looked out at her teammates dancing and remembered that the girls themselves weren't. They were strong. Not only that, they would become even stronger tonight, when standing side by side in their varsity jerseys, as Wildcats.

It dawned on Mel how cowardly her decision had been to treat last season like some kind of dirty secret. Nope. Instead she would help her team face the past head-on.

She just needed to figure out how. And fast.

It came to her when she ducked into Party City to grab boxes of sparklers for the varsity jersey ceremony. She loved the idea of each teammate lighting one sparkler off another, forming a glittering chain that would brighten the midnight dark. On her way down the aisle, she breezed right past the piñatas.

Then Mel stopped. Hustled back. Moved a papier-mâché rainbow to the side. Shifted over a unicorn.

And there it was. A giant golden number 2. Probably made for a little kid's birthday party.

Mel, however, saw an effigy of a runner-up trophy.

Like the best ideas, it came together in a snap, the whole thing playing out like a movie in her mind. Her teammates, blindfolded and spun around one by one, each getting to take a crack at it with a field hockey stick. It would be lots of laughs, watching the girls stumble and sway before getting their bearings. But working together, using all their might and mettle, fueled by their heartache and frustration and disappointment, they would smash that 2 to smithereens and gorge themselves on the candy that spilled out.

I mean, could anything be more perfectly Wildcat?

The only thing Mel hasn't yet figured out is how to string the piñata up at the field tonight. But something will come to her. Today proved yet again, as always, that Mel only needs to trust herself, trust what Coach has cultivated in her. In all of the girls.

Mel closes the trunk and hurries across the parking lot to the Starbucks. Her hand is on the door when her phone rings in the back pocket of her cutoffs. Her heart lifts. Wondering.

But it's only Gordy.

Shit.

Through the window, Mel meets eyes with Phoebe, who's already in line. She points to her ringing phone and mouths, "One sec!"

The first words out of Gordy's mouth are, "Did you make the team?"

It seems so stupid now, how stressed Mel let herself get last night. Making Gordy stay up late with her on the phone, way later than she should have, reassuring her that she wouldn't be cut. Especially after she'd so artfully dodged Gordy's calls and texts these last few weeks, found plausible excuses to decline his repeated invites to hang out with him.

"Yes, I made the team," she tells him sheepishly.

Though honestly? With Coach, you really never know.

Gordy lets out a breath he'd apparently been holding. "When I didn't hear from you, I got nervous."

"Sorry. Phoebe and I have been out—"

"And you're still team captain?" Gordy asks tentatively.

"Yup." Hearing Gordy's sad sigh, Mel reminds him, "Um, that's *good* news, Gordy."

"For you, maybe. I'm about to be dumped."

She could correct him. They were never officially together. Mel was careful about that from the start. Making it clear to Gordy that this, whatever *this* was, was super low-key, a summer thing. Not to say it hadn't been nice. Maybe even really nice. But it didn't change the fact that come September, she would need to devote herself completely to her field hockey team. Anyway, Gordy goes to West Essex. He already knows how it is with the Wildcats.

Mel says sweetly, "I wasn't planning to dump you. Just ghost you."

Gordy lets out a little puff of breath instead of a laugh. Mel can almost feel it against her forehead, the way she would if she were curled up in his arms.

"Wow, that's really cool of you, Mel. Thanks so much."

Mel teases him like this sometimes. As if she didn't care about him. But hearing him pout, already missing her, tugs at Mel. No joke.

She should get off the phone.

Instead Mel walks the curb like a balance beam, setting one white canvas sneaker in front of the other and asks, "Where are you?"

"I just got to the lookout on the Frick trail. Where are you?"

"Starbucks."

"Oh wait. Yeah. I see you down there."

Gordy's turn to tease her.

The first time they hiked the Frick trail together, Mel had sworn she could see the Starbucks from the lookout. Not because she *actually* could, though she did follow the highway with her finger to a spot that was surely a decent guess. It was amazing, dizzying really, to see the entire valley from that vantage point, lush with the greens of summer. Her universe normally fit neatly inside a rectangle of Astroturf.

Granted, she was in a weird place. So much was in flux and none of it in her control. There was her scholarship to Truman, Phoebe's knee injury, whether or not Coach would be coming back to West Essex, whether or not she would be team captain. Mel was haunted by how she'd let Coach down. His lead scorer unable to put up a single point. Not just in the championship game, either. Mel didn't score in their last two regular-season games. That she'd played well in the off-season for her club team coaches was no consolation. Actually, it made Mel feel worse.

Hooking up with Gordy gave Mel a way out of her own head. When they were kissing, she thought only of kissing. It was a huge relief to let go. After all, how could things fall back into place with her holding on so tightly to the pieces?

And now, just as she'd hoped, they have. Pretty much.

"Mel? You still there?"

"Yes."

"Just for the record, I'm happy for you. Last night . . . I've never heard you sound so unsure of yourself. I mean, you're—"

"Ooh. Hey, Gordy?" Mel bites her lip. "That's my mom on the other line."

"Right."

Something in his voice tells Mel that Gordy knows she's lying. Mel likes him. She really does. But the ache that's appeared in Mel's chest only makes her clearheaded about what she needs to do. So, with a finger already hovering over the red circle, she ends the call with a purposefully cool and detached "Bye."

Mel hops off the curb and hurries inside.

Phoebe sits at a table, lips around her straw, draining her usual—a Grande iced mocha, no whip. Mel's usual—a Grande iced mocha, extra whip—is in front of an empty chair. Phoebe's staring at her phone, dragging her finger down the screen, the same steady stroke, over and over again.

"Everything okay, Phoebs?"

"Yup." Phoebe turns her phone over, screen side down. "You?"

Mel tucks her hands inside her sweater cuffs and pulls her cup greedily toward her. She takes a sip. Perfectly sweet. "Never better."

Back at home, Mel finds Psych-Up party prep in full swing. A cleaning crew is spread out across the house, vacuuming stripes into the carpet, cleaning windows, fluffing pillows. The caterers have arrived and are stacking three different sizes of white china plates. Outside, the pool guy is lying on his belly, testing the pH in a little beaker.

Her parents spared no expense. Why would they, with so much

to celebrate? Their daughter got a full ride to Truman. No matter the outcome of this season, Mr. and Mrs. Gingrich are certain they've already won.

There are plenty of other success stories. Most of her senior teammates have already committed to top schools. Jenny Puglisi is headed to Monroe College, Summer Ackerman to DCU. The rest are still weighing their options.

The only senior who hasn't received a single offer yet is Phoebe.

Mel always knew that two scholarships to Truman would be a long shot, even before Phoebe got hurt. But Phoebe's worked so, so hard to come back after her injury. Landing a spot on a college team has to happen for her. And Mel is ready to do whatever she can to help Phoebe shine. Fingers crossed, they will at least end up playing in the same division next year. It will be totally surreal for her and Phoebe to be on the same field wearing different jerseys. But the secret truth is that they could never *really* be against each other. Not in their hearts.

Mel flips through the mail on the kitchen island. Even though she committed to Truman a month ago, she still gets university brochures from schools who aren't targeting her for field hockey. But it's the new September issue of *Vogue* that catches Mel's eye, a glossy behemoth, addressed to her mom. She slips it underneath her arm and heads upstairs.

Mel finds her varsity jacket laid out on her bed, back from the dry cleaner and sheathed in plastic, a *C* in blocky font newly sewn onto her sleeve. She tiptoes over, sits carefully next to it, and snakes her hand under the plastic. Thousands of soft, delicate white loops, like a brand-new fluffy towel.

Coach years ago let it slip to Mel that when the time came, the captain's *C* would be hers. Mel understood that to mean immediately after the championship game of her junior season, as it had been for the previous captains. Knowing the honor was coming to her ahead of time didn't take anything away from Mel's excitement about it. Only shifted it by a few seconds, to right after Coach would call her forward to stand in front of the entire team and give a little speech about her, listing the qualities he felt made her the most deserving.

Would Coach try to surprise her with some new compliment? Or would he say the sorts of things he'd already told her privately? Either way, Mel hoped she wouldn't blush too badly.

Never in a million years did she imagine her junior season ending with the seniors crying in a huddle. Or Phoebe using her stick like a crutch to hobble over to the trainer's table. Ali never even made it back into the locker room. Apparently, she walked straight off the field and onto the bus.

Mel lowered her head and watched as pinpricks of blood speckled through her sports bra. Turf rash from a desperate dive she'd made in the final seconds of the match for a ball that had been stolen off her stick. She knew it hurt, but she felt only the shock that she would not turn this around. That she would have no more chances to pull something off and save the day. It was over.

All the compliments she'd been imagining Coach might pay her evaporated. She suddenly had no idea what he thought of her. Her performance in these last three games like an eraser rubbed over her, exposing her for a fluke. Or, worse, a fraud.

And yet, when Coach finally came in to address them, Mel still glanced up, hopeful and hungry.

He said, "I want everyone on the bus in five minutes," and then left. Without so much as a glance in Mel's direction.

Their team captain, Rose Tynam-Reed, stepped into Mel's sight line with a look of disgust that made Mel pull out her ponytail so she could hide behind her hair.

What a horrible teammate she was. With all the hearts that were breaking around her, Mel even thinking about getting the *C* was the worst kind of betrayal.

She can see now that Coach withholding it from her was just. It hurt at the time, but isn't that why they call it growing pains?

Anyway. It's a new season now. Comeback time.

Mel tears away the plastic bag and slips her varsity jacket on, loving the weight of it, and flops on her bed, her feather pillows catching her in a puff.

This season will be Mel's victory lap. This time she *will* deliver. For Phoebe, for Coach, for all the girls. There's no other choice.

Her phone buzzes in the blankets. Another time her heart skips a beat.

Gordy: I'm having people over tonight. You should come.

Gordy: And before you accuse me of forgetting about your sleepover, you can bring the entire team.

Gordy: In fact, I looked up the field hockey calendar. The Wildcats' season doesn't officially begin until tomorrow's scrimmage. So you can't start ghosting me until then. Deal?

Gordy's persistence makes her smile. Mel respects it. But she doesn't text him back.

FRIDAY, AUGUST 26
3:12 P.M.
PHOEBE

Phoebe Holt drops her duffel bag and closes the front door. The central air quickly, mercifully, overtakes the summer steam she's pulled inside with her. She smiles, hearing Hamburger, the Holt family golden retriever, clamber off the living room couch and come galloping down the front hallway to greet her, his nails scraping against the hardwood floors.

He'd been a handsome dog for most of his life. Silky fur, pink tongue, white teeth, the best boy. But at thirteen, evidence of Hamburger's age is suddenly everywhere. His dull coat, the fatty tumors on his belly, his horrible breath. Cataracts, a drop of oil on the lens of each eye.

Phoebe winces as Hamburger slides clumsily on his last few steps toward her, slipping on the new braided throw rug her mother bought for the foyer, and he knocks into her like a canine bowling ball.

Hamburger couldn't give a shit. After a few happy sniffs, he greedily licks Phoebe's ankles, her skin salty from sweat. "Hammy, quit it," she says. "I feel nasty enough." She gently nudges his soft head away as she steps on the back of her sneakers to remove them, then peels her socks off with her feet. Phoebe would crouch down to give him a good petting if she weren't so sore. Instead she scratches her watermelon-pink fingernails along the span of fur between his ears.

This is how they'd spent the weeks immediately after her surgery, when Phoebe was immobile. She'd lain prone on the couch with Hamburger splayed on the floor beside her, his head lifted high enough to meet her hand, both of them still except for the scratching. Shells of their former selves.

Hamburger lumbers off, his coat rubbing against the Wildcat paw print flag that will be imminently unfurled and slid into the socket mounted outside the Holts' front door. Phoebe brushes away the fur he leaves behind on it, hopefully the last of Hamburger's summer shed. She pushes away thoughts of next summer, when Hamburger likely won't be around anymore, and focuses instead on this dumb-ass rug that has to go.

Phoebe uses her stick blade to lift it up off the floor and carries it toward the kitchen. "Hey, Mom! We need to talk about this rug!" She thinks not just of her dog. God forbid Phoebe were the one to slip and reinjure her knee. She would have no choice but to murder her own mother.

A few steps deeper inside and Phoebe smells something strange. It's plasticky. Strong. As if someone mistakenly blew up a new pool float inside.

Following her nose, Phoebe finds her mother standing in the kitchen directly under the skylight. Mrs. Holt's hair is the same color as the fur on Hamburger's belly, more white than blond.

She's in tan chino shorts and a pink polo shirt, housed inside a clear plastic rectangular tent only slightly larger than her body, almost like the packaging of the middle-aged mother of Barbie.

Mrs. Holt waves and shouts, "Go Wildcats!" A fuzzy circle fogs the plastic in front of her mouth.

"Mom, what the hell is that?"

"A personal spectator tent! Isn't it clever? They'll go right over top of our chairs. Now your dad and I can stay warm and dry on the sidelines all season. And check this out!" She unzips the front plastic panel and presses her hands against a layer of otherwise-invisible netting. Her voice louder now, she announces, "Voilà! A mosquito-free zone!"

Since freshman year, Phoebe's mother and father have made nearly every single one of her games, rain or shine or snow, home or away. Other parents or friends fill the bleachers when they can, casually watching the game as they chitchat, glancing at the action whenever they hear cheers. The Holts choose a spot several feet away from the other spectators, sit side by side in camp chairs—Wildcat navy, of course, his and hers, with MR. H and MRS. H monogrammed in white on the carrying sleeves—their eyes trained on the game.

There's an open cardboard shipping box on the counter. Phoebe peeks inside and sees the packing slip. "You spent two hundred bucks on these."

"Each." Furrowing her brow, Mrs. Holt carefully and deliberately twists the tent in on itself, collapsing it into a surprisingly small disk not much larger than a Frisbee, which she flicks toward the counter. It lands impressively inside the box. She nods pertly, pleased, and then turns to face her daughter. "So, what's the latest with your knee? Any soreness?"

"Nope. No soreness." Phoebe's mother either doesn't hear her or isn't listening. Whichever, Mrs. Holt sets to filling a plastic ziplock bag with ice from the dispenser on the door of the fridge. "Aren't you going to ask me if I made the team?"

Her mother freezes, eyes wide. "Did you make the team?"

"No, I've been cut," Phoebe says wryly, and hops up onto the kitchen island. "So I hope you can return those tent thingies."

"Very funny." Her mother wraps the bag of ice in a fresh dish towel and presents it to her daughter.

Phoebe folds her arms. "Mom! I just told you! My knee feels great."

"Like I don't know how hard Coach makes you girls work today."

"It was brutal," Phoebe concedes. "Borderline sadistic, actually." She can't hide her pride when adding, "And I totally killed it."

As grueling as Coach's workouts are on the last day of tryouts, Phoebe has always, weirdly, looked forward to them. The other girls tend to think of this final day as something they need to *survive* in order to make varsity. For Phoebe, it's a chance to show off her very best qualities as a player. When it comes to strength and endurance, Phoebe is peerless on the Wildcats.

In her very first season, she and Mel were newbies and completely blindsided the first time the older players dropped their sticks and started Coach's warm-up loop over again. Phoebe had eaten a bagel with cream cheese for breakfast that morning, a mistake, and by the beginning of their fourth mile run she was overcome by the urge to puke. Phoebe didn't stop running, didn't even slow down. She kept pace at the front of the pack with the older girls and just turned her head, arching her neck and projecting as best as she could toward the sideline.

The Wildcats talked about that move for the entire rest of the season. Phoebe was an instant legend.

And so, from the minute her eyes fluttered open after her ACL surgery, Phoebe vowed that, by today, she would return to the field in better shape than ever before. It is what pushed her in rehab to do another set of reps, pedal another mile on the stationary bike. It transformed her despair into determination.

She still has work to do. Her timing is stubbornly off, Phoebe knows. And even if she pretends otherwise, Mel knows it too. But that was part of why performing well today was so important to Phoebe. She could show her team and Coach how committed she was to coming back 100 percent. To prove that she would never stop working until she got there.

"I'm sure you did kill it, Phoebs." Her mother shakes her head and sighs. "Just like I'm sure that, if your knee *was* hurting you, you wouldn't tell me." With that, her mother places the ice on Phoebe's leg, holding it there while the cubes shift and slide inside the bag, forming a steady cradle of cold around her knee. "And that's what worries me more than anything."

Phoebe rolls her eyes. Of course she gets why her parents act like this. They've spent the past nine months in limbo, simultaneously in awe and unnerved by their daughter's determination. Torn between cheering Phoebe on and urging her to take it easy. If only they'd quit torturing themselves and accept what they all know to be true. Even if her parents asked her, begged her, to slow down, Phoebe wouldn't. Couldn't. The pain of not being a Wildcat is worse than anything Phoebe ever feels in her knee.

"You'll see at tomorrow's scrimmage that you don't have to worry," Phoebe says.

"Remember that word, okay? 'Scrimmage.' Meaning the outcome doesn't matter."

Phoebe recoils. "Mom. We're playing Oak Knolls."

Her mother turns on the sink. "What about that girl? Who replaced you?"

"Kearson Wagner."

"Is she back on the JV team or . . ."

"She made varsity too." Phoebe sees her mother soften with relief, which royally pisses Phoebe off. "I'm actually glad Coach gave Kearson another chance." This isn't a lie, exactly. Just a slightly more benevolent version of the truth. "But I hope she's not too bummed when she doesn't see much playing time."

"Well, at the very least, this Kearson girl will be there if you need a rest. I'm sure that's why Coach—"

"I won't need a rest." Phoebe hops down. Even though the ice bag feels good, she tosses it into the sink, sending a splash of soapy water up against her mother's polo.

"Seriously, Phoebe? This is exactly what got you into this trouble in the first place!"

Upstairs, Phoebe gets a bath running, hot water tap turned full blast. She shakes in a generous amount of Epsom salts, which her PT said she should be doing after every practice and game. While the tub fills and the air thickens with steam, Phoebe peels off her still-damp layers, a tank top, her sports bra, her shorts and underwear.

Usually, by the end of summer, she's a tan line disaster. A crosshatch made from various combinations of tank tops and sports bra straps. A bronze band between where shorts end and her shin guards begin. To even their skin out, both she and Mel would strategically drape themselves in pool towels so that the sun hit only certain parts of their body.

But this summer, Phoebe's tan is enviable. She twists and turns in the mirror. Baked an even brown over her shoulders and chest, creamy white in one line where her bandeau bathing suit top kept her covered. Even better than the girls who lifeguard at the country club pool.

To Phoebe, it looks weird.

The last thing that comes off is her compression bandage—Knee Spanx is what Phoebe calls it. She sits on the toilet and rolls it down. It's damp and smells musty, having taken a real beating this week.

Phoebe has a hinged brace she wears on the field. She fucking hates it. Black, hard plastic, a hinge on either side, lots of Velcro straps, all parts working to keep her knee stabilized. It is ugly as hell and impossible to ignore when she has it strapped on. But yes, of course Phoebe wears it. She's not an idiot.

The Knee Spanx, however, Phoebe has on most of the time. And like *actual* Spanx, it simultaneously increases her confidence while also making Phoebe aware that she needs a gimmick to trick everyone, including herself, that her body's different than it actually is.

The moment Phoebe first hurt her knee was memorable only because of the injury she sustained. She almost wishes it had been the result of some killer highlight-reel play, an insane collision that would have made the crowd gasp. But no.

It was three games before the end of last season. Phoebe had been pushing a ball up the field, when a defender finally reached her. Phoebe got the pass off her stick, slicing it upfield for Mel, but the defender still swiped at her. Phoebe hurdled the defender's stick so as to not be slowed down following the play. Her body had successfully performed this action somewhere in the neighborhood of a bazillion times before. She landed on her left foot, as per usual. But before her right one came down, Phoebe was flat on her back.

Mel threw down her stick and sprinted over. "Are you okay?"

"Yeah, I think so." Phoebe's knee didn't pop, and to her immediate relief, she wasn't in a ton of pain. But when she tried to get up on her own, she found she couldn't put much weight on her left leg. "Shit."

The ref blew his whistle, stopped time. Every player knelt down as is custom. Not just the Wildcats. The opposing team too. Out of respect.

With her arms slung over Coach and the athletic trainer, Phoebe hopped off the field. Mel followed them to the sideline, carrying Phoebe's stick for her, and crouched down next to Phoebe, listening intently as the trainer assessed her.

"How's it feel, Phoebe?"

Phoebe glanced down at her knee. It was suddenly a balloon. "Better than it looks," Phoebe said, trying not to sound nervous.

She waved at her parents across the field. Gave them a thumbs-up.

Coach lingered over her for a few seconds, but then called in the team and made some quick adjustments. Phoebe tried not to take it personally. He'd be over later to check on her. They had two other midfielders besides Phoebe, but one was currently on the field and the other subbing in on defense. Half the team had to shift around in order to restart the game.

Meanwhile, the trainer went to work. Feeling her knee, moving her leg around. As soon as the game restarted, Phoebe's eyes were on the field. Everyone looked so awkward out there, in these new positions, especially Mel.

"It's not that bad!" Phoebe told the trainer, convincingly until a certain twist brought a shock of pain that took her breath away.

"I think it's an ACL sprain." The trainer threw an instant cold pack onto the bench a few times, then handed it to Phoebe. "Let's see what this does for the swelling. I'll come check on you in ten minutes."

Phoebe made it five. The time was itchy. It was so uncomfortable for her not to be out there. She was always out there.

"I really think I'm good," she told the trainer.

"Phoebe."

The Wildcats were still up three to nothing. But if Phoebe were playing, it'd be four to nothing by now. Maybe five. "Just tape it up and I'll be fine!"

Her plea ignored, Phoebe got up herself, started slowly walking back and forth, putting a bit of weight on her left leg, then a bit more. The trainer was pretending not to pay any attention to her, but Phoebe knew she was watching.

"Please let me back in."

The trainer sighed. "If you can hop up and down on your left leg, I'll put you back in."

Coach, who Phoebe hadn't known was listening, looked away from the field to watch. Which made her want to suck the words back into her mouth. Phoebe tried, despite already knowing she couldn't. Despite the fact that the pain made her wince. It was a pathetic display. Coach turned back to the field, and Phoebe didn't say another word for the rest of the game.

It was indeed an ACL sprain. The doctor so annoyingly cheery with his diagnosis. "It could have been much worse," Phoebe remembers him saying. Ice, rest, and wrap. Four days of crutches. After that, three weeks of rest, and she'd be good to go. Phoebe did the math and immediately burst into tears. She would miss two regular-season games. And the championship game too.

Phoebe had never called Coach before. She could have texted, but the news felt too big to type. He answered quickly, just one ring, as if he'd been hoping she'd call. She immediately started sobbing.

Phoebe doesn't remember what she said to Coach exactly. But it didn't take a genius to decipher it was bad news. The worst possible news. She remembers wanting to ask him a million questions about her injury, wanted him to give it to her straight, since Coach had been through this before. Multiple times. But he stopped Phoebe before she could get going.

"Don't sweat it. You rest up and we'll talk when you're back at school."

When he hung up, Phoebe stared at her phone screen. She was surprised that the call took less than three minutes. Of course Coach had better things to do than play therapist on the phone. Plus she was too upset to have an actual conversation. If she needed comfort and encouragement, she'd call Mel. Still, his brevity stung.

Coach brought Kearson Wagner up from JV to varsity as Phoebe's sub. Even though their last two regular-season games were meaningless—the Wildcats had already statistically qualified for the championship—watching bobblehead Kearson (who Phoebe heard was a decent player) stumble and struggle and bob her bobblehead every time Coach screamed at her for screwing up (rightfully so because what the fuck was she doing out there) was still agony.

Putting Kearson's complete sucking aside, it shocked Phoebe that Mel didn't score a single goal on her own in those last two games. It sucked to watch her best friend—the most confident, competent player on their team—become someone unsure, unsteady, useless.

For that reason, Phoebe missing the championship was unthinkable.

Unthinkable.

So she played. Never thinking the Wildcats would lose. Never thinking her sprained ACL would become a tear. Never thinking it would put a universe between her and Mel for the next nine months.

Phoebe sinks into the tub, her back slipping against the porcelain until the tips of her blond hair begin to dance in the hot water. She needs to bend her legs in order to fit, knees cresting out into the cold air. Her injured one is bulbous, noticeably larger than the other. Scarred by multiple incisions. Pocked by injections and drains and scopes.

She held so much stress this week, put so much pressure on herself to prove to Coach, and to everyone really, that she hasn't lost her edge. There was a moment when Coach was reading off the names that she'd gotten worried. When Kearson was chosen before her. Maybe Phoebe hadn't made the cut. Maybe she would never fully recover. She clung to the strap of her gear bag, clung to it for dear life as Coach read another name, and then another, then another.

When he did finally say her name, Mel immediately reached over, took Phoebe's hand, and squeezed it. As if she'd been just as scared.

They had started the summer with the best of intentions. Both girls quietly determined not to let Phoebe's inability to play field hockey affect their friendship. It proved harder than either one expected. So much of their relationship, they realized, was tied up in this sport. Not just in the games and the practices but in hundreds of miles on team buses, hours in airports, sharing beds in hotel rooms, huddled under awnings during rain delays. Their earnest attempts to untangle themselves from field hockey seemed to do more damage than good. For most of the summer, they avoided each other, choosing to preserve what was left than let it completely unravel.

So while Mel made out with Gordy, Phoebe ignored the emails and phone calls of college scouts looking for an update on her condition. While Mel made out with Gordy, Phoebe rehabbed with her PT specialist. While Mel made out with Gordy, Phoebe practiced drills alone in her backyard.

This imbalance was nothing new. Mel is a truly gifted player. She doesn't need to train to perfect a skill. It's one and done. That's how quickly she absorbs it. Instant muscle memory. Phoebe works twice as hard to play at Mel's level.

If it now takes three times as much work? Fine.

Phoebe's injury nearly cost her everything she loved. Her team. Her sense of self. Her ability. Her strength. Her best friend. Basically all that defined her as a person. Who wouldn't work as hard as they could to come back from that?

There is just a small wound left to heal. A divot where a drainage tube was inserted after she developed an infection post-surgery. Tenderly, and with almost surgical precision, Phoebe uses her pinkie nail like a razor blade, sliding it between her skin and the scab. The underneath is slick and pink. A rivulet of blood, not much more than you'd get nicking your leg shaving, trickles down her skin and into the bathwater.

This will be the last time I pick this scab, Phoebe thinks. It's a thing she always says when she messes with it, but today she means it.

FRIDAY, AUGUST 26
4:58 P.M.
KEARSON

Kearson Wagner opens and closes her fists as discreetly as she can, hoping to flick away the tingles in her hands. She made herself a new mix for this season, only brand-new songs released this summer. The volume is up as loud as her phone will go, earbuds nestled snug in her ears, little vibrating pebbles.

A tap on her shoulder. Her mother, in the driver's seat. Kearson pulls out an earbud. Just one. "What?"

"Everything okay?" Her mother keeps her voice light, pretending to be more focused on an empty intersection, dutifully glancing left, then right, then left again, a performance worthy of a driver's ed instructional video. The sunlight makes her white silk blouse nearly see-through.

Kearson pulls the invisible levers inside her, hoisting a smile to her face. As soon as she guides the earbud back into her ear, her mother tugs the white cord, causing both to drop out.

"Seriously, Mom?"

"You're going to go deaf playing your music that loud, Kears."

"I can't listen to NPR. It makes me carsick."

"All you had to do was ask." Her mother makes a big show of gently pressing the button that turns off the car radio. Lips pursed, a pleased little *hmm* sound escapes through her nose. A check mark on an tally sheet of what a good mother she is.

The driver's side window is still rolled down from her mother's daily cigarette, even though the air-conditioning is on high and the smoke mostly gone. Somewhere in the distance, the rhythmic *chop chop chop* of a lawn sprinkler slicing a stream of water. Kearson closes her eyes and breathes to bring her heart rate down to match its pace. But the only thing slowing is the speed her mother is driving.

"You're going to make me late."

Kearson's mother pauses at the next stop sign and lights a second cigarette from a pack she already put away. After a deep puff, she leans her elbow against the open window, her arm straight up. Her wristwatch remains stationary, but three thin gold bracelets slide to the middle of her forearm. Resting her temple against her fist, the lit end of the cigarette dangerously close to her hairsprayed hair, her mother finally says, "Follow your heart, but take your brain with you." The delivery is soft and slow, drips of honey. "I heard that at a sales conference once, but don't you think it's good life advice?" Her mother wets her red lips. "Follow your heart, but take your brain with you," she says again in the same contemplative drawl.

Kearson rolls her eyes and tucks her earbuds back in.

They used to talk. Two night-blooming flowers sitting opposite each other on Kearson's twin bed. Her mother, clean face slick with night moisturizer, a soft roll of her belly visible through her nightshirt without her Spanx. And Kearson, with wet hair smelling of her apple detangler spray, retainer slid in, dots of Oxy on her problem areas.

Their discussions stretched hours past Kearson's bedtime. Her mother had gone through plenty the past few years, divorcing Kearson's stepdad, switching Realtor companies, and now, the beginnings of menopause.

She didn't get into the nitty-gritty details with Kearson, but instead posed plenty of abstract questions. Would she find love again? If she did, should she even *think* about getting married for a third time? Would she earn Top Producer Midsize Market again this year? Or would it be taken by some younger, prettier real estate agent who was better at social media?

"I keep tweezers in my purse," she once confessed. "I'm growing a beard one wiry chin hair at a time."

"Mom! Stop! You're beautiful!"

Growing up, Kearson was always impressed by her mother's flawless appearance. Stylish clothes. A full face of makeup, a natural yet elevated look. Her whitened smile swung from wooden FOR SALE signs hammered into front lawns across West Essex. She was ambitious as hell, held herself to the highest expectations. Her mother worked hard and she *loved* working hard. It was a beautiful thing for a daughter to watch.

And yet there was something alluring about seeing her mother, a confident, successful woman, laying bare her insecurities in the middle of the night. It made Kearson respect her even more. Her friends talked ruthlessly about their moms, outdoing each other with the goriest details observed behind closed doors, colonoscopy prep, cellulite, varicose veins, hot flashes. Kearson would keep her mother's secrets forever.

Kearson had her own worries, of course. Boys she liked, pressures at school, drama with the JV team. Trivial stuff, really. But her mother treated Kearson's every concern with reverence. She could take a single fear or dream of Kearson's and coax out others Kearson didn't know were tethered to it, gently, subtly, deftly unspooling her.

Kearson loved the dizzy head rush of oversharing, never gave a thought to slowing things down, keeping some parts of her life private. Stupidly, she put the same blind faith in her friends on JV, aligning herself with Marissa and Quinn, trusting them despite already knowing the kind of girls they were. It barely stung when those two stabbed her in the back. But Kearson never thought her mother would betray her. That wound will never, ever heal.

"It's just up here," Kearson says. "On the left."

For the two games Kearson had played varsity last season, she was a passenger in the car that also dropped Mel off. Even still, it would be easy to pick out Mel's house from the other stately colonials on the block. Two clusters of navy blue and white helium balloons float cheerily above the pom-pom topiaries that flank the arched black front door. The house is huge, the lawn perfectly landscaped, with lemon-leaf hedges, a gardenia tree, and a curving redbrick walkway. Mel's Mini Cooper shares the driveway with Ali's Jeep. Coach's SUV is parked at the bottom, blocking both cars in.

Her mother pulls up right alongside it.

Kearson tightens at the thought of Coach and her mother having to make polite small talk. Kearson knows Coach would be cordial and respectful, because that's the way teachers have to deal with even the most overbearing parents. But how would her mother behave? What she might say to him?

At the end of last season, in a meeting with both Coach and the athletic director to discuss a complaint her mother had made regarding Kearson being subbed out of the last regular-season game, Kearson had tried to be as helpful as possible, sharing whatever tidbits she could think of to contextualize her mother's recent erratic behavior—the full-blown menopause of course, but also her two divorces, the antidepressants, at least a half bottle of white wine each night.

It seems her mother hasn't decided how to play the situation. She tentatively peers inside Coach's SUV, her bottom lip caught under her teeth, and then appears relieved he's not inside it.

No surprise. Coach is never late to anything Wildcat related.

Stepping out of the car, Kearson pauses to smooth the front of her chambray jumper and makes sure the bow sash is tied pertly at her hip. From the trunk, Kearson loads up her arms with her gear for tomorrow's scrimmage; a tote with her sleepover clothes, a bathing suit, and a towel; and a rolled-up sleeping bag and pillow. Kearson tries to get away with just a wave goodbye, but her mother beckons her over. Kearson comes as close as the curb.

"I'd like to swing by your scrimmage tomorrow. I have a closing in the morning but—"

"You don't have to do that." Kearson's voice is heavy on the *don't*.

"I'm trying to be supportive, Kears. I've backed way off, which you know isn't easy for me. Can I at least get a little credit for that?"

"If you really want to support me, then you won't come. I just want to play, Mom. I don't want to have to think about you." It sounds meaner than she intended, but Kearson isn't about to walk it back.

Her mother leans across the car to the passenger side, trying to close the gap between them, and says quietly, "Okay," but her voice is uncertain, even regretful. She wants to change her answer. Kearson makes sure to walk away before her mother has the chance.

"Have fun with the girls tonight," her mother calls after her. Less directive than plea.

Defiant, Kearson tells her, "I will."

She surfs that wave of energy straight into Mel's house. Hugs her teammates with equal-if-not-tighter squeezes. Smiles for their pictures and takes just as many pictures of them. The girls go out of their way to be nice, and Kearson is grateful for every undeserved kindness they show her, so grateful that she stays with them for as long as she can possibly bear to.

But the way her guilt hangs on her takes her by surprise, heavier tonight than it's been in months. Or maybe it's easier for Kearson to deflect her guilt with anger when she's with her mother?

When it gets to be too much, she retreats to the den and finds it a good, quiet place to collect herself. She looks at the books on the bookshelf, studies the pictures of Mel and her family. She flips through an old gossip mag predicting a celebrity divorce that actually did come to pass. She slips off her shoes, climbs onto the back of the den sofa, and presses the taped end of a fallen crepe-paper twist to the wall.

Kearson was euphoric when she unexpectedly got called up to varsity last season. Coach came to her first-period class, and that alone made her heart flutter. In the hallway, he explained the unfortunate situation with Phoebe's ACL sprain—he'd gotten the call last night—and that Phoebe would be out for three weeks.

Kearson's hand went to her mouth. "She'll miss the championship?" Most of the JV girls worshipped Mel Gingrich, because she made it look easy. But Kearson looked up to Phoebe for the opposite reason. Nobody worked harder than her.

Coach nodded solemnly. "This is a dare-to-be-great situation, Kearson," he told her, and with a bashfulness that she didn't expect, pulled a Wildcat varsity jersey out from behind his back. "You think you might be up for it?"

Though she loves field hockey, Kearson isn't the kind of player who's after a scholarship, or even to play in college beyond an intramural team. But joining the varsity team still gave her plenty to daydream about. Slipping right in with Mel and feeding her perfect passes. Getting her picture in the newspaper. Earning herself a Wildcats varsity jacket.

Kearson tries to grab hold of those dreams again, fishing around for them like her house keys at the bottom of her book bag. They must still be inside her somewhere since none of them ended up coming true.

She stiffens as a palm presses into the hollow between her shoulder blades, then draws back, the blunt edges of a gel manicure tenderly clawing up the looseness of Kearson's top.

"Hey! I've been looking for you!" Mel tilts her head to the side. "Why are you in here all by yourself?"

"My dad just called to wish me luck tomorrow."

"Oh. Sweet. Can I talk to you for sec? Privately?"

A trickle of sweat rolls down the small of Kearson's back. "Sure." But Mel immediately puts her at ease. Linking arms, Mel guides her out of the den and up the staircase to the first landing. Both girls sit down with their knees angled toward each other. Noises from the party simmer below them.

Keeping her voice down, Mel says, "I'm trying to make this

spoiler free, Kearson, but I have some special activities planned for tonight, and one of them involves the returning players welcoming the new girls to the team." Mel scoots closer until their knees are touching. "I know this is your first Psych-Up, but you're not technically a newbie, either. So . . ." She bats her eyelashes. "What side of that line would make you most comfortable?"

Kearson presses a palm to her forehead, as if Mel's sunny smile actually radiated warmth.

"I'm honestly fine with whatever you decide, by the way. And you don't have to tell me now. I just thought that, if I let it be your choice, then you wouldn't feel awkward when it happened." Mel winces. "But maybe this is more awkward? Ugh. I'm sorry."

"Don't be sorry. It's really nice of you to give me the choice."

Mel is visibly relieved. "Okay."

"The truth is, I'm thinking of tonight as my fresh start with the Wildcats."

"I totally, totally respect that." Mel pats Kearson's leg and then stands up. "That's all I need to know."

Though this might be true, Kearson hurries after Mel, reaching out for her arm, stopping her at the bottom of the stairs.

"I wanted to say congratulations on your Truman scholarship. When I heard you got it, I was so happy. Relieved, actually." Kearson pins her arms against her stomach. "I know how much I cost the team last season. And if I had somehow screwed your scholarship up for you, I don't know if I could have ever forgiven myself."

Mel's mouth falls open. "Oh my gosh, Kearson, you—"

"And, if it's not too weird, would you please let Phoebe know how sorry I am? I'd tell her myself, but I've been trying to keep my distance." Kearson gives a half-hearted shrug. "She has every right to hold a grudge against me, and at the very least, I owe her the courtesy of not having to pretend like she doesn't."

Mel fingers her necklace, rose gold, so thin Kearson hadn't noticed it before. "Kearson. I promise you that Phoebe doesn't hold anything against you, okay? None of us do." Mel finds Kearson's eyes. In a whisper that's barely audible, more air than sound, she adds, "And you're not the only one here who's looking for a fresh start. Not by a long shot."

Mel puts her arm around Kearson and guides her in for a gentle hug. Kearson hugs her back, despite knowing that Mel wouldn't be nearly so kind if she had a clue how close everything was to coming apart at the seams last season. But maybe all that matters is that it didn't.

Over Mel's shoulder, Kearson sees Coach framed in the bright distance down one end of the hall, a jovial conversation with Mel's father wrapping up with typical pantomimes, a back slap, a handshake. All the while, Coach is watching her and Mel with a sidelong glance that Kearson pretends not to notice.

Though she still can't get a touch on her old dreams, Kearson gives up searching. She worked her way back onto varsity to give her all. She requires nothing in return. This is penance for her transgressions. And anyway, it won't be Kearson's dreams that carry her through. This time she knows what to expect and what will be expected of her. This time her eyes are wide open.

FRIDAY, AUGUST 26
5:40 P.M.
ALI

One of Coach's long-standing rules is that every player on the Wildcats must dress up for school on game days. His thinking? If the girls want to be winners, then they need to look the part. He wants it to be crystal clear to everyone at West Essex when they pass a Wildcat in the hallway. It's about projecting confidence, poise, and, most important, pride in being part of his team.

"Basically," Ali remembers Coach telling them once, "you're doing it right if you intimidate the shit out of every other kid in school."

It's always made sense to Ali. When you look your best, you feel your best. When you feel your best, you play your best.

In fact, the transformative power of clothes is why tonight's varsity jersey presentation is such a special moment for the girls. It marks the first time when they see themselves as a team. Ali is hopeful that, when Mel hands Ali's goalie jersey back, and she slips it over her head, Ali will feel ready to play tomorrow. For now though, in the dress she bought specifically for tonight, she feels good enough to fake it.

It gave Ali a thrill when she first saw it hanging on a circular sale rack set far away from the fall wools and tweeds and velvets in the window display. Navy-and-white gingham—a nod to Wildcat colors—strapless, nipped in at the waist, pencil skirt. It fit her like a glove, even in the chest, which has forced Ali to pass on innumerable cute dresses since puberty. The salesgirl brought over a pair of cork wedges, which were super cute, but Ali walked out barefoot from the dressing room and chose a peep-toe leopard-print pair instead. Could a leopard be considered a wildcat? Anyway, they made the look more her style—preppy but with a little kick of unexpected.

The dress was marked down, though not by much, but Ali totally would have paid full price. And she did, for the heels. It was worth it, a perfect outfit for the Wildcats' first Psych-Up of the season. She knew her teammates would love it. And Ali would take their love any way she could get it.

Just as she'd hoped, her teammates have been pulling her aside to pay her compliments since she walked in.

"Where'd you find it?"

"It's perfect!"

"You look like a model!"

Ali feels beautiful. She feels seen. And she eagerly, earnestly returns their compliments.

Honestly? The whole dressing-up thing doesn't even need to be an official rule at this point. The Wildcats seize any opportunity to do it. Dressing up for Psych-Ups helps make their weekends feel more weekend-y, especially when they miss out on stuff other kids do, like going to parties and out on dates. The annual Varsity

Dinner is practically a mini-formal—cocktail dresses, updos and blowouts, manis and pedis. And when the Wildcats are on the road—traveling for club play or tournaments—the girls pack something nice to wear for each dinner, even if they just end up walking over to an Applebee's across the hotel parking lot.

Phoebe once leaned over and joked to Ali that it's as if the Wildcats are dating one another.

The few times Ali's dressed up for boys—the tartan miniskirt, sleeveless cream turtleneck, and whiskey riding boots to Parker Nero's family Christmas Eve party is one instance that comes to mind—her efforts went largely unnoticed.

Not with her teammates. More than notice, they trade accessories with you for a better match, check your butt for panty lines, sit behind you with your curling iron and make sure you don't miss a strand. They happily climb up on beds or chairs or car hoods—whatever it takes to get the most flattering angle—and snap a hundred pictures on your phone so you have options.

Ali's mother says that women actually dress to impress one another. It is definitely true for the Wildcats.

Apparently, even for Grace.

Ali just happens to glance over from the couch when Grace, nearly an hour late, arrives at Mel's, her arms awkwardly laden with her sleepover stuff. She struggles to balance everything while closing the front door.

Ali rushes over both to lend a hand and to get a better look at Grace's hair.

Wildcat blue.

"Grace!"

"Hey, Ali. I'm so sorry I'm late. I had to dye my hair twice to get the color just right. And I didn't want to show up with it looking half-assed. Only the best for the Wildcats!"

Ali reaches out. Grace's hair is soft and unbelievably shiny. And she sees now that it's an ombre, lighter at the tips, darker at the roots. More hues of blue than Ali knew even existed. Though it is totally not her style, Ali can still appreciate how amazing Grace looks. Ali didn't notice before, probably because everyone is so sweaty and gross after tryouts, but Grace is a really pretty girl. And her blue hair actually amplifies it, her eyes like little pieces of amber, her skin dewy and clear and practically poreless.

"It looks awesome," Ali tells her.

"Yay! I'm so glad you like it! I know it's a team thing for the girls to dress up, but this is the fanciest thing I own."

Grace then lifts her arms like a T to show Ali that, technically, she is wearing a dress. Black jersey cotton, shapeless as a bag, the hem over her knees, the arm holes loose loops. Inside, the hint of a black sports bra. The look is modern, utilitarian. It reminds Ali of a YA series she devoured over the summer, bleak dystopian. But on Grace it works. She pulls it off.

Grace works her hands through her hair, subtle adjustments made blindly but with maximum effect. "I just hope it's clear how much being a Wildcat means to me."

Despite how cool Grace looks, she doesn't seem to wear her coolness like a defense mechanism. She's warm. Eager. Excited.

Ali likes her. Truly.

"The girls are going to flip out when they see you, Grace. In the best way."

"I just hope Coach is cool with it. I didn't see anything in the team binder about hair color, so I think I'm technically in the clear."

Of course Coach wouldn't have it in the rule book. Up until

now, all the Wildcats have had a similar look. Fresh faced, girl next door, collegiate. But Ali hopes he'll see the spirit of Grace's gesture. Grace is clearly all in.

And just as Ali expected, Grace steps into the living room and is immediately swarmed by girls, touching her hair, pulling her in for pictures, hugging her. The attention makes Grace bashful. Innocent. Young. In fact, it seems crazy to Ali that she and Grace are only a year apart at West Essex. She guesses Grace probably turned fifteen this summer, just made the birthday cutoff.

There were a handful of JV players who sometimes showed up at upperclassmen parties last year. Like that Marissa girl. Ali sensed how cliquey that team was. It's no stretch to think that Grace didn't fit in there. Or that they might not have even given Grace a chance to fit in.

They really blew it.

Ali's phone buzzes with a text. Her brother James.

JAMES: BIG NEWS.

JAMES: I just took the cutest picture since photography was invented.

ALI: It better be of John-John.

ALI: And not, like, a tiny pot leaf.

Her mother tells people that James works in agriculture. Really, he went into business with some college buddies and now runs a marijuana farm in the rural Pacific Northwest. James definitely gets high and sends Ali pictures of his work, marveling at the beauty of nature.

JAMES: Hey that tiny pot leaf was adorable!

ALI: 😌

JAMES: But this is next level.

JAMES: Brace yourself.

The kitchen is empty. Ali finds a little corner to tuck herself into and presses her back against the door leading out to the garage. Her phone buzzes.

It is a picture of John-John in his hanbok.

JAMES: Dress rehearsal.

ALI: 🖤🖤🖤

Ali's mother had looked in the attic but couldn't find either James's or John's hanbok. There'd been a roof leak a few years ago, and they maybe got thrown out. So Susan had her aunt bring a new one over from Seoul. It's beautiful.

ALI: moremoremoremoremoremore

James indulges her with a picture of John-John asleep and enormous in their mother's petite arms, pleased smiles across both their faces.

ALI: Halmoni!

ALI: 😢

JAMES: I know. It makes me want to get married and have kids.

ALI: Ummmmmmmm

JAMES: Okay, not really. But Mom's so cute with him. She fed John-John duk for the first time and little dude couldn't get enough. Now he's in a food coma.

ALI: So she and Dad made it there safely? They were supposed to text me! 😒

JAMES: Don't blame them for forgetting. This is what they saw when they walked through the door.

James follows up with a picture of a dinner table crowded with dishes of food.

ALI: Whoa! That looks like a damn restaurant!

JAMES: Yeah. Susan's mom has been cooking all day.

Ali's mother and father will make Korean food every once

in a while but never a spread like that, with all the side dishes. Granted, the food at tonight's Psych-Up will be amazing. Mel's parents got Park & Orchard to cater it. But Ali's mouth still waters seeing so many of her favorites on the table. Candied sweet potatoes. Four different kinds of kimchi.

Another text arrives, as if James can see her salivating.

JAMES: Sorry. I don't mean to rub it in. Maybe we can send some food back for you with Mom and Dad.

Ali steps out of the corner and over to the kitchen island. She sends him a quick selfie of herself holding up one of the pretty cupcakes.

ALI: Don't worry about me. 😌

JAMES: 😁

ALI: What?

JAMES: John-John's birthday cake is a three-tiered matcha.

ALI: SHUT UP.

ALI: 😭 😭 😭

There are no Asian markets in West Essex. Definitely no Asian bakeries. You can order some things online—favorite candies, instant noodle soups—but pantry-type stuff. Whenever Ali goes to visit either of her brothers, she gorges herself on things she can get only there, like shaved ice with red bean.

Ali sets the cupcake back down just as Mrs. Gingrich passes by. "Aren't these the best cupcakes, Ali? I mean, who knew vanilla could be so special!"

Ali presses her lips together in a smile and nods.

As long as she's been playing, Ali's been the only Asian girl on the Wildcats. It's not something she's thought much about before, beyond simply acknowledging it as a fact of life. West Essex itself isn't *super* white. Just, like, *mostly* white. Which is how Ali would describe the Wildcats themselves. Thinking back to previous seasons, the most diverse Wildcats varsity roster happened Ali's freshman year, when there were four girls of color. Four out of twenty.

This season there are two—Ali and Luci. She wonders if this is something Luci has noticed too. Someone told Ali that Luci only moved to West Essex last year. Maybe where Luci lived before was more diverse. Maybe not.

JAMES: TTYL sis. Good luck tomorrow!

ALI: Thanks. Tell everyone I love them!

Ali tries not to think about what she'll be missing this weekend. It's rare for her family to be all together, even rarer without Ali. But the Wildcats are her family too, Ali reminds herself. And while Ali's *real* family will always be there, her Wildcat family is forever changing. Tonight's team gets only this one season to be together. When it ends, they'll break apart and spin off in different directions, always connected to each other but never like they are right now.

Ali heads back into the living room. A group of sophomores—some old, some new—clusters around Coach, hanging on his every word. He's talking about field hockey for sure, using his hands to draw the action through the air.

Even though this will be his seventh year at West Essex, Coach remains one of the youngest teachers at the high school. You'll never find Coach socializing around the copy machine in the main office. He eats his lunch in his classroom, which isn't even lunch but some kind of pale, lumpy protein shake.

Ali isn't exactly sure how old Coach is. The consensus between the girls puts him somewhere around twenty-nine. But he seems way closer to their age than, say, a teacher like Mr. Bicehouse or her parents. That's part of what makes it less weird when Coach yells at them. It's 0 percent parental. Parents want you to do your best. Coach wants to win.

Ali took his accounting class as an elective in the spring of her freshman year, hoping that Coach's dynamic energy might unlock some latent math passion inside her. But she was surprised to find that Coach was not a particularly magnetic teacher. The way he'd present or explain concepts was usually hard to follow—completely opposite of the way he communicated on the field—and Ali regularly found typos on his handouts. He often seemed as bored with the material he presented as the students were. Probably because he never wanted to be a teacher in the first place. He only took the job because the math teacher he'd be replacing was also West Essex's field hockey coach.

The Wildcats used to be a mediocre team. Never made it to finals, that's for sure. Lucky to end up with more wins than losses at the end of the season. But once Coach took over, everything changed. Not only has he used his expertise to coach them to victory, he uses his contacts to bring in college scouts. Under his hand, the girls varsity field hockey team has become the most decorated in their high school's history, with five state championships in six years.

After last season, it's a relief to see Coach in an upbeat mood. Ali folds herself into the group. Coach is telling them about the temporary position he took with the Men's Junior National Team this summer, subbing for a strength-and-conditioning coordinator who went on medical leave.

The girls listen intently, but Ali is sure they are thinking the same thing she is: if it *had* been a permanent position, Coach wouldn't have come back to West Essex this season. They are lucky they still have him.

Coach excuses himself to get some water. The girls then turn to Ali and ask her about goalie camp.

"It was good," she says with a shrug.

They nudge her for more details, curious because Ali's position is so different from theirs. Ali normally gets plenty of breaks during Wildcat practice, since many skill drills or formations don't apply to her. Her stick is even shaped differently from theirs, more of a hook than a paddle.

So she tells them. Goalie camp was unrelentingly focused on her skill set. Drills on the field to sharpen her reflexes, increase her agility, extend her reach. Exercises in the weight room to strengthen her quads, her glutes, her core. Frankly, she's never been in better shape. Her tummy has always been flat but she now has actual abs, the beginnings of a legit six-pack. Phoebe couldn't stop touching them when they went hot-tubbing after the first day of tryouts this week.

Still, she's quick to add, "But I really missed being with everyone at Kissawa."

Behind them, Coach clears his throat. Everyone turns and spots him over by the fireplace, his arms folded across his chest.

The girls react with quiet surprise that, unbeknownst to them, he has rejoined their conversation. But for Ali, the sensation is more acute. Closer to a startle. After all, while she yammered on about goalie camp, she kept an eye on the hallway Coach took to the kitchen. It never crossed her mind that he might reenter the living room from a different direction.

"I'm sure your teammates missed you, too, Ali," he tells her grimly.

Ali becomes hyperaware of the girls around her. Not just the ones in this little cluster but also the girls looking at the family photographs on the wall, the girls perched on the couch, Mel and Phoebe doing something with the sound system.

In the days and weeks after the championship defeat, as her teammates emerged from the fog of loss, Ali had wondered if any of them would come to her wanting answers. Maybe not for that first goal Darlene Maguire scored on her, but absolutely for the second, scored also by Darlene, on the very next breakaway.

That time, Ali had just stood there in a daze. She didn't even try to stop the shot.

It was so unlike her. Ali was always on her toes, always in motion inside the goal. She had a twelve-game streak of perfect performances last season, with not a single goal scored on her until the championship. Didn't anyone wonder what happened? Or why?

No.

And not because the girls didn't care. But because there was nothing Ali could say that could change what happened. Excuses were worthless. That was something Coach taught them. Drilled into their heads.

"I hate how these camps put so much emphasis on developing physical strength. As if a certain number of crunches or push-ups guarantees a win." Coach taps the side of his head. "There's a whole other game that gets played up here, and it requires just as much training. I don't care how fit a player is. If she can't play a strong mental game, she's a liability."

The girls nod in complete and total agreement. Ali would nod too if she could. But she finds herself frozen in a painfully familiar way.

Despite the crushing disappointment in herself after Darlene scored on her the first time, Ali had immediately tried to regroup. It was only one goal. The Wildcats could still come back. After clearing the ball out of her net and sending it upfield to the ref, she flicked off her gloves and took a quick sip of water, clinging to the hope that her failure might even serve as the wake-up call her team needed to finally turn things around.

Meanwhile, players from both teams hustled back to midfield for the upcoming face-off. But not Darlene Maguire. She was lingering near Ali's goal. She had her goggles pulled up into her hair like a headband, her field hockey stick tucked under her arm, and a mischievous smile on her face. Waiting for Ali to notice her.

When Ali finally did, Darlene raised the pointer fingers on each of her hands in what Ali initially assumed was a doubled We're Number One! gesture. That is, until she used those two fingers to pull the skin on the outer edges of her eyes taut, lengthening them into slits.

"Didn't see that one coming, did you?"

No.

Ali hadn't.

The thing is, in sports, people are always talking trash. Players, fans. They do it to rattle you, to get under your skin, to break your concentration.

But Coach is right. You can't let them. The best players have the mental discipline to block out the noise and stay focused on the game.

Could that be why Coach is bringing this up? Trying to see if Ali is ready for tomorrow?

If it is, she's figured his game out too late. She glances around and finds he's already left the room.

And then, out of nowhere, Ali is pushed, someone's hand against her left shoulder, and it sends her tipping backward. But she is saved from hitting the floor, her lower back cradled, fingers grabbing Ali's wrist to keep her suspended.

Phoebe grins down at her from above. "Don't look so scared, Ali. I'm an excellent dancer."

FRIDAY, AUGUST 26
6:19 P.M.
PHOEBE

The entire house is wired with speakers, and the playlist Phoebe made especially for tonight streams through all of them, so the music never stops, no matter where she goes. She twirls from room to room, grabbing unsuspecting teammates as she goes, pulling them out of whatever conversation they're having and making them dance with her for however long they'll allow it, spinning each one like a top, dipping them until the ends of their hair sweep the floor.

Phoebe could dance all night. It feels *that* good to be back, the weight of making the cut finally and fully lifted off her shoulders. Phoebe hasn't hung out with some girls since school ended last June. She hears about Stephanie Evans's trip to Disneyland, where one of her cousins dresses up as Kristoff for some *Frozen* live show thingy. Anna Burgess's family bought a new house directly across the street from their old house, because her mother had always loved it and the lady who lived there died. Or was it that the lady got put into one of those assisted living communities? Phoebe can't remember. She's just grateful there seems to be no hard feelings for the way she dropped off the grid.

After her ACL surgery in January, Phoebe scheduled her rehab appointments around the spring club schedule, so she could watch the games from the sidelines. But after her second operation—that staph infection was beyond shitty luck—she couldn't bring herself to keep going.

It was one of the weirdest parts of her injury Phoebe had to contend with, her sudden loss of fortitude. Usually she had more than enough grit to face down any challenge, mental or physical, on the field or off. It was a well she could dip into any time, her reserves always at the highest watermark and instantly replenished by whatever stunt Phoebe managed to pull off.

But this past year took it out of her. Her grit became a more precious resource. One Phoebe needed to conserve for the greater good of returning to the field this season, not waste on dulling the torture of watching her teammates play without her.

Missing spring club was hard. Summer league was harder. It just about killed Phoebe when her doctor said she wasn't cleared for Kissawa.

Mel had gotten her license, and the girls had been so stoked to drive themselves to the camp for the first time. They already knew the best gas stations to stop at for snacks, but now they could hit the outlet mall just past the halfway point, a detour their parents—who would immediately have to drive the return trip home—never let them take. Even though Phoebe couldn't play, she was seriously considering riding up with Mel anyway and then taking a bus or whatever back. Phoebe missed Mel that much. They'd barely hung out at all this summer.

But Mel didn't end up going to Kissawa either. She dropped out when the invitation came to visit Truman and attend a tryout with some other prospectives. Truman was Mel's dream school, and thankfully, the Wildcats' horrible performance in the championship game hadn't completely screwed up her chance of going. This, for Phoebe, was enough good to drown out the bad of not getting an invitation to try out there herself. Phoebe always knew she'd be a long shot. And there were a bunch of other colleges Phoebe was considering. For Mel, it was only Truman.

Phoebe never got the full story from Mel about how it went. Mel never texted while she was at Truman, never sent Phoebe any pictures. There weren't even any general social media updates Phoebe could stalk. Nothing. She knew the silence was Mel being a good friend to her. Mel being sensitive to how badly this sucked for Phoebe, who had been hoping to be there with her. In fact, Gordy was the one who told Phoebe when Mel officially committed. It was totally an unintentional slip; he assumed Phoebe already knew. And of course she played it off like she did.

"Dinner is served!" Mrs. Gingrich says, guiding everyone toward the buffet set up in the dining room.

Phoebe trails Mrs. Gingrich, and in her best impression, adds the caveat, "Seniors first!"

At Psych-Ups, the girls always eat in order of seniority. Seniors make their plates first, then juniors, then sophomores, and lastly—if there are any—freshmen. Only one girl made the cut this year.

Good thing because Phoebe is starving. She fills her plate—lemon chicken, pasta with vodka sauce, steamed veggies—but she barely eats it because she's too busy talking with her fellow seniors, fake bitching about how their Psych-Up dinners are going to suck in comparison to Mel's unless they hire like a sushi chef or something.

When it's time for the juniors to eat, Phoebe stays in her seat and manages a few forkfuls while shooting the shit with Ali. She already chatted with the sophomore players who are eagerly lining up, and plus her food is cold, so she carries her and Ali's plates to the trash.

Out the kitchen window, Phoebe sees Luci sitting by herself at a table in the backyard, staring quietly down at her lap. At least when Phoebe was a freshman, she had Mel to hang out with.

That's partly why Phoebe pushed Mel to drive Luci home today. Mel was making excuses about the errands they needed to run, but Phoebe wasn't having it. "Mel. Why are you being so weird about this?"

"I'm not being weird. I just don't know where Luci even went," Mel said, barely glancing around Coach's classroom to look.

"So go find her!"

It soothed Phoebe that she wasn't the only one with unkind thoughts. And, to her credit, Mel did take Luci home. Phoebe, however, still hasn't said anything to Kearson. She hasn't been a bitch. No dirty looks. No cold shoulder. But she can't bring herself to go out of her way and say something nice to Kearson either. This isn't like her. But like the clicks she sometimes feels in her knee, it's a change Phoebe prefers to ignore.

"Hey, Luci," Phoebe says, walking over. "What are you doing out here by yourself?"

Luci shyly brings up what she's been hiding in her lap. Her Wildcat team binder. "Studying."

Luci reminds Phoebe so much of Mel. Adorable yet intense

AF about field hockey. She teases, "Are you worried that Coach is going to hand out a pop quiz?"

Luci clenches her teeth, revealing two rows of silver braces. "I mean . . . I wouldn't be surprised."

Phoebe shakes her head. "You've passed the test, Luci. So put the binder away, fix yourself a plate of food, and go make friends with your teammates. That's what tonight is about!"

Luci exhales. "Okay."

"*However*. I'm going to require that you memorize the words to the songs I was playing in Mel's car today. I can't allow you to live the rest of your life with that kind of musical blind spot. I'll send you the track list."

Luci laughs and the metal sparkles. "Thanks, Phoebe. I won't let you down."

Phoebe follows Luci back inside. Mr. and Mrs. Gingrich are at the kitchen island, each with a glass of wine, smiling as they survey the party. Mrs. Gingrich calls Phoebe over and gives her a big hug. "It's so good to see you like this, Phoebe. Back where you belong!"

"Thank you."

"Any news on the scholarship front?" Mr. Gingrich asks tentatively. He is in a collared shirt with a Truman University necktie. It's not showy—what looks like a pattern of small polka dots is actually a bunch of little *T*s—but Phoebe recognizes it.

"Dad!" Mel, clearly horrified, zooms in from the living room. She takes Phoebe by the hand and leads Phoebe away from her parents. Phoebe stiffens, trying to resist Mel, not wanting to be rude, but Mel is pulling hard and the last thing Phoebe needs is to tweak her knee, so she gives up.

Over her shoulder, Phoebe says, "Um. Not yet. But hopefully soon!"

Mr. and Mrs. Gingrich call after her, "Well, we're all cheering for you, Phoebe!"

"I'm so sorry about that," Mel groans. "Now that they can't obsess over my college choices anymore, they're moving on to their second daughter."

It's true. Phoebe and Mel are like sisters. Knowing that Mel's entire family is pulling for her is a welcome change from the vibe in Phoebe's own house.

Mel curls up against her. "I bet Coach will be getting plenty of emails from scouts wanting to come see you this season. Not that he'll ever tell." She hooks her chin on Phoebe's shoulder. "Anyway, you know how he is."

Whenever Mel typically says this, it's usually to soften the blow of her knowing Coach better than Phoebe. And most times, Mel does.

Just not this one.

However, all Phoebe says in response is, "Does he honestly believe not telling us stops us from thinking about it? You played every game last season wondering if a scout from Truman was there."

"Yeah, but I get *why* Coach does it. It would mess with our heads if we knew for sure."

Phoebe smiles. She could have predicted that's what Mel would say. She always walks back anything even remotely negative about Coach. Mel might know Coach better, but Phoebe knows Mel better than Mel knows herself.

"You have no idea how much I've missed this," Phoebe tells her.

"You have no idea how much I've missed you," Mel says.

Coach has his favorites. Phoebe's always been a proxy to Mel's stardom. Phoebe didn't get the same accolades Mel did. No picture in the paper. Not that she cared, really. That was never what she played for. Mel might be the star of the Wildcats, but Phoebe has always thought of herself as the heart. And tonight she finally feels it beating again.

Phoebe checks her email, then helps herself to a cupcake, which she eats in three bites while checking her email yet again. Her phone is low on battery, and she sets out to find the charger Mel's family has in the den. That's where she finds Coach, sitting by himself, his phone already plugged in.

He got sunburned from tryouts today, a bit of pink across his nose. His hair, still damp from an earlier shower, hangs down over his eyes. In his dark jeans and polo shirt, he looks like the kind of boyish adult who could play a teenager on television. He's looking at something on his phone, his mouth in a sulky pout, and then clicks his phone off, leans his head back, and closes his eyes.

The Wildcats are not the only ones drawn to Coach. He's mobbed all the time.

The guys at their high school pathetically congregate around Coach's desk, wanting to talk to him about workouts or what supplements he buys from GNC. They beg him to come play Ping-Pong in the gym during free period.

Referees kiss his ass. Parents suck up. Their vice principal is so obviously hot for him. Other coaches always want to bend his ear, shoot the shit, even while he's clearly trying to do his job. Then again, most coaches talk about drills but don't perform them. In fact, West Essex's track coach notoriously drives his car when the distance runners do a ten-miler. But Coach is always on the field with the Wildcats, deftly demoing the drills that don't cause him pain, and gritting his teeth to get through the drills that do. It's like he sometimes forgets his field hockey career is over.

But that's the thing. It's never been about his looks. She's always been drawn to Coach's swagger. His confidence. It's another place where she knows she's still lacking on the field. Phoebe felt so insecure at tryouts this week. Every day she had to shake that feeling, not let it get into her head. Especially the times when Coach would swap her out for Kearson during a scrimmage.

Kearson. Bobblehead Kearson. That's what she looks like, her head slightly too big for her skinny little body, constantly in motion, always yessing Coach.

Anyway.

After checking her email yet again, Phoebe decides to do something brave. And possibly stupid. But she's never let that stop her before. She uses her phone camera to check her makeup, quickly touches up her lipstick, pulls out a few pieces from her fishtail braid. Then, summoning all the confidence she can, she walks into the den and flops down next to Coach on the couch.

"Hey, Coach."

He turns his head and opens his eyes, then closes them again. "Hey, Phoebs."

She loves her new dress, white cotton with a sweetheart neckline and wooden buttons down the front. She didn't want to wear Knee Spanx tonight. She didn't want to think about her knee. But smoothing the dress, Phoebe sees her scar. It used to be pink, but as her skin tanned, it's become white, brighter. Now she wishes she'd picked a different dress. A maxi.

"Nice party, huh?"

"Yeah."

Phoebe blows a few wisps of her hair out of her face. "Wow, you know, I just can't wait to be out on the field tomorrow. Playing in an actual game. Which I haven't done since the championship."

"I'm well aware of the last time you played field hockey."

"Right. Of course. But I've just got this feeling like, once the whistle blows tomorrow, I know it's all going to click."

Slightly irritated, he sits up. "What's going to click?"

Phoebe doesn't even want to say it. But she knows it needs to be said. "Obviously I still need to work on my timing. But I'm going to get there. I'm not worried. Oh, and today's tryout was definitely the hardest test on my knee yet, and I'm passing with flying colors. I don't have a bit of soreness. Just so you know. Or, um, anyone else that might ask."

"You mean like scouts. Phoebe, you know I don't like to talk about that stuff with my players." He scratches his neck and then adds, "Only in the most extreme circumstances."

"It's just that I'm *really* still hoping for a scholarship. Hopefully D1. Obviously not Truman—"

"Truman is off the table. If we had won the championship, it might be a different story." His tone is cool. Matter-of-fact.

"Right. But maybe Wilcox could be a possibility? So Mel and I can be in the same division...." She swallows. "I'd even be willing to consider a lesser option, like Trident."

Before Phoebe had gotten injured, Trident was her safety school. It wasn't D1 but also wouldn't be far from Mel and Truman. They wouldn't play each other, but they could still watch each other play.

Coach's lip curls. "Trident? You're kidding me, right? Come on, Phoebe. You're way too good of a player to slum it on Trident. Forget them."

It's not exactly a compliment, but that Coach believes she's "too good" for anything makes Phoebe's heart swell. However, there's something Phoebe needs to tell him. Something she'd been hoping not to mention.

"I think they've forgotten me, actually." Phoebe bites her bottom lip. "I reached out to Trident's scout on Wednesday. A guy named Jon Dockey." Phoebe looks to see if Coach recognizes the name, but instead his face darkens just like a storm cloud, the kind that sends you scrambling for cover. "I, um, knew Trident was looking at me last season, so I figured it would be a good idea to catch him up on my progress."

Glaring at her, Coach growls, "You did what?"

"I'm sorry." She knew he'd be angry. But he's furious.

A tendon in Coach's neck tightens, straining against his skin. "Did he write back?"

If she were wearing her Knee Spanx, Phoebe would slide it off her leg and roll it down over her face. "No."

"Have you written to any other schools?"

Phoebe shakes her head. "Only Trident, because it was my safety. And I thought hearing they were still interested would give me a little confidence boost. I didn't think for a second they might not want me."

Phoebe hates how hard she's fishing for some kind of reassurance that everything can still work out for her. Mel will talk Phoebe up until she's blue in the face. But Coach is the one person on this team who knows firsthand *exactly* the position she's in right now.

Coach is a former all-star collegiate player, a D1 starter. While playing at Truman, he also earned a spot on the Junior National Field Hockey Team. After graduation, Coach moved up to the Men's National Team and spent two years playing all over the world.

Within that span of time, he'd had a total of eight ACL surgeries, four on each of his knees.

Coach was in the middle of Olympic tryouts when his career officially ended. Both his ACLs completely shredded. Even with the best doctors, there was nothing left for them to repair.

And he's the only one she can trust to tell her the hard truth.

"This is exactly why I don't want my players contacting any scouts on their own. Even with your knee injury, Trident is still way below you. They should be begging *you* to come play there. I don't know what you said to this Jon person, exactly, but it's clear how you came across. Desperate."

"I'm so sorry. Really."

Coach runs his hands through his hair, pulling on his curls, releasing the tension inside him. "All it takes is one email from me to get you back on the scouting radar. An email I will send when and if I feel that you're ready."

"Thank you, Coach. Seriously."

"But let me make one thing perfectly clear, Phoebe," Coach says, his voice low and intense. "You and I will not have another conversation about scouts until I say there's something to talk about. And you and I will *never* have another conversation about you going to Trident again. If you can't follow my rules, you won't play on my team. Do you understand me?"

"Absolutely. One hundred percent."

Coach glances around for someone he seems ticked off isn't already there, poised for action. Mel, surely.

"Do you need something, Coach? I can gather the girls in the backyard for your speech."

"Fine. Go ahead."

Though he's still clearly pissed at her, Phoebe's relieved. It's the best she could have hoped for. Coach is offering her a simple solution to a complicated problem. She has to prove herself on the field. If she can do that, and she will, he'll take care of her.

Coach doesn't want to hear about your cramps, he doesn't want to know if you're breaking out, if you bombed a test, if your mom's being ridiculous, if you've been asked to homecoming, if you've had your heart broken.

He only wants you to perform.

For this, he's made Phoebe into a stronger girl.

Wait. No.

He has made her stronger, no caveat.

FRIDAY, AUGUST 26
7:00 P.M.
LUCI

Luci didn't know for sure if Coach would make a speech tonight, but she hoped he might. Now that it's about to happen, and she's being herded into the backyard by her teammates, she's practically breathless with anticipation.

It's more than mere curiosity for why he's so beloved. Luci's affixed something personal to her expectations of Coach. She has no idea what he'll say and how he'll say it. But if Coach proves he's everything Luci thinks he might be, then maybe she can start to believe in the potential he apparently sees in her.

Her teammates forgo the party tent, where there are plenty of white wooden chairs arranged around banquet tables glittering with white tea lights. Instead they arrange themselves on the deck as if posing for a team photo, in two staggered lines. The alphabet balloons that spell out WILDCATS bob on ribbons behind them, each silver letter twisting and warping their reflections like a fun-house mirror.

Luci stares at her toes, the chalky pink polish she hastily applied. She presses her lips together, hoping to feel a little slick of the lipstick she put on earlier, but it's worn off and Luci didn't think to bring it with her. Getting ready for tonight was one long panic attack. She emptied her drawers looking for something to wear, horrified by all the sequins, the decorative stitching, the matchy-matchy sets. She didn't bother putting the clothes back—they're all still on her floor—because she will never wear that stuff again.

Instead Luci borrowed a dress from her mother's closet that she always loved, slippery and thin, a botanical print of palm leaves and citrus. Her mother never wears a bra with it, but, um, there's no way Luci could pull that off, so underneath she's wearing a white cotton tank top. She briefly considered wearing one of her mother's thongs instead of her Gap briefs to avoid VPL, but Luci chickened out because what if the girls got changed in the same room and everyone saw her bare butt?

A quiet anticipation settles over the backyard, amplifying the ambient sounds of summer. The whirl of the pool filter, a chirp of a bird, a car passing on the street, kids begging for five more minutes outside.

Two of Luci's teammates, the girls standing directly in front of her, drop their heads together and whisper.

"He's going to bring up the championship game, don't you think?"

"Obviously."

"But it's weird, right? That he waited this long to yell at us about it?"

"Um, hi. That was his strategy."

"Ugh, you're so right. My dad does the same thing. He'll tell me I'm grounded, but he won't say for how long. It makes it way worse."

"Only your dad isn't as hot as Coach."

"Eww! My dad isn't hot *at all*!"

Luci attempts to disguise her laugh by clearing her throat. The girls turn and see that she's been eavesdropping, but they regard her warmly, sisterly. One even gently rubs Luci's arm.

"Don't worry, Luci. It's never actually that bad."

"In a weird way, it makes his speech kind of . . . *exciting*?"

"Totally. And, how cute is it that Coach takes the time to write out what he plans to say on a piece of paper?"

"He's much better off the cuff. More relaxed."

"Agreed, but it's his level of caring I'm talking about. He wants to make sure he doesn't forget anything. He takes coaching us *so* seriously that it hurts my heart."

"Yes, yes, yes. That. Also, Luci, even when Coach is mad at us about something, which, I mean, he usually is, he always spins it around at the end and makes it motivational."

"Tough love."

"Tough love from your very hot dad."

"Oh my God, you're seriously depraved!"

"Um, thanks for the heads-up," Luci says, giggling.

The sliding glass door rolls open. The two girls clutch one another with a mix of glee and dread, like they're about to crest the hill of a roller coaster.

Coach steps onto the deck. Mrs. Gingrich and one of the caterers are right behind him, vaguely aware that something is about to happen, and they hurry to collect a stack of dirty plates. Coach centers himself on the impromptu stage the girls have made for him, his jaw clenched, eyes narrowed, and waits.

But once the door slides closed behind the caterer, Coach opens his mouth as if he's going to begin his speech, only to glance down and exhale in frustration without saying a word, like he's changed his mind about what it is he wants to say.

This happens a few times.

Each false start sharpens the girls' focus on him. They stand patient, ready and waiting, which only seems to annoy Coach more.

He begins to pace.

"You have no clue the shit my friends give me about coaching this team. Guys I used to play with? They can't believe I care this much about a bunch of high school girls." He shakes his head, like he can't believe it either. "Why I keep passing up coaching jobs—*seriously* good jobs—in order to stick around here. And it's like . . ."

Coach trails off, the thought slipping away. He falls backward against the deck railing, exasperated.

Something fizzes inside Luci. She's never been talked to like this by a grown-up. But is that what Coach is? A grown-up? The distinction feels so totally wrong—practically a betrayal—even though she'd never thought twice about lumping every adult into the same category.

"Let's be real, though. Their lame insults are being made at your expense. Same for the whispers around West Essex about how I'm supposedly too tough on you girls. That I push too hard."

His hand moves up to the tiny wildcat embroidered on his polo shirt and presses against his heart. And despite it being physically impossible, Luci feels the warmth building there.

"It's not just that most people don't see what I do in you girls," he says bitterly. "It's that they've never even thought to look."

He stares at them, unblinking. "And that should scare you girls shitless."

Coach lowers his hand. Luci is so startled by the phantom ache that appears in her own chest, it takes her several seconds to recover. And with it, also, a clarity. Every lingering question she may have, about Coach, the team, these girls, their intensity, has suddenly been answered.

Just like that, Luci gets it. Understands everything.

Pinching the bridge of his nose, Coach seems to concede a fight within himself. He reaches into the back pocket of his jeans and removes a bulky paper square.

His speech.

Luci watches him smooth out the creases against his thigh. He's written it by hand, front side and back, on pages and pages of notebook paper. So many pages that Luci's surprised he got a staple through the left corner. While she can't make out a word of his penmanship, she finds ample evidence of passion for what he's written in every scribble and cross-out.

It's a beautiful mess.

The girls standing directly in front of Luci find each other's hands and squeeze. Luci follows their cue and braces herself.

Coach scans the first page, as if to familiarize himself with what he's written, and then flips to the second. "I started working on this the night before tryouts began," he tells them, an impromptu preamble. "I figured I'd spend an hour tops sketching out a few rough ideas. But once I got going on it, I couldn't stop. I stayed up until sunrise and wrote it straight through, start to finish." He glances up at them briefly. "Clearly I had a lot to say."

He looks over the third page, then the fourth. Something he's written on the fifth page prompts Coach to roll his eyes. Luci feels herself blush in earnest solidarity. When Coach finally does start giving his speech, she hopes he won't edit himself on the fly. She wants to hear every word.

After that, he flips through another page or two more, giving each a disinterested glance, then jumps forward to the last. And Luci's suddenly not sure if he's going to read his speech at all.

But then, Coach clears his throat and, tracing a sentence near the bottom with his finger, recites what Luci intuits as the very last line.

"'Remember, so long as we stick to our core values, the Wildcats can reclaim what we've lost and become a stronger team in the process.'"

His voice sounds like he's pleading with them, but Luci detects not a drop of resistance in her teammates. Everyone seems pitched slightly forward.

"When I initially wrote that last line, I was referring to last season. And despite how our team ceased to function on any level for the last three games, despite how many chances there'd been for each of you to step up for your team where instead you backed away, I still wanted to end on a hopeful note tonight."

Coach shakes his head and crumples his entire speech up in a ball.

Even if Luci hadn't gotten the heads-up about how Coach's speeches typically go, it would still be obvious this is uncharted territory. The entire team glances around at one another, uneasy.

"But after what I've seen on the field this week? What I've seen tonight? I don't feel hopeful. I feel betrayed."

Coach leans over to one of the candles flickering on a nearby table and drops the wadded-up speech onto the flame. For the quiet seconds it takes for it to catch fire, Luci can't seem to breathe.

Coach, on the other hand, has gotten a second wind. His restless energy from earlier dissipates into an unsettling calm. "You girls may have managed to fool yourselves. You may have managed to fool each other. But you haven't fooled me." He flashes a cold smile. "My team didn't just lose a championship. You girls also lost what it means to be Wildcats."

With that, Coach walks back inside Mel's house.

Until this moment, Luci has mostly felt spared from Coach's ire. Now she feels nakedly complicit, remembering how she so hungrily lapped up all Coach's compliments at his desk this afternoon. Yes, he clearly believes Luci can be something. But right now? She's nothing. Completely untested.

Luci feels woozy. And she's not alone. All the girls seem off-kilter. Even Mel has her hand fanned out and pressed against her chest, as if to keep herself from teetering over.

It takes a few seconds before anyone speaks.

Phoebe is the first. "Looks like someone's on his period."

No one laughs.

"Not helping," Mel chides her, and Phoebe hangs her head. But the joke does seem to break the spell. Mel steps out of the line and briefly occupies the space Coach just left. "That could have been *a lot* worse," she tells the rest of the girls, her voice as steady and sure as she seems to be walking in her high-heeled sandals. "Coach almost didn't come back."

As a newbie, it's hard for Luci to wring much comfort from this caveat, though her teammates seem to do so. Instead, she latches onto Mel's certainty. It's not a huge leap to think Mel knows Coach better than anyone else here tonight. Coach may be having doubts about his team, but Mel doesn't seem to doubt him. So why should Luci?

FRIDAY, AUGUST 26
7:45 P.M.
MEL

Mel replenishes her platter with cupcakes, selecting only the most perfect ones that remain in the cardboard bakery box—ones with the icing curls at the top like tiny ocean waves—and arranging them so they look worthy of a cookbook cover.

Shortly after Coach's speech, Mel followed him into her house, hoping that she could keep him from leaving but without any idea of how she might get him to stay. Thankfully, her mother had already intercepted him and, holding this same platter, insisted he stay for dessert. Coach offered a polite excuse, but then her father came over and selected a cupcake for Coach and one for himself, making it clear that Coach would be sticking around a while longer. Coach forced a smile and took a bite. His furrowed eyebrows lifted after a few chews. The cupcakes were that good.

Which is why Mel now swirls from room to room, interrupting conversations to gently but firmly push them on her teammates.

Everyone must eat a cupcake. Sugar helps the medicine go down.

Of course Mel bristled at the things Coach said. But as the minutes tick on, she feels more and more at peace with it. His words came straight from his heart. He wouldn't be so passionate if he didn't care.

And Mel knows her teammates care too. Deeply.

At the very least, that puts everyone on the same page. Though small, Mel still counts this as a victory. Hopefully the first of many for the Wildcats this season. But for now, it's more than enough to keep Mel afloat as the Psych-Up begins to shift from Coach's portion to hers.

Mel feels her phone vibrate and sets down the platter.

COACH: Save me

This is the first text Coach has sent her in nearly a month.

She bends down and fiddles with the strap on her sandal, shielding herself from anyone who might see her blushing.

This is a secret that Mel's never told anyone, not even her best friend. It almost wasn't a secret to begin with. But when Mel realized, midway through her freshman season, that it was a special thing between her and Coach, she kept quiet. And then, more quickly than Mel would have thought possible, it became too late to ever tell her.

In the beginning, Mel and Coach only talked about field hockey. He would ask her opinions. Who played well, who didn't. Sometimes he would complain to her about the refs, poke fun at other coaches, voice his worries about different girls on the team. Their conversations became as much a part of her postgame ritual as taking a shower.

Never flirty but friendly. Like a friend. A good friend, sometimes, because it was easy to talk to him. That didn't mean, however, that his texts didn't give Mel a charge. Make her feel special. Because they definitely did.

Though they could talk about field hockey infinitely, the universe still expanded. He began to tell her about Truman. His alma mater. The greatest place on earth. The happiest times of his life.

Sometimes he called. Usually late and without warning. Just in case, Mel went to sleep with her phone plugged into her charger and always on vibrate. She would keep her voice quiet, and he'd keep his quiet too, even though he was probably in his condo, all alone.

It's only been talk. Coach would never . . . you know. And the same goes for Mel. They know there are lines that cannot be crossed. Lines that might not be there in the future, but are very clearly drawn in the here and now, and not worth the risk to his reputation and hers. But there is something real between them. Something that's grown over the years, spread roots, and managed to sustain itself despite them both purposefully ignoring it in the hopes it might die.

MEL: Where are you?

COACH: Your dad's office

COACH: I've been trying to say goodbye to your parents for the last twenty minutes

MEL: Sorry

COACH: They just brought out your baby album

Oh God.

Mel picks up the platter and sprints down the hall. She finds Coach on the leather Chesterfield in her father's office, a photo album splayed in his lap. Mel's parents are each perched on an arm, leaning down to point things out. They are both extroverts and terrific party guests, well read and well informed on a wide variety of subjects. But their favorite topic of conversation—at any time, to any group—is Mel.

She's their pride and joy.

She had been difficult to conceive—they tried for more than a year, and then with the help of a specialist, a lone viable embryo was implanted. Mel grew like a weed in utero and was born strong as an ox at eleven and a half pounds. She was too big for the eyelet lace romper her mother had packed for her, so she was taken home from the hospital in only a diaper.

Mel hates most of her baby pictures, hates when the baby album comes out on her birthday and gets passed around to her friends. Bald, androgynous, one of those giant beast babies you see every so often on the news, held in the arms of her swan-like mother. She was a physical baby: killer grip, quick to sit up, then crawl, then walk. She didn't really get cute until around two, when her hair came in, shiny and stick straight.

"Mom. Dad. Coach needs to get going."

Her father says, "Oh, look, sweetie! Annie!"

Her mother taps a photo with a manicured nail for Coach's benefit. "This is the girl who introduced Mel to field hockey."

Her parents had always been athletic—her mother a devoted lap swimmer, her father with three standing racquetball games a week. Mel slipped right in with tennis lessons, swim team. She had a decent golf swing and liked driving the cart. But those sports were quiet. Lonely. A twosome on a vast manicured golf course. A clay court at the country club where no one spoke above a whisper and you never, ever argued with a line judge. A sparkling private pool where your opponents were watery blurs in your periphery.

Mel discovered field hockey through her babysitter Annie

Birch, a high school girl from Dormont who took over watching Mel two Saturdays a month for her parents' date night after her other babysitter left for college. Once Annie must have come straight from a game. Mel, on the front stairs, watched Annie get out of her car, still in her grass-stained gray kilt and maroon shin guards, a wooden stick shaped like a candy cane propped up in the passenger seat.

As an eleven-year-old, Mel had boundless energy. Annie adopted a strategy of running Mel ragged so she'd pass out by ten o'clock, giving Annie a few hours to lie on the couch and enjoy the Gingriches' premium cable.

Mel was curious, so Annie drove them to her house to get an extra stick and some cones she had, and then she put Mel through a couple of drills in the backyard. Mel was good, intense, a quick learner. Later, Annie let Mel stay up past her bedtime and showed her a rough cut of the video Annie was having made for college scouts. The Dormont Lady Knights were in second place behind the Oak Knolls Bulldogs. Annie told Mel that West Essex field hockey wasn't great, but that was a year or so before Coach got hired. Anyway, Mel fell asleep on the couch while watching videos of other girls playing all around the world. England, Australia, India, Germany, China.

Mel awoke the next morning tucked in her bed. Her father must have carried her up. Downstairs, she saw that Annie had left her old stick behind for Mel to keep, plus a ball and a few cones.

In spite of what a feral little monster Mel looks like in the picture—bug bites and dirty fingernails, clutching her borrowed stick, Annie standing proudly behind her, hands on Mel's shoulders—a rush of love for Annie drowns out her embarrassment. How crazy it is, the way certain people can come into your life and change it. It gives Mel a hopeful feeling. Like nothing is set in stone. Like you don't have to steer through life so much as pinball through.

Coach seizes the opening to escape. To her mother, he says, "This was a perfect kickoff to this season." Her father gets a firm handshake. They thank him for coming, for everything he's done for their daughter, and her father promises a draft of the recommendation letter Coach asked for by next week.

"Cupcake?" Mel asks, as a joke more than anything.

"I'm feeling sick to my stomach," Coach mutters, breezing past her.

And now Mel is too. So starved for a win—any win—she completely misread the tone of Coach's texts, if not his entire post-speech mood.

From the doorway, she watches Coach stalk down the hallway. He doesn't stop to say goodbye to any of the girls he passes, doesn't slow down when stepping over sleeping bags or around field hockey sticks. One fluid motion carries him straight out her front door.

"Tonight couldn't have gone better," her mother says. "A Psych-Up befitting the best captain the Wildcats has ever had." She plants a kiss on Mel's cheek.

"We're so proud of you, Melly," her father says, coming around Mel's opposite side to take another cupcake.

She passes him the platter.

Mel follows the same escape route, as if Coach had been demoing a drill, only with a layer of *nothing to see here* camouflage, because the last thing she needs right now is for her teammates to see their captain panicking. She takes an empty cup from

Kearson and drops it in a wastebasket, pauses to adjust the angle of a throw pillow on a bench, pretends to be texting someone. When she reaches the front door, she is careful to open and then close it without causing so much as a tap from the brass knocker.

It hasn't cooled down much outside but Mel shivers anyway. Coach's Escalade is still parked at the end of her driveway. And he's sitting on the bottom step, elbows on his knees, head cradled in his hands.

He glances up and she knows—he's been waiting for her.

"Took you long enough."

Despite her earlier misread, Mel knows for certain what the situation is now. Coach may have gotten a few things off his chest tonight, but he's carrying the real burden in his mind. The unfortunate consequence of having so many hopes and dreams and big ideas.

Whenever Coach got tangled up like this, Mel was the one he turned to for help to sort things out. She'd be his shoulder, his sounding board. It didn't matter if they were texting or talking, by the end of their conversation, Coach would feel clearheaded.

Who had Coach turned to in lieu of Mel during the months of silence between them? Did he have someone else to talk to? Or did he keep everything bottled up inside? Mel isn't sure. Nor does she care. Coach needs her now. That's what matters.

Mel's heels click down the brick stairs. She sits down quietly beside him.

"This wasn't how I wanted tonight to go, Mel. In case you were wondering." He puts his head back in his hands and stares at the ground. "I can't believe I lit my speech on fire. I spent so much time on that stupid fucking thing."

"I'm sure it was really great. I mean . . . the last sentence was very powerful." She resists the urge to rub his arm. Even though that's exactly what she'd do for a friend. "But you did what you had to do. And it got the team's attention."

He plucks some grass that's sprouted between two pavers and tosses it aside. "The Wildcats came pretty damn close to having a new coach this season. I think some of the girls were hoping for that."

Mel shakes her head, emphatic. "There would have been mutiny. We would have set our sticks on fire and marched to the AD's office."

Coach sits up. The beginnings of a smile lift the corners of his mouth, and though it doesn't stick, Mel's anything but discouraged. She's got this.

"Whoever they hired would have given a very different pep talk tonight, I'm sure. Given you girls permission to buy into some bullshit. That last season was a fluke. That it was just plain old bad luck. Factors beyond your control. Blah, blah, blah."

Coach extends his legs straight out and arches his back in a stretch. His polo lifts and exposes a still-tan, flat stomach. Mel glances off to the side, at whatever.

"Yes, your speech was hard to hear." Mel sweeps her hair away from her face. "But we know you wouldn't have said those things if they weren't true."

"Except no one's listening." He shakes his head. "You girls can ignore me all you want, but the fact remains that when the Wildcats show up to play, we win. When they don't, we lose. It's as true as it was on my first day coaching at West Essex, as it was at the state championship. And you'd better believe it will be true tomorrow, when we get our asses handed to us again by Oak Knolls."

"That's not going to happen."

He looks at her pointedly. "It is, Mel. Trust me. The cracks you girls think you're so cleverly hiding are on full display. And if I can see them, you'd better believe other teams will too. They'll dig in any place they can get a foothold. They will work our individual fault lines until they split our team apart."

He stands up and walks away without even a glance back at her.

It is so much harder to have a conversation with him in person, with all his passion and longing and worry focused directly on her, not filtered through a screen.

But is Coach right? Yes, they each have their issues. And, hiding their insecurities from one another does affect the team. Their focus.

Yet, for every failing that Mel could point to from last season, the girls have worked their asses off over the summer to come back strong. Look at Ali, rock solid after goalie camp. Look at Kearson, so eager to right her wrongs. And, God, look at Phoebe. Phoebe put herself in a bad situation, made some really stupid choices. But she certainly suffered the consequences for it. She's more determined than anyone.

And Mel? She hasn't thought of Gordy once tonight.

This is Coach, Mel reminds herself. This is what he does. He pushes them like no one else, doing what is necessary to get the girls where they need to be to win. He knows the difference between being good and being the best. They've all learned that good is not good enough for them. Coach has taught them to want more.

These girls already have it in them. Mel knows they're going to rebound. Come together and take back what's theirs. In fact, though she's put so much effort into her varsity jersey ceremony tonight, Mel would gladly fast-forward to tomorrow's scrimmage, that moment when they'll take the field.

He's halfway to his car when Mel remembers why she came running outside here in the first place.

"Coach, wait!"

"I don't know what else you want me say, Mel. I've done everything I can think of to get this team back on track before tomorrow." He fishes his keys out of his pocket and presses a button on the fob. The Escalade beeps, the lights flash, and the ignition turns on. "And you've made sure everyone's had at least one cupcake. So . . . there's that."

Mel stops short and squeezes her eyes shut. Is that all Coach thinks she's done? She knows now is not the time to sulk. If he leaves without giving her the varsity jerseys, the cupcakes *will* be the only thing she can offer her team tonight.

"The night isn't over. In fact, you could even say it's just getting started." Coach acts like he doesn't hear her. He opens his car door and climbs inside. Mel has to reach out to stop him from closing the door. "I just . . . before you go, I need the varsity jerseys. For tonight's, um, thing."

He gives her a sidelong glance but then it clicks. Or slightly clicks. "Oh. Yeah, okay."

It's Mel's understanding that the Wildcats' midnight tradition is a secret among the girls. Obviously Coach knows *something* about the jerseys, since he gives them to the captain to dole out. But she assumes he doesn't know about the breaking of curfew, the ceremony under the stars, the bonding games, the late-night food. Despite all her conversations with Coach over the years, he's never once asked her about it. Nor did Mel offer up any details of her own accord. She's never even dropped a single hint as to what goes on.

He picks something invisible off his polo and flicks it away. "You girls do a little thing with them, right?"

"It's more than just a little thing." She wants her voice to convey how meaningful this night is, but it has the inverse effect: it makes her sound like a little kid.

"Wait. Was it the jerseys you came running outside for? Or to check on me?"

Mel smiles. "Both."

It takes a second for Coach to smile back.

He reaches for a button somewhere Mel can't see, and the back hatch pops open. Leaving the engine running, Coach climbs back out.

Mel eagerly follows him around to the trunk, barely a step behind. It's full of gear used at tryouts this week. Cones, balls, sticks. Coach reaches in and lifts a Wildcats duffel bag with one arm. He's about to pass it to her, but then pulls it back at the last second. A tease like an older brother. It's enough to get Mel's heart racing.

"I've never asked questions about what you girls do with these jerseys. I've let it be your thing. But you know what, Mel? This season, I need a little more to go on. Because if we don't fix these cracks, and fix them fast, then you girls can say goodbye to any hope of scholarships, say goodbye to scouts making special visits to West Essex. Unless the Wildcats deliver, it's all gonna dry up."

Maybe she should tell him everything? Because maybe if he knew how important tonight is to the girls, he'd understand. Maybe even respect it. Maybe even believe that, come tomorrow's scrimmage, he'd see his Wildcats again.

"I might even have an idea or two for you. My Truman teammates and I used to do the craziest shit."

"I remember. I love those stories."

He wets his lips. "You don't even have to give me credit. Tell the girls it was your idea. I don't care. I just want to help."

Mel fiddles with her necklace. Though it is a seriously tempting offer, she can't betray the secret. Of all her duties as team captain, that is one she absolutely must fulfill.

"Please. Please just trust me. I promise you, I've got this."

When Coach has asked her to trust him in the past, Mel's answer has always been yes. It still is yes. She's also given him every reason to trust her. She's already earned what she's asking for.

"You really think you can do what I need you to do to get this team back on track?"

"I know I can."

He shrugs. "Then I guess we'll see how this plays out tomorrow."

At last he passes her the duffel, which Mel eagerly accepts in her outstretched arms. She pulls it close, gives it a squeeze. Coach pulls down the back hatch then pats down his pockets.

"Hey, I left my phone inside."

"Do you want me to go grab it for you?"

"Nah. I got it. But do me a favor and stay out here, okay? Since I have the car running."

"Sure. No problem."

Coach jogs off toward her house.

Mel takes out her phone and opens up her previous texts from Coach. She does this sometimes, flicks her finger, spins through three years of their conversations. But she is looking for a particular one. Before tonight, the last text she sent to him was a month ago. The day she got into Truman.

Her first text that day was:

MEL: You don't have to say yes.

And his last reply?

COACH: But I did. For you.

For the last three years, Coach has gone above and beyond for Mel. She owes him so much. It's about time she did something to pay him back.

FRIDAY, AUGUST 26
8:19 P.M.
LUCI

The AC in Mel's house feels downright frosty. Luci gets a hoodie out of her overnight bag and pulls it over her head. She knows it looks weird with her dress, but whatever. It's just the girls now. She checks her phone—no missed calls—and puts it in the front pocket.

Someone's in the bathroom off the kitchen. Luci waits for a minute or two. There have to be others, she figures, in a house this massive.

She takes a back staircase up to the second floor, then pads down a long white-walled hallway, her bare feet silenced by thick taupe wall-to-wall carpet. Everything in the Gingriches' house is a neutral: black, beige, white, gray. She opens one door and finds a deep closet with shelves of tightly folded sheets and towels. The next, a library with a fireplace.

Luci doesn't have to guess what's behind the third. It's already cracked.

Mel's bedroom.

Lining up her eye with the open seam, Luci sees simultaneously exactly what she might have imagined and nothing she could have conjured herself.

The bedroom looks staged, like a shot from the pages of a Pottery Barn Teen catalog. Very gently lived in by someone perfect. The furniture is all the same beachy driftwood style. A tall headboard, fluted with crown molding. Over crisp sheets, a lavender comforter is folded halfway down to accommodate an absurd number of pillows.

The curtains, white and barely diffusing the sunset, lift with a breeze. Seconds later, Luci detects a float of gardenia, but the scent is youthful and not at all like the perfume her grandma sprayed so generously along her collarbone that it made her wrinkled skin slick. That's because there's something sweet underneath it. Vanilla. Or maybe honey? Luci breathes deeply but it's too faint, probably just the remnants of whatever lotion Mel put on before getting dressed.

Luci pauses, quickly looking over each shoulder to make sure she is alone. And then she steps inside the bedroom and quietly pulls the door closed behind her.

Though the bedroom floor is carpeted like the hallway, over it there's a thick, creamy shearling rug, on which many bags are scattered, probably from a back-to-school shopping trip. Bloomingdale's, Sephora, Kate Spade, Victoria's Secret. Luci peers into each one.

On Mel's desk, the latest edition of *Vogue*, opened to a dense article.

On Luci's desk, *Chicken Soup for the Soul: Teens Talk High School*. Which, even more embarassingly, Luci's read twice and even dog-eared.

A tall bookcase catches Luci's eye, shelves sparkling with trophies, medals, glossy plastic streamers of pep rally pom-poms. One trophy is so tall, it is tipped on its side to fit. There are several photographs of the team—each matted and framed—along with plenty of candids of Mel and Phoebe as tourists—casting spells in Harry Potter robes, pledging allegiance in front of the White House, up on metal gates at what looks to be a rodeo—sightseeing trips probably fit in between tournament games. Luci tries to determine in which picture Mel looks the youngest, as if that could collapse the distance between them, prove to her that Mel was once Luci's age.

On her way out, Luci spies Mel's Wildcat varsity jacket hanging on the back of the door with its heavy leather sleeves, its striped collar, the terry loops of her *C* letter. Luci pets it before slipping out.

Back in the hallway, Luci carefully pushes the door until it's almost closed. When she turns, she runs right into Coach.

"Luci," he says, a devilish grin gracing his face. "What are you doing sneaking around in Mel's room?"

It is a miracle she doesn't die.

He must see the panic in her face, because Coach lifts his hands in a friendly, disarming way. "I don't actually care what you were doing in Mel's room." His breathing is slightly labored, as if he just returned from a leisurely morning run. His mood seems brightened in that way too. Endorphins, blood flow. "I'm just glad I found you."

"Okay." Luci has no clue why that might be. She thought Coach had left. Luci feels a tickle of excitement at the thought of him hustling back for her.

He scans the hallway and makes sure they are alone. "I know my speech tonight came off a little . . . intense. And most of it probably went over your head. But believe me, the girls needed to hear it. Some problems I'd hoped they'd solve for themselves over the summer have gotten worse, and unless I step in and help fix them, I'm afraid there's not going to be anything here for you in four years."

Luci can't believe that Coach would go out of his way to check in with her like this. That her future would be a consideration is both humbling and validating.

Coach rocks side to side with boyish energy. Nervous and excited. Like they are running out of time on a clock Luci can't see. "You trust me, right, Luci?"

She has no idea why he's asking. But really, isn't there only one answer to give?

"Yes!"

He smiles. She wonders if he thought she would say no.

"Good. Because I came up with a little surprise team-building exercise for you girls tonight. Something to help bring the team together. And I need your help to pull it off. Cool?"

Luci bites her lip and nods. "Absolutely." She's not sure her heart is still beating.

"Excellent." He checks the hallway again. "Do you have your phone on you?"

Their conversation now revving, Luci slips into a faster gear to keep pace. She pulls it out of her pocket, unlocks it, and passes it to him. He taps the screen with this thumbs then hits send. Luci hears his phone buzz in his pocket. Before handing it back, he switches her ringer to vibrate.

"Okay, so here's the plan. On the table near the front door are Mel's car keys. Once I take off, I want you to slip outside and hide your phone somewhere in the back seat. Don't let anyone see you."

Luci has no clue what he is talking about, why she would need to do such a thing, but she nods, like this is a perfectly normal request. "Got it."

"I knew I could count on you, Luci," he says, walking backward away from her.

"Oh. So that's it? That's all you need me to do?"

He winks and says, "For now," and then hustles down the stairs.

Luci presses her back against the hallway wall and tries to catch her breath. She hears the front door open and close.

Her phone doesn't have much charge, only 30 percent, and she contemplates powering it down to conserve it. But Coach didn't say to. So she doesn't. Luci slips downstairs and heads toward the front door.

She's just about there when Mel walks in, a duffel bag in her hands.

Luci freezes. There's nowhere for her to hide, so she spins and pretends to be admiring the family photos on the wall. Out of the corner of her eye, Luci watches Mel drop the bag on the floor and push it with her foot underneath the console table. She lets out a deep, cleansing breath, checks her hair in the mirror, and then walks into the living room.

Luci's heart takes a second to resume beating. She could not do this, come up with some excuse why she was unable to do this very small but very important favor. Instead, Luci tells herself not to be nervous. She does trust him. He's given her no reason not to. In fact, quite the opposite.

With quick, quiet steps, Luci picks up Mel's keys from the table. They are exactly where Coach said they'd be.

It's finally dark outside. That soft, fuzzy dark that happens only in summer. Fireflies are flickering across the front lawn. Coach's

Escalade is gone; Mel's Mini Cooper is parked in the driveway next to Ali's Jeep.

Luci clicks the unlock button on the key fob and opens Mel's back passenger door. As she leans inside, her phone buzzes in her hand, and she startles so badly that she nearly drops it.

COACH: 👍

COACH: 🏆

Luci ducks her head to peek out the rear window. See if she can find where Coach is watching her. But there's no sign of him.

Maybe he's not watching. Maybe he just knows that Luci's going to deliver.

LUCI: 😁

LUCI: 👍

She does exactly what Coach asked her to do, sliding her phone into the space between the cushions that Luci sat on earlier this afternoon. When she locks Mel's car up, the alarm beeps once, but no one inside seems to hear.

Luci hurries up the steps and through the front door, gingerly setting the keys where she found them.

"Cupcake, Luci?"

Luci spins. Mrs. Gingrich is practically on top of her with a platter of them. "Yes, please."

Luci goes into the living room, sits next to Grace on the couch, and takes a bite. The cake is soft and moist. She'll have to check her braces once she's done eating. Despite the pop of sugar, her heartbeat begins to slow.

Luci passed Coach's test. Plus now she knows something is going to happen tonight, even if she has no idea what. And like her two teammates were trying to explain, right before Coach made his speech, it's both scary and exciting all at once.

FRIDAY, AUGUST 26
9:02 P.M.
GRACE

Grace didn't see Coach leave, but it's obvious that he's gone, because all the girls are changing into their bathing suits. Some, like Grace, are waiting for one of the bathrooms to change in privacy, while others strip down behind different pieces of furniture, modesty willingly traded for a chance to claim one of the novelty floats awaiting them in Mel's swimming pool.

Grace is relieved that the overall mood is as buoyant. Since she wasn't on varsity last year, she doesn't take Coach's gripes as personally as others might. But Grace had been in the stands for the state championship game to cheer the Wildcats on, which put her close enough to know exactly how badly it sucked.

That morning was brutally cold and the forecast warned it would only get colder, maybe even snow, so Grace dressed for warmth rather than Wildcat team spirit. A pair of thick tights underneath the only jeans she owned that didn't have holes, two sets of socks, her scuffed white Doc Martens boots, two T-shirts, an itchy lemon cardigan sweater that was warm despite its state of partial unraveling, her grandfather's black wool peacoat that weighed about ten pounds, a shearling-lined striped hat with dorky ear flaps, and a pair of mismatched mittens.

The sky pressed down with thick one-dimensional grayness as Chuck drove Grace over to the high school. He took the turns fast, making up for the time Grace had spent coaxing him out of bed, then to find his keys, then something to scrape the frost off the windshield. But she wasn't late. If Chuck was her ride, Grace always padded the clock.

The JV team had planned to meet at the high school at nine thirty to surprise the Wildcats by decorating the varsity team bus and cheering them as they boarded and departed for the state university's field. Grace was a minute early by those plans, but found she was still the last of her JV teammates to arrive. And that the varsity team bus was already decked out. Windows soaped with paw prints, giant letters cut from construction paper and taped to the body, empty cans tied to the back bumper with blue and white ribbons. Her JV teammates were cleaning up what looked like the remains of a breakfast tailgate. Crushing empty donut boxes, pouring out half-full hot chocolates that had gone cold.

"Do you want me to stick around?" Chuck asked gently. "Or I could take you to the game. I'm not doing anything today."

"One of the girls will drive me," she assured her brother, with no clue who that might be. But Grace was so embarrassed, she just wanted him to go.

She did not call her teammates out for purposefully excluding her. The way to survive was to swallow their drips of venom until you were immune. So Grace acted like she'd been the one who'd gotten the time wrong. She complimented their work—the bus did look awesome—and found ways to involve herself, checking the knots on the streamers and strings. There was one donut left, a jelly that another girl had tasted and put back. Grace ate around the bite mark.

Then the girls formed two lines stretching from the bus to the doors of the West Essex athletic wing and stood at attention like sentry knights in the cold. When the Wildcats emerged, the JV team whooped and hollered, clapping mittened hands together, cheering each player's name and jersey number, someone's phone blasting "We Are the Champions."

The varsity players kept their heads low and their earbuds tucked in as they walked this gauntlet, but they still smiled and some even blushed. Like embarrassed big sisters who love you even when you make a complete ass of yourself.

The only player who didn't look up was Kearson.

Grace did manage to score a ride to the game. She didn't bother asking, just squeezed into the way, way back of a minivan and rode next to her teammate's kid sister.

At the state university field, JV rushed to claim a section of bleachers directly behind the Wildcats' team bench. Though there was already a nice crowd to watch the game, and it continued to fill in, the stadium was so big that the place felt empty. Still, the JV girls were fizzing with anticipation. They hardly ever got to see the varsity team play because they were on opposite schedules—home games when varsity was away, and vice versa. And this game held a significance far beyond anything they'd personally experienced. Even though they had finished their season respectably the week before, with a shutout against Shaler Township to an almost full home field crowd, JV was essentially just practice, a chance to sharpen their skills, learn how their teammates played, scope out the competition. Whether JV won or lost was almost an afterthought.

The Wildcats hardly got off a shot in the first half. Mel and Phoebe struggled to slip back into their rhythm. No one was worried. Even though varsity had lost the last two regular-season games. And Phoebe wasn't in tip-top form. It was still unimaginable they'd lose to Oak Knolls.

After halftime, things started to come apart for the Wildcats but it fused the JV together. The Wildcats were making stupid mistakes and playing sloppily. The JV team had been boisterous throughout but now they screamed their throats raw. They wanted their enthusiasm to smooth whatever was cracking. They wanted their belief in the varsity girls to make them believe in themselves. As the clock ticked down, they abandoned their hopes for an outright win, and prayed the game would remain scoreless and go into overtime.

And then, with just two minutes to go, Darlene Maguire scored on Ali.

The JV girls clung to one another. It took a second to absorb the shock, but Grace and her fellow teammates still applauded Ali's efforts—she'd gotten a finger on it.

When Darlene scored again not a minute later, the JV girls were far less forgiving. Grace heard them cattily pointing out how Ali had barely moved. Marissa even said, "What the eff? Did Ali have a stroke out there or something?"

At the end of every game, all the players on the Wildcats jog down to the end of the field, pick up their goalie, and walk off the field together. It's a sign of unity. But after the final whistle, no one went to get Ali.

Granted, there was a lot of commotion. Senior girls crying.

The team trainer running out to help Phoebe off the field. Mel, sinking to her knees in front of the scoreboard. Still, Ali glanced around for her teammates, dazed at first, then disbelieving. And Grace, despite her distance from the field, felt a familiar sting.

The JV girls glumly shuffled up the bleacher stairs and toward the exit, evaporated adrenaline now exposing them to the frigid temperature. Grace went the opposite direction, fighting the flow of the departing crowd down to the entrance of the players tunnel. There, she quietly, respectfully wished "Good game" to all the Wildcats on their way to the locker rooms, okay that her voice was drowned out by Oak Knolls well-wishers who vastly outnumbered her. But when Ali finally came through, hobbling in her bulky pads, Grace cupped her hands and shouted, to ensure it wouldn't be.

Coach was last off the field and the only one who looked up at the sound of Grace's voice. She briefly thought she saw Coach cringe before he disappeared into the tunnel, though at the time, Grace blamed the cold. After all, the snow flurries had just begun to fall.

Except tonight, in the August heat, he'd done it again. This time, during his speech, the one and only time his eyes had landed on her.

"Grace!"

Ali, in a strapless floral bathing suit, beckons Grace across the backyard, over to where Mel is in the middle of a pre-swim pep talk with the rest of the Wildcats.

"Listen. I know that Coach's speech was a bit of a surprise tonight. But . . . I mean . . ." Mel shrugs. "That's his style, you know? He likes to keep us on our toes. And all he really cares about is what happens on the field when it's game time."

Grace feels herself nodding in agreement. It is a comfort. A place where Grace knows without a doubt she'll measure up.

"But it's okay. *We're okay.* And tomorrow we're going to show Coach, and Oak Knolls, that the girls on this team know *exactly* who we are."

From off to the side, a streak of a voice. "We are the fucking Wildcats!" Phoebe races through them and cannonballs into the pool to the cheers of the team.

Grace hasn't gone swimming much this summer. Once at her uncle's Fourth of July barbecue. A few dips in the lake at Kissawa. The pool in Mel's backyard has a diving board and also a hot tub just off the stairs leading to the shallow end. Grace would love to dive in but she is afraid her blue hair color might run, so she twists it up in a bun at the tippy top of her head, then lowers herself into the bubbling hot tub. The water is searing but it feels so good on her sore muscles.

Kearson approaches and unfurls her towel. Her bikini is cute. Pink gingham. Grace watches Kearson slide in with her, though she doesn't exactly join her. Without a word, Kearson leans back and closes her eyes.

Though she wasn't overtly mean like some of the other JV girls, Kearson never made much of an effort to be nice to Grace either. But Grace knows tonight is about coming together. They are teammates again, but in a new way.

Grace closes her eyes too and clears her throat. "Congrats on making the team."

"Thanks, Grace," Kearson says. "You too."

Grace waits to see if Kearson will volley the conversation back. She listens to the gurgle of the jets, the pulse of the music, the splashes and squeals of the other girls in the pool. Eventually, she peeks to see if Kearson is there. She is. Eyes still closed. Relaxing. So Grace closes hers again too and tries to do the same. This was a friendly enough start but there's no rush. They have an entire season to warm up to each other.

"I'm sorry, Grace."

Grace sits up. "For what?"

"I never thanked you for the cookies you made me last season."

Quinn came up with the idea that the JV girls should each pick a varsity Wildcat and bake them a special championship treat on the last school day before the big game. The treats could go in pretty bags, or maybe an individual Tupperware container, but whatever it was should be decorated with the player's last name and jersey number in cheery bubble letters. And include a handwritten note wishing them luck.

Almost immediately, the JV girls began to shout out the names of varsity players they wanted to bake for. The senior starters were picked first, claimed by the most popular girls. Grace was not given an option. Or rather, before she called out a name, it was suggested she take Kearson. None of Kearson's friends apparently wanted her. They were jealous. And anyway, Grace heard whispers that Phoebe had been cleared to play, her recovery likely sped up by how badly Kearson sucked in the last two games.

But fine. Sure. Whatever.

Grace isn't much of a baker, so she bought a roll of premade cookie dough. They came out of the oven looking okay, but Grace left them to cool on the baking sheet, and by the time she chipped them off, the bottoms were black.

She put the cookies in a bag on the Friday before the game. At first she didn't bother including a handwritten note. It wasn't like they were close. But before tucking them into Kearson's locker, she ripped out a piece of notebook paper and quickly scribbled down a quote. Serena Williams.

> *A champion is defined not by their wins but by how they can recover when they fall.*

"Oh. I'm glad you liked them."

"Don't get me wrong. They tasted awful. But I was really grateful." Kearson smiles shyly. "So grateful that I ate them all anyway."

"Well... that makes me happy and also sad. But mostly happy."

Mel walks around the backyard addressing the different clusters of girls. Eventually she makes her way over to the hot tub and bends down. "Hey, it's getting late. Coach wants lights-out by ten o'clock."

Grace and Kearson lift themselves out of the water. Mel hands them their towels. They follow the rest of the team back into Mel's house. The caterers have taken the food and serving dishes away. In the clean kitchen, the lights are off except for one over the sink and a scented candle flickering on the counter. Mel's parents must have gone to bed.

The finished basement is cooler than any other room in the house, windowless and holding the central air. It's borderline frigid. Grace breaks out in goose bumps as she peels off her bathing suit, changes into her Ramones T-shirt and the bike shorts, and grabs her toothbrush.

The fight for sink space becomes a little game. The girls, like sisters in a too-small house, box each other out to wash their faces and brush their teeth. Phoebe teases a junior for using kids' toothpaste, which Grace defends, because she used the same kind and remembers it being hella delicious, and several girls commiserate that toothpaste companies don't make fun flavors for adults. Ali rushes in, desperate to pee, no privacy needed, which prompts Phoebe to tell everyone a story about how, after getting stuck behind an accident on the highway, they forced the bus driver to pull over on the shoulder and the whole team lined up and peed in the weeds.

Mel suddenly barges in. "One of the girls on Oak Knolls just posted a video and tagged a bunch of us in the comments."

Everyone is pretty pissed, but Phoebe is incensed. She spits, wipes her mouth with her arm. "You're fucking kidding me." She storms out.

"Who was it?" Ali shouts after them and rips off a piece of toilet paper so hard that it sends the roll spinning. "Who posted the video?"

The team gathers into the main room of the finished basement and crowds around Mel's phone. A bunch of girls shout that they can't see, so Mel shouts back, "Okay, okay," and mirrors her phone to the television.

It's Darlene Maguire's page.

The room falls silent. Mel presses play.

First, music. A snippet of "Tomorrow" from the musical *Annie*.

Then a crudely edited slideshow. Pictures of newspaper articles, college acceptance letters. Then a video of championship game footage taken from the local cable channel broadcast and edited down into a Boomerang. Darlene scoring on Ali over and over and over again while Ali remains motionless.

Mel reaches out and gives Ali's shoulder a tender squeeze. Ali doesn't take her eyes off the television.

The video ends with the entire Oak Knolls team on their home field with the state championship trophy and a white bulldog.

Grace tunes into a whispered conversation behind her.

"I hate Oak Knolls but that bulldog is cute."

"I heard their coach never lets him inside. Just trots him around at games like a prop."

"Someone should call animal control. That's cruel."

Oak Knolls waves at the camera. At the Wildcats.

Tomorrow, tomorrow, I love ya, tomorrow. You're only a day away!

Mel quickly disconnects her phone before the video begins replaying.

"You okay?" Phoebe asks Ali.

"Yup," Ali says too quick, too focused on unfurling her sleeping bag.

Phoebe isn't quite buying Ali's answer, but instead of pressing her, she turns to the rest of the girls and announces, "Tomorrow we'll wipe those shit-eating grins off their faces."

Two senior players open up the couch into a full-sized bed already made with sheets and tightly tucked blankets. They climb on and a third girl squeezes in the middle, but when a fourth tries to fit, she immediately slips off the end, which makes the whole room crack up laughing.

The rest of the girls unfurl their bedding—sleeping bags, comforters brought from home—onto the plush carpet.

Kearson waves Grace over. "Grace! There's room over here!"

Mel tiptoes over the bodies, spare pillows tucked under each arm. "Did you forget a pillow, Grace?" She tosses one over.

Grace tries to hand it back. "This kind of hair dye sometimes rubs off."

"It's fine. My mom has a million pillowcases."

She takes her dress and wraps it over top of the pillow, just in case.

At two minutes before ten Mel turns off the lights. Grace

wonders if Mel will sleep upstairs in her own bed. But no, she finds space next to Phoebe.

A comedic round of "Good night" goes from head to head to head. Lots of giggles at first, then a bit of shushing.

Grace settles into her spot in the corner. The AC vent is nearby, with its whispers of cold wind. It's crazy to think of all that crammed into a single day, both physically and emotionally. Grace lets her head sink into the pillow.

Just as she hoped, Grace has finally found her place. Her people. Her pack.

SATURDAY, AUGUST 27
12:00 A.M.
LUCI

Someone's alarm. The terrible one that sounds like a submarine is sinking.

Luci lifts her head and blinks away the bleariness. Some of the girls are up and already dressed. The older girls. Is it morning? Already? It doesn't feel like she was sleeping long.

Across the room, Phoebe flicks the basement lights on and off.

"What's going on?" Luci whispers to no one in particular.

She both does and doesn't know.

Suddenly, Mel is standing over her, clapping her hands. She's out of the pajamas she wore to bed and is now in a pair of jean cutoffs, a thin white ribbed tank top, and her Wildcat varsity jacket. Though they washed their faces at the sink together, Mel's got eyeliner and a sheer peachy gloss on again.

"Let's go, newbies! Rise and shine!"

The new players exchange wary looks, unsure whether or not

to smile. A girl next to Luci reaches for her sleepover bag and digs for her clothes.

Mel toes it away. "Sorry, girls. No time to change. We've got so much to do!"

Luci looks down. She went to bed wearing a big T-shirt and a pair of Mickey Mouse boxers. But at some point she got cold and slid on her hoodie. Thank goodness. She doesn't have a bra on.

"Can we wear shoes?" Luci meekly asks, standing up.

Mel turns, blinks a few times. "Luci. Of course you can wear shoes. We aren't monsters."

Ali walks through the room with a pillowcase. "All phones in here, please!"

The girls turn them off one by one and drop them inside the pillowcase. Not just the new girls, but the returning players too.

"Phone," Ali says when she gets to Luci.

"I . . . I don't have one."

"You don't have a phone?" Ali asks, a blend of pity and confusion. Ali glances backward at Mel. "Luci doesn't have a phone."

"No . . . wait." She shakes her head, starts over, talking mostly to Ali but also to Mel, who edges her way through the crowd toward them. "I mean, I *do*. I just don't have it with me." Which isn't a lie.

Mel is toe to toe with Luci. "Why wouldn't you bring your phone with you?"

For a second Luci thinks about telling her the truth. Not here, in front of everyone. If she could speak with Mel privately in the laundry room or whatever.

Except Coach had said to trust him.

"The thing is, I dropped it in water after practice today and so now it's sitting in a bowl of rice. I don't know if it's ruined or not, but we just got new ones because we signed up for a new plan, so if it is ruined, my mom is going to kill me. She said if it's dead, she's buying me a flip phone. I doubt I'll even be able to text."

Luci crouches down and pulls a pair of sneakers out of her bag, using the time to catch her breath. What the hell did she just say?

Thankfully, the girls seem to buy it. At the words "flip phone," they groan in unity. Mel even chimes in, "I have an old iPhone you can have, Luci. We won't let that happen to you."

A few minutes later, Mel holds her finger to her lips and the girls file past her up the basement staircase. Everyone waits in the dark kitchen while Phoebe slips outside alone and looks up to a second-floor window—Mel's parents' bedroom, likely. Phoebe gives a thumbs-up. Then the team tiptoes into the backyard, through the side gate, and out to the driveway.

While the older girls unlock their car doors, the new Wildcats form a line, ragtag in their pajamas. Luci needs to make sure she rides in Mel's Mini Cooper, so she positions herself as near to it as possible.

Phoebe clutches her heart. "Oh my God, you girls are so adorable.

"Were we ever that young?" Mel says while hip checking Phoebe.

"Nope," Phoebe says. "Okay, newbies. Pick a car, any car, the night is young!"

Luci takes off sprinting. She pulls on the door handle, climbs into the back seat, and sits on the hump. As inconspicuously as possible, she finds the cell phone where she left it and slips it into the front pocket of her hoodie.

Grace, strolling at a more leisurely pace toward Ali's Jeep, says to her, "See, Luci? I knew you and Mel would get along."

The Wildcats split themselves up into a total of six cars and drive off into the night.

Phoebe takes Mel's phone and cues up a song. "Okay, Luci. This is the first song I'm putting on your mix. It's a classic."

"I'm all ears!" Luci says.

They aren't even at the end of Mel's block when Luci feels her phone buzz in her hoodie pocket. Eyes wide, she glances at the teammates sandwiched on either side of her in the back seat. They don't seem to have noticed. Nor have Phoebe and Mel. They are all belting out lyrics Luci doesn't know.

The warmth of her secret seeps into her.

In no time at all, they pull up to West Essex's field. Twelve hours ago they were here trying out. Twelve hours from now, they'll be here playing Oak Knolls. The girls speed in to the empty lot, hanging out the windows, parking wherever they want.

Luci feels an urgency to see what Coach texted and respond if needed. But of course, she needs to be secretive. Otherwise, she'll be caught with her phone, Mel will take it away (not to mention expose her for lying), and she'd fail Coach's test. Phoebe said there wouldn't be one, but that's what this is. A test of her commitment to Coach and to the Wildcats.

Her teammates walk ahead of her. Mel and Phoebe are pulling stuff out of Mel's trunk. Luci crouches down between two other parked cars. She pretends to tie her shoe but pulls out her phone instead.

Yes, she is betraying her teammates. But it is with Coach's instructions. That has to count for something, right?

SATURDAY, AUGUST 27
12:12 A.M.

COACH: Where are you girls?

LUCI: We just got to the high school field. Sorry I didn't answer right away. I was afraid someone would see me.

COACH: No prob. I'll make this quick.

COACH: Like I told you, I planned a surprise team building exercise. No one knows but you.

COACH: When the girls are trying to figure out what to do with my instructions, I want you to say that we had a conversation tonight about my college days and all the crazy stunts we used to do, and that maybe you girls should do something like that.

LUCI: 🤐

LUCI: 🙄

LUCI: 👍

COACH: 😂

COACH: I promise this will eventually make sense.

LUCI: Anything else?

COACH: Just keep in touch. You're my eyes and my ears tonight. Okay?

LUCI: I won't let you down!

COACH: I know you won't.

COACH: 😉

COACH: Btw, I've heard this night is usually super fucking boring. You can thank me later for making it fun. 😎

**SATURDAY, AUGUST 27
12:15 A.M.
PHOEBE**

The Wildcats home field is lit with stars and fireflies and moonlight. Phoebe—field hockey stick over her shoulder, the shopping bags pulled from Mel's trunk bunched at the curve of the upturned blade—pauses at the break in the chain-link fence to take in the beauty with a deep and satisfied breath. It sucks that they never play night games because it's fucking *magical* out here. Teammates brush past as they step onto the field. It's a gentle current that Phoebe eventually relents to.

She lowers her stick like the arm at a railroad crossing, twists the staff so the blade points toward the turf. The bags slide off one by one to the ground. Phoebe takes a knee—her uninjured one, now reflexively favored—and rifles through their contents for the sacks of candy. Phoebe then sets to tearing each one open with her teeth and pouring their sugary contents—Hershey's Kisses, Twizzlers, Dum Dums, Airheads, Smarties, Tootsie Rolls—into the cavernous 2 piñata.

Phoebe senses someone coming up on her right side, the awareness of what might be in her periphery sharpened on this very field. She turns and watches Kearson walk past, careful to maintain a deferential distance, her arms wrapped around herself as if she could somehow be freezing on this sticky summer night.

Another player might blame Kearson for basically leaving her no choice but to get back out on the field for the championship game before she was technically cleared to play. Not Phoebe. And as Phoebe informed her mother this afternoon, she really doesn't begrudge Kearson her spot on this year's team either. Kearson clearly worked hard to improve her game in the off-season and she's gotten a lot better.

But these benevolent feels are deep down inside her, in some dark, damp nook where it's hard for good things to take root. To be honest, Phoebe doesn't know for sure that she's having them at all. They might be ghosts of her former self, haunting her. She used to be the kind of teammate who gave her all for the good of the team. Except how can she play like that this season, when she has so much on the line?

And so what if Kearson feels uneasy around her? So what if she feels like Phoebe's ACL tear is her fault? That works to Phoebe's advantage. Doesn't she deserve an advantage, a leg up, after everything she's sacrificed?

Phoebe bites the inside of her cheek. Hard.

"Yo, Kearson!" When Kearson looks up, Phoebe tosses her a foil-wrapped Kiss. "You look like you could use a little sugar."

Kearson catches it one-handed. "Thanks, Phoebe."

There. Phoebe lets out a cleansing breath and returns to the task at hand, shaking a final bag of goodies into the piñata and then closing the hatch.

Mel had happy danced right there in the aisle of Party City when she found it, then leapt up on Phoebe's back as they hurried to the register, almost knocking them both to the floor in the process. Mel was so excited, Phoebe actually felt bad bringing up the practicalities of stringing the piñata up at their wide-open playing field—namely how and where—but Mel waved Phoebe's concern away. She'd think of something.

Only it's clear Mel hasn't. Why else would she conveniently hang back in the parking lot to get "organized" while asking Phoebe to get the piñata set up?

Phoebe rolls her eyes. It's funny how much their relationship on the field is mirrored in their real life. More than she ever would have thought.

Phoebe looks around, trying to figure something out. She nixes stringing it up at a corner of fencing (no room to get a good swing in), draping it down the backside of the bleachers from the top rung (not enough rope). But if she can hang it from the base of their scoreboard, that might work nicely. The scoreboard is large, mounted on three tall metal polls, and tall enough for the piñata to sway over their heads.

Phoebe carries the piñata over on her back. At the scoreboard, she takes a ball of twine in her hand and shoots it like a free throw. It takes a gorgeous arc, a comet tethered to the piñata at her feet. Phoebe knows it will sail over the crossbar. She doesn't have to watch. But she does, just for fun.

Swish.

Phoebe's first love was basketball.

Her first crush, LeBron.

Phoebe had started playing basketball with the kids on her block after getting a hoop for Hanukkah when she was eleven.

Her driveway became home court for any girls and boys wanting to scrap. It didn't matter how cold it was that winter, every day after school, there'd be a pile of discarded sweatshirts and ski jackets on the ground as stinging-cheeked kids played until it became too dark to see.

Phoebe was tall, taller than any of the boys, and she loved posting up under the basket, ready to receive a pass. She'd do a quick dribble to reposition herself, then a little move, maybe a pump fake. Boys *always* fell for her pump fake—they were so hungry to block her shot—diving for a ball that never left her hands and leaving her with a wide-open shot.

Come spring, her height advantage began to shrink, and Phoebe found herself moving to the point guard position, sinking a gorgeous three-pointer every so often, but mostly working the court to find an open teammate, bouncing a perfect pass their way. She didn't mind scoring fewer points; she took pride in every assist.

By that summer, the boys were becoming more physical. They were suddenly stronger and taller and when they would hold up their arms for passes, Phoebe tried not to notice the hair growing in their armpits. Some of them straight up wouldn't guard her, they'd just throw their hands up, and they definitely got weird when Phoebe got physical with them, pushing her backside into their stomachs as she inched as close to the basket as she could get.

Derek Noble from two blocks over went out of his way to be rough with her, throw an elbow up, push on her from the back. He bruised her good one time, an elbow right in the ribs, but she wouldn't allow herself to cry. By this time, the neighbor girls who used to play alongside her now sat in the shade, watching them, barely keeping score, whining that everyone should go swimming instead.

Eventually J. P. Coakley got a hoop for his twelfth birthday, and Derek and the rest of the neighborhood boys started playing at his house instead of hers. Phoebe could have walked four houses down from her driveway and joined them, but to be honest, none of them were very good. Her father gave her more of a run for her money playing HORSE.

She still loves watching basketball with her father. And since becoming a Wildcat, she's always been number 23, an ode to LeBron.

J. P. transferred to Central Catholic after the end of eighth grade, and as far as Phoebe knows, he doesn't play basketball. Derek Noble, however, goes to West Essex. He is a varsity basketball starter, also number 23.

Last February, Phoebe had a late PT appointment, so she tucked her crutches under her arm and hopped into the bleachers to watch some of the boys varsity basketball home game while waiting for her ride. The stands were barely half-full, the school's cheerleading squad had to beg for answers to their call-and-response chants.

Derek was a physical powerhouse in the first quarter, leaping for the rim, diving for a pass. By the second quarter, he was growing tired, slowing up. By the half, he resorted to using his brute strength as a cover for his lack of stamina. He fouled out before the end of the third quarter and was forced to watch from the bench as his teammates lost the game, a towel draped over his head, directly underneath the two field hockey championship banners Phoebe had helped earn. She snapped a couple of pictures on her phone, a bit of visual inspiration for her PT session. Wasn't shy about it, either. She turned the flash on and everything.

Phoebe focuses now on securing the piñata and gives it a tap to make sure it will hold. The 2 swirls like a top, a golden blur no longer recognizable as a number.

Then she follows the sideline back to the rest of her stuff, at first walking, then moving into an easy jog. In a flash, Phoebe bursts into a sprint. She shouldn't be doing this without her brace, and definitely not without her Knee Spanx, but fuck it. After a few meters, she stops on a dime, spins around, hustles backward at half speed, then spins and takes off again, racing all the way back, a huge smile on her face.

When she stops, Phoebe pulls up her knee and hugs it to her chest. It's a tiny bit sore, but nothing Phoebe can't handle. She's played through way worse.

"Hey, looking good!"

It's Mel, standing center field, fists on her hips. Mel's been watching her. And she's grinning. She might be as relieved as Phoebe herself that her knee is holding up.

Phoebe quickly deflects out of embarrassment. "What do you think?" She gestures to the piñata. "Not bad, right?"

Mel gives her two thumbs-up. "MVP!" She threads her arm into Phoebe's and leads her away from the girls at midfield and toward the deserted metal bleachers. "There's something I want to run by you real quick," Mel says coyly. "I came up with a brilliant plan for when we play Oak Knolls tomorrow."

"Isn't the plan just to win?"

Mel sits down on the bleachers and wets her lips. "Coach's speech tonight got me thinking. I want to do more than just win. I want to make a statement. Set the tone for this season. Do something big to get our confidence back. For Coach, obviously, but also for the rest of the girls." Leaning forward, she takes Phoebe's hand and tugs her down, making Phoebe sit next to her. "And I want us to be the ones to do it, Phoebe."

The backs of Phoebe's legs feel clammy against the cold bleacher steel. "What do you have in mind?"

Mel stomps her feet, a giddy burst of metallic thunder. "Okay! So. You and I are going to make a run at the Oak Knolls goal with the kind of intensity we'd have if the clock were about to run out and it was our last chance to score. Except we're going to do it immediately after the face-off."

"Assuming you win the face-off," Phoebe teases.

Mel swats her. "Please! I *always* win the face-off! Anyway. Instead of passing forward, I'm going to hook the ball sideways to you. Then you and I will sprint straight up the field, full throttle, crisscrossing passes as we go. I'm imagining three total, like boom boom boom, with your last one hitting me right at the top of the key. And then I'm going to fire off a shot as hard as I can, with everything I've got."

Phoebe watches Mel's eyes sparkle. Her chest rises and falls as if she actually completed the play she just described. It is no less exhilarating for Mel to imagine this game than to actually play it. "And this idea just came to you?"

"Yes. On the ride over. Why? Is that weird?"

Phoebe laughs. "Um, no. This is extremely on brand for you, Mel."

Mel tucks her hands in the pockets of her varsity jacket. "Obviously, best-case scenario is I score right away. . . . But even if I don't, then you and I will just go at them again, the very next time we get the ball. Again and again and again, as hard as we can, as many times as it takes." She bites her lip. "What do you think?"

Phoebe had tried to put her earlier conversation with Coach at the Psych-Up out of her mind. She couldn't tell anyone about what had happened, least of all Mel. But Phoebe knew she was the reason, or at least *a* reason, behind his angry speech tonight.

Mel's idea is a couple of notches higher than where Phoebe set the bar for herself for tomorrow's game. Phoebe sees now that higher is where she must aim. After how badly she screwed up with Coach, it won't be enough for Phoebe to simply play well tomorrow. She'll need to play better than her best to repair what she's damaged.

Not only that, but Phoebe suspects that Mel might be in exactly the same spot she is with Coach. Desperate to prove that the Wildcats' top scorer can and will deliver.

How amazing then, that they can attack this problem on the field together. Suddenly, it seems to Phoebe more possible than not that they'll be able to solve it.

"I'm in!"

Mel springs up. "Yay! This is going to be so great!" She jogs backward toward midfield, where the rest of the team is standing around. Phoebe moves more slowly.

The girls were friendly before field hockey, but during their time in the eighth-grade summer skills camp, Phoebe and Mel got tighter by the sheer fact that they were clearly the best of their peers. Mel was on a whole other level, and Phoebe was always working to keep up. But she liked that. On the girls' basketball team, there would have been no one to push her. She'd have been the one carrying the team.

And when they each got the call from Coach inviting them to join the varsity tryouts that summer before high school, both girls were hopeful of course, but also nervous and wanting to be sensitive that the other maybe didn't get the call. They hadn't yet gotten to the point of sharing nearly everything with each other.

Umm. Hi was about as brave a text as Mel could manage to send her.

Ummmmm!!!!!! HIIIIIIIII, Phoebe texted back.

Being the only two freshmen on the team, they would sit together at the front of the bus, claiming the fourth seat behind the driver. As they got older and gained more seniority, the girls could have moved toward the back, but they never did. They liked their seat. They'd memorized the pen graffiti written there, accepted that their window was the only one on the bus that wouldn't open.

Neither girl, individually, was particularly superstitious, but together they developed a hundred little rituals over the years to ensure a victory. They packed certain snacks, depending on the day of the week and type of game. Tuesday scrimmage meant they split a Kit Kat. Saturday mornings, a salt bagel with cream cheese. Before games they tied each other's cleats. They would hit play on their playlists only after the bus had left the school parking lot.

It certainly didn't hurt matters that Phoebe played midfield and Mel left forward, two inseparable positions. They clicked in that way too, a deep trust forming between them. It was beyond intuitive. They always knew where the other was on the field.

Field hockey became a year-round sport. The regular season was followed by spring club league, the Thanksgiving showcase in Florida, Kissawa summer camp, summer league. Plus both girls were alternates in the National U-18 team two years ago.

Outside of their relationship on the field, their personalities complemented each other in real life. Mel was shy and reserved, but Phoebe knew how to get her to be silly, unguarded. Like the time, for Phoebe's birthday, that Mr. Holt took the girls on an overnight trip to see the Cavs play in Cleveland. She made them each a T-shirt to wear, KING and JAMES, and together they would dance to every song played over the PA system, hoping to make it on the jumbotron screen.

As close as they are, Phoebe's injury shed light on some aspects of Mel's personality that either Phoebe hadn't seen before or just straight-up ignored. Like how much Mel actually relies on her. How quickly Mel's confidence, which seemed part of her DNA, could slip away. How uncomfortable Mel is with being vulnerable.

If anything, these revelations make Phoebe feel more warmly toward her best friend. They help her make sense of things. Why Mel wants them so badly to play, if not for Truman, then in the same division. Because it's hard to imagine Mel making many new friends. Or at least the kinds of friends she needs.

Phoebe joins everyone at the very center of the field, where a large navy circle is painted on the turf. Inside that is a smaller circle in white, and inside that is the illustrated rendering of West Essex's school mascot. The wildcat has golden fur streaked with black and white stripes, white fangs bared around a panting red tongue. Though she knows it isn't meant to be, Phoebe has always interpreted it as a female.

The girls sit cross-legged around that outer navy ring. The newbies, adorable in their pj's, are beaming with anticipation. The returning players in normal clothes, looking as excited as they did the first year they made the team.

Mel steps into the center and everyone quiets.

"During tryouts, it's every girl for herself, until Coach makes his final picks, selects the best of the best for his team. But starting tonight, it's no longer about any one girl. Not me. Or Phoebe. Or Ali. Not about the starters or the girls who'll mostly ride the bench. Tonight we all become Wildcats."

Mel's Psych-Up is a perfect blend of old and new like the players themselves. She starts, as in other years, with the Clap Clap Lap Snap name game because it's always a good time. Next they play Two Truths and a Lie, which is another Wildcat favorite. Phoebe and Mel are always out to stump each other, like two poker players betting big on shitty cards. Ali duped the entire team this year—turns out she got a tattoo on her hip when she was visiting her brother in San Francisco this summer. Three little stars that Kearson instantly recognizes as the design on top of every page in the Harry Potter series. Phoebe read all the books at least three times each and she didn't get it.

Next, Mel leads the girls in a new trust game called Willow in the Wind and she's relieved when it's a big hit. But Phoebe knows that it doesn't matter what games the girls play. Swap out Big Ups with a Human Knot. Trust Wave with Slice 'n' Dice. After the stress of tryouts, where any mistake could mean the difference between making the team and not, it's a relief to do dumb shit together, where the whole point is to fall on your ass in front of your team.

That said, Mel's piñata feels not just special but necessary. Cathartic.

Phoebe practically pees her pants laughing as she watches her blindfolded teammates swinging wildly with her field hockey stick.

Luci gets in the first good crack, and the girls all scream and cheer her on as she swings again and again, beating the crap out of it, landing every hit.

Finally, the number 2 piñata cracks open and a rainbow stream of candy pours out. The girls dive into the bounty.

It's perfect. This night is fucking perfect. Phoebe is overcome with feelings for her team, these girls, every last one of them. Even Kearson bobblehead Wagner, which really says something.

Phoebe wants to play field hockey forever.

She hip checks Mel playfully and hands her a lollipop. Mel thanks her and dabs the tears from her eyes with her varsity jacket sleeve. Phoebe immediately tears up too. They laugh at each other.

"I told you I was going to cry," Mel says.

"Happy tears," Phoebe says, wiping Mel's eyes and then her own. That's exactly what they are. Phoebe, maybe more than anyone, knows the difference.

SATURDAY, AUGUST 27
12:50 A.M.
MEL

Mel watches from the center of the circle as her teammates twist left to right, each girl lighting her sparkler, and then passing the fire onto the next, adding clouds to their electric white snowstorm.

She knows Coach will be happy tomorrow. He will see his Wildcats.

When the sparkler circle is complete, Mel takes a breath and says, "As captain, it is my belief that every girl here tonight has proven herself a worthy teammate. And so, it is now my great honor to present each of you with your varsity jersey. From this moment forward until the final whistle, we are the Wildcats. Team first, always."

Lead by Phoebe, the girls begin singing the Wildcat fight song.
We are the Wildcats, the navy blue and white,
We are the Wildcats, always ready for a fight!

*Don't mess with the Wildcats, we won't accept defeat,
For we are the Wildcats, and we will not be beat!*

*Three cheers for the Wildcats, your honor we'll defend,
'Cause when you're a Wildcat, you're a Wildcat till the end!*

Mel shrugs off her varsity jacket and then crouches down before the duffel bag full of varsity jerseys at her feet.

She will slip on her own jersey first. Then she'll fish out the numbers already claimed by the returning players and hand those out. Last of all, she'll call forth each new Wildcat to choose a number from the jerseys that are left. Practical, efficient. Though, if it were Phoebe, she'd take them out with flair and reverence, like when Rafiki lifts up baby Simba and presents him to the pride.

Mel pulls back the zipper and bites her lip.

The varsity jerseys are made of heavy-weight polyester. They are white, slightly boxy, with short sleeves. Short sleeves are good for September games, when it's still hot out, but by mid-October, the girls will layer long-sleeved shirts underneath their jerseys to keep warm. Their jerseys have navy numbers stitched to the back, "West Essex" stitched across the chest.

But what Mel finds in the duffel bag are a tangle of their practice pinnies. The ones Coach hands out for scrimmages. Flimsy mesh tanks in blue and white, damp and slightly musty. Mel doubts they've been washed once all week.

Mel is so suddenly dizzy she sets her hands down on the turf to steady herself.

Phoebe is waving her sparkler, singing, smiling. Mel catches her attention with a pained stare.

"Everything okay?" Phoebe says, stepping into the circle and crouching next to her, careful to hold her sparkler off to the side. Mel doesn't have to answer. Phoebe sees for herself that there are no Wildcat jerseys in the duffel bag. "What the . . ."

Her teammates slow the fight song down to an eerie tempo. Mel glances up at them, and they immediately pick up the speed again, pretending not to see that something weird is happening.

"Sorry, girls. Just one second," Mel announces, her voice high and sharp. She quickly zips the bag closed and walks out of the circle.

"Is everything okay, Mel?" Luci bites on the side of her finger, one foot on top of the other.

"Yup!" Mel says, without slowing down, feeling their eyes on her back.

"This is weird," Phoebe whispers, at her side. "Is Coach saying we haven't made the team yet? That we could still be cut?" Phoebe gasps and grabs Mel's arm, pulling her to a stop. "Oh my God, Mel. Remember Becks?"

"Huh?"

"Becks Altiero!"

"Phoebe! I know *who* you mean!" Phoebe and Mel were sophomores when Becca, aka Becks, Altiero was a senior with long brown hair, blunt cut bangs, and a little gap between her front teeth. Becks was sweet as sugar in real life, but on the field, she was notoriously salty, something the girls attributed to having grown up the only girl sandwiched between four brothers. Not only did Becks have a mouth on her—and the uncanny ability to curse out a ref without him ever hearing—but she loved to showboat. Every time she scored a goal, Becks would bust out a celebratory dance move on her way to retrieve the ball. A twerk, a shimmy, a worm. You never knew what it was going to be. Her victory dances weren't so much a way to annoy the opposing team (though they did) but an expression of Becks' joy in playing the game. "What I don't get is why you're bringing her up now."

"Don't you remember? How Coach benched her for the last half of the season?"

"Vaguely? I thought Becks was having a dry spell."

"No. It all started at one of our practices. Coach was demoing a defensive ball handling skill, and he picked Becks to stand in on offense. Except Becks wouldn't let him steal the ball. She kept pulling it away from him and teasing him about it. At first Coach was laughing, but then he got hella pissed."

"How do I not remember any of this?"

"I have no idea. But at the very next game, Coach benched her. And then the game after that, too. I think Becks even tried to apologize, but Coach pretended like he didn't know what she was talking about."

"Maybe Coach didn't know what she was talking about." Mel certainly doesn't. "Anyway, that's, like, an entirely different situation. None of us are trying to flex on him."

"Yeah. That's true."

"It has to be a mistake." They'd had a straightforward conversation. Yes, he'd hesitated. Yes, he'd wanted Mel to let him in on their secret Psych-Up traditions. But when it came down to it, Mel had asked Coach to trust her. By giving her the jerseys, it meant that he did.

Mel blinks.

Let's see how this plays out.

"I should probably text him, though, just to make sure."

"Mel, don't! It's late. We're supposed to be at your house sleeping. We don't want to piss him off more. If it was a mistake, we can just get the varsity jerseys from him tomorrow. Even without them, we've still had an awesome night. Your Psych-Up was a total success."

Mel smiles at the compliment but there is an uneasy feeling in her stomach. "Don't worry." Phoebe starts to follow her into the parking lot, but Mel holds up her hands. "Stay with the girls, okay?"

"What do you want me to tell them?"

"Have them keep singing until I can figure out what's going on."

She shoves her hands into the pockets of her cutoffs and walks quickly toward her car. The parking lot lights collect moths, confetti that never falls to the ground. Behind her, her teammates sing dutifully.

We are the Wildcats, the navy blue and white,
We are the Wildcats, always ready for a fight!

Don't mess with the Wildcats, we won't accept defeat,
For we are the Wildcats, and we will not be beat!

Three cheers for the Wildcats, your honor we'll defend,
'Cause when you're a Wildcat, you're a Wildcat till the end!

Mel takes out her phone. She's not even sure what she should write.

MEL: Hey.

Coach answers almost immediately. Like he's been waiting to hear from her. His phone expectantly in his hand.

COACH: ?

MEL: I'm sorry to be texting so late.

MEL: But I just realized that the bag you gave me was full of practice pinnies

MEL: Not varsity jerseys

She waits to see if he'll respond.

MEL: And I'm wondering if that was an accident or . . .

Mel's heartbeat fills her ears.

COACH: Seriously?

COACH: 😂😂😂

MEL: I don't understand.

COACH: Yeah. I know.

COACH: That's coming through loud and clear.

Mel looks around. The parking lot is empty. The street quiet. She turns to the field and sees that the sparklers have gone out. All that remains are curls of cinder smoke.

She will have to walk over there and tell the girls there are no varsity jerseys. There will be no ceremony. Phoebe was sweet to say this part didn't matter, that her Psych-Up was still a success. But Mel knows the jersey ceremony is the point. So to have it taken away from her is humiliating.

He's humiliated her in front of her team.

Why?

Her hands shaking, Mel types faster than she thinks, rapid fire, two thumbs.

MEL: You said you wanted me to help fix our team.

MEL: I told you I had a plan.

MEL: So why didn't you at least give me a chance?

MEL: Why did you trick me into thinking that you trusted me?

MEL: Why not just tell me to my face?

MEL: Instead of making me look like an idiot in front of all the girls?

Her chest rises and falls. The gush of adrenaline leaves Mel slightly nauseous. She's never gone off on Coach like that before.

She immediately regrets it. But Mel finds validation in watching Coach struggle to respond. She sees him write back, then stop, write back, then stop.

It startles her when her phone rings in her hand.

"After everything I said tonight, in the backyard and privately to you, why would you think for a second you girls deserve your jerseys?" Coach lets out a loud breath. Impatient static. "Honestly, Mel? You proved my point better than I was able to myself. This should show you just how far off the rails the Wildcats have gone."

Mel slowly sinks to the ground and hugs her knees.

"I'll take some of the blame for us being in this situation. I let you girls get too complacent, pumped up your egos too much. Potential isn't the same as destiny. We're not hungry enough." She hears him switch his phone from one side of his face to the other. "You're the perfect example of that."

"How so?"

"I should have never made you captain after you committed to Truman. After I heard about your boyfriend."

Mel's cheeks burn like they've been slapped.

"He's not my boyfriend."

She's telling the truth. She's never once lied to Coach.

And she wants so badly to bite back. Inform Coach that, on the first day of tryouts, one of the JV players swore on her mother's grave that over July 4 weekend Coach drove past her with Miss Candurra riding shotgun. The news didn't do much for Mel's appetite, but it served as a lip-smacking feast for her teammates, who knew only famine when it came to insights into Coach's personal life. The girls planned to verify this possible new relationship via a crowdsourced scrutiny of body language once school starts up, but Mel could know right now if she wanted.

She bites her tongue instead.

"I'm only saying I don't blame you for having one foot out the door. But if you can't step up the way I need you to as captain of this team, and be willing to do the tough stuff, then I have to take over. You didn't really leave me with a choice. My reputation is on the line."

"So what now?"

"I know I told you girls to be at the field by eleven o'clock tomorrow but I'm changing that to nine. We'll have a team meeting in my classroom. Between then and now, I want you all to think long and hard how badly you want to be a Wildcat. Based on what you come up with, I'll know if I still want to be your coach."

"Okay," Mel whispers. But the line is already dead.

Mel never knew when Coach would go cold. He did it like an ice bath, plunging her into it, a shock to her system, no time to brace herself. Though it stung, there was always an underlying reason. Some injured part of her that he was trying to heal.

Apparently, this part of her never has.

He must know how badly what he's done has hurt her. But the one bright spot—because with Coach there's always a bright spot—is that the door isn't completely closed. He's left it open for her. There's still a chance. And if there's one thing Mel has learned, you don't quit when there's still time left on the clock, especially not if you're losing. You play hard until the final whistle. Until it's truly game over.

SATURDAY, AUGUST 27
12:57 A.M.
KEARSON

Kearson watches the fiery tip of her sparkler travel the length of the rod, hissing and spitting shards of light. They fall, bright but brief, burning out just before they hit the turf. A perfect allegory for her time playing varsity last season.

To think that it was only last summer when Kearson went to Camp Kissawa for the first time, between eighth grade and her freshman year. She and two of her girlfriends quietly decided to sign up together, though they kept it a secret from their other classmates. The girls were hoping for a leg up during the freshman skills camp that would happen later, in August. They wanted to shine. Make JV at the very least, or perhaps even get sent straight up to varsity. Marissa told everyone she was going to the beach. Quinn pretended it was her grandma's eightieth birthday. And Kearson said she had to go see her father.

Unlike the weeklong camp Kissawa ran for players who were already in high school, the one for rising freshmen was only a long weekend. Still, it would be the longest Kearson was away from home for the last few years, basically since Kearson's father moved to London for work and essentially gave up sharing custody. Both Kearson and her mother pretended the time away was no big deal, but then they hugged too long on the front steps and their throats began to close up with emotion, while Marissa and Quinn snickered from the back seat of Marissa's family minivan.

Camp Kissawa was four hours from West Essex, just over the state line, deep in the woods, named for the lake it abutted. Field hockey players from all over the world came to Kissawa for instruction. It had a reputation.

It was everything right away. Brittle pine needles blanketed the ground, making bare feet impossible. The food in the mess hall was mediocre but they licked their plates clean because they were burning through so many calories. Copious amounts of tick repellant were needed. On some nights, more stars than space filled the sky. There were four gorgeously kept fields equipped with nighttime lights and electronic scoreboards. A weight room made for girls, where someone from a long-ago summer had cheekily hung beefcake photos of young male movie stars who were now playing the fathers of a new generation of young male movie stars. Positive affirmations were scribbled on every mirror. Bunks were rustic wooden rectangles with screened doors on either end and eight bunk-bed cots. No place to charge your phones, but it didn't much matter. Every night the three girls pledged to stay up until sunrise with each other but they were always asleep, drooling on their pillows, before ten thirty.

Camp was the best part of Kearson's summer that year. And as the girls had hoped, Kearson, Marissa, and Quinn made the JV team as freshmen. Grace also got picked for JV, which really annoyed Marissa. She didn't like the sounds Grace made when she'd dive to grab a pass. Also Marissa nearly threw up when some of Grace's sweat flicked onto her as Grace stole the ball off Marissa's stick.

Kearson, Marissa, and Quinn had a great JV season together. They befriended a bunch of older teammates—sophomores and a few juniors who hadn't made the cut for varsity. Kearson and Quinn and Grace were all JV starters. Marissa played plenty too, though she was always leaving the game early, getting injured, saying someone tripped her, complaining about the referee.

Anyway, the three of them were excited to return to Kissawa as high schoolers for a full week.

But when it came time to sign up, Kearson's mother made it clear to her daughter that she didn't think Kearson should go. This incensed Kearson. After all, her mother had already forbid Kearson from playing spring club. She wanted Kearson to take some time off from field hockey and basically forced her to try out for the spring musical with Marissa instead.

Kearson relented then, because maybe she did need a break? But she refused to skip Kissawa. Kearson told her mother that if she didn't want to pay for camp, then Kearson would just ask her father for the money. When they'd had this fight, Kearson was calling home from London. She had arranged her own plans to visit her father as soon as school let out. The first time in years.

That did it. Her mother wrote a check.

Marissa and Quinn were riding up with other teammates, and there was unfortunately no room for Kearson in the car. She felt weird reaching out to Grace, since they weren't actually friends. Kearson's mother offered to drive her up but Kearson refused. Instead, she took a commuter bus into the city, and then picked up a Greyhound bus out to the camp. The stops added an extra three hours, nearly doubling the trip, but principle was principle.

By the time Kearson arrived, the skies twinkled with country stars, the check-in tables were folded up and put away, the air smelled faintly of a summer cookout that was clearly over. She carried her things up to the main office, but it was empty and locked.

Kearson followed the smell of burning logs. More than a hundred girls sat around the campfire. It was too dark to pick her teammates out, so she simply stood by herself and pulled her arms inside her T-shirt. She forgot how cool it was up here in the woods. And she was too far from the fire to be warmed by its heat.

When she entered their bunk later, all her other JV teammates seemed surprised to see her, even though Kearson had texted Marissa and Quinn the second she'd signed up. And they weren't exactly welcoming to her either. They smiled and waved, but Kearson wasn't greeted like a teammate. More like some interloper who got placed here because she signed up too late to bunk with her team.

Someone else was missing.

"Is Phoebe here?"

"No. She still hasn't been cleared to play."

"Torn ACLs take like nine months. Plus she had that infection."

"I bet it's killing her. Especially because she would have been fine if she hadn't played in the championship game."

"That was her choice," Quinn said quietly. She avoided looking at Kearson, but Kearson knew this was said for her benefit.

Kearson felt a squeeze in the back of her throat.

"Yeah, some choice," Marissa snarked. "It was either come back and maybe win or not and for sure lose. Hopefully it's not a career ender for her. Plenty of athletes are one-and-done."

"Not Phoebe," Kearson said. "She'll be back."

There was a quiet, the girls reaching for phones, for whatever shield was closest.

Kearson worked her butt off at Kissawa that week. Worked as hard as Phoebe would have, if she could have been there. To give even a drop less effort than that felt unconscionable.

And so Kearson keeps on singing the words of the Wildcat fight song, even after her sparkler goes out. It takes a second for Kearson's eyes to adjust to the dark. When they do, she sees Mel walking back onto the field.

The girls go quiet. This time Phoebe doesn't tell them to start singing again.

Ali walks across center field, straight over the Wildcat decal. "Is everything okay? Where are our jerseys?"

Though she's never gone through this ritual before, it's clear that an unexpected wrench has been thrown into Mel's plans. Inside Kearson, something catches, a prickly little burr snagging into a soft part of her.

Coach.

Mel doesn't appear rattled. If anything, she looks determined, closing the distance between her and them with a wide stride, the Wildcat duffel bag slung over her shoulder. Mel sits down cross-legged in the center of the Wildcat circle and rests a hand on each of her knees. The ring of players sits down too, inching closer to her.

"There's been a slight change of plans," she tells them, her voice steady. "We won't be getting our varsity jerseys tonight."

She unzips the duffel bag and calmly lifts up two handfuls of limp practice pinnies.

Grace glances over at Kearson with an aching look, her eyes so wide and wet that they seem twice their normal size.

"Maybe Coach gave Mel the wrong bag," Kearson whispers to her. "An honest mistake?" She's aware of how hollow her voice sounds when volunteering this excuse for him, an echo reverberating in her brain, like déjà vu.

"It's not a mistake," Mel says. "And if you think about the things Coach said tonight, it's also not a surprise. He doesn't think we're ready. And he's giving us until nine o'clock tomorrow morning to prove to him that we are."

"How are we supposed to do that?" Phoebe asks.

Luci nervously raises her hand, but Mel rolls onto her knees, a bolt of inspiration. "Ooh. What about this? We show up at school before Coach, way earlier than our meeting. That way, we're in the parking lot waiting for him when he pulls in."

"But what if he beats us there?"

"We could sleep in the parking lot, I guess. To be sure."

Kearson glances around at the tepid faces. There's something anticlimactic about Mel's plan. Even Mel seems to realize it now that she's said it out loud.

Phoebe crawls across the circle over to Mel. "It's not a bad idea, Mel. Just maybe not the best idea."

Luci raises her hand again. Though she still looks nervous, this time, she doesn't wait to be called on. "I know I'm new here and I don't exactly understand how any of this works."

"It's fine," Phoebe says. "You're one of us, Luci."

"Well, Coach was telling me tonight about his college days at Truman. I guess his field hockey team used to pull off these crazy stunts? Maybe we could do something like that."

Ali says, "What kind of crazy stunts?"

"Umm. Let me see if I can remember . . ." Luci seems to grasp for words that aren't there, don't come.

Mel lets her off the hook. "Once his entire team ran around Truman's campus wearing only their jockstraps."

The girls bust up laughing. Even Mel.

Mel says, "And another time, I guess the the guys maxed out their credit cards and bought hundreds of these plastic owl statues and filled another college's team bus up to the ceiling with them."

More laughter.

Phoebe rubs her palms together. "Now, see . . . that sounds fun. Way more fun than just showing up early tomorrow to beg Coach for our jerseys." Phoebe adds gently, "No offense, Mel."

Mel lets go a long, low sigh. "You're both right. My idea was actually the *opposite* of what a Wildcat would do." Mel sits back down on her butt and pulls her knees into her chest.

One of the hardest parts of last season was not simply having to see Mel doubt herself, but knowing that Kearson herself helped cause it.

Kearson sees now a chance to assist Mel, rather than hinder her.

"That's it, Mel! Our school fight song is all about what the Wildcats are. I know every other sport at West Essex sings it too, but we could bring it to life in a way that's just about our team. Just for Coach."

The girls' lips move, reciting the first stanza themselves.

We are the Wildcats, the navy blue and white,
We are the Wildcats, always ready for a fight!

Kearson watches as her idea catches like the sparklers they lit earlier. Lighting up one girl after another.

Mel tries again, this time saying, "We could go over to Oak Knolls and take selfies at their field. Like that eff-you video they posted for us today."

"Coach would probably like that swagger," Phoebe says. "We could TP their houses. Put shaving cream on their bus...."

Grace raises her hand. "I have an idea. But it might be a little crazy."

"Says the girl with the blue hair," Ali says sweetly.

"Hey. Crazy isn't bad," Phoebe says. "I think we need a little crazy right now."

Grace smiles. "Okay. Well. What if we kidnapped the Oak Knolls bulldog?"

Mel winces. "You mean steal their *actual dog*? No. We can't do that. Absolutely not."

Phoebe jumps to her feet. "Wait. Oh my God, wait. We would be *legends*."

Mel is still shaking her head. "We could get in serious trouble."

"Not like *kidnap* in a bad way. More like just borrow him for a while. Long enough to take a few pictures," Phoebe says, growing more and more animated by the second. "How badass would that make us look? I mean, Coach would probably flip his shit."

Mel stands up. "Phoebe! Stop!"

But Phoebe is crawling on her knees across the circle over to Grace. "How would we do it?"

Grace says, "Didn't one of the girls say that the Oak Knolls coach keeps the bulldog outside?"

Mel throws her hands up and, to no one in particular, laments, "I can't believe we're actually talking about this!"

Mel's timing is off, Kearson realizes, like it had been when they last played together. And like then, a second's hesitation makes all the difference. Because the other girls are no longer just talking about this. They are sprinting toward their cars. They are already gone.

SATURDAY, AUGUST 27
1:09 A.M.

COACH: Update?

COACH: Update?

LUCI: Hi! Sorry!

LUCI: Everything went great!

LUCI: I said exactly what you wanted and the girls were super into it!!!

COACH: 💯

COACH: Did Mel talk shit about me?

COACH: She was so pissed when she realized I never gave her the jerseys. 😂

LUCI: Mel definitely seemed surprised. But not mad at all.

LUCI: She was ready to get to work and make things right by you. 💪 😊

COACH: What about the other girls? Have you overheard anything negative?

LUCI: Nope! Nothing at all.

COACH: Great. I'm pleasantly surprised.

COACH: Like I said, we've had some trouble on that front.

COACH: So what's the plan? What are you girls going to do to impress me?

COACH: 😛

LUCI: 🤐

LUCI: It has something to do with the Wildcats fight song.

LUCI: We're going to act out the verses as a team.

COACH: 🙄

COACH: Things are worse than I thought.

LUCI: 😂

LUCI: I think it's going to turn out cool! Everyone seems really excited anyway. A bunch of girls are pitching ideas for Wildcat-y things we can do.

COACH: Like who?

LUCI: Grace

COACH: 😬

COACH: If you girls show up at the field tomorrow looking like a bunch of blue-haired weirdos, I'll quit on the spot.

LUCI: My mom would KILL me if I dyed my hair blue.

COACH: I would too.

COACH: 😂

LUCI: I'd better go. We're at a gas station. I said I had to pee so I could text you!

COACH: 😬

COACH: 😂

COACH: Keep up the good work, Luci.

SATURDAY, AUGUST 27
1:11 A.M.
ALI

They descended upon the desolate gas station like a tornado touching down. Their cars barely screeched to a stop in front of the fuel pumps before doors were flung open and girls spilled out. While the drivers gassed up, the rest either sprinted inside to pee or danced to the weird oldies song piped in from speakers somewhere over their heads, half of them in pj's, half in normal clothes, an electrified mix of headlights and fluorescent making them appear to glow.

Ali is just holstering the gas nozzle when Mel shouts that she's found it, the home address for the head coach of Oak Knolls. None of the girls have their phones with them, they'll all follow Mel. The girls quickly climb back inside their rides, click their seat belts. Engines start.

As she drives away, Ali sees the night cashier in her side mirror. He's behind the store window, rubbing his bald head and laughing.

Oak Knolls is maybe fifteen minutes from West Essex, straight north on the highway, two exits past the mall. Ali doesn't love driving on the highway. Merging traffic scares the crap out of her. But at this time of night, the roads are theirs. Over and over, the six cars change lanes and shift positions, pulling alongside each other to beep and scream and wave, then dropping back and crossing three lanes without bothering to signal. Each ride is so overstuffed with girls that their long hair spills out of the open windows.

Ali plays her music louder than it's ever been. Her brother James got her hooked on hip-hop and the bass ripples through her, mini sonic booms. Between that and the rush of the wind at sixty-five miles per hour, Ali feels like she's in a deprivation tank. She couldn't hold on to a thought if she wanted to. Which is great because she doesn't.

Ali takes the long curve of the Oak Knolls exit and feels the pull of inertia, her body straining against her seat belt. The brightness of the highway dims to that of a country road. Stars appear.

Her music is turned way down. Ali glances over at Grace. Quite a bold move for a newbie riding shotgun in an older player's car. "You got something against hip-hop?" she asks, and immediately moves to turn the volume back up.

Grace laughs. "No! I just don't want us to wake the town up."

"Right. Okay."

About a quarter mile farther, they reach Oak Knolls. Ali, the last car in line, sees the traffic light go yellow, and the car ahead of her guns it through. Ali gets stuck at the red. Not a big deal, she can still see them. It's more annoying. Another pause.

She lets out a huff, twists her neck until it cracks, turns her stereo off because the volume is too low to really hear the song anyway. On her left, she sees a grassy postage stamp rimmed with white curb, there to set off a wooden sign proclaiming *Welcome to*

Oak Knolls. Next to it, a smaller sign is pushed into the grass on thin metal stakes, like the kind people put in their front yards at election time. It says *Varsity Girls Field Hockey State Champions.*

After rolling her eyes, Ali scans the intersection, left to right and then left again. Not a single car to be seen. Only the taillights of the last car in the Wildcats' caravan pulling farther and farther away.

Ali tells herself to run the red. Just run it. There's no way she's getting a ticket. And even if she did, even if there were one of those red-light cameras sneakily mounted somewhere, what would a ticket even cost? Like fifty bucks? Her father would probably just pay it, thinking he'd done it. She looks left and right and left again. She looks at that stupid sign.

Kearson leans forward from the back seat. "It's green," she says helpfully.

"Thanks," Ali says.

As Ali continues forward, her passengers—Kearson and two juniors in the back seat, and Grace in the front—chat about how cute the downtown area of Oak Knolls is, pointing things out to one another. A cupcake café with pink awnings. A bookstore called Never Not Reading. A tiny theater with a glowing marquee that looks like it's been around since movies were invented.

"You couldn't pay me to live here," Ali says, announcing her way into the conversation. "Oak Knolls is a complete dump."

The girls laugh and Ali laughs too, even though she used to love going to see movies at that theater. Unlike the multiplex in West Essex, they put real butter on their popcorn, not butter-flavored oil.

If the cupcake café was open when the movie let out, she'd stop in. Not for cupcakes—the best ones really did come from

Park & Orchard in West Essex—but the incredible frozen hot chocolate they made. And it was at the bookstore where she'd first seen a shelf talker for the dystopian series she'd gobbled up two summers ago.

But Ali doesn't come to Oak Knolls anymore. She doesn't want to risk accidentally running into Darlene Maguire. Ali knows she'll face her eventually, but she wants it to happen on the field, when she'll know it's coming. The worst thing would be to get ambushed. What if Darlene made some racist gesture again, only in front of Ali's family? What if baby John-John was with her?

"Ali, you missed the turn," Grace says, but her eyes aren't on the road. She's focused on Ali's hands, gripping the steering wheel, the tendons flexed and taut. "You okay?"

"I'm fine," Ali says, more sharply than she intends to. She tries to soften it with a smile, but it comes to her face like a stick dragged through wet cement.

She's always had a fire inside her. A heat Ali could stoke to help her dig deeper, run faster, work harder. Bright but controlled, like coal shoveled into an engine bolted to the base of her spine. But since the championship loss, it's turned into a different kind of flame. One that's more unpredictable and dangerous, like the spark off a frayed wire. She never knows where or when it might zap her.

When Grace brought up Darlene Maguire earlier, Ali totally stumbled. Same thing when Coach delicately broached the subject at the Psych-Up. Ali barely managed to keep her cool when watching the video Darlene had posted; inside she was screaming. Driving her teammates through Oak Knolls, Ali's about to have a panic attack.

Ali suspected that Coach had been talking about her in his speech tonight. He watched that very first crack appear. Now she's barely holding it together. And tomorrow, when Darlene comes at her again, she's going to fall apart.

The road comes back into focus. Ali pulls a U-turn in the center of the street, doubles back, and makes the turn.

"I bet that's the house," Kearson says.

Ali drives past a generic little box with gray vinyl siding and a waist-high white picket fence. There's a field hockey sticker on the bumper of the car parked in the driveway. Two red field hockey sticks, turned upside-down, their hooks making a heart shape.

The other five cars are parked around the corner and halfway down the next street, next to a small playground. The girls are already outside and conferring with one another. She barely puts her Jeep in park before the girls riding with her bail out the doors and hurry over. Ali moves more slowly, a pace befitting the drag on her team she believes herself to be.

She is the last to reach the team huddle. Same as on the field, when during a time out, the girls circle up and feverishly plan their next attack. Sometimes her teammates will have already reached in, their stack of hands bouncing like a trampoline, and screamed, *Let's go Wildcats!*, and their charge back onto the field spins Ali like a top.

Similarly, Ali expects to find that a strategy to grab the bulldog has formed without her. But no. They're all hesitating.

"So . . . how should we do this?" Phoebe says.

Mel shrugs. "I mean, we want it to be a team effort, but we can't all go up to the house and take the dog. We'd get caught for sure."

For a moment, no one else says anything to the team. But plenty of girls whisper to one another.

"Do you think we could get, like, arrested for this?"

"Probably. I think it counts as theft even if we're only planning to borrow the dog for a little while."

"At the very least, we're all getting suspended if we get caught. Maybe three days, but probably five."

"Definitely five. Principal Meyer suspended Alan Wallows for five days, even though all he did was get caught using fake money in the cafeteria vending machine."

It's not that any of her teammates *want* to back down. It's that, now they're here and no longer just spitballing, it's a lot harder to step up. It's not surprising. They are all good girls, who do well in school, don't drink or do drugs, never get detention. The idea that one of them is going to volunteer to do this potentially illegal and season-ending stunt seems more and more unlikely with each passing second. Oak Knolls is their rival, sure, but only because that's the team who bested them.

Except that's not the way Ali feels. For her it couldn't be personal.

"I'll do it," Ali says.

"Wait," Mel says. "Seriously?"

It's not clear if Mel's relieved or not that Ali has stepped up. But Ali's made up her mind. She bends over, reties her sneakers with double knots, and tucks away the slack so there's no risk of tripping.

The thing is, Ali has always, always felt a part of this team. These girls, some of whom she has known for years, they've traveled together, played together, hung out together. She knows their parents, knows who they've made out with, knows how their sweat smells, knows who bites their nails, who snores, who is in remedial classes, who takes medication.

But Darlene Maguire robbed her of that feeling.

"Yup. The rest of you can be my lookouts. Or just wait here. Whatever you're comfortable with."

"I'll go with you, Ali," Grace says.

"Grace, I can do it on my own."

"I know that," Grace says. "But you don't have to. I've got your back, remember?"

Ali rubs a hand through Grace's blue hair. "Team first, always."

The energy picks back up immediately. Girls bouncing on their toes. Clutching each other.

"Here, Hamburger loves these," Phoebe says, passing Ali a granola bar. "It's our secret. I give him one every night. My mom has him on some stupid diet. Anyway, you can use it to lure the bulldog over."

Mel warns them, "Don't do anything unless it's totally, totally safe. If it's not, we'll just come up with another idea."

The girls cluster up in a tight circle, put their hands in, and do a whispered *Let's go Wildcats!* cheer. This time, Ali's hand is smack-dab in the center, as if held by every single one of her teammates.

The girls skitter through the dark, squatting behind trees and parked cars, spreading out through the night. Footsteps dulled by the runways of grass between sidewalk and pavement. Most houses dark. Quiet of crickets. An airplane high overhead.

Grace and Ali pause behind a tree and scope out the scene from a few houses away.

All the downstairs lights are off. One upstairs room flickers, the flashing blue light of a television.

Ali shares a nod with Grace and the two creep forward,

prowling low past hedges and trash cans and parked cars, until they are each clutching slats of the white picket fence. Peering into the yard, Ali sees a little doghouse, a water dish, some chew toys. But no sign of the actual bulldog.

"Here, puppy, puppy," Ali whispers.

"I guess their coach actually does bring him in for the night," Grace says.

Ali gives a soft whistle.

Nothing.

She unwraps the granola bar and waves it around so he can smell it.

Nothing.

Ali looks over her shoulder. All the eyes glowing in the dark. What will their confidence be like tomorrow, knowing they walked right up to the edge of this moment, with all they had to prove, and then froze? Ali knows better than anyone. She's never quite recovered.

On the field, she is her team's last line of defense. If she can't deliver, the Wildcats don't have a chance. She let them down once. She will not let it happen again.

"I'm going around back."

Grace looks nervous but she still follows Ali, and together the girls sneak around the side of the house. They peer over the rear fence, but the bulldog isn't in the backyard, either. Ali does, however, spot a doggy door flap on the back door.

An idea comes to Ali hard and fast and sudden, a wave breaking on the shore, pulling away everything else in her mind. Coach talked about having a strong mental game earlier tonight. She is laser focused. She whispers to Grace, "Let me see if I can lure him outside."

Grace, for the first time, looks worried. "Ali, please. This was a dumb idea. I'm sorry I said anything!"

"Stay here and tell me if any lights come on."

Ali opens the back gate and silently tiptoes into the yard. She shakes her car keys ever so quietly as she ascends a short set of back stairs. She's got her granola bar outstretched. "Here, puppy, puppy," she whispers. "Where's the good doggy?"

A low growl comes from inside the house. Nothing threatening. More like a cat's purr.

Crouching on her knees, Ali lifts the flap to the doggy door.

Her eyes dart all over the kitchen. A butcher-block countertop. Open shelving on the walls. A white ceramic pitcher holding wooden utensils. A furry blob splayed on a braided rug in front of the kitchen sink.

The bulldog is staring right at Ali. He doesn't lift his head, just blinks his wet eyes.

"Hey, buddy." She fumbles for the granola bar. "Here, puppy, puppy."

He sniffs the air and gives a deep, throaty bark.

Ali freezes, waiting for someone to come downstairs and investigate.

But it's quiet.

She pushes her arm as far through the doggy door as she can get it.

At last, the bulldog lifts himself off the rug and lumbers over, stopping to stretch his squat hind legs, a trickle of doggy drool dripping out from the side of his underbite. Ali is careful as she reels him in, pulling her arm back an inch at a time, beckoning him closer and closer, and finally letting him lick the granola bar. She then takes hold of the bulldog's collar and leads him through the doggy door.

Once he's outside with her, Ali scoops the bulldog up in her arms. He's heavy and warm. Bristly fur. She breaks off a piece of the granola bar and lets him sloppily gobble it off her hand.

"You're such a good puppy!"

"Holy shit, holy shit!" Grace says when Ali carries him down the steps and through the back gate.

"Come on! Let's get out of here!"

She and Grace jog down the driveway and out to the center of the street, barely able to keep themselves from laughing, the bulldog licking Ali's face as she jostles him in her arms. The rest of the girls, shrieking with excitement, peel out from behind their cover. And suddenly everyone is running, a wild pack, close to one another, not letting anyone fall behind. They sprint, hair blowing, high on endorphins. Bare-faced. Some of the girls hold hands, pull one another along. They know love. This is love. Better than with any guy because this is forever.

They dive into their cars, too many girls for too few seats, chests heaving, hearts racing.

Exhilaration.

They already know they will never forget tonight. And it's only just getting started.

SATURDAY, AUGUST 27
1:41 A.M.
MEL

Mel doesn't know exactly where Ali is leading them but she happily follows her taillights as their six-car caravan makes its way across Oak Knolls. The bulldog, which the girls are calling Buddy, is sitting on Phoebe's lap in shotgun, front paws up on the open window frame, head out of the window, wind lifting his jowls. Pleased as the rest of the girls are to be on this joyride.

Mel is feeling so Wildcat. All of them are. The buzz between the girls is tangible. It's always been a joke, how their periods inevitably sync up at some point during a season. Pity which unlucky team would face them at their reddest. The same witchy magic is at play right now. A strength and confidence that comes from twenty girls in lockstep with one another.

Mel knows she will never have this again. Next year she'll be wearing different team colors. Singing different songs. She'll play hard, of course, the way Coach taught her, the only way she knows.

She'll give her all to Truman. But Mel will be a Wildcat until the day she dies.

They drive circles around the perimeter of Oak Knolls High School, then park with their headlights aimed at a huge bulldog mural painted on an exterior wall. Mel sets the camera timer and leans her phone against her windshield. The girls pose in front of the mural, their backs to the camera to obscure their faces, and give it a middle finger salute. The only one looking at the camera is Buddy, who sits obediently at their feet, a toothy, pink-tongue doggy smile.

The first attempt comes out perfect. One and done.

Mel tries a couple of filters, looking for the best one to brighten up the dark. Any other year? The varsity jersey ceremony would be over, and girls would be in bed. But Mel feels wide-awake. Only with this feeling, new, alert, does she see how she let herself sleepwalk for so long, how there can be so much range within a beating heart. One pace keeps you alive, one pace when you're living.

This is Coach. This is why there's no other team like the Wildcats. His methods might be a bit unconventional, but damn it, he gets results. She might have been a little angry with him at first. She wanted so badly for him to trust that she could bring her team together. But he's proved, yet again, why he's the best, why he makes them the best. She can't wait to show him what he inspired the girls to do tonight.

Mel pastes the picture inside a text and then types the first fight song stanza below it.

We are the Wildcats, the navy blue and white,
We are the Wildcats, always ready for a fight!

As soon as she sends it, Mel imagines herself soaring with the text through the clear night sky, arriving with it in Coach's bedroom. The ding wakes him from a deep sleep. He lifts his head off the pillow, his blond hair adorably dented, shirtless, annoyed, squinting at the glow of the screen. And then, boom, there's that crooked grin he rewards her with every so often, when Mel pulls off something crazy on the field.

More than once he's told Mel that watching her play is the closest he comes to feeling the way he did when he still could. More than once he's told her how much of himself he sees in her. At long last, Mel feels like she's living up to that again.

Phoebe lifts the bulldog off the ground and into her arms. "I wish we didn't have to bring Buddy back home just yet. He's having a good time with us."

"He's like our good luck charm," Mel agrees. "Our drooling guardian angel."

"Yeah, let's keep him for a little while longer," Ali says, rubbing Buddy's ears. "I'll drop him off later."

"Speaking of later, we should figure out what we want to do for the next stanza," Mel says. A car drives by slow on the road and the girls turn and silently watch it pass. "But, um, maybe not here?"

Phoebe says, "Ooh! Let's go to Gordy's and regroup. He said we should swing by tonight if we were bored."

"We aren't bored," Mel says pointedly, ignoring the excited smiles of her teammates. "We're having the time of our lives." She's annoyed that Gordy told Phoebe he was having people over too. Was it because he knew she wouldn't come? "It's probably dying down anyway by now."

"Doubt it. It's the last party of summer, Mel." Phoebe squirms to keep Buddy's tongue from licking her face. "I just figured you'd want to go."

"I don't *not* want to go." Mel sighs. "But we need to stay focused. It won't have the same impact if we send Coach the picture for the next verse an hour later." Mel glances at her phone to make sure her first text went through. It hasn't. She's got only one bar. "Ugh. I'm getting horrible reception."

Phoebe passes Buddy to one of the new girls and leans into Mel's ear. "Did something happen between you and Gordy?"

"No."

"Okay. Good. Then it's no big deal to swing by, so long as we just make it quick? We can just run in, say hi to some people, make our plan. Then we're out."

Honestly? It isn't a big deal. Not the way Mel's feeling right now. With a certainty that Gordy was a rebound hookup Mel never wanted in the first place. In fact, it might actually be a good thing to make an appearance. She'll stay close to the pack, show Gordy her team is all she cares about now. He'll have to take the hint.

"Fine. We can stop by Gordy's for fifteen minutes." Mel tosses her keys to Phoebe. "You drive. I need to make sure this text to Coach goes through."

Mel gets enough signal as they merge back on the highway. While waiting for Coach's response, she scrolls through some of their past conversations.

COACH: I shouldn't tell you this but a scout from Truman will be at today's game.

COACH: TO SEE YOU SPECIFICALLY!

This is from early November of last year. Mel bites down on her smile. It's a favorite.

She immediately raised her hand and asked Ms. Mondadori for the bathroom pass, then hurried straight to Coach's classroom.

He must have been expecting her, because as soon as Mel stood on her tiptoes and squared her head in the chicken-wire glass window of his classroom door, Coach excused himself from his students and met her out in the hallway.

Coach had been talking up Truman to Mel since her freshman season. At first it was the kind of pitch you'd find in any college catalog. Truman was a storied university, not quite Ivy League, but still with an excellent reputation for humanities. Their field hockey team produced nationally ranked players, many of whom, like Coach, went directly into the Olympic pipeline. But as they grew closer, Coach shared more personal stories with her about his time there. What his different dorm rooms were like, interesting classes he took, crazy stuff he and his teammates used to do. He loved telling her about his college days as much as Mel loved hearing about them. It really brought the school to life for her. By her junior year, Truman was Mel's top pick.

Which is why she was practically hyperventilating. "I almost wish you hadn't told me. I don't know how I'm going to relax."

It was Coach's policy never to share scouting information with the girls. Mel suspected there'd been scouts at previous games that season, but Coach kept it close to his vest. It made her heart swell that he was breaking his own rules for her. She was a special exception.

"I've trained you for this, Mel." He put his hand on her shoulder. "Trust me. You're ready."

He was calming. He could be that sometimes. Another teacher walked past them. Coach pulled his hand back. They both got quiet, shared a goofy smile, and didn't speak again until she passed.

"Just do me a favor and don't mention this to Phoebe. I want to give you both the best chance at playing together at Truman next year. If Phoebe's rattled, neither of you will get to shine."

Mel played brilliantly. Three goals, all assisted by Phoebe, which was great news for her, too. It was so hard not to tell Phoebe how well they both performed for the Truman scout. Mel managed to keep her lips sealed. Her only slip—if you could even call it that—happened during the final goal they scored together.

It was such a thing of beauty, the only two players in sharp focus, everyone else background blur, passing and sprinting, passing and sprinting, and then Mel firing a shot so hard, the crack of wood like a thunderclap, that she wondered if she'd broken her stick in half. She picked up the ball from the back of their opponent's net and ran screaming to midfield. Phoebe looked amused, and maybe slightly concerned for Mel's sanity. Mel leapt into Phoebe's arms, knocked them both to the ground, and then she laid a big fat kiss right on the top of Phoebe's sweaty head and said, "I freaking love you, Phoebe Holt."

Hours later, Phoebe was sound asleep, cuddled on her favorite side of the bed, and Mel was wide awake, still completely hopped up on adrenaline, when Coach texted her. She crept out of Phoebe's bedroom into the Holts' family room, Hamburger following close behind her in case Mel made a detour to the kitchen.

COACH: YOU KILLED IT MEL!

COACH: I told Truman you were something special and you proved I know what I'm talking about!

COACH: I was so fucking proud of you, I almost hugged you.

MEL: 😍

MEL: Phoebe did great, too! Don't you think?

MEL: Hopefully the scout saw how well we play together and wants us both.

COACH: I actually got some news from the Truman scout.

COACH: But not about either of you two.

COACH: 😬

MEL: 🔥

COACH: 😩

COACH: He said a head coaching position is opening up at Trident.

MEL: But aren't you waiting for Truman's coach to retire?

COACH: Yeah.

COACH: For the last four years.

COACH: 😒

Coach had long ago confessed to Mel that his dream job would be to return to Truman and become head coach of the team he once played for. He tried to stay regularly in touch with his former coach, who was still in charge over there. The guy was so old, he didn't text or email. Coach sent him actual letters, which Mel found pretty adorable.

COACH: Trident is nothing special but I could make a big impact there. Put them on the map then leapfrog someplace else in a couple of years.

COACH: I can't stay at West Essex forever.

COACH: It's been too long already.

COACH: Colleges are impressed by what I've made happen here, obviously, but at the end of the day, I'm still coaching high school girls. I'm only getting interviews because people remember me from when I used to play.

Mel also secretly harbored the idea that she and Coach might overlap at Truman at some point in the future. But, really, she just wanted him to be happy.

MEL: Where is Trident?

COACH: About an hour away from Truman.

COACH: My friends and I used to make the drive there every couple of weeks to hit up the bars.

COACH: It's close enough that I can come and see you play.

COACH: You'll have to call me by my real name.

Mel's eyes went wide. She held her phone up to Hamburger and whispered, "Am I dreaming or is he flirting with me?" Hamburger licked her face.

MEL: Well, of course.

MEL: Because you wouldn't be my coach anymore.

COACH: Exactly. My. Point.

COACH: I'd be coming there to see you as a . . .

COACH: 🤭

MEL: 🤭

COACH: 🤷

MEL: 🤷

COACH: 😂

MEL: 😂

Mel startles, feeling a tap on her shoulder. "Hey! Did Coach write back?" Phoebe asks.

Mel looks up from her phone, disoriented. Though it felt like she'd been in the car only a minute or two, Phoebe was already parked a few houses down from Gordy's. And her teammates were all spilling out of their cars and hurrying inside.

"No. Not yet."

"Then what are you smiling at?"

In the time it takes for Mel to unbuckle her seat belt and climb out, Phoebe and Buddy have made it all the way up Gordy's front lawn.

"Why are you in such a rush?" Mel calls out after her.

"You're the one who said we only have fifteen minutes!" Phoebe teases.

Buddy gives a throaty bark.

With a sigh, Mel closes the passenger door, tucks her phone into the pocket of her cutoffs, and rakes her fingers through her ponytail.

Gordy's Volkswagen is parked on the driveway—along with a bunch of mountain bikes and two kayaks—likely dragged out to make space in the garage. Two garage doors are lifted up, and the inside is open and bright and inviting, with clip-on construction lights running on bright orange electric cords.

It seems like a lot of people were here at some point, judging by the sea of empty beer cans and stacks of discarded Solo cups, but it's a smaller group now. A game of beer pong is in progress, but the two players—juniors, Mel thinks—are the only ones focused on it. The other kids are staring vacantly at their phones. A girl and a guy are asleep on an air mattress.

Mel approaches the Ping-Pong table. After sinking a ball, one of the players tells her, "Gordy's inside."

Great. So does everyone in West Essex know she and Gordy were hooking up this summer?

"Is that whose house this is?" she answers casually.

Mel makes her way inside, trying to find her teammates. She's never had to untangle herself from a relationship. But Gordy came into her life at exactly the right time, when Mel was bored and lonely. Or maybe the wrong time for those very same reasons.

Whatever.

Depending on how the calendar weeks fell and if there were snow days that had to be made up, the girls could count on having roughly three weeks where there was zero field hockey between the last day of high school and the beginning of summer leagues.

Most of them went on family vacations during this gap.

Coach still expected them to keep up on their fitness. It wasn't so much about losing your edge, but gaining one over the girls who wouldn't work as hard as you.

Mel hated to exercise during break. She preferred to go full-blown couch potato, sleeping in, bingeing bad TV, eating garbage, lying on a pool float. Some days she wouldn't even shower, wouldn't ever change out of her pj's. Phoebe could usually guilt Mel into it, and Phoebe was good about finding things they could do that didn't necessarily feel like exercise—water aerobic exercises for the pool, an hour at the trampoline park—but it still wasn't something she enjoyed. It was more about having an answer in case Coach happened to text her wanting to know what she got up to that day.

But Phoebe's knee still had her completely out of commission and Coach had barely spoken to her since her surgery. Not only that, but Coach had neglected to email any of the girls with important dates the way he normally would before school let out, which Mel took as another big sign he didn't plan to return to West Essex next season. She wasn't captain; her team might not have a coach. Not to mention, there'd been nothing but radio silence from Truman about Mel potentially playing there. So the prospect of working out alone was extra, extra miserable.

During the first week of break, Mel and her parents headed off to Montreal, and the closest she came to exercise was a daily walk to get poutine. For the second week, she dragged her parents' treadmill in front of the big-screen television and logged about five miles day in the basement. But even with a movie going it was torture. Once, Mel zoned out and lost her balance. She got a terrible rash from the belt, but if she hadn't been wearing the emergency clip, she definitely would have broken her leg.

Running around West Essex felt too showy, so Mel drove thirty minutes to the big county park, where they had running paths and hiking trails and a river that kayakers loved.

She saw Gordy in the parking lot.

Though they were in the same grade at West Essex, Mel didn't know him. He didn't play any sports, though she remembered him being into skateboarding when they were at the lower school. Sometime during high school, Gordy had shifted into more of an outdoorsy guy. There were echoes of his former interest—like his black Clark Kent glasses, his slip-on checkerboard Vans—but the rest of him looked ripped from the pages of a Patagonia catalog. Fleeces, puffer vests, beanies, a carabiner holding his keys to his belt loop. His Volkswagen GTI also had the earmarks of someone athletic: bike rack mounted to the roof, mud splatters, a bumper sticker from the closest ski mountain.

That day, Gordy had his mountain bike flipped upside down, handlebars and seat on the ground, wheels spinning in the air. He wore a pair of jeans cut into shorts, a pair of black socks pulled up around his calves, and a Marmot T-shirt.

Mel wasn't going to disturb him. He seemed hard at work on something with his gears. But he said hello to her and so they chatted for a while. When he apologized for holding her up from her run, Mel admitted she actually hated running. Since Gordy couldn't get his bike working, he offered to show her the Frick trail, one of his favorites.

Along that hike, she remembered how comfortable he looked in the cold when everyone else was shivering at the January bonfire.

Sitting behind him at a drunk driving assembly before Junior Formal. How tanned the back of his neck was.

Had Gordy gone to Junior Formal?

With someone?

Over the rest of June and practically all of July, Mel and Gordy went on hikes nearly every day. If Mel had a summer league game, she'd meet with him afterward and do something small, an easy loop. Other days, when she didn't have a game, they'd tackle more ambitious trails. Steeper climbs with bigger rewards. She liked how easy Gordy was to plan things with. Never a firm schedule, always up for whatever, happy to detour, never embarrassed if he took a wrong turn, if he lost his footing. They'd conquered every trail in county park several times over, and so sometimes they'd drive an hour or two for a new route. She liked those long trips. They never ran out of things to talk about. They actually had to stop themselves from talking to make out.

Mel had Gordy pegged as a loner, maybe because of his skateboarding days, but Gordy always said hello to the people they passed on their hikes, stopped and pet their dogs. He had lots of friends in different towns besides West Essex. Kids he rode mountain bikes with, kids he snowboarded with, kids he kayaked with. His life seemed so much bigger than Mel's, so many facets.

During the week Gordy went with his family to visit his half sister in Maine, Mel hiked alone. Most days she did the Frick trail and spent hours at the vista, looking out across the valley. She'd think about what senior year might be like if Coach didn't come back to West Essex. What it would feel like to walk down the hallway on the first day of school holding Gordy's hand. Going on hikes with Gordy in the fall, when the leaves would be turning. If Truman didn't come through, where she might want to go to college. These daydreams, though not unpleasant, still felt to Mel like an upside-down world, an alternate universe.

Something abstract to consider, like what her life might be like if she were born a boy.

The email finally came in late June. An invitation from Truman to attend a weekend of practices at the university.

Mel's first thought was to tell Coach.

It had been weeks since she felt a rush for him and the quick surge of adrenaline made her a teensy bit nauseous. Instead of texting, she decided to forward the email to Coach's West Essex address, even though it was summer and she doubted he was checking it. She included a quick note. *Thank you for everything you've done to get me to this point. I'll let you know how it goes.*

Truman was still her number one choice. She might have a shot at getting in on academics alone, but it was slim. Her GPA was solid, her SATs respectable. But she'd had only two AP classes this term. And her extracurriculars outside of field hockey were weak. Playing at her level didn't leave time for much else.

Mel put the practice weekend on the family calendar in pen. It would happen in July during her Kissawa week. She wanted to tell Phoebe but it felt almost cruel. So she decided to wait, especially because it wasn't an offer or anything. But Mel was excited to tell Gordy. Even though she had plans to see him later, she called him right away. He was thrilled for her, and later, surprised her with a dinner picnic of some prepared foods he'd gotten from the fancy grocery store in town. They ate at the lookout on the Frick trail.

As Gordy set up their spread, Mel felt her phone buzz.
COACH: What's with the email? Did you forget my number?
MEL: Sorry. Didn't want to bother you.
COACH: Shut up, Mel.
COACH: 😉

COACH: Keep me posted.

It was the first kindness he'd shown her since the championship loss.

"More good news?" Gordy said, uncapping a bottle of lemonade.

Mel slipped her phone into her back pocket. "Maybe."

Both her mother and father traveled to Truman with her, all upgraded to first class on her father's airline points. He charmed the ticketing agents into letting Mel bring her stick on board, likening it to a classical musician's professional instrument. It was stored with the men's suit jackets in the little closet near the flight attendants' service kitchen.

Mel's parents had booked a hotel near the campus, and after a tour with the admissions office, they spent the rest of the day just wandering around. It was fun to see the places Coach had been telling her about over the last few years. She took a picture outside his old dorm. She ordered the chicken tenders from a food cart near the science labs, which he said were the best chicken tenders in the entire world. She even found one of his team pictures in the athletic center.

His freshman year, standing in a line, his hands clasped behind his back, chest puffed out, a confident smile. He was so handsome. And really, she couldn't find many places where he had aged. Back then, he only had one scar, his first ACL surgery.

On Saturday, Mel was a jumble of nervous energy as she made her way across campus with her gear bag to a gorgeous athletic center, all glass. About thirty other girls had also been invited. A handful she recognized from different tournaments; many she didn't. She overheard a few accents. Australian. Indian.

She took a smiling selfie with her stick and her Wildcats

Varsity T-shirt. She sent it to Gordy and Coach. Separately, of course.

GORDY: 🐾 ♥ ♣

Truman's women's team head coach is a woman named Karen Backman. She's a former assistant coach of the Women's National Team, an Olympic alternate.

Mel was instantly struck by how cool Karen was. Karen's long hair was streaked with gray but because she was a blonde, it looked fashionable. She had zero makeup on but still glowed, and she was incredibly fit. Karen had on a fitted Truman T-shirt, a pair of expensive-looking yoga leggings—purple and silver marble—and a hip-looking pair of sneakers.

Mel couldn't wait to get out on the field and impress her. While Karen was introducing herself to all the girls, Mel hopped from side to side, the way she sometimes does on the sidelines when she's waiting to get subbed back in.

Except the girls never went to the field. Instead they took a tour of the athletic facilities and went on another campus tour, though this one focused more on student athletes who attended Truman. Then they had lunch with the current players.

After lunch, the hopefuls boarded a bus—without Coach Karen—and drove away from the field and across campus to the fine arts building. There they were led into a studio full of mirrors, where an elderly man from the dance department dressed in a skin-tight black leotard and wide-legged linen pants led them in deep breathing, movement, and yoga poses like doggy-down-something-something. At one point, Mel made namaste hands at some of the other girls as a joke, but they barely smiled at her.

Back at the hotel, she was supposed to be getting ready for dinner with her parents, but instead Mel was in bed with the covers pulled up over her head. She thought about texting Gordy about what a letdown the day was, but would he even get it? Unfortunately, Coach hadn't responded to any of her other texts about Truman. But Mel didn't let that stop her.

MEL: First day kinda sucked.

She waited.

MEL: Haven't taken my stick out of my bag once.

MEL: You'd hate this coach.

MEL: She made all the girls do yoga.

MEL: Everyone hated it.

He'd like hearing that, Mel thought. Coach loved comparing himself to other coaches. The ones they faced in high school who'd never even played on the collegiate level.

MEL: I know you had an amazing coach at Truman but this lady is a weirdo.

MEL: It's got me thinking Truman might not be the best fit.

He was probably doing something. Maybe at a movie. But they'd been out of touch for so many months, she was hungry for that connection.

His came back rapid-fire.

COACH: Are you kidding me with this shit?

COACH: First of all, I'm in fucking Barcelona right now.

COACH: It's five in the morning.

COACH: There's some kind of loud as fuck festival thing happening on the street outside my hotel window.

COACH: We have a tournament game in a few hours.

MEL: Oh my god, I am so sorry.

COACH: I called in A LOT of favors to get you this opportunity.

COACH: I don't care if the coach asks you to ballet dance for her.

COACH: Don't fucking embarrass me.

Mel's head was spinning. Had she earned her Truman invite? Or had Coach gotten it for her?

MEL: No... of course I wouldn't. I'm just saying...

COACH: DON'T TEXT ME AGAIN.

What was she saying? She spent the entire rest of the night trying to figure it out.

The following morning, Coach Karen pulled Mel aside as she was about to take the field.

"Hey, Mel, hang back, will you?"

"Sure."

There was an awkward pause. "Damon mentioned an incident in the yoga studio yesterday. He didn't feel you were taking it seriously."

Mel felt her cheeks heat up. "I didn't mean any disrespect. I've never done yoga before."

"I take a holistic approach to training. Breathing, flexibility, balance, and concentration are the foundations of yoga but they apply to field hockey, too."

"I guess I'm just eager to show you what I can do on the field."

"I've seen your video. I've read up on your stats, talked to my scout. He had a lot of good things to say about you. I understand that your coach used to play for Truman. He's definitely kept me abreast of all your accomplishments."

"Yes."

"The thing is, every single one of the girls here with you is a talented player. A big part of this experience is to assess our chemistry. Make sure you are a good fit for the culture I'm trying to create here. If yoga isn't your thing, I want to know what is. What kinds of interests do you have outside of field hockey?"

The urge to weep hit Mel hard. She pulled from every resource not to cry, not to make a fool of herself. And when she couldn't stop the tears, she hated herself for it.

"It's okay. I know this is a lot of pressure. And . . ." She paused to choose her words. "I'm aware that West Essex is an intense place to play. Take whatever time you need and come out to the field when you're ready."

"I love to hike. My boyfriend and I have hiked almost every trail in a fifty-mile radius of my hometown."

Coach Karen paused at the locker room door to give her a quick nod. Nothing more than an indication that Mel's words had reached her ears.

After several minutes of sobbing, Mel splashed some water on her face and headed out to the field, with the sense that she was starting the day at a huge disadvantage. Like she'd done something irreparable to Coach Karen's opinion of her. Which, maybe she had. Maybe they wouldn't offer her a spot.

She played hard. Harder than hard. She didn't take her foot off the gas, not once. Stealing passes and outrunning her competition, be it onto the field, from drill to drill, to the locker room. She was hoping to undo the damage she'd done, prove to Coach Karen that she was someone they needed on the team. But every time Mel managed to catch her eye, she felt as if she were doing something disappointing. The harder she worked, the more it seemed like she was failing.

It feels almost embarrassing to her now, on the other side of it, how quickly Mel had given up on herself. She was so sure that none of her dreams would come true. To have wrecked things so disastrously actually brought Mel a strange comfort in those final weeks of July. With nothing left to salvage, the only thing she could do was try to move on.

But everything worked out just as she'd hoped. First with her Truman acceptance, then Coach coming back to West Essex, then finally getting the captain's *C*.

And the buzz Mel suddenly feels from the phone in her back pocket? The cherry on top.

She hears Phoebe and Ali laughing in a nearby room. Mel pivots and heads in the opposite direction, through the kitchen and into a little laundry nook. The lights are off, and though Mel finds the switch, she ultimately chooses not to turn them on. Instead, she hops up on the washing machine and pulls out her phone.

COACH: Holy shit. I didn't think you had it in you, Mel.

COACH: I mean, I'm legit impressed.

Mel extends her legs straight out and flutter kicks the air.

MEL: YAY!

MEL: I'm so glad!

MEL: That was definitely the point!

MEL: 😂

COACH: Want to hear something funny?

COACH: It took me a couple of seconds before I even noticed the bulldog.

COACH: I was too distracted by that weird girl with the blue hair.

MEL: Grace?

Mel types, *She's really great*, and deletes it.

Then, *She's got so much heart*, and deletes it.

COACH: Does she honestly think that looks good?

Mel's stomach clenches. It had surprised Mel when Grace walked in tonight. Mel made eyes at Phoebe, who was across the room, and they both mouthed "Holy shit" at each other. But they meant it in a positive way.

COACH: Why couldn't she have done that before tryouts ended?

COACH: Then I would have known not to pick her.

COACH: 🙄

MEL: I think it's one of those Halloween sprays.

MEL: I'm sure it'll wash out.

And then, to change the subject:

MEL: Thanks for pushing us. You're a great coach. And this has turned into such a great night.

MEL: More soon!

Mel clicks off her phone and her eyes adjust to the dark. She's excited to find the girls and let them know that Coach is pleased with their efforts. But when she looks up, she sees Gordy sitting on a table directly opposite her, piles of neatly folded towels on either side of him.

"Hey, Mel."

Her hand flies to her chest. "Jeez, Gordy! You scared me!"

He reaches over and clicks on the light. "I didn't mean to sneak up on you. You were just so focused on your phone."

Mel tucks her phone into her back pocket. "We just stopped by to say hi." She hops down off the washing machine. "So ... hi."

Gordy hops down too. "Is that Phoebe's dog?"

"No. She's just taking care of him for a while."

"Well, it seems like you girls are having fun."

"We are." Mel tucks her hands into her varsity jacket and rocks back on her heels.

"Cool. I'm glad things turned around from last night. It sucked hearing you that upset."

"I wasn't really upset," Mel says. "I was just ... too in my own head. I shouldn't have called you."

She tries to walk past him but Gordy stops her. Just a gentle touch. "No. I'm glad you did. We've barely had a chance to talk for the last few weeks. I missed you. And, well, I want you to feel like you can talk to me if something's bothering you. I know things on your team can be . . . intense."

Mel presses her lips into a line, refusing to confirm or deny Gordy's assessment. He might be glad she called, but Mel deeply, deeply regrets it.

"We'd better get going."

"Okay. Good luck tomorrow. I'll be cheering for you."

Mel stops. "Sorry. Do you mean 'cheering' in a general sense?"

"I don't think I understand what you're asking."

She's annoyed that he's not getting it. Or pretending like he's not. "Are you planning to come to my scrimmage tomorrow?"

"Oh. Yeah. Why?"

"Because you'll distract me."

"I never seemed to distract you at your summer league games. In fact, wasn't the first game I went to where you scored four goals?"

"Summer league is one thing. This is our season. This is for real."

"But it's just a scrimmage, right?"

Gordy should be able to read her face right now. She isn't playing around. "I need to be completely focused tomorrow. I'm the captain. And this is the team that beat us at states last year."

Gordy clears his throat. "I get that you need to focus on field hockey. I've given you a lot of space these last few weeks. But . . . I mean, we can still talk at school on Monday, right?"

Mel swallows hard. She could just let things happen naturally. Gordy has his own life. His friends, his interests. And Mel has field hockey. But Coach already brought Gordy up to her today and she'd told him they were done. The last thing she'd want is for Coach to think she was lying. Especially about that.

Before she can say anything, Gordy grumbles, "If it's an official team rule, just let me know. Then I don't have to take the fact that you're blowing me off so personally." His voice is impatient. Annoyed. And it catches Mel off guard. "Because I'll know it's not you. It's your coach."

"Coach doesn't have rules like that." He doesn't.

"Well, how come since he came back you've barely talked to me? What else am I supposed to think? And, you know, I remember my friend Dave's older sister Becks saying Coach was a complete psycho."

"Becks Altiero? Please. She was pissed because Coach stopped playing her." Mel's phone buzzes. She hopes Gordy doesn't hear it. She tries not to react. "And of course we can still talk on Monday," she says breezily, hoping the lie buys her a way out of this conversation. "But hey, it's late, the girls and I should get going. Thanks for letting us stop by. This was fun." She steps past him.

"Was that him just now?" he calls after her. "Why is he texting you at two in the morning? I mean, you see how weird that is, right?"

Mel walks as fast as she can. Instead of grabbing her teammates, she heads out of Gordy's house. Her heart is in her throat.

COACH: So where are you girls right now?

MEL: 😬

COACH: C'mon.

COACH: Tell me.

COACH: Unless you think I'll be mad?

COACH: 🤔

MEL: I just don't want to ruin the surprise.

COACH: Is that right?

MEL: 😇

Mel leans against her car, tips her head back to the sky, and exhales quietly.

Gordy was a rebound Mel never wanted. But she did bounce back, thank goodness.

SATURDAY, AUGUST 27
2:19 A.M.

COACH: Hey.
COACH: Luci?
COACH: You there?
LUCI: Hey. I'm here. Sorry.
COACH: I saw the bulldog pic. Can't believe you girls pulled that off.
LUCI: 😊
COACH: This team owes you a huge thank-you.
COACH: Is everyone being nice to you?
LUCI: OMG yes
LUCI: These girls are the best
LUCI: 🥰
COACH: I'm glad they're keeping their jealousy in check.
LUCI: LOL no one is jealous of me!
COACH: I wouldn't be too sure.
COACH: Mel took credit for tonight.
LUCI: Well . . . she is our captain! I just said the one thing you told me to.

COACH: Where are you?

LUCI: We just stopped by a party.

COACH: 😂

LUCI: 😬

COACH: Wait seriously?

COACH: WTF

COACH: You brought the dog back though right?

LUCI: Ummm . . . not yet.

LUCI: We're regrouping here and planning the second verse of the fight song.

LUCI: I'm sorry.

LUCI: I hope you're not mad.

COACH: Whose party?

LUCI: I think his name is Gordy?

COACH: Huh.

COACH: Interesting.

COACH: That's Mel's boyfriend, you know.

LUCI: Really?

COACH: I never would have imagined she'd date someone so . . . dorky. 🤷‍♂️

LUCI: She must like him. I bet she could have her pick of guys at school.

COACH: That's going to be you this year.

LUCI: Yeah right.

COACH: Believe me. The guys at WE get obsessed with the girls on my team.

COACH: Prettiest girls in school.

LUCI: Awww

COACH: I bet even Grace gets a boyfriend this year.

COACH: 😂

SATURDAY, AUGUST 27
2:23 A.M.
LUCI

Luci clicks off her phone. She only has a little battery left. Honestly, she wouldn't mind if it died. Did Coach seriously not realize that every time he texts her, Luci must find some way to peel herself off from her group unnoticed to answer him?

She'd spent the last mile of the car ride from Oak Knolls to the party with her phone pressed into her stomach, trying to deaden his urgent buzzes so the girls sitting on either side of her in Mel's back seat wouldn't notice. The longer Luci waited to respond, the more frequently he'd text.

As soon as they pulled up to Gordy's party, Luci started looking for a potential hiding spot. She noticed a small space between the garage and the bushes of the neighboring house, closed off by two large trash cans—one for garbage, one for recycling. Luci hung back as her teammates entered the party. Then, when the coast was clear, she squeezed between the trash cans and shimmied sideways along the skinny corridor. The thorns of the bushes clawed at her bare legs, but she wanted to make sure she was far enough back that if someone came to throw something out, they wouldn't see her.

While her eyes adjust back to darkness, Luci hears a sound. Footsteps. And a laugh. She watches a boy lead a girl away from the party and into the darkness.

Luci did what Coach asked. She got the night started. Can't he text Mel directly from now on?

Hopefully she's not going to get her team in trouble for having told Coach they're at a party. That part of the conversation was a little weird, Coach telling her about Mel's boyfriend. And when he made the joke about Grace's hair. It wasn't mean. More like the way Luci's older guy cousins teased her. There's a closeness in those kinds of relationships, a sense of trust, that makes it okay.

His methods are a little strange. Or are they? The other girls have played under Coach for years. They know him way better, and they don't seem to be fazed by it. In fact, the opposite is true.

Luci remembers one moment during tryouts. She reached her stick out to stop a perfect pass lobbed to her by Kearson, but the ball was quickly stripped from her by Grace. Coach shouted, "Quit reaching and get your feet around the fucking ball, Luci!"

Luci chased it down the field, apologizing to Kearson—who pretended not to hear her—and also to every other girl in earshot. Every time Luci screwed up, she would sheepishly do this. *Sorry, sorry, sorry, sorry,* spewing out of her. And the other girls would ignore her. Or so she thought.

Coach blew his whistle with all the air in his lungs, stopping play, and grabbed Luci by the arm, halting her as if it were a leash.

Luci's heart just about stopped. A teacher had never laid hands on her before, not even accidentally. She wanted to melt into the turf. Maybe it would be better if Coach cut her right then and there, a mercy kill. In fact, she was pretty sure he was about to do just that.

Coach ripped off his sunglasses and, gleaming white teeth bared, he growled, "Luci, do you think I give a shit if you're sorry?" Reflexively, her mouth opened and closed like a fish's. She nearly said sorry again, though thank God she had the wherewithal to swallow it. Still, Coach must have seen it bubbling up inside her, because he brought a finger close to her nose for a final warning. "The only thing I give a shit about is you getting your feet around the fucking ball! So get your feet around the fucking ball!"

She nodded.

"And next time I hear you say 'sorry,' I'm sending you back to play with the freshmen. Period."

Luci answered, "Yes, Coach," trying to mimic the unemotional way the other girls on the team answered him. But she was humiliated. On shaky legs, she jogged onto the field, and the girls circled up for a face-off. No one said anything to her, but they did all look her in the eye when they each tapped their stick blades on the ground, a signal that they were ready to resume play.

This time Luci got the cue. What else the stick tap meant. *Just keep playing*. Their way of silently supporting her. Telling her it was okay. No big deal.

Luci took a deep breath and tapped her stick back. Ready.

Whistle.

Surprisingly, the urge to cry had vanished. In fact, Coach's directive seemed to free something in Luci that was already unleashed in her teammates. Yes, she still got shouted at for being in the wrong spot, for taking a shot when she should have passed, but it stopped stinging.

Luci also found it strangely liberating that none of the girls ever apologized to one another. They just worked harder. They grinned and bore it, the same way the women in Luci's family did.

And honestly, Luci had already spent years overapologizing for stuff she shouldn't have. For her mother not having the time to bake brownies for a stupid PTA bake sale. For why Luci was academically so far behind the West Essex kids in her grade, save for her Spanish class, obviously. For having a father who wrote checks but never birthday cards. In an instant, Coach's directive helped her regain focus, helped her hurdle the sand trap of inadequacy and land someplace greener, more fertile.

Ready to go.

So Luci slides her phone into her hoodie pocket, reassured that she is doing the right thing, that it makes sense. That what Coach has asked of her fits right in with all the other nontraditional coaching methods he used on the team. After making sure the coast is clear, Luci wriggles back through the trash cans and onto the driveway.

She walks across the front lawn intending to finally go into the party. But then she sees Mel in the middle of the street a few houses down, all focus and control, completely oblivious to the rest of the world around her, batting a ball back and forth with a stick so fast, it becomes a blur of color.

There had been a fender bender in the middle of a scrimmage on the fourth day of tryouts. Someone in the high school parking lot—a newly licensed driver, no doubt—backed hard into another car, and the sickening explosion of metal on metal stopped the girls in their tracks, including Luci, the ball on her stick during a halfway decent run up the midfield.

Then, two more collisions, a chain reaction that began with Mel thrusting her body between Luci and the ball and ending with Luci flat on her back. Luci was slow to get up. She rolled to her side and pushed up onto her knees, pausing there to get her bearings. It wasn't a hard hit. Luci just hadn't seen it coming.

Down the field, Mel fired off a shot into the back of the net. Only then did she realize there was no goalie. She spun around and saw the other girls jogging off the field, calling out to make sure no one had been hurt as a plume of steam rose over the parking lot. Mel's jaw fell slack, clueless as to what happened.

Luci approaches gingerly. "Hey, Mel."

Mel glances up from the ball, but only briefly. "Hey, Luci. Why aren't you inside?"

Luci shrugs. "I don't really know anyone. Well, besides the girls." She takes a seat on the curb.

Mel laughs to herself. "Honestly? Sometimes I feel the same way."

"Wait. Isn't this your boyfriend's party?"

Mel stops abruptly, the ball centered on her stick, blade angled to take aim at Luci. Luci freezes as Mel pulls back and fires off a shot. Luci winces reflexively but it's not a rocket. Instead, the ball chips off Mel's stick blade in a soft high arc, the way you might toss something to a friend across the kitchen. Luci reaches up and catches it barehanded.

Mel walks over and sits down on the curb next to Luci. "Did Phoebe tell you that?"

"No. I overheard one of the girls say it . . . though maybe I heard wrong?"

Mel slides out her ponytail holder and gently pulls her fingers through her hair. "Gordy's not my boyfriend. We hooked up, like, for a few weeks this summer. Nothing serious. And now it's totally and completely over. You know what I mean?"

"I don't have any firsthand experience in that department, but yeah. I get it."

"Just so you know, I don't have that much experience either. That's a nice thing about being on this team. Wildcats field hockey inoculates you from relationship drama. You're too busy to get caught up in it." Mel leans back, her hands behind her, and looks up at the sky. "You'll see how the other girls in school are always in the hallways with their boyfriends, breaking up and making up over and over again." She shakes her head. "I don't know why anyone bothers until college."

"You seem like you've got it all figured out."

"Is that how I seem?" Mel smirks. "I guess that's the way I looked at each of my old varsity captains." She sighs. "Anyway, don't forget, you're the one who came up with this whole idea tonight. I owe you big-time."

Luci thinks back to what Coach said. That Mel hadn't given her any credit. Maybe that was true. But it's not now. "I'm sorry if I stepped on your toes."

Mel sits up and turns her body so she's facing Luci. "Luci, I'm honestly grateful. The Wildcats have been doing this special Psych-Up night before any of us got to high school. But it's basically the same every year. Yes, traditions are important and I've always believed that there's something really special about tonight being ours. But why wouldn't we want to try something new, especially after the way last season ended? Why wouldn't we shake things up?"

"I'm glad you think it's helping."

"I know it is. Watching Ali come out holding that bulldog was . . . just awesome." She pauses. "You wouldn't be able to tell, but she's been different since we lost the championship. And it was nice to see the old Ali back." Mel grins. "I wish we could post our picture and tag Darlene Maguire, the way she did with their stupid video tonight, but, you know, we'd probably be suspended."

"Expelled." Luci laughs. "Well, it's not for them. It's for us, right?"

"And for Coach," Mel says.

Mel looks over at Luci with such tenderness, it's hard for Luci not to look away. She puts her hand on Luci's knee. "This is going to be a big year for you, Luci. And I'm here if you need anything. Okay?"

A tingling giddiness comes over her. "Coach said the same thing to me today," she confesses. "But I'm still having trouble believing it. It's a lot of pressure, and I don't want to let anyone down, especially not him, you know?" Though Luci expects Mel to understand, she stares blankly at her for a few seconds. "So, um, really. Thanks for saying that."

Another moment or two of silence.

"Hey, Luci, can you go in and round up the girls? I'd text but I've got everyone's phone. We need to get going and figure out the last two stanzas if we're going to get any sleep tonight."

"Sure. Absolutely."

Luci heads into the party house and circles through the room tapping her teammates on their shoulders. She stops briefly at a cooler and reaches around beers and lemonade Smirnoffs, hoping for a can of soda. She could use some caffeine.

Phoebe and Ali are deep in a discussion, each of them perched on the arm of a recliner, the Oak Knolls bulldog snoring asleep between them on the seat.

"What's that on his nose?" Luci says, crouching down.

Phoebe squints. "Dorito dust."

Ali wipes it off. "Hey, Luci? Settle something for us about the Wildcat fight song."

"Okay."

Ali says, "So you know the line 'We are the Wildcats'..."

And then Phoebe interjects, "Do you think the 'We' means, like, 'we'? As in 'us' collectively?"

Ali holds her arm out like a seat belt across Phoebe. "Or! Do you think it means 'WE,' as in the initials for West Essex?"

"I don't know if I'm the right person to ask. I mean, what do I know?"

Phoebe claps her hands. "That's exactly why we're asking you! Because you haven't been indoctrinated yet. So what's your feeling?"

"Yeah, what's your vibe!"

"I guess it could go either way? Anyway, Mel wants everyone outside."

"Is that where she is?" Phoebe looks over one shoulder, then the other. "I thought she was talking to Gordy."

"Wait," Ali says. "Do you mean 'talking'"—air quotes—"or actually talking?"

Phoebe puts her arm around Luci and teases, "I guess it could go either way."

The girls get up, and Phoebe pats the bulldog lightly on the rump. He snorts and lifts his head, gazes dreamily at her. She snaps her fingers, coaxing him off the recliner, and heads for the door.

"Gordy! We're taking off!"

Phoebe hurries ahead to say goodbye to a guy moving through

the room with a trash bag, cleaning up. Luci thinks he's cute. Hair buzzed short like a little kid in summer, bristly like the fur on the bulldog. Coach had called Gordy dorky. Probably because of his thick black eyeglasses. But Luci thinks they make Gordy look thoughtful. Smart.

As Luci passes, she overhears a snippet of his and Phoebe's conversation.

Phoebe bites her finger, thinking. "Look. She's just stressed. It's been . . . a night. After tomorrow's scrimmage, she'll—"

"She told me not to come."

"Wait, seriously?"

"I think Coach was even texting her as we were talking. She was trying to play it off."

"Well, hold on. He's just checking in on us tonight. It's not that weird."

"It is weird. It is."

Luci feels a hand on her back, gently nudging her along. "Don't worry," Ali says, leaning down to whisper in Luci's ear. "She'll catch up."

SATURDAY, AUGUST 27
2:38 A.M.
KEARSON

Kearson and Grace walk out of the party and across the front lawn, stepping apart momentarily to allow for the bulldog peeing in the grass. As they come back together, Grace playfully knocks into her and nudges her chin across the street.

"Is it weird seeing your mom's face all over town?"

Across the street, a house is for sale, and one of her mother's real estate signs is near the curb, perfectly positioned so her coiffed portrait is illuminated by a streetlight.

Kearson laughs. "Yes. It's like she's stalking me."

It's a good thing Kearson's mother can't see her tonight. The athletic director would have a full voice mail of her complaints when school starts back up on Monday. Anything Kearson might say to contextualize what she and the girls are up to would be dismissed prejudicially. West Essex field hockey is forever tainted for her mother.

Her mother didn't make it to any of her JV games last season, and so, when Coach gave Kearson the tap, she didn't expect the fact that she was playing varsity to make any difference. Besides open houses taking up the weekends, private showings and closings on the weeknights, sports weren't her mother's thing. Still, Kearson was excited to share the incredible news. Her calls went straight to her mother's voice mail, so eventually she just left one. Kearson could hear how high-pitched her voice sounded, reverberating off the bathroom walls as she explained how the opportunity to replace the injured Phoebe and play alongside the top talent of the Wildcats was a dream come true.

When Kearson walked through the door after her first varsity game, her mother was waiting with a special dinner for them, rainbows of take-out sushi to celebrate, which she had plated in the shape of a W.

"Gah! My varsity girl!" Her mother had gone to West Essex herself, but there hadn't been much in the way of sports for the girls back then, besides cheerleading, to which Mrs. Wagner was abjectly opposed. "I'm so proud of you!"

Kearson immediately started sobbing. Her mother, totally blindsided by this emotional bait and switch, pushed back from the table and rushed over to comfort Kearson, soy sauce splashing out of the little bowls.

"Kears, what happened?" Her mother looked her over frantically, as if Kearson had just walked out from the wreckage of a car crash. Which wasn't that far off.

"I played so horribly, Mom!"

"What? No! How can that be?"

Kearson didn't expect it to make sense to her mother because, though she never made it to games, her daughter was a JV starter. She couldn't name Kearson's position but she knew Kearson loved field hockey.

Kearson went straight upstairs and fell on her bed in a heap. Her mother followed her. "Tell me."

Kearson tried to catalog all her failures from the day's match. How she couldn't seem to connect with Mel, as if they were speaking two different languages on the field. How Phoebe had started off the game by trying to cheer Kearson on only to grow so frustrated with her, she wouldn't say two words to her. And Coach, the way he screamed at her. His voice was like ice in her veins, freezing her when she needed to stay warm, stiffening her when she needed to play loose.

Annoyingly, her mother kept interjecting with some vague defense of her. That this was Kearson's first game. That she was still learning. That she had never played with the varsity team before. That it was supposed to be fun. It began to occur to Kearson that she could never explain this. Her mother wouldn't ever understand. Kids who just wanted to screw around and have fun did intramural sports. On the Wildcats varsity field hockey team, fun was not the point. Fun was the by-product when the girls won. The varsity girls played with an eye on college scholarships and state titles and national competitions. This was the big time, which made Kearson's shortcomings a big-time failure.

Kearson pretended to fall asleep so her mother would leave, and once her mother had, Kearson quietly wept until she actually did.

The next game, the final one of the regular season, the Wildcats were the visiting team at Franklin Lakes. Technically the Wildcats had already clinched a spot in the finals, and the game didn't mean anything, except it meant *everything*.

Kearson didn't perform any better. In fact, she played worse because in her heart Kearson knew she simply wasn't good enough to compete at this level. Failure was her inescapable destiny. And like an infectious disease, she would take the entire team down with her. Coach wasn't the only one exasperated with her. Now her teammates were too. Mel stopped making eye contact in team huddles. Phoebe lost her voice trying to steer Kearson's actions from the sidelines, and now she sat mute with a blank stare. They all seemed to know Kearson was a lost cause. It may have been a meaningless game, but for the Wildcats it was hospice.

And then, about ten minutes into the second half, Kearson saw her mother arrive in a black wool coat trimmed on the collar and cuffs with faux leopard fur.

The Franklin Lakes bleachers—one for home fans and one for away—were located on the same side of the field, next to the high school building. But Kearson's mother wanted to be close to her daughter, so she walked around to the opposite side of the field and stood in the parking lot, behind a chain-link fence, just a few feet away from the Wildcats' team bench.

Having Coach narrate Kearson's endless missteps was one kind of misery. But to have her mother attempt to drown Coach out with her cheers was next-level torture. Her mother's shrill encouragements for a game she clearly didn't understand blasting at the backs of all Kearson's teammates and Coach was the most humiliating experience of her life. Kearson was already on edge; her mother pushed her over.

Kearson was subbed out near the end of the second half, after almost accidentally colliding with Mel in the midfield. She went to the bench and sobbed her eyes out. That's finally what shut her mother up.

Later, Kearson found her mother waiting for her in the

kitchen. There was no sushi this time, not even false pretenses of celebrating. Kearson could tell her mother was upset, the string on her tea bag wrapped so tightly around her finger that the tip was changing color.

"Just tell me, Kears, does Coach yell like that at all the girls?"

"Yes."

"I don't understand." She sounded genuinely boggled. Like it was impossible. Wouldn't other parents have complained? Wouldn't she have heard something?

"Mom, please. It's my fault. I screwed up like a hundred and one times."

"I don't want anyone screaming at you like that, Kearson. Hell, I don't even do it, and I'm your mother!"

"You don't get it," Kearson told her, exasperated. She was already so upset with herself, she didn't want to now have to go over everything a second time, justify that her fuckups were indeed big enough to have warranted Coach's wrath. "I'm going to bed."

"What's that on your face?"

"What?" Kearson lowered her face to look at her reflection in the toaster. There was a big red mark on her cheek. A perfect ripe raspberry of broken blood vessels. Her stomach hit the floor. "I got hit with a ball."

"When? Is that why Coach took you out? Is that why you were crying on the bench?"

"No. It happened in warm-ups. I wasn't looking."

"Kearson . . ."

Kearson should have stood her ground. But she knew her mother would eventually disarm her, unspool her the way she always did. She simply ran to her room and locked the door.

Kearson dials back into the conversation. The girls are throwing out ideas for the next stanza of the Wildcat fight song. She murmurs the lyrics to herself.

Don't mess with the Wildcats, we won't accept defeat,
For we are the Wildcats, and we will not be beat!

Ali says, "Remember that sign when you first drive into Oak Knolls, about how they are the state champions? We could steal it and"—she shrugs—"I don't know. Burn it or something?"

Luci says, "We do have to return Buddy anyway."

"I don't think we should make this stanza about Oak Knolls," Mel says. "Tonight's supposed to be about us showing Coach that we know what it means to be Wildcats."

Kearson says, "What if we sneak into the West Essex gym and take a picture of us standing underneath the spot where our champion banner *would* have been?"

"I love it!" Mel says. "But how are we going to get inside?"

Kearson informs the girls, "The athletic director always keeps his office window unlocked. He hides a pack of cigarettes and an ashtray on the ledge so he can secretly smoke."

The girls laugh. It is kind of funny to think of him being a secret smoker.

"Do you think it would still be unlocked? The school's been empty all summer."

Grace says, "He was in his office this week. I saw him when I was filling up the water bottles before tryouts."

"Okay! So we'll go in, take a team picture, and then get out. We still have one more stanza to do after this and then we're going straight to bed! We have a game in a few hours!"

"Way to go, Kears," Phoebe says, patting Kearson on the shoulder. Kearson beams like she's just had a medal pinned to her chest.

It's become clear to Kearson that her mother's interference is what left her so vulnerable. In fact, she likely preferred Kearson to be weak, because it wasn't like her mother tried to make her strong. With her mother, it was always the underbelly. The space she's put between them has done Kearson wonders. But here, with the girls, she feels stronger than ever.

The girls drive over to the school. They park in the far parking lot and, after cracking windows for Buddy, creep like ninjas to the school, Kearson at the head of the pack. The building looks spooky at night, no lights on, all the windows turned reflective in the darkness.

"Don't worry," Mel says, helping to hoist Kearson up to the ledge of the athletic director's window, which is only a little higher than her head. "Even if someone did call the cops on us, I'm like ninety-nine percent sure I could talk us out of it."

The crazy thing: it feels true. When the girls are together, they feel invincible.

Her tennis shoes scraping the brick, Kearson scrambles up, then crouches in the small space of the window frame. Just as she suspected, there is a new pack of cigarettes and a little glass ashtray, which looks like it was swiped from a diner. With a few upward thrusts, Kearson is able to push the window open and climb inside.

She had been called into this office exactly three weeks after they'd lost the state championship.

The athletic director was behind his desk, and Coach leaned against a file cabinet in the corner, looking just over Kearson's head, jaw clenched. Before either of them said anything, Kearson lowered herself into one of the two wooden chairs facing them and stammered, "I—I returned my varsity uniform before Christmas break. I put it in a plastic bag and hung it on the doorknob." Because that's what this was about, right?

Coach and the AD shared a confused look.

Maybe not.

"Also, please know that I absolutely *do not* expect a varsity letter." She twisted in her seat so she was talking to Coach. Even if she technically earned one by playing those two games and also dressing, though not playing a single minute, for the championship, she didn't want it. "I would rather try for one next season." If Coach didn't flat out cut her, which would be completely in his right to do after her dreadful performance.

But again, Coach and the AD were perplexed. The AD cleared his throat, that way smokers do, deep and phlegmy. "So you don't know why I called you down here today, Kearson."

"No," she said softly. "I guess I don't."

Coach actually laughed then, tension uncapped, as if he saw through some magic trick or sleight of hand that was being pulled on him. His eyes pinned on Kearson, he said to the AD, "Now do you believe me?" The AD glanced over at Coach, wholly sympathetic, and drummed his pen on a blank notebook page.

Now Kearson imagines herself in that chair across the office, what the two of them saw, a too-tall freshman, wringing her bony hands in her lap, wide-eyed and looking back and forth between the two men, afraid to breathe, wondering which of them was going to tell her what this was about.

Kearson wonders now if looking so completely clueless actually helped her case. As soon as the AD said, "I received a call from your mother this morning, Kearson," the office became a vortex, a hole opening up directly underneath her chair, pulling her down down down. It hadn't begun as a performance, but it became one very quickly. Kearson needed to take control of her story. She was no victim. And this was an opportunity to do something heroic.

Which isn't all that different from what she's doing back here tonight, come to think of it.

"Hey! Kears!" the girls whisper from outside. "Is the coast clear?"

She hurries back to the window. "Yup! Who's next?" She smiles, reaching out her hand.

The high school has a fresh, clean smell. Almost antiseptic, but not entirely unpleasant. It's dark, but with the emergency lights and Mel's phone, they can see pretty well. And inside they are lit up with excitement. The girls tiptoe together in a cluster, padding silently down one hall, then a stairwell, toward the gym.

The floors are buffed to a reflective shine. The bulletin boards feature cheery back-to-school scenes, glued-down announcements on construction-paper backings, ruby-red apples, perfectly sharpened pencils, fall foliage that's yet to appear IRL. Everything is pressed in tight with pushpins and staples. Every locker is opened wide, a hallway of gaping metallic mouths. The desks inside classrooms sit in perfectly straight rows.

Kearson is reminded of the possibility the new school year brings. Forget New Year's Eve. The first day is when real resolutions are made. Earnest pledges fill their hearts, promises they fully intend to keep. *This year, I won't be late on homework. I'll keep my locker clean. I'll study for tests, not just cram. I'll get better sleep. I'll dress up more than just game days. Shower every morning. Wake up early enough to do my hair.*

But Kearson has a feeling that her teammates all share a single dream tonight as they step inside the darkened gym. *Whatever it takes, this season, the Wildcats will be winners again.*

The gym is a dark cave of shellacked wood. Retractable bleachers folded up tight against the walls. Basketball hoops cranked up and out of the way. Navy blue mats Velcroed to the walls. An equipment closet with all kinds of sports paraphernalia in the midst of being reorganized.

And above their heads, rows and rows of championship banners, rectangles of thick navy wool and hand-stitched white letters. It makes Kearson so proud to look up and see the five this team has won, the only banners in the gym that haven't faded or collected dust over the years. This is their history, but in the scope of time, it is the here and now.

Mel passes the first three, championships won before Mel's freshman season, and stops under the fourth. The girls crowd around her.

"I was talking with Luci before about captains, and it occurred to me that some of you girls might be interested in a mini Wildcat history lesson."

She points up at the fourth banner.

"Joli Sands was team captain my freshman season." Mel's voice takes on a godlike echo. "Joli was all-state midfielder, leader in assists and penalty shots, and she got a full ride to Quayle University. When we won states that year, Joli's parents rented three limousines to take our team to the varsity banquet dinner and afterward drove us all down to her parents' beach house. It was one of the most fun nights of my life, though I still gag if I even smell raspberry vodka."

The girls giggle.

Mel takes a few steps down the line, to the fifth banner.

"Olivia Mills was captain my sophomore season." A couple of the older girls hoot and holler. "National Team alternate and goalie of the year, to the surprise of no one, because Livvy had a perfect season, zero points scored against her. Livvy was crazy superstitious. She wouldn't ever take off her goalie gloves unless she had both feet on the sidelines, she wouldn't step onto the field until every girl on the Wildcats had tapped the top of her helmet with their stick blades." Mel scans the crowd, stopping when she sees Ali. "In the locker room after winning the state championship, Livvy presented her gloves to our freshman backup goalie, none other than Ali Park." A few girls rub Ali's head. "And right after, Livvy accidentally leaned against the master knob of the locker room showers, where we had apparently been standing, and doused all of us in ice-cold water."

"Even Coach?" Grace asks, her hands covering her mouth.

Mel nods her head incredulously. "Yup. Even Coach."

Everyone has a big laugh. Even Kearson. She'd love to see Coach like that—laughing and proud. Hopefully this season.

Mel takes another step, just past the last banner. You can hear a pin drop.

"Rose Tynam-Reed was our captain last year. All-state defensive player of the year, full ride to Danford. I know we had good times last season. . . ." Mel shrugs. "But I can't forget the sound of her crying in the locker room after we lost the championship. And how, after Coach told us to get back on the bus, she was the first to walk out. And the rest of us did the same thing, quietly packed up our stuff and left. I don't remember any of us saying one word to each other." She shakes her head sadly. "Is it any wonder why we lost? Because that's not what Wildcats do." She places a hand on her heart. "This is what Wildcats do."

The girls all nod.

"Coach may have helped us to remember what it means to be a Wildcat tonight. But now it's our job to never, ever let ourselves forget. If we can do that, there'll be another championship banner hanging in this spot next year."

The Wildcats erupt in screams and claps and hoots and hollers, the gym exploding with sound.

Mel scurries a few feet away, balances her cell phone upright on a stack of exercise mats. The girls grab sticks from the equipment closet and cuddle up against one another, readying their pose.

Ali says, "Did anyone find a ball in there? Might be nice for the picture."

"I did," Phoebe says, strutting out from inside the closet. And then, coyly, "The question is, how badly do you *want* it?"

In a matter of seconds, Phoebe has her loaner stick on the floor and is batting a ball back and forth. Ali jokingly tries to snatch it away with her stick. At first Phoebe deftly pivots and laughs deliciously, swaggering, but Ali stays on her, like a tango, stepping forward with each of Phoebe's steps back, a Cheshire-cat grin on her face.

"Phoebe, you don't have your brace on!" Mel cautions.

"Thanks, Mom!"

Indignant, Mel picks up a stick, darts forward, and steals the ball from them both. "I've always thought I could play defense," she says, all bravado.

But then Ali crosses in front of her and steals it back. "You'll need to be faster than that!" She calls out across the gym, "Grace! Grace!" before chipping her a pass.

And just like that, an impromptu game begins, spreading out from a few girls in the center of the gym to everyone who is here. Sides take shape without much deliberation, and half the girls peel off their shirts, play in just their tanks and sports bras.

First one girl calls for a pass, then another yells for sideline. Sticks slap the floor; sneakers rub the wood with bright squeaks of friction.

It reminds Kearson of how good she used to feel when she played. And she's both grateful and humbled that this joy hasn't been completely extinguished.

Mel and Phoebe are completely in sync. Kearson saw them struggling a bit during tryouts this week but they've slipped back into a groove. It is all love. Every shot, every play, ends with them hugging each other.

They scrap like this for who knows how long. Kearson's bra is sticking to her with sweat and the score is tied, three goals on each side.

"Next point is game," Mel announces. "We still have one more verse to do!"

After a face-off, Kearson grabs the ball, spins, and fires a pass over to Luci. It lands right on her stick. They could make a good twosome, Kearson thinks.

But the action stops like a freeze-frame.

"Shit," Luci says, and drops her stick.

Kearson spins around and sees Phoebe is down on the floor, holding her knee.

The rest of the team rushes over. All except Kearson. She can't move.

Mel kneels down and tries to tend to Phoebe. "I told you not to play without your brace! I mean, haven't you learned your lesson?"

Even in the low light, Kearson can tell Phoebe is bright red, but Kearson's not sure if it is from embarrassment or anger. "Don't worry. I'm fine." Phoebe tries to stand. A few girls reach down to lend a hand, but Phoebe refuses. It's as painful to watch as what Phoebe must be feeling. How much effort she requires to get to her feet.

"You don't look fine!" Mel grabs her hair in two fists and pulls hard. "Coach is going to kill us."

"Just take the picture." Phoebe hobbles across the gym, unable to put any real weight on her knee, until she's underneath the empty banner space. "Hello! Someone take a fucking picture so we can get out of here!"

So they gather together with their borrowed sticks and pose underneath the spot where this year's banner would be hung. Five minutes ago, they could all see it. Now no one can bring themselves to look up, least of all Kearson.

SATURDAY, AUGUST 27
3:06 A.M.

COACH: Luci

COACH: Luci

COACH: Luci

LUCI: Sorry.

COACH: You girls better not still be at Mel's boyfriend's house.

LUCI: No. We left a while ago.

LUCI: Also they aren't seeing each other anymore.

LUCI: Mel told me herself.

COACH: 😒

COACH: Whatever.

COACH: Where are you? What's happening?

LUCI: We're waiting outside the high school. We snuck inside to take a team picture.

COACH: Waiting for what?

LUCI: Mel and Phoebe are still inside.

COACH: Doing . . . ?

COACH: Luci.

LUCI: You should probably ask Mel.

COACH: 🫨

COACH: Why would I need to ask Mel when I'm asking you?

COACH: You're my eyes and ears, remember?

LUCI: Yes.

LUCI: I think they're getting ice. Phoebe might have hurt her knee.

COACH: Are you kidding me?

COACH: Tell me that you're fucking kidding me.

COACH: Luci

COACH: LUCI

SATURDAY, AUGUST 27
3:08 A.M.
MEL

The girls quickly collected their things, returned the sticks to the equipment cabinet, and hustled out of the gym and back to the athletic director's office. But Mel and Phoebe are still in the gym together.

Using a field hockey stick for balance, Phoebe wobbles on her good leg while testing how much weight she can bear on her re-injured one. Her teeth are clenched, and she sucks air through them in painful gasps each time she sets her tiptoes briefly on the floor, wincing, but her lack of success—of even a glimmer of improvement—doesn't prevent her from trying again and again and again, hoping for a different result.

Mel—helpless and heartbroken—stands watching.

"Phoebe . . ."

"I'm fine."

"Please, Phoebe. I—"

"Mel!" Phoebe pauses, momentarily shocked by her own

volume. She pulls her ponytail tight. It's started to slip out. When she speaks again, her voice is softer but no less urgent. "Just . . . give me a second. Please."

Mel folds her arms tight across her chest.

A good friend would do no such thing.

A good friend would say, "No, Phoebe, you're clearly *not* fine."

A good friend would say, "I'm calling your mom."

A good friend would say, "I'm driving you straight to the ER."

Which is why Mel's just as furious with herself as she is with Phoebe right now. Mel's *not* a bad friend, but that's what this whole mess has turned her into. That's who Phoebe keeps pressuring her to be.

Mel barely slept the night before Phoebe's ACL surgery and was wide awake at 5:00 a.m., right around the time Phoebe and her parents would have been en route. Even though the girls had texted plenty the previous evening, Mel couldn't help but send one last bit of encouragement Phoebe's way.

MEL: Good Luck!

MEL: You're the strongest and toughest girl I know!

MEL: You've got this!

PHOEBS: I can't believe you're awake.

MEL: I was too nervous to sleep.

PHOEBS: Lol meanwhile my mom slept through her alarm

MEL: 😂

MEL: Make sure she texts me the second you're out of surgery.

PHOEBS: K.

MEL: And I'm coming straight over after my club game.

PHOEBS: Thanks for being such a good friend.

PHOEBS: See you later!

PHOEBS: Or, if not, I'll see you on the other side! 😇

MEL: OMG I HATE YOU! 😈
PHOEBS: 😈 😂

Phoebe talked about her surgery like it was no big deal. A couple of snips here, a few stitches there, and her knee would be good as new. She didn't even have to go to an actual hospital for it, just a fancy outpatient surgery center where they mostly performed plastic surgery. Phoebe kept joking about a potential paperwork mix-up where she'd wake up with a brand-new set of double Ds.

Though Mel never let on, she knew Phoebe was full of it. Mel had googled the real story of what the surgery would entail. First off, your ACL doesn't "tear" so much as "explode." It can never be sewn back together because the ligament completely liquefies. The operation is actually a very involved procedure that lasts nearly three hours. Phoebe's surgeon would construct an entirely new ACL by cutting away a strip of the tendon that currently connected her kneecap to her shin. He would then thread that piece into place via holes he would drill into her bones, and later, those holes would be plugged up with screws. Mel found a video of an ACL surgery online. She closed her laptop as soon as the scalpel pressed into flesh for the first incision.

Not only was Mel alarmed by what Phoebe was about to endure, but also she was dumbfounded that Coach had undergone ACL repairs four times for each of his knees, a grand total of eight operations, before being forced to retire. She'd asked about each one, but the details were vague and hazy. A torn meniscus his sophomore year; a cadaver ACL after getting flown home from England during an international showcase. It expanded Mel's notion of his loss, rendered his emotional pain into something physical, and carved out an even deeper place for him inside her heart.

And knowing that, how could Mel not forgive him for shutting her out? For suddenly regarding her as a thing that took up space on his field, like a plastic cone? Coach never wanted to coach high school girls field hockey. And he certainly never wanted to teach high school. He took this job only because there was nothing else out there at the time. He never wanted to care about any of this. The championship loss had wounded him. And all his scar tissue made it hard to heal.

Anyway.

Gruesome as it was, Phoebe was raring to go. Though she was diagnosed with a torn ACL the day after the championship game, she'd been forced to wait an entire agonizing four weeks to have the operation. Her surgeon felt this time was critical to allow the swelling to go down. Unfortunately, the delay only increased the time before Phoebe could play again. And patience was never her virtue.

Once the operation date was set for January 22, Phoebe bought a wall calendar and began plotting her comeback. Certain events she marked with a Sharpie . . . every spring club game, plus the weekend tournaments, summer leagues, the week at Kissawa. With those set, Phoebe plotted out her physical therapy goals in pencil, erasing and moving imagined milestones.

"If there are no complications, I should be cleared to start running in four months. That puts me out of spring club for sure. But fingers crossed I'm good to go for summer leagues. And there's no way I'm missing Kissawa."

The whole thing seemed to Mel a cruel exercise. From what she had read, Phoebe was going to be completely out of commission for at least six months, minimum. And it could be a whole year until she had fully regained her strength and range of motion.

But of course, Mel said nothing. Just like she said nothing when Phoebe had decided to play in the championship game, when her ACL was only a sprain. Her job as Phoebe's best friend and teammate was to support her. She wasn't a doctor. And she'd always been impressed by how hard Phoebe worked at everything she did. If there were an exception to the rule, Phoebe would be it.

It was just before study hall that Mel got the text from Mrs. Holt saying Phoebe was out of surgery and the procedure had been a success. Mel sent a text to all her teammates and then decided to stop by Coach's classroom. He'd want to know, of course. And, also, Mel was looking for any excuse to talk to him.

Mel felt Coach's absence like a breakup. She often got the urge to text him. Just something funny she heard. Sometimes she would write these texts in the Notes app on her phone. But she would never send them. She knew, somehow, that no good would come of it. Instead, she respected his space, tried to give him room to cool off. But really, she was stupidly eager to barehand what was surely still searing hot.

Knowing she'd have the opportunity, she dressed up that morning. Disregarding the below freezing temps, Mel wore a corduroy miniskirt with bare legs, a cropped Fair Isle sweater, cable-knit knee highs, and riding boots.

He wasn't in his classroom. Or the cafeteria. She was on her way down to the gym when she bumped into him walking out of the teachers' lounge. He seemed surprised to see her.

"Hey, Mel."

"Phoebe's out of surgery. Everything looks good."

"I heard. Her mother just texted me."

Oh. Well, of course. "A bunch of us are planning to go over tonight. A little personal Psych-Up."

Another teacher pushed out, accidentally hitting Mel square in the butt with the door. Mel was so embarrassed she didn't register who it was. But thinking about it now, she remembers.

Miss Candurra.

After Miss Candurra passed, Coach cleared his throat. "I have some news. I landed a gig with the Junior Men's National Team. I'm going to be their strength-and-conditioning coach. It's a temporary position for the summer, but they are looking to hire someone on full-time."

Her last-ditch hope, of course, was that good news from Truman would eventually come for her and help smooth things over between them. Then Coach would get hired at Trident, and she'd graduate high school, and they could reconnect and start over.

But in a little more than four weeks, he'd landed an amazing opportunity. He'd be traveling the world this summer. Coach had shifted his sights to bigger and better things.

She lowered her head and her throat got tight. "That's great."

Perhaps he sensed Mel was about to cry, because he quickly said, "You should probably get back to class. You don't have a hall pass and I don't want to get in trouble for not writing you up."

The girls ended up at Phoebe's house that evening. They brought flowers, balloons, pizza. It was the first time the Wildcats had gotten together as a team after the loss. Mel swallowed the news Coach had told her. They'd all hear about his new job eventually. She didn't want to bring anyone down. And she wasn't even sure she could get it out without bursting into tears.

The team reunion was short-lived.

Phoebe was obviously in a lot of pain, and for it to show on her face meant it had to be excruciating. Phoebe stayed very quiet.

Didn't make jokes. Didn't initiate conversation. Mel could tell Phoebe was scared. The girls stayed for maybe twenty minutes.

Phoebe missed the next two weeks of school. Mel brought her homework every day after spring club practice. She could tell Phoebe was going stir-crazy. She was also rapidly losing weight.

"All my muscle is wasting away here on this couch. And my pain pills make me nauseous. I can't keep anything down."

"Can you switch to Advil or something?"

"I tried. But unless I take the strong stuff, the pain is so bad that I can't sleep."

"Have you talked to Coach? Maybe he could give you some advice."

"I haven't heard from him. And I don't want to. Not when I'm in this bad of shape." She leaned back and stared at the ceiling. "I don't even like *you* seeing me this way."

Back in school, on crutches, Phoebe was always irritable. Then she got put into a big walking brace, which was so ugly, but allowed her to finally put weight on her knee. Once she began physical therapy, Mel saw a shift in Phoebe's emotions. Her depression lifted. She was back to being fiercely determined.

On Presidents' Day, Mel came over and found Phoebe doing exercises in her room. She was red-faced, pushing hard. Her body trembled with exertion.

"Wait. I thought you already had a PT appointment today."

"I did. I'm doubling up."

"Phoebe, is that really a good idea?"

"I already have my parents breathing down my neck. I don't need it from you, too."

"Okay. Sorry."

About a week later, in early March, Mel was in third-period

English when she looked up and saw Phoebe beckoning her out to the hallway. Something was wrong. Mel could see it in Phoebe's face. Mel raised her hand and didn't wait to be called on, interrupting Mrs. Sandoz, who was reading aloud a passage from *Little Women*.

When Mel stepped into the hallway, Phoebe was nowhere to be seen. Mel whispered, "Phoebs!" and walked quickly on her tiptoes.

She found her in the stairwell, draped over the banister, all weight lifted off her leg. She was still in her big walking knee brace. "Fuck!"

"What's going on?" Mel put her hand gently on Phoebe's arm. Her skin was warm to the touch.

Phoebe glanced up at her, pale and glassy-eyed. "Do you have any Advil?"

"Advil? You look like you need an ambulance."

"I'm fine. I think I've just been working my knee a little too hard."

Mel gave her a look. "Phoebe. Let me see it."

Reluctantly, Phoebe lifted her dress and unhooked the walking boot. Her leg was vibrating. The skin was angry red and swollen around her knee, and her incisions oozed a milky liquid.

Mel put her hand to Phoebe's forehead. She was so hot it scared Mel. "I'm taking you to the nurse."

Phoebe's eyes looked a little unfocused. Like she might suddenly faint. "Don't tell Coach, okay?"

Mel positioned herself up underneath Phoebe's armpit and helped her hobble. "It's going to be okay."

The nurse sat Phoebe in a chair and crouched on the floor in front of her like a shoe salesman. She stuck a thermometer in

Phoebe's mouth. "It's 102," she said soberly. "Phoebe, what's the best number to reach your parents?"

Mel ran straight to Coach's classroom. They were in the middle of taking a test; everyone had their heads down. She walked quickly up to his desk and said, "Something's wrong with Phoebe."

Coach didn't say anything. He just walked right out of his class. Mel followed as he hurried to the nurse's office, his gait awkward and stiff from his own knee injuries.

As soon as Phoebe saw him, she started to sob.

Mel hung back by the nurse's office door to give them space. He sat next to her on a cot, letting Phoebe lean against him and cry. And when Mrs. Holt pulled up a few minutes later, Coach carried Phoebe out to the car in his arms.

Mel loved him in that moment. Knew for sure she loved him. For weeks, as an act of self-preservation, she had tried to convince herself she didn't. But accepting she did allowed her to release whatever muscles she'd relied on to hold the pieces of her heart together. And his treatment of Phoebe was proof that he cared about them despite how hard he tried not to. Which gave her hope.

Phoebe had developed a joint infection. It wasn't clear if exercising too hard had caused it but it did not help. She was admitted into the hospital, had drains put in her knee and another surgery to clear out the infected tissue, then spent three days on a course of IV antibiotics. She didn't allow visitors. Not even Mel. It set her progress back a month.

That was the real stress point in their friendship, Mel sees now. As soon as Phoebe was able—or, honestly, even before—she returned to her crazy rehab schedule. Mel asked her a few times about her knee, but Phoebe never gave her a straight answer. More than that, Phoebe made it clear it was a conversation she didn't want to have.

Is it any wonder that Phoebe is stuck in her own feedback loop all over again? Mel listens to her talking to herself with a sinking feeling.

"I really don't think it's my ACL," Phoebe says. "There wasn't a pop like last time." Hop, wince, hop, wince. "It doesn't even hurt that bad." Hop, wince, hop.

Mel pulls out her phone, intending to check the time, but she finds several texts from Gordy waiting for her.

GORDY: I don't want to fight with you, Mel.

GORDY: If you honestly don't want me at your scrimmage, I won't go.

She writes out, *I think it's for the best that you don't*, then deletes it.

Writes, *I'll call you after my game*, then deletes it.

Writes, *Please leave me alone*, then deletes it.

Suspiciously, Phoebe asks, "Who are you texting? Coach? Don't say anything—"

"It's Gordy." Mel returns her phone to her pocket, annoyed. "We need to go. Can you walk?"

"If I had my Knee Spanx, I'd be fine."

Mel rolls her eyes. "Coach has a first aid kit in his classroom. I bet there's an Ace bandage in there. And maybe one of those instant ice packs too."

Mel offers Phoebe her arm, but Phoebe opts to use the field hockey stick instead. Silently, they head toward Coach's classroom.

Mel doesn't bother turning on the lights. She drops Phoebe off at one of the desks in the front row and then opens Coach's supply closet, using her phone as a light to see what's inside. Everything is neat and tidy.

"God, he really is anal, isn't he?" Phoebe calls out across the classroom. Trying to make a joke to cut the tension.

But Mel doesn't laugh. There's nothing even remotely funny about this. They've come so far tonight, worked their asses off to make things right with Coach and with each other. For nothing. He's going to completely lose his mind when he finds out what's happened. And Mel knows she'll be the one who'll take the brunt of it. She'll be the one held responsible. She's team captain, after all. What if Mel struggles without Phoebe in the same way she did last season? How could her team, and Coach, ever look at her the same way again?

She finds the Ace bandage and the ice bag. When she turns around, her stomach drops. Phoebe has hopped her way around Coach's desk and is now sitting in his chair. She opens up his laptop. The glow of the screen in the dark makes a halo around her head.

"Phoebe! What are you doing?"

"Nothing . . . ," she says, completely focused on the screen. A couple of clicks brings the sound of emails arriving to his mailbox.

"Are you crazy?" Mel hurries to put the things away in the supply closet without disturbing anything. "Turn that off right now!"

"I want to see if any of the scouts have written to Coach about me."

"Are you completely insane?" Mel pushes the laptop screen down. "What does it matter anyway? You can barely stand, Phoebe!"

"Relax. I was only going to take a quick peek." Phoebe says it so casually, like none of this is a big deal. Like the biggest problem they're dealing with right now is Mel overreacting.

"If Coach finds out you went into his email, he'll kick you off the team. You know that, right?" It's outrageous that she even needs to say this. Mel begins straightening Coach's desk, putting papers in a pile. "And he'll kick me off too, because I was in here with you!" She finds a pencil on the floor. "Where was this?"

Phoebe shrugs. "I don't know. And I doubt a misplaced pencil is going to give us away."

Mel crouches down to make sure nothing else has been disturbed. "Forgive me if I override your judgment on this, Phoebe. You haven't had the best record of making good decisions." She feels anger building up inside her. "Just wrap your knee so we can get out of here."

Phoebe snatches up the Ace bandage and begins doing exactly that. She's gotten good at it. Slow, dutiful, pulling tight, making sure the bandage lies flat.

"Why are you being such a bitch to me, Mel?"

"I'm not being a bitch. But I can't do this anymore, Phoebe."

She wrinkles up her nose. "Do what?"

"I can't pretend like this situation"—Mel lassoes the room with her pointer finger—"isn't happening in order to protect your ego. I need to put our team first."

"Because I haven't?"

"No. You definitely, definitely haven't."

Phoebe laughs incredulously. "Um, okay. Whatever, Mel."

"See? That's what I mean. Not only did you ruin tonight, you've also basically guaranteed that we're going to lose tomorrow." Mel feels her eyes getting hot. "I was so excited to play with you. We had our plan. We were going to do it together. But now that's over because of your stupid decision to play without your brace! I mean, how reckless can you be?"

"Who said I'm not playing tomorrow?"

"You think Coach is going to put you in?" Mel actually laughs. "Kearson's playing. And you know what? She's going to totally fail because she's so afraid of you! She was practically in tears at the Psych-Up dinner asking me to pass along an apology to you."

"I'm playing tomorrow." Phoebe's voice chokes with emotion. "I'm fine."

"Great idea, Phoebs, double down on your bad decision. It worked out so well for us last season."

"It only worked out for you, Mel." Phoebe slumps back in Coach's chair. "And I was okay with that."

Mel doesn't understand. And actually, she doesn't care to. Phoebe is clearly delusional. "Do you think I owe you some kind of *thank you*? I don't think what you did was noble. You made a bad decision—several bad decisions, actually—and all of us have to pay the consequences." Mel feels herself begin to shake with anger. "I've worked so hard tonight to try to keep this team together. And the girls have stepped up in a big way. Except for you."

Phoebe's chin starts to quiver. She lets go of her bandaging, and the whole tight coil unravels, goes slack, useless.

"I would do anything for this team!" Phoebe's voice would probably be louder if it weren't so shaky. "And for my best friend. That's why I'm in this situation, Mel. Except unlike you, I never needed any credit. I don't need the validation you do."

"That's funny coming from someone breaking into Coach's laptop for scout emails!"

"Quit acting like you're upset for our team. The only person you're thinking about right now is Coach. He's the one you don't want to disappoint. He's the only person you play for."

Mel sets her jaw. "Coach came back this season and he didn't have to. Sorry I don't want to let him down! Sorry I don't want him to regret it!"

Phoebe pauses and Mel can see something running through her head. Regrets. Mel knows she must have them. But Phoebe still has to accept responsibility. No one made her play. She's accountable for her own choices.

"Why don't you ask Coach what a horrible, selfish teammate I am? Text him right now." Her lip curling, Phoebe adds, "I know how much you two chat."

Mel stiffens. It looks like Phoebe is gathering her courage or something, which freaks Mel out, so Mel keeps talking. "Look. I don't want to fight with you." As soon as Mel says this, her eyes well up. Because it's true. She wishes she could take back everything she's said. But she can't. It's out there.

Phoebe quickly finishes bandaging her knee and then gets up and slowly approaches. "Have you two talked about me? Has Coach said anything to you about how I've been playing this week?"

Mel goes cold, fight-or-flight kicking in. "Are you serious? He knows you're my best friend!"

Phoebe begins to cry. "Are we, Mel? Are we still best friends? Because it doesn't feel like it. It's like we barely know each other anymore."

"Of course we are!" Mel starts backing up. "Seriously, Phoebe. Coach hasn't texted me once this entire week."

"Then give me your phone."

Phoebe grabs for it. It's almost playful at first, but Mel holds on tight and twists away. It should be over. But Phoebe is relentless. And Mel is lying.

She and Coach have texted about Phoebe. Plenty. Their last exchange before tonight had been about her. Never anything bad. Never ever ever.

But what's on her phone is dangerous to Coach. Mel can't let Phoebe see how much they are in contact. Mel pushes Phoebe off her and Phoebe yelps in pain.

"Phoebe—"

"Forget it. Let's just go." Phoebe wipes her eyes. "Can you bring my stick back to the gym?"

"Yeah. Okay. Sure." Mel picks up the loaner field hockey stick Phoebe's been using as a crutch. "You sure you don't want to hang on to it?"

"If I lean on you, I can probably manage without it."

"Okay. I'll be right back."

Mel's entire body is shaking as she walks briskly to the gym, her phone still gripped in her hand. She realizes she never sent Coach the picture she took in the gym. She quickly puts it in a text, along with the second verse of the Wildcat fight song.

Don't mess with the Wildcats, we won't accept defeat,
For we are the Wildcats, and we just can't be beat!

He texts back immediately.

COACH: It's after three in the fucking morning.

COACH: We have a team meeting at nine sharp.

COACH: And an enormously important scrimmage tomorrow.

MEL: I know, I know. We're almost finished. Just one more stanza left.

COACH: Do you think any of this is going to matter tomorrow?

COACH: When Oak Knolls shows up fully rested?

COACH: Do you think this is going to give us an edge?

MEL: I thought this is what you wanted...

COACH: Don't even think about turning this around on me, Mel.

COACH: This "plan" is yours.

COACH: Own it.

COACH: I'm going to bed. Don't text me again.

Mel rubs her arms and looks around the empty gym. Weren't they just having the time of their lives ten minutes ago? Maybe everything is irreversibly screwed up. Maybe it is all her fault.

The shame begins to drain her, her sense of self spiraling down like a bath with the plug pulled out. Underneath Mel's confidence has always been the unnerving worry that, without Coach there pushing her and shaping her and guiding her, she would never shine the way she has. After the championship loss, it became something far more haunting: that Coach had her pegged all wrong. Mel's not the player he thought she was. Not even close.

Even if Coach is pissed at her tomorrow, at least Mel can say she didn't give up. It is for him but it's also for them.

After putting the loaner stick away, Mel glances around and makes sure the gym looks just as it did before they snuck in. Then she doubles back to Coach's classroom. Though she swore she left it open, the door is closed.

Mel peers in the window.

Phoebe is gone.

And so is Coach's laptop.

Mel sprints down the hall, calling for Phoebe. She sticks her head out of the athletic director's office window and looks at the girls. "Did Phoebe come out this way?"

Ali shakes her head. "No. Isn't she with you?"

Mel takes a deep breath. Tries to think clearly. Tries not to panic. "She must have walked out a different way." Mel sweeps her leg over the sill, crouches on the ledge, and pulls the window closed. "Let's spread out and see if we can find her."

One of the girls says, "Hey, Mel, is that your car?"

Mel hops down to the ground. Indeed it is. Headlights click on, the engine purring already. She steps forward, expecting Phoebe to pull around to where the team is.

Instead, Phoebe guns Mel's Mini Cooper straight out of the parking lot so fast the front end scrapes the little speed bump, a million sparks brightening the night for a brief, scary moment.

SATURDAY, AUGUST 27
3:22 A.M.
ALI

Ali stares into the dark as if waiting for Phoebe to pull a U-turn and come back. Mel does too, because a joke like that would be totally Phoebe.

Ali swallows. "Did Phoebe say where she was going?"

Mel is visibly shaken. "No."

"What happened? Did you two have a fight?"

Mel doesn't answer. Which is an answer all its own.

Ali knew Mel and Phoebe were in a weird place for most of the summer. But it wasn't until she got a call in the middle of the night from Phoebe's phone that Ali understood just how weird.

It was nearly one in the morning. Ali had been streaming a K-drama on her phone and must have fallen asleep. When it started to buzz and she saw Phoebe's name on the screen, Ali felt terrible. She'd dropped the ball with Phoebe big-time. Ali knew Phoebe was struggling after her second surgery, but she hadn't reached out. Not because she didn't care. Because Ali was struggling too.

She picked up and heard someone else's voice. One she didn't recognize.

"Umm, is this Ali?"

"Who is this?"

"This is Tracy Costello. I'm Pete Costello's little sister. On the basketball team."

Ali's head was swimming. "Okay . . ."

"I'm sorry to call you so late, but I'm at a party at Derek Noble's house with Phoebe and she's pretty wasted." Tracy sighed. "Like . . . shooting-baskets-in-her-underwear-level wasted. I found her clothes but she won't put them on. Everyone else is passed out, and you were the first person in her contacts who I kind of sort of knew and . . . sorry."

"Don't be. I'm on my way."

Ali stripped out of her nightgown and pulled on a romper. She grabbed a pair of sweatpants and a T-shirt as backup for Phoebe and got to the party five minutes later.

There was Phoebe, shooting three-pointers in a cotton bra and panties, swaying on her feet but nailing every shot. Tracy sat cross-legged on the edge of the driveway, watching. She had Phoebe's clothes neatly folded next to her.

"Ali!" Phoebe was jovial enough.

"Hey, Phoebe," she said.

Tracy pulled Ali aside and quickly filled her in.

That afternoon, Tracy had posted a random old picture and tagged everyone in their neighborhood crew. She held it up for Ali to see. The kids were lined up on someone's front lawn, everyone in swimsuits and wrapped in too-thin towels. Phoebe was the only girl in a bikini, basketball on her hip, her legs bruised and scraped and pocked with bug bites. Derek was next to her, flexing nonexistent muscles.

After Tracy posted the picture, she and Phoebe began messaging back and forth. They were friendly at school but Tracy was a freshman, the little sister, and they hadn't properly caught up in years. Tracy mentioned the party at Derek's house that night. It was a lot of the basketball guys, but pretty much everyone from the old gang would be there too. Phoebe agreed to stop by.

Actually, the way Phoebe put it in her text was *It's not like I have jack shit else to do.*

Ali remembered then that this was the third day of Kissawa camp. Their entire team was there, except Mel, who she'd heard was at Truman. Ali hadn't told Phoebe she wasn't going either since she'd chosen to attend the goalie camp instead, mainly because there would be no chance of seeing Darlene Maguire there. She felt bad all over again.

"I'm glad you called me," Ali told Tracy.

"Phoebe was the coolest girl around when we were growing up. I always looked up to her. She never gave a shit what the guys thought of her. It was like . . . she was invincible."

"Yeah. I totally know what you mean."

Ali corralled Phoebe into getting dressed. She was too drunk to bring Phoebe back to her own house, so Ali used Phoebe's phone to text Phoebe's parents. They'd reached out twice already, asking when Phoebe thought she might be home. It was a no-pressure ask. After the year she'd had, they were happy Phoebe was out of the house.

PHOEBE: Hey I ran into Ali at the party. Okay if I sleep over at her house?

MOM: How nice! Have fun!

"Where are we going?" Phoebe asked her.

"My house. We're having a sleepover."

"Yay," she said, like a machine powering down.

Later, tucked into Ali's bed, her eyes already starting to flutter shut, she murmured, "You want to hear something hilarious, Ali? Derek's penis is so small." That was the last thing Phoebe said before she passed out.

The next morning, Phoebe woke up looking like crap. When she realized where she was, she was embarrassed but also grateful. And she gave Ali the full story.

She told her how weird it was to be going to a party without any of her teammates with her. To know that none of them would be inside to welcome her, to talk to her, to make space for her on the couch. She had a pang of fear, almost turned around and went back home. But then Tracy spotted her from the front porch and waved Phoebe over.

"I had never been inside Derek's house before. The foyer was filled with framed pictures of him and his family when we were kids. Dorky sweater vests, pressed khakis, and his basketball sneakers. I always thought he was cute."

After some puberty awkwardness between them on a driveway basketball court, they'd spent the last several years pretending like the other didn't exist.

"Anyway, he was surprised to see me walk in the door. Totally checked me out so long that the kid sitting next to him gave him a shove to play his card." Phoebe shrugs. "It made me feel good."

They did not speak to each other. Not even a hello. It wasn't antagonistic. Phoebe didn't feel unwelcome. It was a flirtation born of the competitive thing they used to have with each other.

It was like a game of chicken. Which of them would acquiesce first and acknowledge the other.

Him passing her too close in the kitchen, his hands finding the divots of her hips, steering her body out of his way. Gentle but firm. Confident. Her reaching across Derek to tap someone else, letting her hair sweep across his arm, letting her perfume drift into his nose.

Phoebe drank too much. Those twisted lemonades where you can't taste the alcohol. She could feel herself getting wasted but the drinks helped her courage. Phoebe knew they were going to hook up. It was fun. She missed fun.

The party thinned out around midnight. It became harder for her and Derek to hide the game they were playing with each other. Fewer buffers to keep them apart. At some point, he cocked his head toward a hallway. Phoebe set down her drink and headed in that direction.

She wasn't sure which room was his but then Derek was behind her, reaching around her for the doorknob, nudging her inside with his body, like a shadow.

Phoebe took quick glimpses of the room in the dark like a camera snapping shots without a flash. His unmade bed, his dresser with cologne bottles lined up, a set of dumbbells on the floor, a chin-up bar in the frame of his closet.

She turned to face him and then they were kissing. Hungry kisses, like they'd both wanted this for years. It wasn't romance, but more the release of something bottled up that had always existed between them.

Her hands over her mouth, Ali asks, "Did you ... have sex with him? Because you did mention his penis last night."

Phoebe laughs. "I mean, I would have. Probably. But Derek

passed out cold in the middle of our hookup. That's why I went outside and played basketball."

"Do you like him?"

Phoebe shook her head. "No. I'm just . . . so bored. It's like nothing gets my heart racing anymore. I think I just needed a win."

Phoebe made Ali promise not to tell anyone about it and thanked Ali for saving her. Ali was hoping she'd stay and hang out, but Phoebe took a shower and headed home. She had a PT appointment.

After she left, Ali had a weird feeling like she should call Mel and tell her what had happened. Not everything, but something like "Have you talked to Phoebe lately? Maybe you should check in on her."

But she hadn't. It's something Ali deeply regrets right now.

She puts her hand on Mel's shoulder and gently suggests, "Maybe we should go back to your house and wait for Phoebe there. The rest of the girls are looking tired. And it's getting late." Mel turns toward her, eyes wide and blinking, and Ali's not even sure if Mel heard her. But instead of repeating herself, she feels the urge to say something reassuring to Mel. The best she can come up with is "At least Phoebe's not alone. She's got the bulldog to keep her company."

"Is Phoebe okay?" Kearson asks. She looks anxious.

"She's fine," Mel says automatically.

Ali wants to believe her. Mel knows Phoebe best. But, glancing over to their field, Ali can't help thinking of their last team practice before the championship game.

"Holy shit, is that Phoebe?" Rose said in an astonished whisper. Even though Ali was halfway finished with Rose's French braid, she pulled free and the whole thing unraveled as she began to jump up and down, waving with both her hands.

One thing Ali already knew was that once Phoebe got it in her head to do something, it was nearly impossible to talk her out of it. Like when they were at last year's Thanksgiving showcase in Florida, and she decided to wear her face goggles out to dinner. Or when, at Kissawa the previous summer, she went skinny-dipping in the lake all by herself, because the rest of them chickened out.

So when Ali turned and saw that, indeed, Phoebe was walking toward their field, dressed in her practice gear and carrying her stick, she should have just smiled and shaken her head, tried to push down the worry in her chest.

"Please, please, please, God, tell me that you're cleared to play for the championship game," Rose said, falling to her knees.

Phoebe placed her hand on Rose's forehead. "Your prayers have been answered, my child."

Rose jumped up. "It's a miracle! Hallelujah!"

Ali said, "Weren't you on crutches, like, this morning?"

"Umm, yes. I'm never giving my crutches up. When you've got crutches, teachers let you leave class with a buddy ten minutes before everyone else to avoid all the hallway traffic. It's a pretty sweet perk." Phoebe flopped down on the bench and stretched her arms and legs out like a star. "Anyway, don't worry, I'm not going to do *everything* today. My plan is to take it easy until the big game."

"But are you sure doing *anything* is a good idea?" Ali glanced down the sideline at Mel for backup, but she was focused on taping up her stick blade, either not listening or not getting involved.

"I appreciate you looking out for me, Ali. But I talked it over with Coach and—"

"What about your doctor, though?" Ali sat down next to Phoebe. "Because when my dad sprained his ACL, it was a full month before—"

"Coach said—"

"Well, it's not like Coach can see your X-rays—"

"Ali! Let me finish, for fuck's sake!"

Ali put her hands to her cheeks. They felt hot. "Sorry."

"Don't be sorry. I love you."

"I love you, too."

"Can I finish now?"

"Yes."

"Coach said he trusts me to know what's right for my body. If my knee starts to bug me, I'll sit down and he can sub Kearson in. But right now I'm feeling really strong." To prove it, Phoebe stood up, held her field hockey stick out in front of her, horizontal like a tabletop, and started doing high knee lifts.

"Okay, okay," Ali said.

Rose wrapped Phoebe in a hug. "Well, this is the best news ever! Kearson was seriously killing us out there." After letting go, she passed back her hair tie and asked Phoebe to braid her hair for her instead of Ali. "Don't worry. She's still in the locker room."

"Poor thing. She wasn't ready," Mel said, finally entering the conversation.

"Big shoes," Phoebe said with a grin.

Ali looks back over from the field and finds that Mel is addressing the team.

"Girls, I know we're tired and it's getting late. Let's head over to Waffle House, chug some maple syrup, and then finish strong and come up with something great for the final verse of the fight song."

"Wait. So we're still doing this?" Ali's surprised, and also not.

"Absolutely. Phoebe would want us to."

Maybe so. But what's clear is that, when Phoebe feels desperate, she doesn't make the best decisions. And maybe the same thing goes for Mel, too.

Still, the girls squeeze into the five remaining cars.

Mel, sitting shotgun in Ali's Jeep, keeps checking her phone.

Ali sees a head tipped back and bobbing asleep, a pale exposed neck. One of the sophomores.

Kearson is chewing the shit out of her finger. Nervous, obviously.

Grace is pinching herself to stay awake.

"We'll be there in ten minutes but you can sleep. I don't mind," Ali tells her.

"Nah. I'm good."

That's what makes them Wildcats. Team first, always. Isn't that what Coach always asks of them? But what does it mean?

Putting the team before yourself?

Or protecting your teammates at all costs?

Ali isn't sure. She's too tired to think.

SATURDAY, AUGUST 27
3:27 A.M.
PHOEBE

Phoebe pulls over to the side of a quiet road and parks Mel's car in the dark seam between two streetlights. It was dangerous the way she sped off from the high school, all gas, no brakes, through one stop sign and another, the Wildcats getting smaller and smaller and smaller in the rearview mirror. Except it's Phoebe who feels like she's disappearing, everything but the throbbing in her knee. A broken heart inside a wound.

How broken?

After everything, she still wants to play.

This humiliating deficiency of common sense leads Phoebe to reach for Coach's laptop on the seat next to her. She lifts the screen and it brightens the car like an oncoming headlight. His school email program is already up and loaded from when she opened it in his office so she doesn't need to be connected to the internet. Phoebe types her name into a search bar and a bunch of emails pop up. At the top is a thread exchanged with Jon Dockey, the Trident recruiter, subject line "PHOEBE HOLT UPDATE."

She'd brought up Trident to Coach hours ago at Mel's party. Told him their recruiter never responded to the email she had sent on Wednesday. Why didn't Coach mention that they'd been talking about her, apparently as recently as this week?

Instead Coach told her not to even bother with them. He told Phoebe she was too good for Trident.

She clicks on the thread and scrolls down to the first message.

>Monday, August 22
>
>Coach,
>
>I'm seeking some information regarding Phoebe Holt.
>
>As you know, we were initially very excited about her, but I'm aware that she sustained an ACL tear last season that required surgery. While I did not expect to see Ms. Holt during spring club, I was surprised that she missed summer showcases and Kissawa.
>
>You and I have always had a good, straightforward relationship regarding recruitment. I'm wondering if you can shed any light on her current status as we finalize our offers for the following academic year.
>
>Thanks,
>
>Jon

Phoebe pauses to take a breath, hoping it will slow her racing heart, only she forgets to exhale.

>Tuesday, August 23
>
>Jon,
>
>Phoebe underwent two surgeries in the

off-season—one for the ACL tear and one for an infection developed from rehabbing too aggressively—which is why she was sidelined longer than anticipated. Today was our second day of tryouts. I'd say she's at maybe 75%, and might very well get to 85%, but I don't believe she'll ever fully regain her edge.

It's disappointing because her initial injury was a minor ACL sprain. Unfortunately, Phoebe disregarded the advice of her doctor and misled me that she'd been cleared to play, when in fact she had not. I've always admired Phoebe's heart but I would hate to see Trident invest time and resources into a player whose recklessness has proven more of a liability than an asset.

So yes, I would advise you to seek another midfielder. Oak Knolls had a surprisingly decent one. I don't remember her name or if she's already committed elsewhere, but you might throw a call over that way.

That said, I do have an incoming freshman that will be making some serious waves. I watched her play today and will pull her up tomorrow. If you get in early this season with an offer, you can scoop her up before she's on anyone else's radar. I'd be happy to make an introduction.

And now I have a favor to ask. Any news on the men's head coaching position? It's been total radio silence. Frankly I'm surprised. I can't imagine another candidate has the experience I do. And aside from the championship loss this winter, my record speaks for itself. I'd appreciate it if you would put in another good word for me.

Phoebe leans forward, her lungs collapsing like the bellows of an accordion, causing her to emit a similar groan. She scrolls back up to the top of the message, intending to go over Coach's entire response again. There are so many dissonant bits to parse through. But she can't seem to pull her eyes off one particular sentence.

Unfortunately, Phoebe disregarded the advice of her doctor and misled me that she'd been cleared to play, when in fact she had not.

She grips the piped leather sides of Mel's driver's seat, as if to remind herself she is not in free fall.

That's not what happened.

Not even fucking close.

She never told a soul about the conversation she'd had with Coach about playing in the championship game. Before they talked, Phoebe was already thinking of coming back. Had already butted heads with her doctor at the last follow-up appointment, because honestly, was one more week of taking it easy really that essential?

His answer was annoyingly definitive. "Yes."

Phoebe could have gone straight home after leaving the doctor's office, but no, she drove herself to the field, even though practice was nearly over. She had never missed a practice before her injury, not a single one since making varsity. Phoebe wasn't about to start now. There would be only one more after this one, before the championship game. She purposefully left her crutches in the car.

It was December. The girls were puffing tiny clouds. Phoebe felt like a complete asshole in her winter jacket, so she took it off. When she played she never felt cold, and now she hated that she couldn't stop herself from shivering, like she had already lost something from being sidelined for two weeks.

Coach didn't say anything to Phoebe. Maybe he hadn't noticed she'd arrived. He blew his whistle, stopped play, and let loose on Kearson, a snarling dragon's cloud of hot angry breath pouring from his mouth and his nose straight into Kearson's face.

For those last two games of the season, Phoebe wrung a dark glee from watching Kearson's repeated screw-ups. Each time Coach would chew Kearson out, she'd return to the field totally dazed, her bobblehead bobbling in a crazy dizzy blur, and before it had settled and steadied, she'd make another mistake and start the whole cycle over again.

For whatever reason, Kearson couldn't seem to absorb Coach the way the rest of them did. Then again, though Coach yelled at all his players, what he aimed at Kearson that afternoon was a level of vitriol Phoebe had never seen before.

Phoebe actually felt bad for her.

Ordinarily Coach actively weeded out the girls who couldn't take his style of coaching. Under normal circumstances, Kearson would never make the cut. But these weren't normal circumstances. He'd been forced to make an exception. And the entire Wildcat team was suffering for it. With the state championship hanging in the balance.

After a whistle to restart play, Coach turned his head slightly toward her and said, "How was your appointment?"

Phoebe had asked Mel to tell Coach, because she knew she'd be late for practice. Not that it mattered. But Phoebe wanted to still feel a part of things.

"He thinks I still need more time to heal."

"But you're not on crutches."

"I still have them. I just hate them."

He sighed. "Not having you out there is killing us."

"Believe me, it's killing me, too."

He blew his whistle. Another Kearson fuckup.

Phoebe was trying to muster up the courage to say, *Fuck it. Can't you just play me?* She hated herself for being too scared to do it.

Coach turned his attention back to the field and restarted play. Once the girls were again in motion, he let the whistle fall from his lips. "You and I, we're a lot alike." He swallowed. "That's why I'm going to tell you something I probably shouldn't. Because if it were me, I'd want to know."

"Okay."

Keeping his eyes on the field, he said, "There's a Truman scout coming to the championship game. Finally. I've been bugging them for months to come, but they've been focused on recruiting defenders." He stuffed his hands into his pockets. "I know it's shitty timing. But this is your shot. Yours and Mel's. So just know that if you want to take it, I'm not going to stand in your way."

It was everything Phoebe had wanted to hear. Tacit permission to disobey her doctor's orders. But still, Phoebe hesitated before responding.

"Does Mel know?"

"I've decided not to tell her. Her performance in the last two games . . . it's clear her head's messed up. I've never seen her play so badly. The pressure of the championship, and then to throw Truman into the equation? I'm afraid she won't be able to handle it."

"I'm just worried that I might not be physically up to it."

He glanced sideways at her. "That's true. I mean, you aren't at your best." He licked his lips. "But . . . in my experience, a situation like this, when you have no choice but to play, helps you bridge that gap. And in this case, you've got all the reasons in the world to step up."

He left it to her to decide.

Weird though, that Phoebe doesn't remember expressly telling Coach, "Okay." Or "I'm in." Or even something cheesy like "Let's fucking do this!" while holding up her hand for a high five that Phoebe knew he'd never give her, but that was the joke of it. She didn't say anything then, or after practice, or the next morning.

It now occurs to Phoebe that there was no need for such a moment. The decision had, in fact, been made for her.

About halfway through the first quarter of the championship game, it became clear that Phoebe's knee was still very much an issue. That's the distinction between just walking around and playing to win. Two very, very different speeds.

Mel was surprised to see Phoebe struggling. She'd assumed Phoebe would be closer to 100 percent. Why else would Phoebe be playing?

That question weighed on them both. Still, Phoebe killed herself to create opportunities for Mel. And there were a few beautiful passes that broke through Mel's overall gloom and lit her up again, her strong, beautiful, confident best friend. Phoebe imagined the Truman scout making notations, shooting some video.

"We're so close to breaking through," Mel kept saying after every missed opportunity. And Phoebe believed it for as long as she could. Eventually the pain won out over the adrenaline. She paused by the sideline.

"Coach, I don't know if I can keep going." If he heard her, she couldn't tell. There was no reaction. "Coach?"

"I know what you're capable of, Phoebe. And I know you'll hate yourself forever if you step off the field. You'll always wonder what if I hung in there a little longer. What if I just kept going?"

He meant *keep going*, of course. So Phoebe did.

Team first, always.

Everyone was counting on her. Everyone had been so glad she'd come back. She'd do anything for Mel. And Coach knew it.

She played until the final minute.

She may have walked herself up to the edge of that cliff, but it was definitely Coach who gently nudged her off.

> *Unfortunately, Phoebe disregarded the advice of her doctor and misled me that she'd been cleared to play, when in fact she had not.*

Phoebe closes the laptop and carelessly pushes it over to the passenger seat.

The day after the championship game, Phoebe's surgeon explained the extent of the damage visible on her MRI. Phoebe struggled to follow. Before her ACL sprain, she'd been blissfully unaware of her own anatomy, beyond that her body did exactly as she instructed it to.

"But how could it be torn? I played the whole game!"

"It happens more often than you think."

"I don't mean to be rude, but I want a second opinion."

The surgeon tried a different, low-tech approach. "Here. You can diagnose yourself." He had Phoebe extend her right leg. "Instead of feeling firm," he explained, before pressing gently on the injured knee with his fingers, "it feels like mush." Her knee reacted to his touch the exact disgusting way he'd described.

Had she torn it again tonight?

Phoebe unwraps her hastily bandaged knee. She takes a few deep breaths, trying to psych herself up. Her hands are quivering. Shaking.

She feels the terrible truth for herself.

Phoebe cries so hard it is difficult to breathe. Sobs. Smashes the steering wheel. The pain—both physical and emotional—that Phoebe's trained herself to keep mute rises in volume, cranking to dangerous, deafening decibels.

Buddy barks in the back seat.

Phoebe had forgotten he was there.

A sinister thought appears from that dark place she seems stuck in. Let Buddy out on the side of the road. Someone would find him, return him, hopefully ask questions. Mel took the pictures, texted them to Coach. Phoebe could let it slip. She could ruin Coach. Ruin the Wildcats.

She eyes the bulldog in the rearview mirror. He's nervous. Panting. But still trusting. After all, they spent the night together. And as if to prove his faith in her, Buddy balances his front paws on the center console, leans forward, and licks her tears.

He knows she'd never.

Phoebe takes him home. Turns out she's still a good teammate, even without a team.

SATURDAY, AUGUST 27
3:29 A.M.

COACH: Luci

COACH: What's happening?

COACH: I want an update on Phoebe's knee

LUCI: I don't know anything.

COACH: THEN GO FIND OUT SOMETHING

LUCI: You're putting me in a weird situation.

LUCI: And I'm almost out of battery.

COACH: Are you back at Mel's?

LUCI: I think the plan is to go get food. Everyone's pretty hungry.

COACH: WTF

COACH: I told Mel this night is over.

COACH: I want you to go up to Mel and tell her you want to go home.

COACH: Right fucking now.

COACH: Say that you know that's what Coach would want.

COACH: He wouldn't want us to lose sight of Oak Knolls.

COACH: That's what really matters to him.

COACH: And so long as we show up ready to play, you know in your heart that I'll give you girls the varsity jerseys.
COACH: Okay?
COACH: ???
COACH: LUCI

SATURDAY, AUGUST 27
3:35 A.M.
GRACE

Grace is one of the last players in a line of Wildcats shuffling quietly into the Waffle House. Out of respect, the girls hide their yawns as they pass Mel, holding the glass door open for them, instructing every few heads to "Order whatever you girls want, okay?" Mel seems determined to keep her voice cheery and upbeat, despite her visible weariness, what sounds to Grace like the beginnings of a sore throat taking hold, and ... everything else.

Even though she's putting one foot in front of the other, Grace's mind is working backward, tracking the night all the way back to her idea that they should steal the Oak Knolls bulldog. Now Phoebe's missing, along with the bulldog, and her team could be in some serious shit.

If only she'd kept her mouth shut. Her teammates were already pitching their own ideas for what they could do for the first stanza of the fight song. And yeah, maybe they were boring ideas, but they were also way less illegal. Grace had drowned them out. She'd wanted to impress everyone. Wanted her new teammates to think she was so cool.

As she nears Mel, Grace stares deferentially down at her sneakers.

If they don't get the bulldog back before the Oak Knolls' coach realizes he's missing, it could spell big trouble for the Wildcats. Grace runs through the possibilities. The police could get involved. They certainly weren't careful enough. Plenty of people have doorbell cameras these days. Mel's pictures, texted straight to Coach's phone. They could be arrested. Their season canceled. The twenty of them expelled from school.

All thanks to Grace.

Mel grabs Grace's arm, stopping her cold. "Oh no! My wallet is in my car!" Mel helplessly looks out to the road for any sign of Phoebe. A traffic light clicks needlessly from red to green at a deserted intersection.

Grace, meanwhile, goes through the motions of patting herself down. Though she would do anything to help, it's a pathetic charade, because it's not like she'll find any money in her bike shorts. "I'm sorry, Mel."

Mel closes her eyes and rubs her face with her hands as if washing it. She's starting to unravel. That it's taken this long for even a crack to show strikes Grace as proof of Mel's leadership skills and devotion to getting them through this night, though Mel would certainly take no consolation in her assessment.

Ali sidles up to them and leans against the railing. "I got you, Mel." She unzips a small pink leather pouch attached to her key ring and passes Mel a credit card.

"Thanks," Mel tells her.

The Waffle House is normally packed on weekend nights. Grace has come a few times with her brother and his friends after tagging along to one of his shows and seen kids from her high school file in drunk and ready to carb load. But it's completely dead at this time of night. Just a few random men eating their meals in silence and a single waitress leaning forward against the counter, watching a show on her phone.

The girls head toward the very back and commandeer several tables. A few use the bathroom. The rest drop into seats and pass out menus, rubbing their eyes in order to see clearly.

Grace takes a seat across from Kearson and picks up a different frequency. Over the top of her menu, she watches Kearson pull the sweetener packets from their white ceramic holder and begin grouping them by color: Equal, Stevia, Sweet'N Low, sugar. She's mostly focused on the task, though every few seconds or so, she glances out the window.

"Kears. You all right?"

"I'm worried about Phoebe." Kearson shakes her head, quickly stuffs the sweetener packets in willy-nilly. "Do you think she's okay?"

"I guess that depends on your definition of 'okay.' I mean, she did manage to sneak out of the school and steal a car without any help."

"This whole week, Phoebe thought I was gunning for her spot. I could tell. She kept her eye on me all the time. If I got close to her when we were running laps, she'd run faster. If Coach subbed me in, I could tell it killed her." Kearson shakes her head. "Maybe she ran off tonight because of me. She probably thinks I'm happy she got injured."

Even though something must have really upset Phoebe to

make her take off the way she did, Grace can't imagine it was Kearson. "No way. No one here thinks that."

Pleading, Kearson whispers, "The only reason I wanted to play well this week was so that Phoebe would know I was ready to step in if she needed me. That if she needed to take a break, she could trust me not to screw up like I did last time. But I feel like my being here at all is making everything worse for her." Her eyes fill with tears. "And you want to know the saddest thing? I'm actually *terrified* of playing tomorrow. I mean, what if I cause us to lose again?"

"Unless Phoebe undergoes an emergency leg amputation between now and our scrimmage, I'm guessing she'll be on the field tomorrow, ready for action."

Finally Kearson laughs. It's small but seemingly enough to pull her back from the brink. She lets out a breath. "I really hope you're right."

"But even if I'm not . . . you are a great player, Kearson! Plenty of girls wanted your spot. But Coach picked *you* for a reason."

Grace leans back and holds up her menu. But the type is sadistically small and the laminated plastic coating reflects the overhead lights straight into her eyes. It's too late at night to try to parse through the different combination plates, so she puts down the menu.

Kearson now has her head down, her face replaced by a stripe of luminous scalp running between her braids. Her tears hit the table one sad plop after another.

"Kearson!" Grace quickly takes a paper napkin from the dispenser and wipes up the tears, then lays a second napkin out to catch the rest as they fall. "Did I say the wrong thing?"

"You're right," Kearson concedes, "but you don't know the reason, Grace." The muscles in her jaw tighten as she works up the courage to make a few more words. "Coach didn't have a choice. He had to let me on the team."

Grace wrinkles her nose. Before she can ask Kearson to explain, Ali and two other junior girls claim the remaining open seats at their table. As they do, Kearson grabs Grace's menu and uses it to shield her face.

Mel hovers near their table, her phone pressed to her ear. Grace is so close to her she can hear everything, one ring and the beginning of Phoebe's voice mail.

"Does anyone know what time it is?" It doesn't occur to Mel to look at her own phone.

"Ten minutes to four," Luci answers. Her eyes stay on her watch as she quietly says, "Maybe we should think about calling it quits for tonight."

"No," Mel says, pacing between the tables. "Obviously this night's taken something of a turn. I can't get in touch with Phoebe, and we should have been asleep hours ago, but we *have* to finish the fight song for Coach. We cannot quit on this when we've only got one more stanza to do."

Ali yawns and stretches. "I'm so tired I can't even remember it."

"'Three cheers for the Wildcats, your honor we'll defend,'" Mel sings, pausing to yawn herself. "''Cause when you're a Wildcat, you're a Wildcat till the end.'"

A bell from the kitchen. Grace didn't realize how hungry she actually was until she smelled food cooking. She isn't the only one. Everyone turns their heads.

The waitress arrives, looking tired and not exactly happy that her quiet section is suddenly full. "So long as you girls aren't planning to make me split the check twenty ways, I'm ready to take your order."

"One check is fine, thank you," Mel says.

The waitress scratches the back of her head with her pencil. "Is this some sorority hazing thing?"

Mel smiles thinly as she slides into her seat. "No. We're teammates."

"Let me guess. You're the mascot?"

It takes a second or two before Grace realizes the waitress is talking to her.

"I'm kidding. I admire your bravery, sweetie." Using her pencil to draw an invisible circle around Grace's head. "Not every girl has the guts to walk around with blue hair in public."

Grace ignores her. "Can I have an order of—"

"You know what's funny?" Ali twists in her seat and stares the waitress down. "I was thinking the same thing about your root situation. Talk about brave! The contrast between your grays and that ashy brown . . . it's the kind of look that says, without apology, 'World, I give up.'" The waitress sneers, and Ali leans tenderly against Grace. "Split a chocolate chip waffle with me?"

After their orders are taken, Grace slides out of the booth and walks to the bathroom to wash her hands. She focuses on the anemic squirt of foam, crackling in the cup of her palm, focuses on triggering the motion sensor to pony up another, but then gives up and focuses on conjuring a lather from what she's already got. The soap smells suspiciously like nothing. Grace focuses on the sink; the sensor on the faucet is too sensitive, the blasts of water annoyingly brief. She focuses on the dye underneath her fingernails.

Grace generally avoids looking at herself immediately after interactions like the one with the waitress. From experience, she knows that whatever insult was lobbed will inevitably get reflected back at Grace like a fun-house mirror, warped and distorted.

That said, her preference—and yes, she knows how tragic that makes her sound—is actually this sort of disparagement, what Grace thinks of as Hot Takes from Passing Strangers. A clean, quick, straightforward punch in the ego, always a version of, *Hey, no offense, but you're fucking weird.*

What Grace has always found much harder to shrug off were the slights she endured from her JV teammates. Cold shoulders, eye rolls, thinly veiled revulsion, or being rendered invisible. These behaviors rarely manifested into an insult, something Grace could process, or perhaps even proactively address. Like those superpainful chin zits that last forever and never come to a head, leaving you no way to squeeze out what's festering. Instead, you're forced to simply reabsorb your perceived grossness.

She has felt none of that tonight from her new teammates. No edge on Grace that they wish she'd sand down. Surely walking in with her bright blue hair tonight threw at least a few of them for a loop. But her teammates took it in stride and their reactions were overwhelmingly positive. Even if it wasn't necessarily their style, they respected it was hers.

Coach was the only one who hadn't directly commented on it, one way or the other. Yes, there was that one time Grace maybe caught him staring at her during his speech, but she was still operating on the assumption that, if Coach truly hated her hair, he would have said something to her. He's not the kind of guy who holds back. Quite the opposite, in fact. The only girls who escaped Coach's wrath this week were the girls who didn't make the team. They weren't spared so much as ignored.

But now, rewinding the evening, Grace can't think of a single interaction she had with Coach tonight, good or bad. If anything, he regarded her as if she'd wandered into the wrong party.

And perhaps, in his mind, she had.

After all, the JV girls had known for years that Grace was different. But Grace doubted she was on Coach's radar. Before tonight, he wouldn't have seen her with crazy colored hair. And only once—in the moments just after the championship loss—was she in his orbit dressed in anything other than workout clothes.

She's always held on to the belief that, so long as she played well enough, Coach would make a spot for her on the Wildcats. But Grace never exactly tested that theory either. Not until tonight.

Grace finds Mel standing outside the bathroom, one shoulder leaning against the opposite wall, looking down at her phone. Her lips, pursed and pouty, seem oddly pale, until Grace realizes that it's because the pink gloss she always wears has worn off. Even though she is hunched over in exhaustion, her hair wrapped in a messy bun at the top of her head, Mel still shines with a radiant beauty that appears effortless but is actually impossible for normal people to pull off.

Even if Grace put on the very same clothes—the white tank and denim cutoffs and varsity jacket—and you stood the two of them side by side, it would be like comparing a leopard with a trout.

"Sorry, I didn't know anyone was waiting."

"I'm not waiting. I'm just . . . I don't know." She holds up her phone gamely. "Hoping Phoebe will text me back."

"Are you worried?"

She shakes her head. "She's had a hard time these past few months, and a lot of it she's had to deal with on her own. But no. I'm not worried." As if she needed to prove it to herself, Mel takes one last look at her phone before putting it away. "How are you holding up?"

"Fine."

"I hope that stupid waitress didn't upset you." Grace shakes her head, which makes Mel smile tenderly. "Good. I want you to know that I'm a very generous tipper, especially when I am using other people's credit cards, but I won't give her a penny more than fifteen percent." She laughs, glancing over her shoulder on her tiptoes. "I can't believe Ali burned her like that! You know, this is the first season Ali's taken a younger player under her wing. She clearly sees something special in you. We all do."

Mel's compliment is almost enough for Grace to swallow down the question rising up in her throat. Almost.

"Can I ask you something about Coach? Did he say anything to you about my hair tonight?"

Suddenly Mel stands up straight. "Umm, why do you ask?"

"I just want to make sure I didn't screw up somehow. I checked the team binder, but I didn't see any rule about hair dye in there. Unless I missed something. . . ."

"You didn't miss anything, Grace." Mel grimaces. "I just think it's never come up before. We've never had a girl like you on our team." She's quick to add, "And that's a *great* thing, if you ask me."

"If Coach hates it, you can tell me. I'd rather know."

Mel looks somewhat relieved, though not entirely unburdened, by Grace's earnestness. "I'm sorry, Grace. I thought it was such a cool thing to do. But Coach is . . . not exactly a fan."

Grace takes a deep breath. "I'll dye it back tomorrow." Mel gives her a thin smile. "Unless you think I should tonight?"

"I don't want you to feel pressured to do that." Mel bites on her knuckle, clearly uncomfortable being the messenger here. "It's just that I honestly don't know how Coach is going to react when we show up for our team meeting tomorrow." Mel reaches out and rubs Grace's upper arm.

Grace spares Mel from having to finish the thought. "It's really no big deal. When I was in the lower school, I changed my hair color every week."

If Grace had her choice, she'd have Chuck bleach it. But it's too late for that and would require too much to explanation. She'll have to cover the blue with something darker from the drug store.

Mel lunges forward and wraps Grace in a huge hug. "We love having you on our team, Grace. And I want you to have the best experience possible."

"Thanks for being honest with me. I know that wasn't easy."

"It was absolutely horrible."

Mel threads her fingers through Grace's and brings her back to the tables. As the girls pass the kitchen, Grace sees their waitress pointing her out to the cook.

Grace takes a deep breath and works it out in her head. The Walgreens just up the road is open twenty-four hours. She could walk over there now and grab the dye while the rest of her teammates finish eating. That way, she wouldn't take any time away from whatever the girls come up with for the last stanza.

The girls are practically melted with exhaustion. The food has been served but no one is eating.

Or, it occurs to her, maybe Grace's dye job could be the last stanza.

Mel sits down but Grace remains standing. She doesn't think it through so much as just start talking about what she's going to do and why. Everyone seems to be following her rationale enough to not put up much of a fight, especially once the girls realize that they can head back to Mel's and finally go to sleep.

The only holdout is Ali, who strangles her napkin. "I don't understand what any of this has to do with our fight song."

Grace makes a feeble attempt to link the two on the fly. "'Three cheers for the Wildcats, your honor we'll defend' . . . and I'm a defender!" Ali groans, but Grace stands her ground. "Does it really matter at this point?" And, instead of waiting for Ali's comeback, Grace motions to their waitress and says, "Check please."

Grace gives shotgun to Mel again on the ride from the Waffle House to the Walgreens. Ali stays silent on the ride, despite Mel's best attempts to make small talk, and when Ali does talk, her voice is clipped, answers short. But when Mel asks her, Ali hands over her credit card, which Mel then passes to Grace.

They will get through this together. What other choice do they have?

The girls don't bother to park, just leave the cars running in a line outside the store while Grace goes in by herself. The lights are way too bright.

Boxes of hair dye are spread in front of her. Smiling women looking their best. None looking like Grace.

What was the message Grace wanted to send with her blue hair tonight? That she wanted to belong? Or that she was different?

She can't remember. She's too tired. She picks Clairol in soft black.

Back at Mel's house, the girls sneak down to the basement and hope to find Phoebe waiting for them, but she's not there.

Mel gets Grace set up in the bathroom. "Do you need anything to do this?"

"Just a towel." Quickly, Grace adds, "Not a nice one."

"Do you want company? I'd be happy to sit with you."

"It's okay. You and the other girls get ready for bed."

"I know you said it's not a big deal to do this, but I just want to tell you that it's a big deal to me."

Grace mixes the dye and the developer. The room quickly fills with fumes of ammonia. She cracks a window.

Thirty minutes and it'll be over.

Somewhere outside, Grace hears Ali getting into it with Mel again. She pouts, "I don't get why her hair color is an issue at all."

Mel says, "Come on, Ali. What is and what isn't an issue is Coach's call. You know that."

Ali is insistent. "Grace did it for us, Mel."

"I know. And she's doing *this* for us too."

Grace's eyes fill up and she lowers herself down on the side of the tub.

While she's glad to have worked out a way that dyeing her hair can help them, Grace knows in her heart that what Mel just said is wrong.

Grace isn't doing this for her team. Because her team would never, ever ask her to.

SATURDAY, AUGUST 27
4:03 A.M.
PHOEBE

Phoebe's not at all tired, even though she should be. Then again, Phoebe never sleeps great the night before a game. It doesn't matter if they are playing a shitty team or one that could really give the Wildcats a run for their money. It's always impossible to get comfortable in her bed, even with two Tylenol PMs and the new feather mattress topper she'd gotten as her big Hanukkah present. She'd spend the night flipping over from back to belly, kicking off her sheets, refluffing her pillow. The stress of knowing you aren't sleeping when you need to be sleeping is its own particular kind of suck.

She'd think about the game all day too, which could be super unfortunate if she has a test or a project to present. This is one of the things Coach taught them. To visualize the game, how you are going to play it.

Right now Phoebe's strategy is not to hold anything back.

Why would she, with nothing to lose?

Up until now, Phoebe has held on to her decision to play in the championship game as her own. It made her feel powerful. Strong. Even though she'd needed that little push from Coach. That's why it was so hard for her to hear Mel talk the way she did tonight. Painting her like such an idiot for what she'd done. Reckless. Stupid.

How could Mel have it so twisted?

Phoebe wants every single one of her teammates to know it. She's got the proof right here in Coach's emails. That she was manipulated, played, lied to, her body sacrificed. And for what? So Coach could throw her under the bus and earn a good word for a new job he wanted?

Oh, she would fucking l o v e to call Coach out on what she's discovered tonight in a one-on-one tomorrow. Stroll into his classroom before all her teammates arrive and watch him squirm as she sets down his laptop, already open to the Trident email exchange. She'll play it totally cool, lay her cards out, tell him how it's going to go. She'll keep this "miscommunication" between the two of them, so long as Coach gets her recruited to play at a different college. Wait. Actually, fuck that. For all she's sacrificed, Phoebe wants to play at a D1 school and have her happy ending with Mel. It shouldn't be too hard to do, right? He has the contacts. He's made so much happen for other girls. Now he needs to make it happen for her. Or else.

It's kind of fucked-up but Phoebe totally would do it if not the fact that she reinjured her knee. The thought of enduring another ACL surgery, and then another grueling six months of rehab, is just too much for her to bear. Even if it went well, even if she worked just as hard as she had the first time, Phoebe would miss her entire varsity season. And even with Coach giving his network of scouts a full-court press, no college was going to offer her a spot on the roster after she blew out her ACL twice in a year.

There is no way out of this hell. It's only fair that Coach get trapped in hell with her.

She got a glimpse of what this hell looks like tonight. She noticed, when she was in Coach's classroom with Mel, how he's made it into a weird museum celebrating his glory days. His collegiate team pictures professionally framed. His national jersey in a glass shadow box. His sticks, medals. All reminders of his unfulfilled potential. The life he imagined he'd have looming like a shadow over the here and now.

Coach has always given off the vibe that he's too good for West Essex. He dresses like he is. He walks down the hall like he is. He teaches like he is, barely caring. What she interpreted as cockiness, Phoebe now sees is misery.

There've been so many times Phoebe has felt that same misery inside her. Pulling her down, making her unkind, ungenerous, competitive. She hates who she is becoming, and she sees her future in Coach. Her one hope for tonight is that by blowing him up, she'll detonate those terrible parts of herself, too.

Phoebe parks Mel's car in her driveway, rewraps her Ace bandage, and gathers her things. She digs her phone out of the pillowcase in Mel's trunk. There are a million text messages and missed calls from Mel. Her voice mail is full.

MEL: Phoebe are you okay?

MEL: Please let me know you're okay.

MEL: We will get through this together. I promise.

Phoebe shuts her phone off before she reads any more. She grabs Coach's laptop, slides it underneath her arm, and limps around to the back of the house, where she knows the sliding glass door will have been left open for her.

Mel's parents sleep like the dead. Memory foam, expensive sheets that stay cool and slip against your skin, tufted headboard, shades that block out all light, a sound machine emitting steady rolls of ocean waves. Not to mention their nightcaps, an Ativan for Mel's mother and a tumbler of Scotch with a tennis-ball-sized ice cube for her father. For these reasons, Phoebe feels no need to be quiet as she moves through the kitchen toward the basement stairs.

But hobbling down the steps, her breathing turns shallow. The other girls are deeper in, talking, laughing, getting ready for bed. She freezes like an intruder when she hears someone coming; the instinct to turn and run before she's discovered kicks up her pulse. Even if she could run, it's too late. She's caught.

"Phoebe!" It's Mel, now changed into her pj's. She rushes over, takes the handful of steps separating them in two long leaps. "Are you okay?"

"I ... don't know."

A flash of panic. "Where's Buddy?"

Phoebe says, "I took him back, let him loose in the front yard."

Mel exhales. "I knew it." She threads their hands together, tugging her down into the basement. "Everyone's going to be so relieved to see you."

"Wait." Phoebe pulls herself free. The wind that filled her sails just moments ago has gone still. She came in here intending to blow up Coach's spot in front of her entire team. But now she hesitates. "Can we talk for a second? Privately?"

"Phoebe ... I'm sorry about everything I said." Mel smothers Phoebe in a tight hug, as if Mel knows that if she lets go, there's a good chance Phoebe will slip away again. Phoebe hugs Mel back the best she can, one arm trying to do the job of two because she's also holding Coach's laptop.

Mel pulls away and sees it. Fear comes over her. Her eyes widen. She forces down a swallow. Her voice is thin, shaky. "Did you find something?"

It's hard for Phoebe to grab hold of how she got to this place. She'd wanted to prove that she was a good teammate. That she'd made the ultimate sacrifice. But she's suddenly not sure if what she's holding actually proves that.

Phoebe chose to play in the championship for two reasons, to help her team win, and so she and Mel would have their best shot at getting into Truman. One of those things happened. And before she read Coach's emails, it was enough for Phoebe to feel like it had been worth it. Learning that Coach fucked her over afterward with the Trident recruiter is what set her on the warpath.

Phoebe doesn't want Mel to feel guilty about her place at Truman. Doesn't want her to think this was, in any way, her fault.

But of course Mel will. Phoebe already sucker punched Mel with her own poorly kept secret. That Mel has a close relationship with Coach. What if she feels culpable in this somehow?

Phoebe has known for years that Mel and Coach text. It never bothered her. In fact, Phoebe felt cool knowing her best friend was the one with this special relationship. She knew it was nothing more than a harmless crush, Mel idolizing Coach.

Mel had been so sad when she feared Coach wasn't going to come back. Depressed. When she started hooking up with Gordy, Phoebe was happy that she'd finally moved on. But then Coach came back, and suddenly, Gordy was being dumped. Even though Phoebe knows Mel *likes* Gordy.

What Phoebe is about to tell Mel will shatter her.

Mel says it again. "Phoebe. Did you find something . . . ?"

Before Phoebe can answer, Luci stumbles on their hushed conversation.

"Phoebe!" Luci rushes over, hugs her, and runs back into the main part of the basement. Phoebe can hear the news of her arrival spread like wildfire.

It heartens her.

She loves these girls. If she could somehow be sure that revealing what Coach did to her wouldn't come back to hurt the rest of the team, she'd do it in a heartbeat. But she doesn't want to burn the house down, to take away everything from them just because she let herself get screwed.

So, to Mel she says, "No. Nothing. I was just freaking out, I guess." And she gives up the laptop, hands it over to Mel, who Phoebe knows would never look inside. "Maybe you can get this back into his classroom before Coach sees it's missing." She shakes her head. "No. Wait. I want you to hand it to him. Tell him that I took it."

That's better. Then Coach will know that Phoebe knows. He'll have to clean up his act. The threat that Phoebe could expose him as a lying, manipulative prick is a power she can wield to protect anyone else from getting screwed by Coach again. Suddenly she feels lighter. And now that the computer is out of her hands, she can hug Mel the right way.

"But he'll throw you off the team."

Phoebe releases her, limps into the basement, leaving Mel to find someplace to ditch the laptop. Mel calls out. "Phoebe! Hold on a second!"

The girls have gathered in the main room, happy to welcome

Phoebe back. But something wrenching must show in Phoebe's face, because their smiles take a huge collective dip.

Phoebe tries to remind herself that there was a time when she didn't even know what field hockey was. That there is surely something out there in the world that will fill this enormous black hole.

"Okay," she says, puffing a few breaths, cracking her neck, psyching herself up. "None of you are allowed to speak until I've said what I have to say. Otherwise I'm not going to be able to go through with this."

"You don't have to, Phoebe." Kearson stands up, and for once, her bobblehead stays steady. "I quit."

SATURDAY, AUGUST 27
4:16 A.M.
KEARSON

Kearson is in utter disbelief. Not over the act of quitting itself but because this is the first time since being called up to varsity that she was ahead of the play and not behind it.

Timing has been a huge issue for Kearson since last season. She's always getting caught flat-footed. Always the last to see what's coming. Not only on the field but in life too. She's been burned just as many times on breakaways as she has by people she thought she could trust. Her reflexes are set on a frustrating time delay, her intuition suffocated by her overthinking.

And yet, somehow Kearson knew what Phoebe was about to do before she did it, anticipated exactly what was coming before it came. It's a slight edge, gained perhaps because Kearson herself had been thinking about quitting the team since the girls hit up Waffle House; the words were already in her mouth. That Kearson would get to save Phoebe from having to speak them was all she needed to act.

Kearson lets out a sigh of deep relief. And then she steps over and wraps Phoebe in a big hug.

Phoebe is stiff with shock. "You can't quit. I was going to quit."

Kearson laughs, wipes her eyes. "I know." She's smiling. "Now you don't have to."

"Um, hello! Neither of you is quitting!" Mel says, throwing her hands up.

But Kearson is insistent. "Phoebe, I'm so sorry. I never wanted to make things harder for you. You should be focused on having a great senior season and getting a scholarship. I don't want my being here to mess with your head."

"Hold on, hold on. If anything, I'm the one who owes you an apology. I've been a really shitty teammate. Believe me, even when I was being a bitch to you, I hated myself for it. If you quit, I'll never forgive myself. And . . . look at me."

Mel nods. "Last season you were given a spot on this team. This season, you earned it. You deserve to be here."

"Plus, do I look like I'm in any shape to play tomorrow? Our team is going to need you!"

Kearson looks out at the rest of the girls. "I've caused so much trouble for this team. More than you girls even know."

Phoebe eyes her. "What do you mean?"

Kearson feels her chin quiver. She lowers her head. "My mom called the athletic director and made a complaint about Coach at the end of the season. She tried to get him fired."

Blurred in her periphery, the entire team exchanges uneasy looks. She wouldn't blame them if they asked her to pack up her stuff and leave right now. She'd have to call her mother to be picked up.

No. She'll just find someplace to go until morning. Maybe a park or something.

The girls begin to speak.

"Honestly? I'm surprised no one has complained before with the way he acts sometimes."

"I used to think it was funny. The looks other teams gave us when Coach would lose his shit."

"Oh my God, me too. I took this weird pride in it. Like it made us tougher than them."

"This is my third year and I still get freaked out by how upset he gets."

Kearson allows herself a small smile of relief. Someone puts a hand on Kearson's shoulder. Mel.

"I get why you feel bad, but you really shouldn't, Kearson. The girls are right. Everyone knows that's Coach's thing. Which is why I doubt Coach's job was ever really in jeopardy," Mel says, her voice getting warmer, brighter. "Plus we all know not to take it personally. It's his way to motivate. I'm not saying it's the best way, but it's his way, and it has worked. We work harder than other teams because he pushes harder." She sighs. "That's something I think is tough for people to understand. From the outside looking in, it seems cruel. From inside we understand what Coach is trying to do."

Kearson bites her lip. "It wasn't just Coach's yelling. My mom was upset about something else." She sinks down on the floor.

The brightness on Mel's face dims. "Oh. Okay."

Ali hugs a pillow to her chest. "Do you want to talk about it, Kearson? You don't have to. But . . . it might help."

Kearson takes a deep breath. She doesn't have to tell them, but the crazy thing is that she wants to. She knows the girls won't spin her story into something bigger than it is . . . like her mother did. Nor will Kearson have to tell a watered-down version of events to not trigger any alarm bells . . . like she had to with the athletic director. And she won't have to worry about anyone taking secret gleeful delight in the painful details . . . like with Marissa or Quinn.

She's ready to share her truth. Kearson is in a safe place.

It happened during the last game of the regular season, immediately after Kearson's near collision with Mel. The ref blew his whistle, recognizing Coach's call for the Wildcats' last available time-out.

Having almost injured Mel, Kearson was sick with shame. Not only was she unable to replace one injured star player, she nearly knocked their other star out. She was surely about to get eviscerated by Coach, probably the worst he'd ever given it to her. And with her mother there, watching.

Coach screamed for Kearson to come over for a sideline conference. She adopted the posture she'd found worked best for her—eyes on the ground, imagining the laces of her cleats were a ladder she could climb up to get herself out of here. But unlike other times, she went into a sort of fugue state. Like her body was shutting down. Her mind shutting down. Because she couldn't take it anymore.

"I guess I didn't hear something Coach said to me," Kearson tells the girls. "Probably when he was telling me to get off the field."

Out of frustration, Coach spiked his half-empty water bottle as hard as he could on the ground. He'd thrown it with so much force, it popped straight back up, end-over-end inertia. Kearson didn't see it until it hit her square in the face. It came fast. An ice-cold fist. There was no time to protect herself.

The bottle then landed at her feet, water seeping out from a crack in the plastic onto the turf.

Kearson held still. No matter that her cheekbone took the

brunt of it, the wind had been knocked out of her like a blow to the chest. With a shaky hand, she gently touched the epicenter of the sting on her cheek and then looked at her fingers, expecting to see blood . But there was none.

"When I looked up, I could tell Coach was as surprised as I was. Because it really *was* an accident. I know in my heart. He hadn't meant for the bottle to hit me in the face. It was an unlucky bounce."

Everyone is silent. Kearson can feel it, the elephant suddenly in the room. She knows what the girls are hoping she'll say next. That—intentional or not—Coach immediately apologized for what happened.

"So . . . we just stared at each other like that for a few seconds. And then I walked over to the bench, like he'd told me." Kearson shrugs. "That was the last time I was on the field as a varsity Wildcat."

There is a part Kearson leaves out of the story. It is too humiliating to share. But she actually picked up the water bottle and handed it back to Coach before sitting down on the bench.

"My mom and I had a big fight about it. I kept telling her over and over again that I'd gotten the bruise during warm-ups. But after the season ended, she called the athletic director and told him what she suspected had happened. She never even told me she was doing it. I had no clue why I was suddenly getting called down into a meeting with the AD and Coach. Luckily I was able to smooth things over. I made her seem like some crazy helicopter mom. And I've barely spoken to her since."

Ali says, "Kearson . . . maybe she waited until the end of the season because she wasn't sure what she should do. And because she knew you still wanted to play."

Kearson says, "She absolutely knew that. But my mom should have trusted me."

Phoebe lowers herself onto the floor next to her. "But you *were* lying, Kearson. And she probably could tell."

Luci says, "Maybe your mom never wanted you to know. She could have been hoping to have the incident documented or to just give the AD a heads-up or something."

Kearson feels the squeeze of guilt come back and wring a concession out of her. "Maybe," she says. Then, "Probably." She forces a swallow. "But it doesn't change the fact that I need to quit the team."

Mel, the only one who's still standing, folds her arms. "Nope. Request denied. I'm team captain and no one is quitting tonight. Not you and not Phoebe."

"But what if my mom makes another complaint? I was able to talk Coach out of trouble once, but I don't know if they'd believe me again." The girls plead with her, but Kearson is resolved. "I've had the best night with you all. I love this team, but not enough to stay. Not when I'm a liability."

Ali tosses her pillow aside, crawls toward Kearson on hands and knees, and hugs her. Ali pulls back, looks Kearson deep in the eyes, and says, "I know exactly how that feels. I'm a liability too."

SATURDAY, AUGUST 27
4:27 A.M.
ALI

Ali lets go of Kearson and picks up her pillow again, hugging it the way a kid who's afraid of the boogeyman hugs his teddy bear in the dark.

What is she scared of?

It's not seeing Darlene Maguire tomorrow. Ali's known this day would come.

It's not what Darlene Maguire will do. Of course she'll pull the same stunt again, seeing how well it worked last season. Tomorrow she, or someone else on Oak Knolls, will most certainly pull her eyes into slits. Maybe call Ali a Chink, too. Throw in some Ching Chong Chinaman, because who cares if Ali is Korean? Gooks all look the same. Maybe bust out a karate move, a high-pitched *hieeeeeeeeeee yah*, a jump kick, the crane.

Ali's not even afraid that her teammates won't be sympathetic. She knows they will.

So she finally spills her guts. Tells them exactly what happened after that first goal during the championship game, Darlene's charming little "bet you didn't see that one coming" setup for the eye slits.

It certainly wasn't the first time someone had said or done racist stuff to her. She's gotten plenty of little comments like "You speak perfect English!" Or, the opposite, when people come up to her and start speaking in whatever Asian dialect they know, expecting Ali to understand it. And that's just the normal, everyday stuff. There'd been plenty of bigger, more agressive moments too. But it always threw Ali when a person her age did it.

The girls on her team look ashamed that they had no idea this sort of thing happened. They must be shocked that a girl like Darlene Maguire, who seems like the kind of girl they are, could ever do such a disgusting thing. Embarrassed, maybe, that they never thought of all this before, what it might be like for Ali. And so deeply sorry, because Ali is clearly hurting, has been hurting for months.

And finally, after peeling back all the layers, Ali sees the thing she's afraid of.

She tilts her head back, pulls her long hair over her shoulder, takes a deep breath. But it catches, that shuddering that happens right before you start to cry.

"My whole family is away this weekend at my nephew's first birthday party, which is a big Korean thing. My brother's wife's family is flying in from Seoul. I wanted to go so badly. But I didn't even ask. I didn't want to have to explain it to Coach, and also, I thought it was better that my parents won't be there tomorrow." Ali begins to lose it, tears spilling out. "Even though the same thing has happened to my mom and dad too. Multiple times. And to both of my brothers. And will happen to baby John-John, and that breaks my heart. It's just a part of life that I know I need to get used to. But I don't think I ever will."

Luci has her eyes narrowed, fierce with determination. "Coach needs to know about this before tomorrow's game. If you feel weird going to talk to him alone, Ali, I'll come with you. I will stand next to you."

Ali feels a surge of love for her. "Thank you for offering that. But Coach already knows. I told him right after it happened the first time."

Luci flinches. "Wait, what?"

Ali had immediately signaled for time from the ref. Something she'd never done before. None of the girls called for time-outs. That was Coach's decision.

She looked across the field to their sideline and Coach speeding at her, a practically lethal look on his face. She immediately regretted what she'd done. But it was too late to take it back.

"Why the fuck are you using a time-out?"

Ali pulled her mask off her face and wiped away the tears. "That girl, she . . ." It felt so disgusting to say.

Coach snarled, "She just scored on you!"

"That girl . . . she just made Asian eyes at me."

Coach seemed taken aback. "Are you sure? Maybe she was . . . I don't know, wiping her eyes or something."

"I'm positive. There's no question what she did." Ali said it loud, hoping that the girl, the girl she didn't yet know was Darlene Maguire, would hear Ali tell on her. Ali wanted her to be thrown out of the game. Maybe suspended. Maybe banned from ever playing field hockey again.

Coach groaned. "Ali, some players just talk trash. It's part of the game. Any game."

"It was more than talking trash. It was racist."

"Either way. She was trying to get under your skin and you let her. Look at you right now. You've lost all focus." He gave her a tap on the helmet. Not light. Kind of hard actually. A wake-up call. A slap to the back of the head. "This is the state championship, Ali."

"Well . . . can you go say something to her coach?" Ali glanced over at the Oak Knolls bench. And then back at Coach, who was shaking his head at her like she was a tattling child. "I don't want her doing it again."

He stared at her hard, unbelieving, disappointed that they were still discussing this. "If I do that, you'll only be made a bigger target. This is a *you* problem."

The ref came over, the whistle held between his clenched teeth. "Everything okay?" His eyes went to Ali. "You okay?"

"I'm going to sub you out," Coach said, and spun on his heel.

"No." Ali reached out, grabbed his arm. "I'm . . . I've got this."

And now, to the girls, Ali concedes with deep regret, "Except I didn't. I'm sorry."

"Darlene Maguire is the one who's going to be sorry." Mel presses her lips together and lifts her chin. "Ali, I know I speak for the entire team when I promise we will do everything in our power to make sure this never happens to you on our field again."

The girls nod in agreement. All except for one. Luci. She's deep in thought, a fist pressed to her lips.

"It's okay. I'm over it," Ali tells her. With a sly grin, she adds, "Mostly," because she knows Luci gets it.

Luci doesn't acknowledge Ali's jokey caveat. "I can't believe Coach would say something like that to you. That it's a *you problem*." She shakes her head in disbelief. "I mean, is it any wonder you froze up for Darlene's second shot? How could you ever get your focus back after that?"

Mel puts a hand on Luci's back. "I'm sure Coach didn't understand what was happening at the time."

"Really?" Luci twists to face Mel. "Because it seems pretty clear-cut. And even if he didn't, Coach should have had Ali's back regardless." To the rest of the girls, she pleads, "I mean . . . isn't that what he's always preaching to us? Team first, always?"

Mel struggles to answer Luci's charge for a few painfully awkward seconds.

Ali, on the other hand, doesn't even try. Instead, she lets herself get swept away, imagining an entirely different version of the Darlene Maguire incident. If Coach had shown Ali more support in those moments, would that second goal have gotten past her?

Hell no.

Though it might not have made a difference in how the championship game ultimately shook out, it would have made all the difference to Ali.

"Hold up," Phoebe says, scanning around the room. "Where's Grace?"

"Oh my God." Ali jumps up. She never should have let Grace do this. Never ever ever. She rushes to the bathroom, pounds on the door. "Grace, it's Ali. Let me in, okay?"

Phoebe and Mel arrive next to her.

"What's happening?" Phoebe whispers.

Ali says, "She's dyeing her hair."

Phoebe jerks her head back. "Now? At four in the morning? Why?"

Ali is livid. She knew it was wrong at the time; she should have been more forceful. She will not make the same mistake now. She turns to face Mel as she answers Phoebe's question. "Mel told her that Coach didn't like it."

"Oh my God, Mel. You didn't," Phoebe says.

"Grace asked me. And I didn't want to lie. But I didn't tell her to dye it!"

"But you didn't tell her not to either," Ali snaps. "All you care about is finishing the thing for Coach tonight. I bet you probably led Grace into feeling like she needed to."

Mel is incredulous. She puts her hand up to her mouth. "How could you think I'd do that?"

"Because you'd do anything Coach asked." Ali's hands go to her hips. She knows the team is watching. But she doesn't care. She's so upset for Grace. For Kearson. For herself. So upset at everything. So tired. She's never once had a fight with one of the girls. But she can't stop herself, even seeing the flush drain from Mel's cheeks. "Always so quick to defend him. Always happy to shine a positive light on him."

Grace's voice, small, comes from behind the bathroom door. "Please don't fight. Ali, it was my decision. Mel didn't pressure me at all. And I was the one who asked her, basically forced her, to tell me what Coach thought about my hair, because I already knew it."

Ali's mouth snaps shut shamefully. "Mel. I'm sorry."

Mel shakes her head, as if to say *forget it*, and fiddles with her necklace. Ali can tell Mel is upset. She tries to reach for Mel's hand, but Mel slips away before Ali can grab it. Ali turns to Phoebe, ready to offer another apology to her in Mel's stead. Phoebe scratches her cheek and turns her attention back to the bathroom door.

"Grace. Please. Just come out."

The door creaks open. Grace walks out with her head down, her hair still blue. "I couldn't do it. I'm sorry. You know I would do anything for this team. I'd do anything you asked me. But this wasn't about you. The only one who cares what my hair looks like tomorrow is Coach. And if he doesn't give me a varsity jersey because of it, I'm okay with that."

Ali wraps her arms around Grace, kisses her square on the forehead with a smack.

The basement lights flash on and off and on and off and on and off.

Mel is standing at the switch.

SATURDAY, AUGUST 27
4:40 A.M.
MEL

Okay, girls! That's it! Time for bed!" A few of them murmur to each other, so Mel flicks the lights a couple more times like she's their annoying mother. "Let's go! Let's go!"

Phoebe hobbles down the hallway toward Mel as quickly as she can. In the flashing lights, skipping forward in choppy segments, her limp looks even more pronounced. "What are you doing?" Mel doesn't answer, just keeps flashing the lights until Phoebe squeezes her body between Mel and the switch. Careful to keep her voice down, Phoebe pleads, "You can't shut the conversation down, Mel."

"We need to sleep, Phoebe."

"The girls are being really brave right now. If someone has something to say, then they deserve the chance to say it."

"I'm not saying we *can't* talk about this. I'm only saying there's a better time to have these kinds of very emotional conversations. And not when we've been awake for almost twenty-four hours!"

Mel tilts her head back and sighs. "You saw how Ali came at me just now!"

Even though Ali immediately apologized, the sting of her words lingers inside Mel, an uncomfortable vibration, an itch impossible to scratch. Worse, though, is that Ali said those terrible things about her in front of the team. Thankfully, Grace came to Mel's defense, set the record straight. But still. She's mortified to have been accused of betraying her team. These girls are everything to her.

Phoebe lifts her hands. "Fine. It's late, the girls are upset, and we definitely don't want to start fighting with one another. But at the very least you should call a team meeting so we can figure out what to do about tomorrow."

Mel steps away from Phoebe and peers down the hall and into the main part of the finished basement. Though she ordered the girls to go to bed, none of them have listened. Instead, they sit clustered together, as many as could be crammed on the couch and the rest cross-legged on the floor. Girls are chewing on their fingers, biting down on their lips, rubbing their eyes with their hands. And very clearly trying to eavesdrop on Mel's discussion with Phoebe.

Mel stands up straight and ticks her volume up. "There's nothing to figure out. We're going to show up at Coach's classroom exactly like he asked us to, at nine o'clock sharp. He's going to give us our varsity jerseys and we're going to play field hockey."

With a huff, Phoebe takes Mel's hand, laces their fingers together, and tugs Mel deeper into the hallway, to allow them more privacy. "Do you honestly think Ali wants to play tomorrow after how Coach handled what happened?"

Mel doesn't even need to think about it. "Yes. I do. She's

our goalie. And like I said before, Coach didn't necessarily understand—"

"What about Kearson? Coach hit her in the face with a water bottle, Mel."

"That was an accident. Kearson said so herself."

Phoebe runs both hands through her hair. "What if Coach doesn't give a varsity jersey to Grace because of her hair? Are you going to be okay with that, Mel?"

Mel puts her hands on her hips. "We both know that's not going to happen. Grace is too good of a player. He might hate her blue hair, but not as much as he hates losing."

Phoebe lifts her chin. "You mean like Becks?"

This again? "I don't remember that the way you do, Phoebe. I'm not saying you're wrong, but—"

"But you'll do whatever mental gymnastics it takes to defend Coach."

Mel rolls her eyes at Phoebe's sarcasm, but inside, her heart is racing. It's exactly like she told Phoebe: it's too late for these kinds of heated conversations. Nothing good is going to come from this. Only terrible things. Mel is certain of it.

"Look. It might be hard to see it right now, but I really do think tonight was a success. Coach led us to this moment. He was spot-on when he told us we had cracks we were hiding from each other. But none of us are hiding anymore. And guess what? We are stronger for it."

Phoebe blinks. "You're forgetting that Coach caused the cracks."

"That's not fair, Phoebe." Not to mention completely unhelpful.

"Please don't talk to me about fair." Phoebe gingerly lowers herself onto the basement stairs and stretches out her injured leg. It's clear she's in a lot of pain.

"Let me get you some ice." Because Phoebe needs it and also because it's an escape hatch from this conversation.

"Ice isn't going to help. I tore my ACL again, Mel. I'm out for the season. Maybe for good. I mean, it's not like I'm getting a scholarship now. I'm totally and completely fucked."

Suddenly light-headed, Mel reaches for the banister to steady herself. This can't be happening. "You don't know that for sure, Phoebs. Don't make any decisions tonight that you might regret tomorrow."

Phoebe smirks. "You're about to regret saying that to me."

"Why?"

"You know what I decided tonight? To take one for the team. I came back here to tell the girls that I quit and hand you Coach's laptop. I was fully prepared to give myself amnesia about what I found on it because I thought I was the only one Coach had screwed over. But it's clear that's not the case. Not even close."

Goose bumps prick on Mel's arms. The stairway, suddenly too dark and narrow, the door to the kitchen a million steps away.

Phoebe says, "Aren't you going to ask me what I found?"

She wants to say no. She knows she should say yes. But seeing as either answer would drag Mel more deeply into this terrible night, she says nothing.

"I had a conversation with Coach tonight. I told him that I had reached out to a scout from Trident to see if they might still be interested in me, and I was kind of freaking out that he never wrote me back. Coach told me to forget them. Put them out of my mind. I was too good for Trident."

"That sounds like a pep talk to me. You are too good for Trident!"

"Except what Coach conveniently left out of our conversation was that he'd already told the Trident scout to pass on me. He told them not to even bother coming to see me play."

"Okay. Well." Mel holds up her palms. "I'm sure Coach had a reason for that. He must have another plan for you." A plan which Mel hopes Phoebe hasn't completely screwed up for herself.

Phoebe points her finger at Mel. "Then why did he write such terrible things about me? Making it out like I tricked him into letting me play in the championship."

"I don't know, Phoebe. But . . . I mean . . . isn't that kind of what happened?"

Mel is careful to say this differently than she had earlier, when they were fighting in Coach's classroom. Softer. Gentler. Way less accusatory. Zero percent confrontational. She's trading on the fact that they are best friends, and therefore know and accept the best and worst of each other. But the change in Mel's delivery makes no difference to Phoebe. If anything, it slices into Phoebe even more deeply now, because of how Mel's already scored her.

"No, Mel. That's not what happened." Her chin quivers. "I planned on never telling you this. But Coach told me that Truman was sending a scout to the championship game. He said he'd been trying all season to get them to see us, but that they'd been focused on recruiting defenders." She pulls her hands inside her sleeves and wipes her tears. "And before you say Coach doesn't tell us about scouts, trust me, this time he did."

With Phoebe's lead-in, Mel had been bracing for a truly horrible revelation. But this? This makes zero sense.

"Phoebe. What are you talking about?"

"You don't believe me. Amazing."

"I just . . . don't understand." Why would Coach have told

Phoebe that? The Truman scout had come to see them weeks before. She knew it because he'd broken his scouts rule for her. Not to be a jerk about it, but that's another part that doesn't add up for Mel. If Coach were going to break his rule about scouts, and that scout happened to be from Truman, he'd tell Mel. Not Phoebe.

"Do you think I invented the conversation?" Phoebe leans back. "Have you forgotten how he yanked the rug out from under you tonight when he switched out the varsity jerseys?"

Even though she still can't quite wrap her head around the things Phoebe is saying, Mel answers, resolute, "He did that to help me."

"You didn't need his help! Your Psych-Up was amazing. The best we've ever had. The piñata was perfect. The girls were all having an amazing night until he butted in uninvited. He took tonight away from you for no good reason, Mel." Her breath catches. "Or a reason that we haven't figured out yet."

"You sound crazy, you know that? Like, where are you coming up with this stuff?"

Phoebe stares at Mel so hard it makes her shiver. "Every single one of us can see what's happening here except you." Phoebe glances around and spots Coach's laptop where Mel had set it down, on a wicker basket filled with old magazines. She picks it up and places it in Mel's lap.

"Here. Read the email he sent about me to Trident. Then tell me I'm crazy. Actually, come to think of it, don't stop there. I bet you'll find a lot of illuminating emails in there. Maybe even some about you."

"I'm not going through Coach's laptop. I'm not going to be part of this." Mel tries to hand it back, but Phoebe refuses to take it. "You want me to have some horrible story about him, but I'm sorry! I don't!"

Phoebe seems torn between anger and sadness and is trying to choose her words carefully. At last she says, "I think you're already living inside a horrible story, Mel. You just can't see it."

With that, Phoebe walks away from her and returns to the team.

Though she is entirely off-kilter, Mel stands up and begins to follow, intending to first give the laptop back to Phoebe without another word, then to shut off the lights and order her team to bed once and for all. But Mel only makes it a few steps, halted by the idea of herself a few minutes from now, the basement lights off but every one of the girls staring at her through the dark.

So instead Mel turns and hurries up the basement stairs, through the kitchen, down the hall, and up to the second floor. She closes her bedroom door and locks it. She is panting as if she were being chased, but no one is following her.

Coach's laptop is in her arms. It's heavy, too-large, ancient technology that's labeled PROPERTY OF WEST ESSEX HIGH in marker, not like the new light-as-a-feather MacBook Air Mel got last Christmas. With framed photographs of her teammates smiling down at her, she sets it on her vanity, this dangerous thing, and backs away from it until she hits her bed.

Through the central air vents, Mel hears the girls talking in urgent whispers.

She climbs underneath the covers and closes her eyes, hoping she's so exhausted that sleep will overpower her mind, which spins wildly, a too-fast ride. To try to steady herself, Mel plucks from the swirl her very best memory of Coach. When Mel knows for certain she was her happiest.

* * *

Mel's official offer to attend Truman on a full-ride scholarship came by way of a FedEx envelope on the last day of July. It was ten o'clock on a Saturday morning. Her father had just returned from racquetball with a bag of warm bagels.

Mel and her mother were sitting at the kitchen island looking at their phones. He set the envelope down in front of her without a word. Mel shifted her eyes off the screen and TRUMAN UNIVERSITY ADMISSIONS DEPARTMENT came into focus.

Her parents were overjoyed.

Mel felt a different emotion, something closer to bewildered surprise. She'd been stumbling through the wreckage of her imploded life this summer, trying her best not to glance down at the broken pieces. But here was a dream that had survived intact, a relic from a future Mel assumed she would never get to live.

Her father disappeared to the basement and returned with a bottle of champagne, opaque black with a gold foil label. Mel had drunk this kind only once before, a single golden glass poured for her on her sixteenth birthday. She knew it was very expensive, so she forced herself to swallow every last drop, though she was disappointed it didn't taste sweeter. Thankfully, this celebration was closer to brunch, so once the crest of bubbles subsided, her mother topped the champagne off with a float of orange juice. One sip and Mel's eyes bulged hearts.

They'd go to Park & Orchard for dinner, of course. It was where the Gingriches celebrated every milestone. An elegant, dimly lit restaurant with oversize windows, black tables that were so shiny with lacquer they looked wet, flickering tea-light candles, and enormous glass vases of lush greenery, willow branches, and mandarin oranges in the white-tiled foyer. Park & Orchard was always included on "best of" lists. Though West Essex was forty miles outside the city, they all said it was worth a trek to the suburbs. Mel loved their cheesy scalloped potatoes, served crusted and bubbling in a white ramekin. Oh, and their homemade steak sauce, thick as molasses. She always ordered a Shirley Temple, extra cherries.

Her father called for a reservation, asked for his favorite table to be held for them, the one in the back left corner that overlooked the whole room, and bragged about Mel's full-ride scholarship to the girl who answered the phone. It made her warm, how proud he was of her, grinning ear to ear. Her mother gently pushed away some of the hair around Mel's temples and kissed her tenderly.

This felt like the beginning of a long, loving goodbye.

She was the luckiest girl.

Her father said, "Why don't you invite Phoebe? Tell her we're ordering every dessert on the menu." A joke, from one of the first times Phoebe came with them to dinner.

"She's out of town," Mel lied, still working over in her head how best to break her Truman news. Obviously Phoebe would be happy for her. But it felt weird, maybe even a little gross, to be so showy, especially when she knew Phoebe was still going to PT several times a week. She would tell Phoebe some other time. Maybe closer to school, when they'd hear who would take over from Coach. She could deliver the news to her teammates all at once.

Mel thought about asking Gordy. Her parents had been bugging her to meet her mystery man. But before she had a chance to ask, her mother said, "What about inviting Coach?"

Right. Mel would need to tell Coach.

After her texting freak-out during Truman tryouts, Mel

refused to let herself even think about reaching out to Coach for the rest of the summer. It was too easy to imagine him rolling his blue eyes and tossing his phone aside seeing her name pop up.

"Mom. I doubt Coach wants to go out to dinner with us. He's not even my coach anymore."

"Did you hear for certain that he's leaving West Essex?"

"No. Not officially."

"Well . . . your success is still his success!"

It was. Absolutely.

Mel's father had already whipped out his phone. Mel took a quiet sip from her champagne flute. It was like when your friends approached a cute older guy, and you hung back in their wake, trying to play it cool. It was a relief to have someone else, even if it was her father, absorb the brunt of the embarrassment.

Her father left a voice mail. "Hey, Coach, it's Rick Gingrich. Our sweet baby Mel got some fantastic news today about Truman. The best news possible. And we couldn't be prouder of her." To Mel's horror, her father began to tear up, his voice cracking. "We're planning to celebrate tonight at Park and Orchard and I know she'd love nothing more if you would join us."

Cheeks hot as fire, Mel sprinted upstairs and texted Coach.

MEL: You don't have to say yes.

Though in her heart, a small part of her hoped he would. This was an accomplishment she knew he would respect.

She waited for Coach to text back.

And waited. And poured another mimosa.

With the initial shock having worn off, Mel dutifully went through the paperwork. There was the official Truman offer of intent, which she immediately signed, some financial disclosure paperwork that Mel set aside for her mother, medical forms, a copy of the Truman alumni magazine. And, last but not least, at the bottom of the FedEx envelope, Mel found a trifold map that looked like something you'd pick up at a trailhead. There was a Post-it stuck to the front.

> *There are loads of great hiking trails not far from campus, but truthfully, I hope what excites you most about coming to Truman is the chance to forge your own path. I can't wait to see how far you go.*
>
> –Karen

Mel pressed the map to her chest. That Coach Karen had thought to include this for her was the kindest and most considerate gesture. It also marked the first piece of Truman that belonged solely to Mel. She snapped a picture and sent it to Gordy, remembering that she'd referred to him as her boyfriend in that conversation with Coach Karen about hiking.

GORDY: WHAT?!?!?
GORDY: NO WAY!!!!

It was easy to match Gordy's excitement. By this point, Mel had a good buzz going.

MEL: My parents are taking me out to dinner tonight.
MEL: Would you maybe want to come with us?
GORDY: Absolutely.
MEL: It's a nice place so you'll have to dress up.
MEL: Your fanciest fleece.
GORDY: You think I don't own a suit?
MEL: Is it made of water-wicking fabric?
GORDY: 😂

GORDY: You'd better prepare yourself, college girl.

GORDY: Your boy cleans up real nice.

Mel was excited about dressing up for Gordy, too. She'd spent their summer dirty and sweaty. Bug spray instead of perfume. SPF instead of foundation. Sometimes Mel didn't even bother washing her hair. Gordy didn't care. She'd often catch him staring at her instead of the view.

She had just stepped out of the shower when her mother popped her head into her bedroom. "Coach can make it. He'll meet us at the restaurant."

"Wait. Seriously?"

A towel cinched around her, hair dripping on the carpet, Mel raced across her room and checked her phone. Coach still hadn't texted her back. But he had, apparently, returned her father's call.

She flopped down in front of her vanity. "I invited Gordy to come with us."

"That's fine, sweetie. The more the merrier."

Nope. Not in this case.

"It's okay. We'd have to change tables."

"Mel, your dad can handle sitting at a different table. Plus he and I want to meet Gordy."

"Another time."

She picked up her phone.

MEL: Hey. Sorry but my parents are being weird.

MEL: They kind of want this to be a family thing.

MEL: I should have asked them first before inviting you.

GORDY: No worries.

GORDY: Text me later.

GORDY: I'll come by in my suit.

GORDY: I just put it on and I'm looking 🔥

Mel typed, *k!*, then deleted it.

Even though she had every intention of seeing Gordy later—this was just a dinner and Coach was very likely taking a job someplace else—it still felt safer not to commit.

It was easier than she'd expected to redirect her enthusiasm for dressing up from Gordy to Coach. Mel and Coach hadn't seen each other all summer. She picked a forest-green wrap dress, her new school color. She curled her hair and wore heels, the lilac suede ones she'd worn on Easter, and the diamond solitaire from her grandmother. She put on lashes. Though Mel would rather die than ever admit it, she did want to look pretty for him. To look like a college girl, not a high school kid on his field hockey team. It was a chance to make a new impression.

Mel had a flutter in her heart as she followed her parents into the restaurant. Coach was waiting near the hostess stand. He looked hot. Raw denim, a pale blue oxford button-up, Truman green tie, navy blazer, brown chukkas. His hair was longer and blonder than she'd ever seen it. He was using new product in his hair, the curls perfectly messily clumped. Immediately, Mel was struck by a bolt of jealousy. Was he flirting with the hostess?

But boy, she felt a swell as he pivoted away from the hostess when the Gingriches came through the door. It was clear Mel made the impression she'd been hoping to. He hugged her, his nose sneaking into her hair. She could feel his eyes on her as they were led to their table.

Mel had the distinct sense that she had been infused with a newfound power. How to wield it was less clear to her.

Dinner was stiff at first. Her father had selected a bottle of wine, which Coach took one sip of—trying to be a good sport—and clearly did not like. Her mother quickly told him to order something else. He got a beer. Light beer in a bottle. The same kind at high school parties. The waitress brought it out with a glass, which he did not want. The sweating brown bottle made the table feel lopsided somehow.

For the first course, it was mostly her parents and Coach who conversed, where Coach's international travels this summer intersected with their past vacations, with Mel interjecting every so often to correct something her father had remembered wrongly.

Mel wanted Coach to try the things she liked, and she'd pushed him to order the calamari, but he was perplexed when it arrived to the table not breaded and fried, but smoked on a plank with a squeeze of lemon juice and snips of fresh parsley.

"That's a little too adventurous for me," Coach said, leaning back from the table as the waiter set it down.

Mel caught her mother making an amused face.

"Speaking of adventurous," her father said, "Mel's been hiking just about every trail in this part of the state with a friend from school. He was going to join us tonight, but I believe something came up."

Coach took a sip of his beer but it was pantomime. Mel knew the bottle was already empty. "Oh? Who?"

"Gordy Ackerman."

Coach blanched. "Gordy Ackerman? With the glasses?"

"He's just a friend," she stressed. But inside, Mel swooned. It was Coach's turn to feel jealous. Long overdue. The first ever time she could recall.

Over entrees, the conversation shifted to Truman, the intersection of Coach's past and Mel's future, and there was never a lull. Mel's future, Coach's past. Many of his anecdotes were ones

Mel had already heard, but she remained engaged and attentive nevertheless. Because she detected something new in his framing, a wistfulness, as his experiences and accomplishments became things that Mel herself would also have a chance at. They were not equals by any stretch, but the distance that had always been stubbornly between them, and which had vastly widened this summer, felt like it was collapsing at warp speed. She boldly ordered herself a mimosa—which did confuse the waiter, and also the bartender, since Park & Orchard was only open for dinner—but after a permissive nod from her mother, they obliged her. Coach got himself another beer.

The rest of the meal went too quickly. Coach passed on ordering dessert, no surprise to Mel, but she convinced her mother to get the flourless chocolate cake. And then she urged her father to get a second cappuccino. When the waiter delivered it, they were the last diners in the restaurant. She didn't want it to end because she wasn't sure what sort of ending it would be. Coach had avoided any reference to his future plans.

As he stirred in some sugar, her father said, "I think this is going to be Mel's best year yet. Now that her future is set, she can take her foot off the gas. Have some fun."

"Contractually speaking," her mother added, "she doesn't even have to play field hockey this year."

"I'm still going to play," Mel said. And, thanks to her newfound confidence, she mustered up the nerve to casually add, "I just don't know who for."

Coach fiddled with his napkin.

Her mother, harking back to their earlier conversation, deftly nudged a little harder. "Mel mentioned you might be joining the Junior National Team permanently?"

Coach pressed both palms on the table. "I've decided to stay at West Essex, actually. Don't get me wrong. It was a great opportunity. Just not the right one at the right time. I know this might sound silly, but I've always had it in my head that I'd stay through Mel's senior season. She'll be one of the first players that I've gotten to coach all four years. I want to see this through with her."

Mel put her hands to her water glass, then pressed the cold to her cheeks, while her parents gushed over the wonderful news.

And then Coach pulled something out of his interior blazer pocket.

Mel gasped audibly. The waitstaff looked over expecting a proposal, only to give a quizzical look when they saw Coach passing her the captain's *C*.

"The only reason I didn't give it to you sooner is because I wasn't sure if I was coming back."

"Please! It's fine. You don't have to explain. I'm just so happy you chose me."

He grinned. "It wouldn't look right on any other Wildcat."

Her mother excused herself to the ladies' room.

Her father, to pay the bill.

And then it was just them.

Mel had the urge to say so much to him but she was afraid to open her mouth. She knew she was a little drunk.

Coach's hand found hers under the table. And he held it, very softly, and didn't let go until the last moment, when it was time to leave.

In the parking lot, before one final round of goodbyes, Coach asked her parents, "Mr. Gingrich, Mrs. Gingrich, I was wondering, would you consider writing a letter of support for me? Like a general reference? I'm trying to get my teaching portfolio in order."

Her parents were happy to oblige.

"How funny was he with that calamari!" Mel's mother said on the ride home, turning around to face Mel in the back seat. "As if he thought it came out of the sea breaded and fried."

Though Coach's aversion had embarrassed Mel a few hours earlier, she now felt more sympathetic. "It does look kind of gross, if you think about it."

Inside her clutch, Mel sees a few missed texts from Gordy, sent in hour-long intervals.

GORDY: You home yet?

GORDY: Rabih is having people over, but I'm still dapper 😉 so just text when/if you want me to come by.

She had already decided she would not be writing him back. But Gordy's final text erased any lingering doubts she had about it.

GORDY: Hey. Did you tell Phoebe the good news? I ran into her and brought it up thinking she would have been your first call. But she reacted a little surprised? Ugh. Sorry. Hope I didn't screw that up.

Mel closed her eyes, intending to think about how she should handle this mess, but it was easier to not think. There would surely be lots of these kinds of moments coming, senior year purgatory, as she stepped out of one world and into another.

Later that night, after her parents had gone up to bed, Mel pulled her leftovers out of the fridge. She'd been too excited to eat much at the restaurant, but now she gobbled up slices of cold steak with her fingers. She made herself one last mimosa.

COACH: You awake?

MEL: Yes.

MEL: Tonight was so fun.

MEL: It's fun to think about the future.

COACH: I hope by 'future' you mean three weeks from now when Wildcat tryouts start

MEL: Don't worry. I've been dreaming about being varsity captain since my freshman year. My dad already talked to the manager about having P&O cater my Psych-Up.

COACH: So I was thinking about something that your parents said at dinner.

COACH: How you can take your foot off the gas now.

COACH: Maybe don't even need to play.

COACH: Was that something you discussed with them?

MEL: Of course not!

COACH: Good. Because you haven't played well since the end of last season.

MEL: I know that.

MEL: But I think you'd have been pleased if you had seen me play spring club and summer sessions

MEL: And clearly I did okay at Truman, right?

COACH: 😬

MEL: What?

COACH: After you sent me all those crazy texts while you were at Truman

COACH: I got concerned.

COACH: I emailed Truman's scout to find out how it went.

MEL: Okay . . .

COACH: You're lucky he owed me a favor.

COACH: And that Truman's first choice decided to go to Schuyler

COACH: He was able to put your name forward again.

MEL: Oh.

MEL: Thanks.

MEL: Seriously, thank you.

COACH: You don't need to thank me. You know I'll do whatever I can to help you.

COACH: But here's the thing, Mel.

COACH: I only have a certain amount of personal favors I can call in to help you girls.

COACH: I spent a lot of them on you.

COACH: I kept thinking about Phoebe tonight. I really want her to end up someplace great. But it's going to be an uphill battle.

COACH: Frankly, us winning a championship is going to be the only way she gets top scout attention.

MEL: I am willing to do whatever it takes for Phoebe.

COACH: I'm taking a screenshot of that text

COACH: Receipts I can pull out when I'm pushing you harder than you've ever been pushed.

MEL: Bring it.

COACH: You know I will.

COACH: Remember. I didn't have to come back, Mel.

COACH: But I did. For you.

Mel tosses and turns, as if trying to stave off this memory from warping.

The feelings, the emotions, the connection she felt with Coach were real. Coach taking her hand might seem tame, but their relationship had previously only existed inside the most secret spaces. Late at night. Pixels on a screen. In her head. No wonder his touch had given her such a thrill. In scale, it was as if Coach had shouted her name from mountaintops.

One bit of praise from him lit her up. And that night, she glowed brighter than ever before. Was it her accomplishments that Coach was most attracted to? And if so, was that bad? He said he saw so much of himself in her. So what if those parts were the parts he liked best?

His texts to her post-dinner spun her light down like a dimmer switch. And the realization that she hadn't been able to get into Truman on her own snuffed her out.

Is that why things cooled off so suddenly afterward? Because he'd seen through her confident routine from the start? She heard nothing from him for the next three weeks. Three weeks she spent on edge, preparing to be captain, planning her Psych-Up, worrying she'd let Phoebe down, trying to untangle herself from Gordy, afraid she wouldn't be able to meet Coach's expectations of greatness. It was state championship or bust.

Oh, Gordy. God, she screwed that up.

She chose to see it as a challenge. Coach only broke her down so he could build her back up. He always led her places she never thought she could go. If Coach believed she could do it, she would do it.

It's never been her place to question him.

It's her job to trust him.

And she did trust him.

Did.

So why can't she bring herself to open the laptop?

Because the reasons that make things more simple for her teammates are the same reasons that complicate this for Mel. None of the girls are in love with Coach. None of them have worked as hard as Mel to make themselves in his image. None of them owe Coach as much as she does.

Worse, Mel feels culpable in every dark moment the girls shared tonight. She's been his little puppet, his sounding board. Mel has never felt so ill equipped, so unprepared.

Mel doesn't need to read a single email to know that she has failed her team.

Maybe she's the one who should quit.

A soft knock at her door. Mel holds her breath. It will be Phoebe. Here to see if she's opened the laptop. No. She is such a coward.

"Mel? Are you awake?"

It's Luci.

Mel gets up and unlocks the door. Opens it only halfway. "What is it?" She makes her voice sound sleepy, so Luci will think she's woken Mel up. She could use that, Mel thinks, should she need to end the conversation quickly.

"Can I come in?"

Mel sighs and opens the door a touch wider. Luci enters and sits herself right down on Mel's bed, the mattress bouncing. She's not fueled by bravado. Her teeth are clenched in worry, tight as the wire threading her braces.

"I was waiting for you to come back downstairs," she tells Mel. "But then I decided it might be better if I just came up here to talk with you. So we could have privacy."

"Okay."

Mel sits beside her, and Luci immediately twists to face her, curls her legs up neatly with her on the bed. Mel sees that Luci's holding something in her hands, something Luci squeezes for courage, before allowing her fingers to unfurl like petals.

A phone.

Mel's eyes narrow. "I thought you said you didn't bring your phone with you tonight. I thought you said it was drying out in a bag of rice."

Dropping her chin to her chest, Luci says, "I'm so sorry I lied to you. But I only did it because Coach asked me to."

"What?"

"He pulled me aside at the Psych-Up right before he left. He said he was planning a surprise and he needed my help to pull it off. He took my phone, put his number in it, and then told me where to find your keys so I could hide it inside your car."

Mel's so startled, the memories hit her like flashes of light, brief and blinding. Coach pretending to have left his phone in her house. Passing Luci on her way back inside with the duffel bag Mel thought contained varsity jerseys. Luci rushing up to be the first one to sit in Mel's car as they were about to drive to the field.

Luci continues, "He's been asking me for updates all night long. Wanting to know where we were and what we were doing, what the girls were saying about him." Luci's neck is flush and she wafts her T-shirt to cool herself down. "He knows that we went to Gordy's party. He was saying weird stuff to me about Grace, making fun of her hair."

Mel's hands grip wads of her comforter. She's thinking of all the effort Coach put into his plan tonight. All the traps he set for her. The missing varsity jerseys. A secret spy. Why? What had he been trying to prove? Why would he go out of his way like this to undermine her?

"Does he know about Phoebe's knee?"

"Just that something happened. The last time I texted him was before we went to Waffle House. He sent me like a million in a row and"—she shrugs—"I pretended my battery died."

Mel, in spite of everything, smiles. "Clever."

"It was too much." Luci shakes her head, clearly uncomfortable, and sets her phone down on Mel's nightstand. "I'll leave this here in case you want to read them. I might be leaving something out." Luci stands up, takes a deep, cleansing breath.

"Why did you tell me?"

"Because you're our captain. And I wanted you to have the full picture when you decide what it is we should do tomorrow."

Luci closes the door quietly. Mel listens as Luci's footsteps grow fainter.

It was such a simple, honest declaration of support for Mel, said with no hesitations, no second-guessing if Mel even deserves to be the leader of this team. Luci believes that Mel will come up with something. And it terrifies her.

Mel always believed she was special to Coach. That he texted her because they shared a deep and meaningful connection. But her senior year hadn't even started and he'd already marked her replacement. Mel 2.0.

Phoebe insisted tonight that Luci was a little Mel. Mel's enormous ego wouldn't even let her pretend to entertain the comparison. But in less than twenty-four hours of being on this team, Luci had the courage to do what Mel couldn't, wouldn't, which is to turn down Coach's volume inside her head and listen instead to the voice in her heart. She smelled the house burning and ran out while Mel took the batteries out of the alarms.

Thank God Coach underestimated his newest asset. He thinks Luci gave him the full picture about what the girls were up to tonight. But he doesn't know that she flipped and outed him to Mel. He doesn't know about the stories they've been sharing with one another. He doesn't know that Phoebe stole his laptop.

Phoebe.

She was driven to do something desperate tonight. She, too, had a sense that the things Coach had been telling her didn't add up. Phoebe laid all the pieces out for Mel, hoping Mel would help her solve the puzzle. But as soon as Mel started to see how one piece—this weird supposed Truman scout appearance at the state championship game—might link with another—throwing Phoebe under the bus to the Trident scout, where Coach just so happened to be job hunting—she shut her eyes before anything else came together.

Fighting the drag of her deep shame, Mel forces herself to stand up. After locking her bedroom door once more, Mel picks up Coach's laptop from her vanity and carries it back to her bed.

She owes it to herself, to her team, and most of all to Phoebe, to have the full picture of just how terrible Coach is before they face him tomorrow.

Unfortunately, tomorrow is already here.

SATURDAY, AUGUST 27
8:00 A.M.
MEL

Mel's phone buzzes next to her. Not a text. Not a call. The alarm she set at Coach's instruction.

Mel bolts upright, knocking Coach's laptop off the bed in the process. Her chest heaves like she's hyperventilating.

She doesn't remember falling asleep. Or how long she was out cold. There was never much time. Whatever she's accidentally wasted was precious.

Coach is expecting the girls in his classroom in one hour, even though their scrimmage with Oak Knolls isn't until noon. He'll need that extra time to decide whether or not they have lived up to his expectations. He will make sure each of them truly understands what being a Wildcat entails. He will decide if they've sufficiently proven their loyalty, their commitment, their heart. And, should he deem them deserving of the honor, he will bestow upon them their varsity jerseys.

Coach's presentation of the varsity jerseys couldn't be more different from the traditions guiding Mel. Hers was to be a celebration, a way to unite them, reinforce them.

All Coach wanted was to break them.

He's in for a rude awakening. This team meeting will not go the way he's expecting.

But beyond that declaration, Mel has no handle on what she should do. She so desperately wants to fire off a shot at him, but it is as if Mel is standing in the middle of a prism, a ball on her stick, with Coach's face reflected back at her ad nauseum. She doesn't know where to aim. How best to confront Coach. What is her team willing to risk? Their entire season? What do they hope to gain?

Whatever the approach, the girls must be united. They can't have a single girl slip. But there are so many angles, so many individual voices to consider, so many grievances that need to be addressed. Does everyone want to come into the classroom? Or should Mel take it on herself to be a messenger?

These were the things Mel had planned to discuss with the girls last night, once she'd read the email Phoebe had asked her to. But one led Mel to read two more for context, led to another ten for a deeper understanding, led to twenty, forty, sixty.

As with all things Coach, once Mel got sucked in, it was nearly impossible for her to climb back out.

The alarm buzzes again. Fifty minutes left. Mel hits snooze once more. Then she picks Coach's laptop off her floor. She rubs her finger across the track pad, hoping to wake it, but the battery is dead.

No matter. She's carrying the proof in her heart. Is it any wonder it feels so bruised? What Mel has discovered about Coach is so much worse than she ever could have imagined.

Coach didn't turn down the job with the Men's Junior National team, as he had framed it during Mel's Truman celebration dinner.

It was never offered to him.

At first, this truly surprised Mel, but as she worked her way down his inbox, it became clear that Coach hadn't been offered most of the jobs he sought, despite sending out a steady stream of résumés since receiving his West Essex email address.

For the ones he did manage to get, Coach was never happy with some aspect of the contract—nine times out of ten it was the salary, which Coach always felt was "offensively low"—and negotiations would inevitably break down.

More often than not, he shined up his applications with the aspirations of his Wildcats. Parlaying interest in his players to curry favors, information, recommendations. It was always done carefully, casually, friendly, subtly. It certainly put Coach's policy of keeping scout information from his players in a new context. By controlling their access to who was and wasn't interested, Coach gave himself an infinite number of aces to play.

Mel was excited to spill this tea, let the girls know just how many schools had been in touch with Coach to express interest in recruiting them. Ali, especially. It seemed like every single D1 school had her on their radar.

But when Mel came across an email from Coach Karen, she almost couldn't bring herself to open it, afraid to see the ways Coach had inserted himself into orchestrating her acceptance to Truman.

It turned out, however, that he had not needed to call in any special favors, or beg them to take a look at her. In fact, Coach Karen herself had made it clear she was very interested in Mel as early as sophomore season. Nor did Coach have to send a last SOS to pull Mel out from the reject pile, as he'd claimed less than an hour after her celebration dinner. These were all lies to make her feel beholden to him.

If anything, Coach was the one reaching out to the scout and Coach Karen, under the guise of checking in about Mel, but he pivoted immediately to tout his own accomplishments.

Coach Karen rarely, if ever, responded.

Maybe that's why Coach Karen had hinted, as Mel had sobbed in the Truman locker room, that she was aware of just how intense it was to play at West Essex.

Thinking back, Mel can't believe how quickly she bought into Coach's narrative. How fast she made herself dismiss that personal note Coach Karen had included in her offer letter. She let the narrative Coach had fed her—that her accomplishments all hinged on having Coach's wind at her back—completely override her own experiences.

Plenty of these kinds of revelations have already occurred to Mel. And surely more will come to her in the days, weeks, months, years it will take Mel to unpack just how gaslighted she allowed herself to be. Hopefully she'll be able to forgive herself for this, but right now, she doesn't imagine she ever will. She imagines second-guessing and third-guessing and fourth-guessing herself for the rest of her life. He's permanently disfigured her with a reflex of believing the worst about herself.

Her phone buzzes. Forty minutes.

Mel sets the laptop aside and hurries down to the basement.

How long did the girls wait for Mel before giving up hope that she'd come back down?

Did Luci come knocking on her door again? Discover that Mel had been sleeping peacefully while the rest of them were in turmoil?

She tiptoes away from the daylight and down to the basement, where it is cool and silent and pitch black.

Maybe none of the girls are here.

Maybe they abandoned her.

If they did, Mel wouldn't blame them.

But no. The hallway opens up to a room full of bodies. Nineteen girls snuggled into blankets and sleeping bags. Peaceful. Mel tiptoes over, stepping soundlessly between them. Not a single one stirs. They are that exhausted, that emotionally spent. She feels an aching tenderness for them.

Mel's bedding is still on the floor, where she first laid it out so many hours ago. She usually brought a sleeping bag to Psych-Ups but since this was her house, Mel had constructed a bed for her and Phoebe to share. A bed Phoebe is currently in, her limbs tucked in tight, careful even in sleep to leave space for Mel. But tonight she's shared a bed with a phantom.

If she had any tears left, Mel would cry them for Phoebe.

She'd confirmed, via Coach's correspondence, that the Truman scout had only come to see the Wildcats play once.

It was not at the championship game, as Coach had told Phoebe. A lie Phoebe still believed.

It was the game in November. The one Mel had kept secret from her best friend, per Coach's request. That glorious game.

Clearing up this misunderstanding led Mel into the worst discovery of this whole disgusting mess. One that finally broke her, tears silently spilling down her face, her chest hitching in silent sobs.

They'd played so spectacularly, their hearts straining the seams of their varsity jerseys with the love they had for each other and the game, that Truman was interested in Mel *and* Phoebe.

And they'd planned to invite them both to their summer tryout weekend.

Obviously there's no saying Truman would have taken both of them. But Coach robbed Phoebe of her chance. He'd lied to her, exploited Phoebe's love of Mel to coax her back on the field before she was ready. And for what? The only reason Mel can think of is that Coach had wanted his best accomplishment as a field hockey coach—earning six state championships in six seasons—to remain intact.

Had he felt any remorse?

No. Because he continued to use Phoebe—or rather sacrifice her—to advance himself as a candidate at Trident.

Mel knows she can never tell Phoebe about Coach's Truman scouting lie. She will take this to her grave. Not to protect Coach, but because Phoebe believes her sacrifice had helped Mel. Mel getting into Truman made it all worth it.

Another buzz. Thirty minutes left.

Even if Mel has no idea what they'll say when they get there, if the girls want to be at Coach's office on time, she needs to wake everyone up now. So she doesn't hit snooze, and instead lets the alarm continue to buzz, buzz, buzz.

The girls begin lifting their heads. All nineteen, undone and unrested, barely coherent.

Mel too. The fumes that carried her down here have now evaporated. She's got a headache, a pulsing knot of regret in the center of her forehead.

She never should have let Coach take this night away from her. Not take. Steal.

He had to steal it from Mel because she refused to willingly give it to him.

That must have come as a shock to Coach. Mel never went against his wishes. When he wanted something from her, she delivered. Except this time.

But why?

Because Mel knew in her heart that Coach wanted something that didn't belong to him.

It belonged to the girls. The team. The Wildcats.

And just like that, it comes to her. Mel knows exactly what to do.

"It's okay," Mel whispers, turning off the alarm. "Everyone go back to sleep."

There is not a peep of resistance.

Mel wriggles underneath her comforter, shivers to warm up. Phoebe rolls over. Her eyes flutter open for a moment, then close. Mel isn't sure if she actually saw her, but then Phoebe curls against her, as if she knew Mel would sleep best clinging to something she loved.

SATURDAY, AUGUST 27
11:00 A.M.
PHOEBE

Someone whispers, "Mel, Mel," but it's Phoebe who first lifts her head off the pillow.

She has no idea how long she's been asleep. Or what time it might be. Or when Mel came down from her bedroom and joined them. But Mel is lying next to her, cradling her pillow, grinning in her sleep. A pleasant dream, which Phoebe takes as a good sign. Good enough to make Phoebe grin too.

Mrs. Gingrich is leaning over them, one hand clutching the top of her robe closed, the other gently patting Mel. She looks hella hungover. "Mel!" she says again. "Sweetie. It's eleven. Only an hour till game time."

The time check is like an air horn. On her way out, Mrs. Gingrich flicks on the lights. The girls pop up and glance around at one another, panicked. They've missed Coach's 9:00 a.m. meeting.

The only one not freaking out is Mel, who stretches her

arms like a cat. She leans up on her elbows and smiles, fully refreshed, and she gives Phoebe's hand a knowing squeeze.

To the rest of the girls, Mel announces, "Don't worry. I have a plan." This in and of itself grants the girls a palpable relief, but when she adds, "Everyone get dressed in your uniforms," the mood rises to hopeful. Because whatever Mel has cooked up for dealing with Coach includes a possibility that they'll still get to play field hockey today.

But Phoebe's hope slips along with her kneecap the moment she tries putting weight on it. Thankfully, the rest of the girls are militantly focused on getting ready. Packing up their sleeping stuff, moving in and out of the bathroom like jets taking off and landing at an airport, putting on their uniforms.

She beams a big grateful smile to Kearson as she passes by on her way to the sink, her toothbrush conjuring up a rabid foam. Kearson cut her off last night before Phoebe had a chance to explain why she was quitting. The only person who knows is Mel. And Mel had begged Phoebe to wait and see how her knee felt and not make any rash decisions. It felt slightly patronizing to Phoebe last night but now it is what keeps her heart beating as she works out another way to get herself up off the floor, piking up like a tripod, her injured leg dangling like a pendulum. It isn't pretty, but once Phoebe's standing, she can walk. Mostly.

The first thing Phoebe takes out of her duffel bag is her Knee Spanx. She refuses to let herself think about how things could be different if she'd been wearing it last night. As she rolls it on, she takes a quick glance at her injured knee. She wants to believe that the swelling has gone down. She wants to believe that perhaps she hadn't injured it as badly as she thought. But the Knee Spanx is up and over it before Phoebe can take a closer look.

Phoebe dresses in her Wildcat uniform just like everyone else. But the experience for her is singular. Practically religious. She hasn't worn any uniform in nine months and she likes the feeling it gives her, like she's a virgin who's saved herself for her true love. She can't believe with how hard she worked to get back to this place that there was a point last night where Phoebe was okay with maybe never wearing it again.

She loves the weight of the pleated navy kilt, dense polyester, bloomers sewn in. The compression of her navy-and-white-striped knee socks, which Phoebe keeps slouched for now at her ankles. When she gets to the field, she'll strap on her shin guards and then hike them up.

Yes. She's decided that she will go to the field. She won't play. That would be stupid. But she can sit on the bench and watch and cheer the other girls on. Maybe, if they are doing well, and her knee isn't bothering her too much, Phoebe might try to see what she can do.

Grace is the first to ask, "Hey, Mel? What should we wear on top? Since we don't have our varsity jerseys."

"Whatever you girls want. A T-shirt, a tank top. Then hustle upstairs and grab some food. We're going to have a team meeting on my front lawn in five minutes."

Upstairs, the kitchen island is beautifully set for a breakfast buffet—platters of croissants, little glass cups of yogurt parfaits, a crystal bowl of summer berries, fresh squeezed OJ—but there's no real time to eat. So the girls just grab stuff. Whatever they can palm.

Phoebe doesn't take any food. She's doesn't feel hungry. She's focused on the pain in her knee, which seems to be getting worse now that she's up and using it. She heads for the powder room off the kitchen, knowing Mrs. Gingrich keeps Advil in the medicine cabinet. But it's not there. She hobbles back into the kitchen empty-handed and gets a glass of water.

Out the window she sees Mel's parents together on the patio, drinking coffee, sunglasses on, the missing bottle of Advil between them. No sense of what happened last night. It's for the best.

Phoebe could walk out and get herself some, but she doesn't want to take the extra steps.

Halfway to the front door, she stops, unzips her duffel, and straps on her much bigger and bulkier knee brace, the one that's hinged and made of hard plastic. The one she hates to wear.

"Hey. You okay?" Mel asks, hanging back to rub Phoebe's back.

"Yup," she says. "Just a precaution."

Mel looks concerned. "Promise me you'll take it easy until you get checked out by a doctor."

"I promise."

Phoebe fiddles with the straps, allowing Mel the chance to get ahead of her. Mel doesn't bother closing the front door, leaves it open for Phoebe. Outside, the girls have already gathered on Mel's front lawn, while Mel opens up her trunk and grabs the duffel bag full of pinnies and the bag where she'd placed all their confiscated phones.

Phoebe joins the circle without her teammates realizing the pain she's in. But this small victory only makes her future defeat inevitable. No matter what Mel has planned, Phoebe won't be part of it. She is a broken piece of this team that will never be fixed.

Mel passes out everyone's phones. Ali grabs hers first, turns it on, and squeals, "John-John picked the ball! John-John picked the ball!" and then explains the significance while showing off a picture of her nephew in a brightly colored outfit.

But more texts come in, rapid fire.

It happens to all the girls. As soon as someone powers a phone on, it dings with a stream of newly received messages, like they are inside a pinball machine.

COACH: You're all late.

COACH: This is not a good look.

COACH: Okay now I'm worried.

COACH: Hope you girls are getting some rest.

COACH: We'll just have a quick chat on the field before the game.

"He knows something's up," Ali tells them. "You can see where he suddenly switches from pissed off to concerned."

Luci laughs dryly. "Now all he wants is a 'quick chat' with us."

"What are we going to say to him?" Grace scratches her leg.

Mel answers calmly. "Nothing."

Kearson holds her stomach and asks Mel, "Okay, but . . . what do you think he's going to say to us?"

"He's either going to try and manipulate us or intimidate us." Mel smiles. "Either way, it doesn't matter."

Phoebe immediately recognizes the look on Mel's face, though it feels like she hasn't seen it in forever. That confident, strong, capable girl. She's got this. She's one step ahead of all of them, and Phoebe's the first to catch her. Phoebe chimes in. "He's not our coach anymore."

Mel beams. "Exactly. We won't even have time to talk. We've got a game to play." She bends down and unzips the duffel bag with the pinnies inside. "But at some point, I will thank him for inspiring us. If he hadn't tried to take last night away from us, we would have never thought we could take our team back from him."

The girls grin, enthusiasm building.

"Okay. So. I've got a pinny for each of you. They are not nearly as glamorous as our varsity jerseys. Some of them are ripped." Mel lifts one to her nose and winces. "None of them have been washed. But we sure as hell earned them. And I'm giving the first one to Phoebe Holt, because she truly embodies what it means to be a Wildcat, putting her team first, always."

The girls all applaud as Mel slips it over Phoebe's head.

Phoebe pretends to fix her ponytail. She takes it out, pulls it back, smooths the sides, then pulls out the elastic and starts it all over again. Only then does Mel, and the rest of her team, realize that Phoebe's fighting back tears.

"I can't come to the field with you." Phoebe abandons her ponytail with a groan, opting instead to wipe her eyes, as if she might grind the tears away with her palms. "Ugh. I'm sorry. It's just . . . this is so hard. I have to quit."

The whole circle collapses around her. Voices urging her, *No, Phoebe! Wait! Don't quit! Please!*

But her mind is made up. "It'll be too hard for me. I'll just be dying to be out there with everyone." She needs to put herself first. At long last.

Mel lowers herself and looks up at Phoebe, and when Phoebe nods, she wraps her in a hug. "We'll drop you off."

"You don't have time. The game starts in twenty minutes. I'll just call my mom and have her come get me."

"It's not up for debate."

Their varsity jersey ceremony is cut short again, but this time, no one cares. The girls grab pinnies for themselves.

All the girls take the ride over to Phoebe's house to drop her off. Phoebe puts on the playlist from her and Mel's first season together. She can see that Mel is trying to keep a smile on her face, but that she's in as much pain as Phoebe.

When they reach her house, Phoebe takes a deep breath, unbuckles herself, and turns to face the back seat.

To Luci, Phoebe says, "I'm still going to quiz you, Luci. Don't think you're off the hook."

And then, to Kearson, "I'm bequeathing you my shotgun seat for the rest of the season, so get your butt up front." Kearson's chin quivers. "Don't worry. You've got this," Phoebe tells her.

Phoebe exits the car. In the time it takes her to climb out, Mel has unbuckled herself and come around to the passenger side.

"You're going to be late," Phoebe says.

"I'm coming over right after the game. And we're going to figure out what to do next. I know it was hard on you last time you got hurt. But this time, I promise I'll be with you every step of the way."

She will miss this. But not losing her best friend will make it easier.

"Good luck, Mel."

"I'll see you later."

The closer it got to game time, the more Phoebe could feel the tension building up. Starting after lunch, if any teammate passed you in the hall, you'd high-five her. Not a casual slap but a high five with force, intention. Once the bell rang, and girls would go to their lockers, they'd sing the Wildcat fight song, and you'd hear the voices of your teammates in other parts of the school, voices that would converge and get louder and louder as the girls made their way down to the locker rooms.

Seasons of passivity, of never questioning, of acquiescing, of deference, of never challenging, of never saying no, of being screamed at, of feeling like a failure, of feeling like a joke . . .

It rises in them.

And even though Phoebe's being left behind, it rises in her, too.

As the girls drive off, Phoebe screams, "Go Wildcats!" at the top of her lungs over the jubilant honking of six car horns.

Her parents are on their way out the front door with their club chairs and spectator tents. They see their daughter and both of them just know.

The shock of this being it, the end for Phoebe, knocks the wind clear out of her. But as with any fresh injury, the first bolt of pain is usually the worst. Phoebe knows if she can get past that, she's already started to heal.

SATURDAY, AUGUST 27
11:45 A.M.
LUCI

Six cars enter the crowded West Essex parking lot and claim the farthest spots from the field, side by side. The team bus from Oak Knolls is already parked along the side of the athletic building.

The girls get out. Everyone is anxious, but excited, too.

"You girls ready?" Mel asks.

"Yes," Luci says, adding her voice to the chorus.

On the walk across the parking lot, Luci holds her stick so tightly she can feel her heartbeat in her grip. The girls slip into the same stride, a marching beat for this battle. And they even manage to score a few early victories along the way.

Grace waving at what must be her family—a college-aged guy and a grandmother type—both with hair dyed as blue as hers.

Kearson folding into her mother's waiting arms.

Mel rushing over to Gordy and giving him a big kiss.

But the vibe shifts to all business as soon as they step onto the field.

Oak Knolls has already warmed up. They've been waiting for the Wildcats to show, excited to see if the video Darlene Maguire posted last night had any effect. Full of bravado, they lean on their sticks.

Ali points out Darlene Maguire to the girls, which Darlene totally sees happen, and there's a team-wide stare down, the eyes of twenty Wildcats issuing a silent warning. *Don't you dare mess with our girl.*

Darlene's face turns beet red.

Luci doesn't want to look for him, but she finds her eyes scanning the field, the stands. Where is he? She feels her senses sharpening, a focus taking hold.

Eventually, he comes out of the heavy metal doors to the side of the field. He's carrying a duffel bag, presumably full of their varsity jerseys. He stops on the sidelines, watching them.

The girls toss their gear down on the sideline bench, directly across from where Coach is standing. Mel leads them to the center of the field, slinging an arm over Luci's shoulders.

"I want you to lead warm-ups today," Mel says with a tender touch on her head.

"Are you sure?"

"Captain's orders."

"What about Coach?"

"Don't worry. We've got your back."

The girls circle around Luci.

She pulls her left arm across her body for one, two, three. *Clap.*

She pulls her right arm across her body for one, two, three. *Clap.*

Luci tries not to watch Coach too closely but she does notice his mouth twist. And then, as she moves from tiny arm circles to big arm circles, he walks toward them, toting his duffel bag, easy and unhurried. As if this is all going according to his plan. As if he were not the slightest bit unnerved.

Except Luci knows he is. She can see the sweat rings under his arms.

There's something delightfully reassuring in how transparent he suddenly is to her. Not only that, but Mel's decision to have the girls play him this way is clearly the perfect choice. They would have gained nothing by storming into his classroom and pointing fingers, hurling accusations. He would have thought them hysterical. But this, to have cut him off from his one source of power before he was even aware of it, is beyond satisfying.

And she can tell the other girls feel the same way. All of them are standing proud and tall when he finally reaches them.

"Everyone have a good nap? Ready to play?"

Luci hugs her right knee to her chest for one, two, three. *Clap.*

Then her left knee for one, two, three. *Clap.*

Coach begins to stroll around their circle as if taking attendance.

"This is funny. You girls are funny. I like your little pinny statement."

The girls are silent. But it doesn't mean there isn't a ton of communication happening between them. Little glances, wry smiles, head nods. All symbols of encouragement. The girls checking in on one another.

His face hardens. "Where's Phoebe?" His eyes narrow on Mel. "What happened to Phoebe, Mel?"

Luci claps a position change. The girls step their legs apart into a wide V shape, cleats touching cleats, and bend forward to touch their toes. Mel sees her strategy and gives a small, grateful nod.

"Okay, look. I see what you girls are—"

Luci clears her throat and begins to sing the Wildcat fight song to drown him out. They all join in.

We are the Wildcats, the navy blue and white,
We are the Wildcats, always ready for a fight!

Don't mess with the Wildcats, we won't accept defeat,
For we are the Wildcats, and we just can't be beat!

Three cheers for the Wildcats, your honor we'll defend,
'Cause when you're a Wildcat, you're a Wildcat till the end!

The referee runs over to the center. He's got his whistle in his mouth. "You girls have jerseys or what?"

Coach straddles his duffel bag, crosses his arms and says smugly, "Nope."

But Mel quickly adds, "Our pinnies should be fine, right? It's only a scrimmage."

The referee looks from Coach to Mel to Coach. Something's going on, but he doesn't seem to want to get involved. And the girls are clearly ready to play.

"Yeah. I'm fine with it. Finish up your stretches, girls, and then I'll need captains for the coin toss."

She smiles sunshine. "You got it."

Coach looks stricken. An itchy red flush creeps up his neck.

"Oh my gosh, you guys!" Ali says. "Look at Buddy!"

Across the field, the Oak Knolls bulldog has spotted the girls and is straining at his leash, barking excitedly, his tag wagging. He pulls so hard that the Oak Knolls coach loses her grip on the leash, and he sprints over to them, bounding into the center of their circle, bouncing and tail wagging, and trying to lick all their faces.

Coach, completely thrown for a loop, launches into a new angry tirade.

"So you girls think you don't need a coach? You think you can have a season without me? Who do you girls think you are?"

It's clear to Luci that these are questions Coach is asking himself. He's finally starting to put it together. Realizing how screwed he is.

Unfortunately, the clock's run out. It's game over.

So Luci, with her hands on her hips, decides to just give Coach the answers. "We are the Wildcats. And as of this moment, you're fired. Now get the fuck off our field."

Whistle.

Acknowledgments

My thanks to:

Molly Pascal, for investing so much of your time and your incredible talent in these pages.

Jenny Han, Jennifer E. Smith, Morgan Matson, Adele Griffin, and Mary Auxier, for their brilliance.

Andrea Mondadori-Llaguet, Lizzy Cimilluca, Katie Kurtzman, Tracey Garripoli-Rodriguez, Dr. Anne Tilley, and Dr. Gregory Thorkelson, for their collective smarts.

Emily van Beek of Folio Literary, for a decade of her expertise, wisdom, and unwavering support.

The all-star team at Simon & Schuster Books for Young Readers, including Zareen Jaffery, Justin Chanda, Anne Zafian, Chrissy Noh, Devin MacDonald, Lizzy Bromley, Dainese Santos, Jenica Nasworthy, Michelle Leo, Lauren Hoffman, Lisa Moraleda, and Anna Jarzab for championing this book.

And three shiny gold medals awarded to my husband, Nick, and my daughters, Vivian and Marie, for being the absolute best.